No Other Choice

A.J. Kohler

Cover Art:
Michelle Crocker
www.mlcdesigns4you.com

Publisher's Note:

This is a work of fiction. All names, characters, places, and events are the work of the author's imagination.

Any resemblance to real persons, places, or events is coincidental.

Solstice Publishing - www.solsticepublishing.com

NO OTHER CHOICE

A Novel

A. J. Kohler

Dedication

Always and all ways, for Cynthia, who has always believed.

Prologue

Like any other predator, Kendra lies in wait. Her prey is not there, but he will be, sooner or later. She need merely have patience. Only her prey matters to her — her prey and her own objectives. Others may interfere, but they will not distract her from her purpose. In the meantime, she can research, she can survey, she can plan. She has done this before; she can do it again. Not for her the slow processes of civilization. She prefers the direct approach. It is much faster, much more certain. It suits her better.

She sees what directly matters to her, although she is not the most observant. Others do not matter. Anyone who gets in the way of her efforts will be dealt with, but in no particular fashion, merely in some way, whatever convenient way, as to ensure that their interference is unsuccessful. Her own desires matter. Other people's ... don't. Other people ... don't. She alone has true existence, in her own mind.

She is directed. She is determined. She will have to see where she can achieve her objective, some place where her prey can be found. If not now, then some later time. How? That will have to wait for where. And when. She will plan.

She does not hate. Hatred is for those who care. Hatred is for those who are weak, and who care out of their weakness. She is strong. She despises those who are weak. Her prey cares. Her prey is weak. When the time is right, she will seize the moment. Then her prey will no longer be a problem. And she can move on. She can do this. She has done this before. She can do it again. She *will* do it again. Soon.

Chapter 1

One year ago:

The remains of an early pizza supper lay on plates precariously set on end tables. The two ever-hopeful dogs, Sasha and Bruno, lay where they could watch for any hand that might offer bits of crust. Amy was getting into the trip she and Alec had just returned from. "I suppose you're now really wondering just what in the hell we were doing in Golondrino."

Calmly, suppressing her intense curiosity with long practice, Becky responded, "Well, yes, the question had occurred to me."

Amy pulled a package from her suitcase and handed it to Becky. "This is for everything you do, have done for us, and, I hope, will continue to do."

Underneath the wrapping paper was a box that Becky recognized. She gasped. "Amy, you shouldn't have!" Opening the box, Becky found one of the most elegant and incredible necklaces she had ever seen. She loved it on sight and, coming from that store, knew it had to have been impossibly expensive. After a lengthy pause, she gently closed the box and looked up. "All right, Amy, give. What bank did you rob? What is the 'special news' you have for me? And generally speaking, what in the hell is going on?"

"Well, first," Amy said, holding up her left hand, "as you've probably figured out by now, Alec and I got married. I'm sorry we did it without you, but it was a Las Vegas quickie because he wasn't going to take any chances about losing me again. Talked me right into it, the old smoothie. We'll do it again, a little more formally, when the rings they" — she gestured at the box — "are doing for us arrive, and you and they" — her glance included Bruno and Sasha — "will be included. Included, hell. You three will be it. Beyond that" — she dug in her suitcase again — "look at this."

Amy handed over an envelope. The announcement inside simply read, 'The Republic of Golondrino is pleased to announce the retirement of Chief Executive Officer Raymond Escarton Fields …' Becky read the last out loud, the volume and pitch of her voice both rising. "His designated successor, A.M. Youngston???"

She looked at Amy, who simply sat there silent. Then at Alec, who was nodding slowly. She was all but speechless. "Oh, my *God*."

Chapter 2

I first began keeping sort of a journal, in novel form, at Becky's suggestion, almost a year and a half ago. Becky — Dr. Rebecca Swan — is my best friend, fourth cousin and a psychologist. Journaling is her answer to almost everything (chili is mine) and I finally gave in, although I've never told her. I've been keeping it up sporadically ever since, but I really should try to do it more religiously. I still have problems putting my innermost thoughts down on a computer screen, but at least if I do it in novel form, I can sort of pretend that it's not really me. It worked for me when I started, but then I pretty much let it go for a while. I need to try again, so once more, here goes. And if I can't do it this time — Becky, I'll get even with you. Somehow. I promise.

Becky has a new boyfriend. Alec and I haven't met him yet, but according to Becky, he's a psychiatrist from Phoenix that she met at some psychological conference. A nice fellow, fairly good-looking, she tells me, even if he's not as well-built as Alec. I was going to have the Family look into him, because as I said, she's my best friend and has been for all our lives, but as soon as his name came up in her Family surveillance file, a link to his file came up as well. He was Family, too, and neither of them knew about the other. This could be … interesting. I noted in passing from his photographs that her description of him was fairly accurate. Hair a bit darker brown than Alec's, about the same height, but judging from his pictures, not as muscular or good looking. Not bad, overall, as these things go. Not to my taste, but that's not my problem. Anyway, I'm prejudiced where Alec's concerned.

I was sitting in my office at the time, waiting to see what sort of case came in the door next, killing some time.

Marketing is something I certainly can do, but it's not something I really enjoy doing. The excuse to take a day off was appealing. I have to admit that I'd never really gone over Becky's file in any depth before, mostly because I already knew pretty much everything in it and in fact knew her far better than the surveillance office did. We've been best friends ever since we were able to walk, maybe before. Well, before she could, anyway. She's a couple of years younger than I am.

There's a tease for at least a hint of background. She really is my very best friend — well, other than my other very best friend, my husband, Alec Trevethen. She and I are quite opposite. She's several inches taller than I, and at least on weekdays when she's working, she's very elegant, always immaculately coiffed, made up and dressed to the nines. She can be quite the fashion queen, in addition to being a makeup queen.

As I've said on other occasions, she knows the difference between ecru and taupe. I know beige when I see it. We're both in jeans and t-shirts when we're just hanging out, of course, but that's different. I'm in jeans and t-shirts virtually all the time, trying to be ready to fade into the woodwork. Well, adobe or stucco around here, I guess. Tucson isn't all that big on woodwork. She's built like the proverbial brick — well, she's still got an incredible figure, even now that we're in our mid-thirties. I — have a figure. Barely.

That's fine with both of us, we're not competing. Anyway, we were raised so close that we pretty much had four parents together, rather than each of us only having our own two. My parents held me back so that I only started school a year before her, but she took all the classes she could possibly manage and we graduated from high school at the same time. We then roomed together all through college before splitting up for grad school and her psych internship. Really the very best of friends, much closer than mere sisters or even most twins.

I doubted that she'd mentioned me to him. For sure, if she had and she'd done as I'd asked her to, she'd mentioned me as Amy Trevethen, not as either A.M. Youngston, which, being Family, he'd recognize immediately as the Family CEO, or as Alannah Meav Youngston, which he might conceivably figure out. If he had figured it out, he'd likely already have given himself away to her trained observation. That's if she even remembered 'Alannah Meav.' I generally try not to (but Alannah was my beloved grandmother's name, which is why I keep it). She'd certainly never brought him around here. Of course, given the tiny mid-town house Alec and I live in at the moment, seeing it might have kept him from believing who I am anyway.

The house is on the one hand very well-placed, because it's directly behind my office, and on the other, it's now pretty temporary for us. We're in the process of acquiring some serious property out on the west edge of town, overlooking Tucson Mountain Park and Saguaro National Park West, to build our dream house. But that's taking time, and we can certainly manage where we are while we get exactly what we want.

I've lived here for years, and before Alec and I got married about a year ago and he moved in with me, he lived just a couple of doors down and his office was next door to mine. Anyway, the dogs are used to it. It's just the four of us right now, and while Becky's certainly spent more than her share of time here, she hasn't been around quite as much lately. Understandable. Another point is that if Alec and I have children — it's still an open question — they really should wait until we're in the new house. Better not be too much longer, my biological clock is ticking.

It's not much of a surprise, as these things go, that she hadn't mentioned me to him. Other than as her very best friend, outside of the Family, I'm just another woman. Understand that the Family is *very* private. You could even call it secretive. Oh, hell, it *is* secretive. Very. As a Family member, you do *not* speak of it to outsiders.

You may open up about it to your spouse, if you choose (some members don't), and there's certainly no way to enforce the secrecy if you choose to shout it from the rooftops. If you did, though, I'd be quite upset with you, and you do *not* want me to be upset with you, since I'm currently the big boss of the Family. Well, no, that isn't the *official* title. Officially the title is CEO, or in some circles, Director. But every so often, I just *like* being the 'big boss' of something.

Anyway, at last count, there are eleven thousand, four hundred and twenty-nine living Family members. We're currently seeing an uptick in the number of families with multiple children; we used to have more single children. That's good for the Family, I think. Being the CEO gives me access to these numbers, of course.

Of those, seven thousand, give or take, are currently in relationships. Forty-eight of those are gay relationships, and nine of those are between two Family members. Seven of those nine are between two Family members where neither of them knows the other is Family. Of the heterosexual relationships, ninety-seven involve two (or more) Family members. All but four are not less than tenth cousins; this isn't an incestuous sort of thing. The heterosexual relationships are mostly pairs, but there are a couple of triads — three with two women and one man, one the other way around. Of the other ninety-three, twenty-three of those don't know that each other is Family. The triads all know, and all four of them have at least two Family members. One is all Family. Now you have more facts than you probably ever cared to know. However, there's more (isn't there always?).

Let me explain the Family briefly. We're a very old and very wealthy Family, far older and wealthier than any family you can probably name, such as the Rockefellers or Astors, or even the Rothschilds. We actually date back to a boy who grew up in the London slums in the late 1400's, apprenticed himself to a merchant and learned — very well — how to make his fortune. He originally conceived of the concept of the Family and set it all in motion.

The Family was organized as a corporation through the efforts of his oldest son (it's one of the oldest corporations in existence), and it's headquartered in a teeny-tiny country in Europe that's so small that you won't find it on a map. The Family pays for all of its members' education, and completing educational levels, getting professional licenses and certifications and earning positive income, other than Family dividends, earns you more shares or fractional shares, beyond the ones you're given at birth (this ability to differentially reward members for success seems to have been the primary reason for organizing the Family as a corporation instead of, say, a trust).

I do mean *all* education. I just had one request come across my desk last week for a Family member who wanted to get an educational course paid for, and the request struck somebody as so unusual it was booted up to me for my approval. The member is 87 years old, and the course he was trying to take was a nude photography class at his local art center. He'd been a dentist until he retired. I just chuckled; his file showed that he'd been cutting quite a swath through the ladies until about five years ago, although he'd been slowing down for about a decade. Not a fidelity issue, as he'd been a life-long bachelor. I told my secretary to send the request back downstairs and tell them to pay it. Nude photography!

Back to what I was saying. Doing better than average, like graduating with honors or making more income, gets you a greater number of additional shares.

The Family is headed by a board of directors and one Chief Executive Officer, or CEO. At the moment, that's me. I've been CEO for just over a year now, having taken over from a fellow who decided to retire after about fifteen years at the helm. As I said, my full legal name is Alannah Meav Youngston, although as the CEO, as well as for most of my life, I officially go by A.M. Youngston, and there is no public notice within the Family of me, the CEO, as female, at least not so far.

In addition to my duties as CEO, I'm also a private investigator here in Tucson. I'm known as Amy to my friends, and I took that name from my initials about the time I started kindergarten because I didn't want to be called Alannah or Meav. Nowadays, though, if anyone calls the office and gets me, unless I already know who they are, I'm Amy Trevethen (Alec and I were married days before I assumed the office of CEO, and we just celebrated our anniversary about a month ago), and A.M. Youngston is not available. No, I can't take a message for you, because I handle all incoming cases. What is your issue, sir (or ma'am)? If it's needed, and it usually is on the rare occasion that they ask for me by name, then yes, I'm Family, too. Go ahead, please.

So as I said, Becky had a new boyfriend. Going back to his file, it didn't have a lot in it. Presumably he hadn't been of all that much interest to the surveillance office. No surprise, as most Family surveillance of members is sort of hit-and-miss and generally not horribly detailed beyond whether one's spouse knows of the Family, unless special attention is requested, usually from my office.

Anyway, he'd gone to a very expensive and very well-respected private New England boarding school

(Boston Latin), then Princeton undergraduate, Johns Hopkins for medical school, Mass General for his internship and residency, then a fellowship at the National Institute of Mental Health. Well, since all tuition and fees are paid by the Family, there was certainly no reason to scrimp anywhere along there, and clearly he hadn't.

Excellent grades (of course), very good evaluations, and all that sort of thing. A rising star, in other words. Until — the record wasn't completely clear on this point — he apparently wrote a couple of articles that caused a major stir and then it developed that his data never quite existed.

Well, no, not necessarily. Apparently the surveillance department had felt this needed a closer look, because the level of detail stepped up somewhat. There seemed to be a bit of a dispute there. A few people claimed that the data had been fabricated. He produced his original notes and data, but the problem was that nobody else could replicate his results.

The final consensus, apparently, was that he had rushed to publish with aberrant data when he should have gathered more, repeated his research, and would then have found that he couldn't duplicate his results. In general, it was chalked up to 'youthful enthusiasm,' but it threatened to kill his academic career. So rather than fighting any more, Robert J. Frankton suddenly relocated to Phoenix and opened a private practice as R. Jon Frankton.

Interesting, to say the least. He's about two years older than I am, so he's got almost four years on Becky. No biggie; with us in our mid-30's now, what's another couple of years?

He and his current wife had met about three years ago and dated for pretty much a year before they were married. Hm. A divorce after two years of marriage? Would this mean trouble ahead for Becky? As far as I could tell from his file, he'd apparently not had any involvement with anyone for close to two years when he and his wife first got together, so he was probably easy pickings for her if she were on the prowl. Let's table that for later.

The upside, for me, was that Becky wasn't casting these wistful looks at Alec and me when she thought I wasn't looking. Not that I was worried about her there. I've known for some time that she was sort of interested in him. She'd let it slip — well, I don't think her mother would have noticed, and certainly nobody else would have. But as I've said, we're *awfully* close. It was a couple of months before Alec and I got married, when I was still holding him at arm's length physically. When I called her on it was one of the only times I'd seen her blush since college, if not before. But she'd never do anything about it.

Besides, dammit, she deserved to have a really good relationship with someone. If he was as good a guy as she believed, then I was thrilled for her. If he clearly was not, then it would probably fall to me to try to derail it, which I didn't look forward to, not one bit. There wasn't any need to come to a decision right now. I'll worry about it if it becomes necessary.

I had just closed his file when the phone rang. I was getting ready to go through my routine when I recognized the name the caller gave on my machine. It was an attorney up in Scottsdale whom I'd completed a job for at the specific request of his client, a Family member, also about a year ago (it was quite a busy time). For him, when I picked up the phone, I answered as Amy Trevethen, and since he seemed just a tad nonplused, I told him I'd gotten married since I dropped off my card and the pictures I'd taken for his client (he himself isn't Family).

He had a job I could do for him here in Tucson, could he send me a copy of the file? I had no reason to avoid a trip up there, and one or two things I could certainly get if I were in Phoenix, so I told him I'd be willing to come to Scottsdale to see him and pick up the relevant file, if that would work for him? We settled on a time for the very next day. Good enough; he had struck me as a decent attorney and a potential additional source of work, so it was nice to see that happening. I didn't have anything on my plate for tomorrow, and there really were a couple of items I needed to pick up there, so why not?

Boy, it never rains but it pours. This was one of those times when I knew far too much and didn't dare say a word about what I knew, much less how I knew it. This attorney is a very good divorce lawyer. As I found out while sitting in his office, in this particular case, it seems that his client's to-be ex-husband was, putting it delicately, fooling around, and had, so far as his client could determine, a woman on the side.

Well, yeah, he did and I knew it, all too well. The problem was that this woman, this client of his, was Kendra Frankton, the wife of Becky's new boyfriend, and the 'woman on the side' just happened to be my very best friend. Of course, since virtually all of my information on this was strictly Family-related and as largely the product of Family surveillance, it was all quite confidential even within the Family. Outsiders and even other Family members were absolutely not privy to it.

I mean, Becky had told me all about him, but only by his first name. Well, his middle name, but that's what he goes by these days. The only reason I knew his full name at all was because of their Family surveillance files. Therein lay my dilemma. I couldn't say a word to this attorney about it. I couldn't sit there and turn down the case, because — since he hadn't given me Becky's name (I don't think he had it yet), just some oblique references — I figured that I had no way I could explain to say how I knew who he was talking about.

Add to that the fact that as the subject of an investigation, I couldn't breathe a word to Becky about it, either. Well, I suppose I could have, but since I'd never actually met the man in question, I felt more comfortable doing it this way. 'Comfortable' is a relative concept here, of course.

This is not a pleasant position to be in, as it were, between a rock and a hard place, and having to derail her new relationship, which was starting to look more and more necessary to me, didn't exactly make it any more pleasant to consider. Driving home from Phoenix was not the most enjoyable time I've ever spent in the car. I was also regretting not having Alec along to talk to about it on the way home, but he'd stayed back in Tucson with the dogs for the day because he had work to do. I needed to bounce this information off him as soon as possible.

It got worse the very next day. Alec and I had talked some about the situation that night, and we were discussing the problem further in my office — he usually uses the study in our house as his office, since he no longer practices law, except for me and the Family as his sole client — when the phone rang once again. We both listened as the machine picked up. "Ms. Trevethen? This is Family member Jon Frankton. I'm a psychiatrist in Scottsdale, and I have need of your services. The Family business office told me to ask for you rather than Mr. Youngston; I hope that is correct. When may I come to see you?"

Oh, shit. I picked up the phone. "Dr. Frankton? This is Amy Trevethen. Before you go any further, I need to warn you that if this is in connection with obtaining a divorce from your wife, I'm currently unable to take your case." I'd tell him I had a conflict of interest if he needed me to, but I hoped he'd figure that out without being told explicitly.

It seemed to rock him back for a moment. I could almost hear the wheels turning as he considered various reasons why I might not be able to take it. I didn't think he'd like any of the alternatives he came up with. Oh, hell, I didn't, either, really. I mean, if Becky was as crazy about him as she seemed to be, then we were likely to wind up getting to know him a lot better in the not-too-distant future anyway, and this wasn't a good way to begin the acquaintance. Downright lousy, in fact.

Frankly, given a choice, I'd far rather be working for him than his wife, but her attorney got to me first. Presuming I'd choose to be working for either one of them, given Becky's involvement in the situation. We exchanged a few pleasantries — 'Yes, A.M. Youngston is the same A.M. Youngston who is the Family CEO. No, A.M. Youngston is not available and does not return calls. Yes, emails and letters will always get replies. Thank you very much, doctor. I'm really very sorry I couldn't be more help to you at this time, doctor.' That sort of thing — and then he hung up. Reluctantly.

I simply looked at Alec. "So now what do I do?"

Okay, so Becky had found this fabulous fellow and she was crazy about him. Totally crazy, in my untutored opinion. He certainly seemed like a nice enough fellow over the phone, judging by the one brief conversation. Either he had charmed his way out of a really bad situation that he'd gotten himself into, and having spoken to him even briefly I thought I could see how he might have done that, or he really had just made a 'youthful error.' I don't know which, and it really isn't my issue anyway.

From the things Becky had told us and me (sometimes all three of us socialized, often just she and I did, the way we used to before Alec and I got married), he was separated from his wife, amicably, during the pending divorce and they had each other's blessing to lead their own lives. Apparently that wasn't an accurate statement of affairs — whups, poor word choice. Let's make that 'less than the truth.' A lot 'less than the truth,' in fact, if she was trying to get enough information to name Becky in the divorce or else use Becky and her involvement with Dr. Frankton to help her force a better settlement for herself.

Alec looked at me for a long minute. Finally he said, "Shall I answer now, or would you like some coffee first?" We're both serious coffee addicts, unfortunately. Well, maybe not 'unfortunately,' but we definitely are addicts. At least it's legal. The Family is broadly invested in coffee, now, too, thanks to me, so it's to our benefit that way, as well.

"Oh, hell, I can use a walk, and I'll bet the dogs could, too. Let's go to the coffee shop." The four of us — me, Alec and the two dogs — had heavily patronized one particular nearby coffee shop during the run-up to my assuming the CEO position last year, and we still often visit it when we want a break. I clucked to the dogs and they both came for their leads.

Luckily it was between terms at U of A, so we didn't have to fight for a spot. When we were settled in at one of our favorite patio tables with coffee for us and part of a stale bagel to split between the dogs, Alec began to address the issue. "It's really very simple. First, you call the attorney in Scottsdale back and tell him that on doing some preliminary investigation, you will have to decline the case as you have a serious conflict of interest."

I had my mouth open, but he held up his hand to stop me from interrupting. "You *can't* investigate your best friend and her boyfriend. You know that, if you stop to think about it without getting your emotions all tangled up in the process. Be the CEO here for a minute and try looking at it that way. That's also a conflict that any attorney worth his salt would understand, and you tell me this fellow is pretty good. At the same time, you couldn't possibly do this investigation without saying anything to Becky about it, and if you were trying to do it, you'd have to keep it from her. She's much too good a friend to both of us for you to do that.

"If it turns out to be necessary, then take the time to spell it out for him. You don't have to volunteer the information, but by all means tell him if he asks. Make that when he asks, because he will. No, on second thought, do volunteer it. He probably won't like it, but you really should let him know that the 'other woman' in question has turned out to be your best friend. He'll not only understand, but in the long run he'll be a lot happier with you off the case. And if you handle it that way, he'll be more likely to keep you in mind the next time he's got work for you down here. Giving it a day or two makes it look as though you really didn't know who she was when you were in his office, but you've just found it out." He stopped for some of his coffee. Sasha stood up and put her head in his lap, hoping for another piece of the bagel. She wouldn't get it until she was lying down again, but she could certainly have some attention and she got that.

"Then what do I tell her?" I asked. "She's been my best friend for longer than I can remember."

He nodded. "I know. What you *should* tell her is to find someone else. As far as we can tell from what's going on, he's already lied to her, big time, telling her that he and his wife were separated and so forth. Even if just from that, my own take on him is that he's bad news, at least until he's finalized his divorce. She, of course, will do what she damn well pleases. I've only known one more stubborn woman, and I married her." He smiled at me as he said it, and I grinned back at him. He was right about that. "Aren't the two of you on for dinner tomorrow?"

Becky and I have been getting together once a week, just the two of us, for drinks and usually dinner, ever since she moved out of the house, now the office, on Speedway, where she and I had lived when we were both relatively new in town. She moved out at the same time that I bought the place on Helen Street, which was about six months before Alec came to town, hoping to renew our acquaintance. Sometimes now it's the three of us, but less often. Becky and I try very hard to keep our private times together. "Yeah, we are. Margaritas and Mexican food."

"Good. Let her know that we'll bring dinner Friday, by the way. I may grill a steak. Anyway, you tell her about the investigation that's going on. You'll have to tell her that you were approached and then turned it down, as well as why. I'd suggest you not tell her about Dr. Frankton's call, but that's up to you. You also better be sure to spell out for her what she has to do if she's not going to give him the boot. Make that 'since she's not going to.' You know the drill. Nothing of import over the phone, no compromising emails, nothing near a cell phone whether it's in use or not, all shades drawn, no physical contact in public — everything."

I was nodding. I ought to know; I'd been doing investigations like that for years, and I knew exactly how to frustrate me. None of which guaranteed that she'd do all of it, or even any of it, and it didn't take much of a slip to obviate every precaution that had been taken up to that point. I felt sort of sick about it, to tell the truth.

Chapter 3

I still felt pretty bad about it the next evening. Usually when it's Mexican food, Becky and I will nibble chips until the meal arrives — not gobble them, but we'll pretty well finish the basket and the salsa bowl between us as we talk. This evening she spent most of her time just waving her second chip around, while she raved on about this fellow. A few things, ones she leaned over the table to tell me without anyone overhearing, were things that I wouldn't have told her about Alec and me. If I hadn't had my background, they would have made me blush. Not now, as she and I were almost equally immune to that (professional training for her).

I mean, I'm not quite completely immune, but it definitely takes a lot more than some almost-explicit sexual accounts to do it for me. Daddy used to write pornography as well as the science fiction he's known for. He published the porn under pen names, for obvious reasons, and when I began editing his science fiction for him when I was thirteen or fourteen, about a year or so after Mom died, I was awfully curious about the things he'd written but didn't show me (what I used to call his 'writing trance' was too unmistakable for him to hide what he'd been doing).

Being a snoop by nature, I dug around in his computer when he was out until I found it and read it — all of it. So I'm way used to hearing about that sort of thing, and generally in a much more salacious and explicit fashion than Becky was giving me. Overloaded, in fact. Different story. Finally she ran down. "Becky, can I give you some sisterly advice?" Becky's actually my fourth cousin, but we've always been together, either inseparable during the day while we lived with our parents or as roommates in college and then here. I've said that before, haven't I? Oh, well, I repeat myself. We're closer than most of the sisters

I've known, lots closer. We've been known to claim that we are sisters; we'd always back each other up on that claim, if asked.

"Of course you can. Would you and Alec like to meet Jon?" Oooh, this wasn't going to go over well at *all*.

"Becky, let him go." She looked shocked. "Becky, if nothing else, he's lied to you. A very *big* lie. He and his wife are apparently *not* separated and they most definitely are *not* okay with each other leading their own lives. They're getting a divorce, and you are going to be named as 'the other woman' just as soon as she, well, her attorney, finds out who you are and gets some proof." Her eyes got as big as saucers.

She was speechless, which left a void I filled. "Here's how I know this. I just went up to Scottsdale two days ago because I got a call from an attorney about an investigation he needed to have done. You remember Jim Briteman from last year?" She nodded dumbly. "His attorney remembered me when he needed some work done in Tucson. I couldn't turn it down then because he didn't know who the 'other woman' was, and you've never given me Jon's last name, although once I saw the file I realized it had to be you. I've got to call him tomorrow and back out of the case due to a conflict — tomorrow, so I can reasonably claim that I didn't know who you were from the beginning. I've lost two cases on this 'boyfriend' of yours." Oops, that was just a bit more than I should have allowed to slip out, and she noticed immediately.

Her eyes narrowed. "What do you mean, two cases? What's the other one?"

Mentally I sighed. This was already not going well. Not going well at *all*. Well, when you've already put your foot into your mouth, it does you no favors to let it sit there. Or to start chewing, for that matter. "The first case was Mrs. Frankton's investigation of her husband and his other woman, i.e. you. The second — I got a call today from Dr. Frankton himself, trying to get me to investigate his wife."

Becky seemed stunned. It didn't last. "Why you? Where did he get your name from? I've never mentioned Amy Youngston to him at all. The few times your name has come up at all, it's always been with Alec and both of you are simply the Trevethens, friends of mine. Good friends. And why would he be calling an investigator in Tucson when he lives in Scottsdale?"

"Yeah, I know. Well, I figured as much. No, he called today and asked for me, Amy Trevethen, by name. He also referred to 'Mr.' Youngston, so he clearly doesn't really know who I am."

I could see the wheels turning. Damn it! I hadn't wanted to get into this, but of course I'd opened my big fat mouth. Idiot me. "Wait a minute. Where did he get your name from? Why would he be asking for you by name?"

I gave her one of my patented sour looks. "Confidential? *CEO* confidential?" This was the little private routine I'd begun to use when I needed to refer to things that she and/or Alec only had access to because of me, whenever I wanted their advice or input on a Family matter and whatever I told them had to be kept utterly private. Both of them were experienced secret keepers from their professions, well-versed in keeping matters confidential. She knew exactly what I was talking about.

Becky hesitated for a moment before nodding. She didn't really look thrilled, but she also knew that when I decided to do things this way, they had to be done my way or not at all. Like Alec suggested, I can out-stubborn her. Barely. "Okay. CEO confidential."

"He got my name from the Family business office. Becky, he's Family. His wife doesn't know about the Family, but he is."

My, what interesting emotions played across her face in those moments before she put her professional visage on and shut it all down. I could only imagine that her mind was working a mile a minute. Then she got a bit of a smile that spread until it kind of took over her entire face. "Oh, that's wonderful. He's Family! He and I ..." I held up my hand to stop her.

"Nah ah. How are you going to tell him? CEO confidential, remember? He's just another outsider to you now, and you're not married to him. You can't tell him that you are, and for *sure* you can't tell him that you know he is, too. And he's been *lying* to you, Becky." I hated to have to keep driving this one home, but it seemed necessary.

Working against me, she hadn't realized that there'd been several times when I'd seen the wistful looks she gave Alec and me when we weren't supposed to be noticing. I had a pretty good idea of how badly she wanted to have a really good relationship with someone. Probably better than she did, at least consciously. If she let him go, we'd be going right back to that, and it would hurt her badly. Of course, in all likelihood, so would continuing a relationship with him, if it played out. Some choice.

The evening kind of went downhill from there. We're much too close as friends to let something as minor as a mere man come between us, but I now disapproved of her new guy a lot more than I had before, and it was pretty clear to her. And this without so much as meeting him. She was also going to do exactly as she pleased, and that showed, too. I tried stressing how she had to act to frustrate the inevitable investigation that somebody would be doing, but while I know she heard me — she'd gotten some small degree of exposure last year, during the ... run-up ... to my becoming the CEO, I had some serious doubts that she would really exercise the discipline necessary to do it.

Keeping a good investigator from getting the information on you and your habits is not easy to do consistently and successfully; you have to be paying attention to what you're doing every moment and stay in the proper mindset all the time. Oh, well, I'd let Alec work on her Friday. Tomorrow is another day.

Friday we loaded up the car with cooler and dogs to head for her place. Becky's home is up in the Catalina foothills, a fairly upscale part of Tucson, and the dogs love it there. She keeps them for us when we travel, like for board meetings. The midtown area where Alec and I live at the moment is, let's be kind, not 'fairly upscale.' It's largely made up of students and the economically disadvantaged; I'd liked it because I had the office, I didn't give a shit about the neighborhood and the house couldn't have been more convenient for me without being inside the office.

Bruno, the Belgian Malinois — think of an elegant, long-legged, very fine-boned version of a German Shepherd, tan body and black mask — hopped into the car quite quickly. Sasha, the long-coat Akita — think medium-sized brown and white bear — took her time as she gathered herself and finally hopped in. It's not quite as amusing a sight as usual, since she's been sheared for the summer. Long-coats carry a *lot* of hair, and since she spends a certain amount of time lying around in the yard — her choice — it makes warm weather easier on her. After all, this is Arizona.

There's a corner of Becky's pool that's shaded at this hour, and Sasha, as always, made a beeline for the exact spot. She hooked her forefeet over the edge of the pool and lay down, toes in the water, watching the water surface and occasionally drinking from the world's largest water dish. Why she won't jump in is simply beyond me. Bruno's attitude is more like, 'Mom, if I get in, you'll put shampoo on me and call it a bath.' I wouldn't, not really, but he keeps his distance, even if we're in the water. Perhaps especially then.

After we had the dinner things arranged in Becky's fridge, Alec announced that he was up for a swim before drinks, and who was going to join him?

I gave him a half-smile. "You just like looking at Becky naked." She and I have been swimming nude since we were in our early teens, and Alec joined us after he and I were married. Neither Alec nor I even own suits, and Becky's still got pretty much the same Playboy-model figure she had when we were in college.

In fact, somebody claiming to be from the magazine tried to recruit her when we were sophomores in college. Becky thanked him for the compliment, told him no, and then she and I just shared a major laugh over it when he was gone. He might even have been for real. I suppose I could be jealous, if I were so inclined, but I'm not; she's no threat to me and I love them both. Pity she hadn't found somebody more like Alec. Or at least single, like he had been.

He laughed. "Should I deny it? You were the one who taught me to appreciate beauty whenever the opportunity arose." I had my mouth open, but he motioned me to hold it. "And as much as I appreciate her appearance, which I certainly do, seeing her always makes me think of the real greatest treasure in my life, which is you."

Becky snorted. "Now he's got you, Amy. Alec, you're good. Awfully good. I'm up." With that, she pulled her t-shirt over her head and began to unhook her bra. Not to be outdone, Alec and I were ready just about the same time.

Becky was about to be the first into the water when I finally noticed her back. "What is *that*?"

She looked over her shoulder. "You like it? It's my new tattoo." I suppose it was quite nice, as these things go — one of those lower-back designs, fairly broad, good-sized and centered on a large red, blue and yellow butterfly.

Becky loves butterflies, although this — was a surprise. That's putting it mildly.

I shook my head. "After all of the discussions you and I have had over tattoos, piercings and the like, you are absolutely the last person I ever expected to do that. Other than me, that is."

She shrugged. "Jon likes tattoos. Anyway, this is just ink and paint. It's good for maybe a week, if I leave it alone. I'm having it redone twice a week right now just to keep it looking fresh. I didn't feel like going all the way. Not yet, anyway."

Well, that was a relief. I mean, yes, it's her body. But she'd never expressed any interest in such a thing before, and we'd both been rather critical of those who did get piercings and tattoos in our discussions. But — 'Jon likes tattoos'? 'Not yet, anyway'? I didn't like the sound of those. "Uh, Becky, have you thought about what I said the other night?" Bruno rolled his eyes in my direction. Did I sound to him like I was upset? Sasha was busy watching the floor jets in the pool stir up the bottom water and generally ignoring us.

A while later, when we were setting up dinner, the doorbell rang. Not exactly the most common occurrence out here, but not unheard of either. I was still cutting up things for the salad, and Becky was setting the table. Alec got the door. When he came back in, I asked him who it had been. "No idea. Some tall blonde. Said she apparently had the wrong house, apologized and left."

Over dinner, Alec and I both tried to warn Becky off him. Not the tattoo, well, body paint; that was harmless enough, I guess. Even a real tattoo probably wouldn't have been all that serious an issue in the greater scheme of things. But this Frankton fellow was something else. We both tried to get it through her head that if he'd lie to her and involve her in his divorce while reassuring her that everything was just peachy, then he was bad news for her, even if he *was* Family. Regardless of whether he really believed what he'd told her, being with him before his divorce was final would still potentially leave her in some very bad straits indeed.

I never did tell her about his earlier problems; I figured that wasn't my place. Now that he was in private practice, it probably didn't matter, at least not on the same scale. Unless it indicated a fundamental honesty issue, but without more recent evidence, that question could wait.

Didn't work anyway. She wasn't having any of it. I have to admit that as long as I've known her, and that was since long before we both decided boys were icky (a phase which didn't last all that long for either of us), I'd never seen her like this. It was almost as though he had some sort of Svengali-like hold over her, although nothing in his file suggested what it might be. I could only presume that she was *really* crazy about him.

Finally we tried to emphasize what she had to do to frustrate an investigator — mostly my efforts — and what her vulnerabilities were in terms of the divorce proceedings, both personally and professionally. Especially professionally. That was mostly Alec. I'm not sure how much of it got through.

Damn it, I know she's a big girl now and she's not *really* my kid sister, but I need and depend on her for advice in Family matters, and, at the very least, this makes me question her judgment at some level. I can't afford that. The Family can't afford it, either. Besides, no matter how old we get, I don't think I'll ever quite shake the feeling that she *is* my kid sister and I have to look out for her.

I believe it was three days later — might have been four; I wasn't keeping track. I was sitting in the kitchen at breakfast, working on a bowl of chili (it still drives Alec crazy that I eat chili for breakfast, but he was in the study with his toast, catching up on world and local news), with my second cup of coffee, watching a financial program on the TV.

Suddenly Alec rushed in, grabbed the remote off the table and changed to one of the local channels. My first reaction was a flash of anger. I'd been watching the program closely and actually getting something from it, which is important when you've got the sole responsibility for the investing of a huge fortune.

Then I really looked at the picture on the screen and my anger evaporated in an instant. I knew that house; it was Becky's. The voice on the screen was talking about the doctor's body being found in the house, and I had a flash of terror. Had something happened to her? Then they shifted to a picture of Becky in the back seat of a sheriff's car, apparently either trying to hide her face or else crying. Maybe both. Oh, *shit!*

No matter what was going on, this was definitely going to be lots worse than simply being named as the 'other woman' in a divorce case. Alec watched me long enough to see that I understood what I was seeing, then he said, "I've got to change. I'd rather be dressed a bit better when I get to the holding facility."

Numbly I nodded. "Me, too. Well, hell, I'm just going as her sister, I can stay like this." I was in my usual jeans and t-shirt. So was he; we're normally very casual. Not a lot of call for more, these days.

Alec looked at me as he was leaving the kitchen. "Lose the gun." I hated to admit it, but that was probably good advice. As an investigator, I sometimes wind up in … difficult situations. I go armed all the time as a matter of course. I carry a pistol and several knives concealed about my person. My usual gun, the one I had on now, is a little Kahr PM40 in .40 S&W caliber, which rides in a shoulder holster under my left arm. I wear the gun all day, every day under virtually any and all circumstances. I hardly notice

I've got it on any more. At times I've been very grateful that I had it.

But going to the jail was a different circumstance. They wouldn't let the gun in, so it was either leave it here, leave it in the car, or let the police log it in and hold it for when I left. None of which I liked, but leaving it here at least kept the issue as low-key as possible. I pulled the t-shirt up to my neck so I could get the holster off. It felt more than just a bit strange to be without it, but I'd keep the knives. The blades were short, if very sharp and well-designed, and either the deputies wouldn't notice them or they might not care that much if they did. Besides, those they could hold if they had to.

By the time I'd let the dogs out back for a quick spin ('quick' is a concept which is not normally in Sasha's vocabulary, but she seemed to understand the urgency today) and they'd come in again, Alec was back in a suit and ready to go. I grabbed the fanny pack I usually wore in lieu of a purse and we were out the door almost before I could catch my breath.

Chapter 4

I hadn't even pushed the button on the remote to set the alarm, much less locked the door, when I heard the phone ring. I ducked back inside and sure enough, it was Becky calling Alec to be her lawyer. What I could hear on the robocall sounded lousy. I hollered for him and went out to start the car while he took the call.

Her home is outside of the city limits, so she'd been taken into custody by the Pima County Sheriff's Department. When we got to the jail, she was still in an interrogation room, although apparently she wasn't being questioned any more as she'd asked to have her attorney. They wouldn't let me go in, too; I was merely her sister and had no right, apparently, to go in to see her. I lied. As I said earlier, she'd have backed up my claim. I had to sit outside and wait while Alec, as her attorney, got to go in and talk with her. He was in there for a long time.

When he came out, I could barely contain myself, but I managed. Just. He looked around and simply said, "Let's get out of here." We found an almost-acceptable coffee shop not too far away and sat. Instead of jumping up and down with schoolgirl impatience like I wanted to at some level, I sat quietly. It wasn't easy. I had to call on a lot of my CEO and investigative experience to manage it.

"Here's the deal. She and this doctor boyfriend of hers were out for the evening and got back to her house about ten last night, maybe a bit before. That's the last thing she remembers until she woke up in her bedroom about two or three this morning. The light on her nightstand was on and the room was covered in blood, apparently all his. He was lying on the bed, face-up and very dead. Very messily dead. She woke upon the floor next to the bed, pretty much face-down, largely covered with blood and lying partly in a pool of his blood.

When she was able to calm down enough, she checked him for a pulse and then called the sheriff. You really know the rest. I did ask that the crime scene techs not cut up or otherwise damage the little rug in her bedroom, because it's quite valuable and has significant sentimental value besides, and they said they'd pass the message along. No guarantees beyond that."

I was all but speechless. Well, we'd been right about one thing, Frankton was bad news, at least for her. Now, it seemed, he was even more bad news. Not the greatest news for himself, either, but wherever he was now, he was probably beyond worrying about such things. Also beyond any repercussions from his earlier missteps. Becky could eventually have weathered his getting a divorce, even with 'other woman' status. The hit to her professional reputation might have diminished her practice for a while, but probably not completely, and it would eventually have recovered.

This was a whole new ballgame, a much worse one for her. "What sort of shape is she in?"

Alec shook his head. "Well, I'm not the mental health professional here, but I'd say she's either in shock or seriously depressed. Maybe both. No sign of emotions, precious little interest in anything going on around her. She didn't seem to care what was going to happen to her or what could happen to her. What information I got out of her, I pretty much had to pry out. Kind of like pulling teeth."

This was not good. "She didn't do it. The only way I could see that she could really have done it would be either accident or fury, and if it had been accidental, she would have tried to tell them that. Still be trying, I expect. I also think that if she'd been furious enough with him, she probably wouldn't go into such a funk so quickly, like that.

"I mean, killing a man isn't easy, and I presume it's worse if it's someone you care — cared — about. That ought to take a *huge* amount of rage, and that's just not her. I think it'd take an awful lot to work her up to that point, and she wouldn't come down easily. Or quickly."

Alec was doing his best imitation of a cocked eyebrow. "So what do you know about what killing a man is like?"

I took a long pull at my coffee, then put the cup down and looked off into the distance and spoke more quietly. Another episode of telling Alec something I'd never tell anyone else. I ought to be used to it by now. I'm not, not completely, but Alec, like Becky, is so completely inside of me, inside of any of my defenses, that I can do it.

Becky had a word for it — internalized, that was it. He and she are so much inside me, in my heart and in my head, that I've internalized them. "I was twelve. A couple of months after Mom was killed, I was home alone, watching TV in my bedroom. Daddy was out for the evening. I heard the glass break at the front door, so I turned the TV down, got my .45, the one I shot in competition, from the nightstand and racked the slide. It already had a full magazine.

"Then I got on my knees by my bed, on the side away from the doorway, and I waited. It wasn't long before they came to my room, and the one in front started making comments about the little girl with the big gun, and how I'd better put it down before I hurt someone. I didn't care what he said. He could have walked away even then and I'd have let him go. But when he started to raise his own gun, I started shooting. Five rounds in all.

"Made a mess of the hallway, but he dropped like a rock and never stirred. His partner headed for the door, leaking blood. They caught him later that night." I sighed. "No, it wasn't easy, but grief really wasn't any part of it. Mom deserved my grief, and I wasn't done there, so what grief I had, she got. Those two ... didn't. Oh, I admit I had some bad dreams, and I spent a fair amount of time talking to Daddy and even to Becky's parents about it."

I straightened up in my chair. "But dammit, I'm alive and whole, and they could have been if they hadn't broken into our home, or even if they'd walked away from my bedroom. I'd also bet my dreams would have been a whole lot worse if I hadn't done what I did, too. Assuming I'd been around to have any.

"I don't know what the DA was thinking of doing to me, but I expect the lawyer Daddy got probably pointed out to him that both by my account and all of the forensic evidence, this had been two armed men who had broken into our house and come to my bedroom, and trying to prosecute a twelve-year-old girl for defending herself under those circumstances wasn't going to fly and probably wouldn't look good come election time, either. It all went away."

Alec laid his hand gently over mine. "Are you sure it's all gone away?" he asked quietly.

I shook my head sharply, not to argue but simply to reorder my thoughts. "Oh, by now, definitely. Enough of it, anyway. I was a nine-day wonder at school, for all that Daddy tried to keep it under the radar. But I wasn't going to play that game, and they tired of it pretty fast. The boys, that is; the girls gave me plenty of room for quite a while longer than that. But I grew up reading and listening to Col. Cooper, and his position was that after a shooting like that, you should be glad you survived and don't fret about what he called the goblins.

"Since everybody who really knew what had happened supported what I'd done, I made it without too much trouble. It made me tougher, although I suspect my reputation in school was more that I was hard, not tough. Believe me, though, I've never forgotten, not one bit." I'd slumped down a bit as I related the account, so I straightened up again. "Does it shock you?"

He thought for several moments before responding. "Shock? No. Surprise, yes, but I've always known you were strong and … ready to defend yourself, I guess I'd say. So not shocked."

I patted his hand in response. "Good. Let's get back to Becky and her situation. What do we do now?"

Alec looked more thoughtful than usual, although his eyes never quite left me. I could see the concern in them, but we needed to get down to business. "Well, the first thing is that we're not going to be able to get her out of there. She's being held on murder one and a couple of related lesser counts. No bail for capital cases, of course. I've got to go over to the west side tonight for her initial court appearance and no, you can't come. Well, you can if you want, but you're just going to be sitting around again; they won't let you in to see her.

"Besides, she won't even actually be there; she'll just appear from the jail by TV. Sorry, but it's not my call, that's just how the county works. Then I think we'd better see who we can get to represent her. This sort of case is way beyond my expertise, and while I plan to stay very involved in her defense, we need someone who really knows what he's doing to run this case."

My mind was racing. Capital case? Becky? Oh, *God!* "You're going to represent her. There's simply no other choice here. You're the one she knows, and you're the one she trusts. Both of us trust. But we can certainly use someone high-powered and experienced in cases like this to do it with you. Let me get back home. I'll find out who the Family has, to start with. If we have to go outside the Family to get the right person, we'll do it, of course, although I'd rather not if there's an option, if only for the expense. How about forensic experts?"

Alec shook his head. "Not yet. Nothing can or will happen until they've finished their own processing of the scene anyway, and that's going to take some time. Figure it's likely to be about a week, and could be more."

Not even the CEO can get the Family business office moving fast enough to suit me — although 'fast enough to suit me' at that point probably meant that they should have had the list ready for me before I picked up the phone, and even I, when I'm entirely rational — this isn't one of those occasions — realize that that isn't reasonable, especially with the seven or eight hour time difference from Tucson to Golondrino, where the Family offices are.

Luckily the business office is staffed 24/7, since the Family ranges all around the world. I had the list delivered by email and was going over it when Alec returned home shortly before bedtime. He stopped into the study and took the time for a quick kiss before announcing that he needed a drink. I said I'd take one too, but I was still stuck on one of the names on the list. "Look at this, will you? 'John Tolliver, Lake Tahoe, California.'"

If you've lived in the United States over the last ten years or so, and you've been paying even the least bit of attention to the news, you don't need to be told any more than 'Yes, *that* John Tolliver, Esquire.' Not after the major criminal cases he's had. The major cases he's *won*, with all of the attendant publicity. All of which seemed to be just what Becky needed. The expertise, not the publicity, although it looked like she already had plenty of that. This case was far too public and making much too big a splash in the news to suit me, at least in terms of trying to keep the Family under the radar. Hopefully nobody would pry that far into her background.

Alec's eyebrows went way up. "Tolliver? But he's ..."

"Black? Yeah, he is. So what? A lot of the Family is white, but not all of us. You just haven't been around enough yet. We've got all types. I don't have actual stats, and I'm not sure if they even exist, but let's take care of this first."

I picked up the phone. It was getting late — actually, it *was* late, almost into the evening news. We were on the same time as California nowadays, since Arizona doesn't do daylight savings, but I could at least leave a message. "Mr. Tolliver? This is Family member Amy Trevethen in Tucson, Arizona. I'm calling you on behalf of Family member Rebecca Swan, also from Tucson, who is in dire need of your services." Just then the phone on the other end was picked up.

"This is Tolliver."

"Oh, Mr. Tolliver." I wasn't particularly disconcerted or upset; I screen my calls the same way. "You're in." At quite a late hour, too.

"Actually, I was on my way out the door when I heard your call come in. You said that both of you are Family?"

"Yes, sir. I'm an investigator with A.M. Youngston and Associates —" He cut me off.

"The CEO? That A.M. Youngston?" Alec came back into the room and set a drink down on the coaster in front of me.

"That's the one, sir. And Dr. Swan —"

"Is that the same Dr. Swan I saw on TV this evening? Arrested in Tucson for the murder of her lover?" One of these days I was going to get to finish a sentence.

"Yes, sir, that's her. We need to clear her and get her turned loose."

He was silent for several seconds. "If you want to clear her, you're much better placed for that than I am. Clearing her is not my business. Investigating might accomplish that, at least if it can be done at all. If you want me to help, you need to understand that my job will be to defend her and, if there is any way possible, get her a 'not guilty' verdict. Clearing her is just not something that you hire me for. Or any lawyer, for that matter."

Alec had been listening to both sides of the conversation; the phone is loud enough. His voice was low enough not to carry to the other end of the line. "He's right. Don't worry about it now. Just get him."

Dammit! I wanted her cleared, not simply acquitted. She *needed* to be cleared, too, for her own sake. Simply being found 'not guilty' didn't really establish anything beyond the prosecution's failure to prove its case, and I knew she was innocent here. But first things first. "You're right, of course, sir. But can I, uh, prevail upon you to take the case?"

"I'm not licensed in Arizona. I'll need local counsel to affiliate with."

"No problem, sir. My husband is an attorney. He's already her attorney of record."

He wasn't quite silent this time, I could hear the tapping of his keyboard. "Okay, I'll be there Friday. Get me a room, please. No, on second thought, don't bother, I'll get it myself. Will you pick me up, or should I make my own way from the airport?"

"What time, sir?"

"Hm. Flight time … pick me up at, let's say, 3 o'clock sharp at the executive terminal of Tucson International. Will that work?"

I looked at Alec, who just shrugged. "Certainly, sir. We'll see you there. Or at least I will."

Chapter 5

I spent the next two days on pins and needles. I would be allowed to see Becky for one half-hour per week, no more, and I tried to get in to see her the day after her initial court appearance.

No such luck; I couldn't see her until Friday morning. Most of what communication I had with her was what Alec could tell her or carry back to me, and as her attorney, he spent quite a bit of time with her. When I did see her — on a TV screen, not even through glass — she looked, well, awful. Not just the lack of makeup and unkempt hair; I'd been prepared for those. Alec had warned me about her appearance. But at some level, she just looked emotionally flat, almost as though she were dying inside.

It was as though she had nothing left to live for any more and was letting go of her life from the inside out. I spent most of my precious half-hour trying to buck her up and to find some spark, some tiny degree of animation inside of her. I don't think I succeeded. I left the jail feeling worse than when I had arrived. Alec was heading in to consult with her when I left.

For just an instant, I almost wished — *almost* — that he and she had been having an affair. At least we wouldn't be going through this mess. Then I considered the idea just a tiny bit more. Well, no, not this mess, but there'd sure be a different mess when I found out about it. Shit. And Alec's not like that, anyway. He's too much of a Boy Scout, bless his heart. She wouldn't do anything like that, either.

Picking up Tolliver held more promise. I was early to the terminal, and after badgering the people running the place, I found out what plane he was flying on — his own, apparently — and watched him land. I was hard-pressed not to let my turbulent emotions show when he came inside, but I waited with feigned patience while he took care of berthing his airplane, or whatever it is you do with them, while he was here.

He was just as tall, slender and well-dressed as he appeared on TV. When he was done, he turned to me. "Mrs. Trevethen?" I nodded. I actually had my mouth open to respond when he added, "Or should I address you as CEO Youngston?"

That did it. Of all of the things he could have said, that was probably about the last line I could have predicted. All of my pent-up emotion went as flat and as fast as a punctured balloon. "And just what makes you think that, Mr. Tolliver?"

He smiled. It looked honest, but I reminded myself that in his business, appearances were everything and nothing whatsoever about them might indicate his actual feelings. "I could, I suppose, say that I did my due diligence in investigating exactly who was engaging my services, but the simple fact is that I actually remember you from when you were just a kid. I was one of the guys who managed to shut Ray Fields out of our group because we thought he was a stick-in-the-mud, back at the occasional Family gatherings we used to have, and I remember a girl who hung around him one year with all of the enthusiasm of someone who was having a tooth pulled without anesthetic. Your name was Amy Youngston then, and I put two and two together. Call it a bit of an educated guess, if you like."

I snorted. I've spent most of the past year trying to keep my actual identity hidden from anyone who didn't already know me. Being public about who I was, at least within the Family, would have made it almost impossible to continue being an investigator, and damn it, I *like* what I do. I wasn't about to stop doing what I love just because I also happened to be running one of the richest enterprises on the planet.

He seemed to understand. "Don't worry about it. I have little or no need to call on the CEO as the CEO, and I certainly don't go spreading around what I know. I just find it amusing that you try to hide your identity, although I believe I can understand why you do. But thinking back to that summer, if I may ask, what do your parents think of your becoming the new CEO?"

"My father is … impressed. My mother died soon after that summer."

He touched my shoulder; I got the impression that it was a significant gesture by his standards. He didn't seem like a hugger. That's too bad, I appreciate huggers. "Please accept my sympathies. I expect that it still hurts quite a bit; I'm not sure you ever quite get over something like that. I'm very sorry for you." Well, he certainly knew how to say the right things. That's why they pay him the big bucks, I guess. That's certainly why the Family was going to pay him big bucks in this case.

I stopped at his hotel so he could check in. He'd gotten quite a nice room, I expect. Certainly the hotel was a nice one. What the hell, the Family was paying his bill, and this would be going into it. The Family could afford him. I knew that as well as anyone. Better than most, probably. Then we went to the house to meet Alec and the dogs. After shaking Alec's hand and petting both dogs, John looked around the living room with an air of slight amusement. "So this is where the CEO lives." Well, yeah, it is kind of on the tiny side, the neighborhood isn't the greatest, like I said, and we're very aware of it nowadays. But it's also temporary.

Alec's eyebrows were about to climb into his hairline, but I just looked at him and mouthed, 'later.' To Tolliver, I just said, "For now. We're buying property on the west side where we're going to build. I've had this place for the last six years, and since it's only the four of us, it'll do for the time being."

One thing that did impress me about Tolliver was that he was clearly dog people. He was not in the least concerned about getting hair on his clothes, thank God. In this house, there's precious little choice. Then when Sasha put her paw on his knee to ask to have her tummy rubbed, he understood and reached down to oblige her.

Professionally, I don't think he and Alec quite hit it off. Tolliver was clearly accustomed to running the show and calling the shots, and Alec had been running his own practice for years. His days of being a junior associate were long behind him. Now he was apparently back in the same position again and, judging from his body language, he definitely didn't appreciate it, although I figured he could manage when he had to, like now.

The two of them talked case background and initial strategy for about two hours. When they finally took a breath, I broke in — I'd been listening without speaking, something I do a lot of as the CEO — to ask about dinner and drinks. I left them to their devices while I went into the kitchen. I decided on a stir-fry and only cut my fingers three times — not badly — while I was peeling and dicing the kubocha squash. I wasn't really paying attention to what I was doing.

For damn sure I wasn't. I couldn't shake the vision I had of poor Becky, trapped inside the jail and trapped inside her own head as well, in all likelihood, judging from how she'd seemed this morning. I'd have managed in there a lot better than she was doing. Well, certainly somewhat better, anyway. In the jail, that is. I probably had at least as many pitfalls inside my head as she did, or at least I used to. I've had a lot less since Alec and I got married. Even about being in the jail, I couldn't honestly say 'a lot' better. Not that it would have been a pleasant time for me, but let's be fair here. I think I'm a lot tougher than she is, in situations like that.

Oh, sure, she's real strong professionally. Being a psychologist is not a profession for wussies, and she's definitely not one. But on a personal level, her life was always on the right side of the law, and it always had an organization, a — a niceness, I suppose you could say — and a certain predictability to it. At some level, Becky is a gentle soul, I suppose is the way I'd put it. This was, it *had* to be, turning her entire world upside down and likely inside out as well. Just the experience of awakening to find what she had … I couldn't imagine it. I figured I'd probably be able to handle it (not if it were her or Alec, a small voice inside my head reminded me), at least better than she was doing.

I also figured she would have freaked out over some of the things I'd been through about a year ago, like having my house shot up twice, with me and the dogs in it both times, and then being grilled by some Tucson PD detectives for hours on end. There had even been worse, right here in this very kitchen. Another story. Or what I'd gone through in my own bedroom, shortly after Mom was killed. But Becky knew I'd shot and killed one of those intruders.

Admittedly, what she was going through right now was significantly worse than the shooting up of the house and the grilling had been. I looked at the counter. Several bowls of cut-up vegetables sat there. Had I done all of that? Well, Alec sure hadn't, and while Bruno and Sasha were waiting expectantly — I usually feed them before doing our dinner, so they were probably wondering just what in the hell was going on — I didn't see either one of them stepping up to the cutting board, either. I must have been on autopilot. Bruno, sitting down, inched himself a bit closer to me, smiling broadly. Can I take a hint?

Not usually, it's not my strong suit, to say the least. But right now, yes, I suppose I can. Especially when it's as unsubtle as his are. Take a break and get their dinners — they were happy. A dog's life was simple and repetitive. I wished mine was. By now, I could have directed the investment of literally tens or even hundreds of billions of dollars — yes, I said billions, with a 'b' — in one fell swoop and been less upset than I was by the simple arrest and imprisonment of my best friend. Simple, my ass.

I poked around in the freezer until I found the bag of cooked shrimp. If they were going into the wok frozen, I couldn't see starting with raw, and anyway, I buy mostly shell-on raw shrimp. I can't peel them frozen. It took a serious effort of will to stop the tears I could feel welling up as I ran tepid water over the shrimp to partially thaw them and then tailed them.

Understand that I'm not an easy crier. I can certainly cry if there's enough emotional stress. Some of the history Daddy used to have me learn, especially when I had to work to get into the heads of the people living it, the way he taught me to do, well, that could make me cry. Some of it, not a lot. Much of written history is fairly dull stuff.

I cried when I used to give up my guide dog puppies, although they were going in a good cause and hell, all of the other raisers cried rivers when their puppies left, too. I always figured I could manage to do some crying then without anyone thinking less of me.

I also cried my eyes out when Mom was killed, although Daddy was making just as many tears as I was then. That was a really horrid time. But on anything like a normal, day-to-day basis, I don't cry much at all, regardless of the provocation.

I've learned to be tough, and I *am* tough. But as I've said, I've internalized Becky. I can't armor myself with that toughness I've spent so much time building, not to help me against what's happening to her, any more than I could if it were Alec. I don't believe I'd cried for Becky since we were both barely teenagers. I think it was probably the first time she had a serious thing for a boy and he treated her very badly. I cried then. *After* I beat the crap out of him.

Of course, word of *that* got around the school by the next morning, and neither of us had many dates, or even much interest from boys, for quite a while. Maybe I overreacted. Who, me? I looked down and found that the two-pound bag of shrimp I'd been working on only had two shrimp left in it. Oh, what the hell. They went into the bowl, too. I hoped the wok was big enough. I took a few minutes and dug around in the fridge and pantry, pulling out various liquids, spices and such for a sauce. When everything was done, I had to get up on the three-step to get the huge pasta bowl to hold it all. With luck, there'd be enough containers around to hold the leftovers, and then there'd be enough room in the fridge and freezer to store them. I set the table in the dining room for three, and when I carried in the bowl, I'd blotted and wiped my face very carefully with a dishtowel. I was glad I don't normally wear makeup, because it definitely wouldn't have survived.

I might as well not have been at the table, with or without makeup. Tolliver knew, without even being told, that dogs don't get to beg at the table. Both of them tried him, but not all that hard. He was gracious enough to compliment my cooking and my choice of wine, but it all seemed just a bit *pro forma*, and that was almost the entire sum of what he said to me during dinner. Besides, the wine wasn't that good. Decent, sure, but not as good as he made like he thought it was. Maybe he's just not a wine connoisseur.

Oh, God, how I wanted to break in, to take charge of the conversation and the planning. But I know my limitations. I don't practice law. If I'd been interested, I could have done that after law school instead of becoming an investigator.

But at the same time, I just *hate* to be relegated to playing the part of the 'little woman.' I don't blame Alec for this evening, and I really shouldn't blame Tolliver for it either, since I'm not the lawyer here, although by now Tolliver had thoroughly rubbed me the wrong way. For no real reason I could even think of, he just had. But only after I'd gotten coffee for all of us was anything more directed at me, and that was mostly just to explain, by Tolliver, that he'd appreciate a ride to his hotel, and he'd fly back to Tahoe in the morning. Apparently he had some cases going there, relatively minor ones, and they could be handled by his associates for the most part, but he had to set them up that way and oversee them periodically. He'd be back here early the next week. Nothing was going to happen to Becky's case in the meantime that Alec couldn't handle. This was the easy time, as these things go. The last two weeks or so before trial were going to get crazy, but there was no reason to let things go off the deep end now. Numbly I nodded.

Alec was back from dropping him off about the time that I finished cleaning up and putting leftovers away. We didn't have to say much to each other. Not angry or upset, we just didn't have anything to convey. I did say something stupid, but all kidding aside, he assured me that with Tolliver's help, Becky had the best possible legal team in place. He had the names of a bunch of forensic experts to call Monday and everything was under as much control as it could possibly be.

Like I said, I'm not an easy crier. I'd go so far as to say I *hate* to cry. It feels like weakness to me, and I refuse to show that to anyone voluntarily, although admittedly I wasn't worried about either Alec or Becky seeing me that way. That night, though, for the first time since we were married, I just dug myself into Alec's right side as close as I could, encircled by his arm, laid my face on his chest and cried myself to sleep as he held me.

Chapter 6

I woke up less than refreshed and still feeling like hell. Alec seemed to understand when I just wanted to cuddle before getting up instead of doing something more. This morning I simply wasn't in the mood for much of anything, and I needed some serious comforting. I was heartsick in a way I'd never been before, worrying about my best friend. Way too internalized, and there's not one damn thing I can do about it. Or would do about it, either. It all keeps coming back to that, doesn't it? I hate not being able to close myself off like this.

After a while I felt hot breath on my back. That had to be Bruno, as I could see Sasha on Alec's other side. Oh, well, they have needs, too. I get to pee first; that's the privilege of being human, although the way I felt this morning, it was more convention than conviction.

Breakfast was subdued, to say the least. I could, I suppose, just claim that my heart wasn't in it, but it was a lot more than just that. I still felt utterly sick to the depths of my soul about Becky. I knew she was innocent. Not just of the murder, but also of whatever she needed to really manage behind bars. As I've said, I'd been her big sister for our entire time together. Not all that much older, true, but I was still generally the protector, or so I felt and had for all of our lives. Now I'd failed miserably. Miserably. What an apt word for how I felt. Could I feel any worse? If it were Alec in there, I figure I'd probably feel just as bad. Maybe if both of them were there … Let's not go there.

Alec fixed the coffee and handed me my first mug of the day. "You need to stop beating yourself up over this," he said. Do I look guilty? Or does he just know me that well? Both? Could be. He continued. "We both tried to make her see the situation and quit involving herself with him in plenty of time for her to avoid this. You can't run

her life for her, and neither of us could have predicted this
mess, anyway. So just ease up on yourself, okay? At least a
bit?"

It made sense, I'd give him that. Becky's a grown
woman and can make her own decisions. The worst we'd
really expected her to have to face was being publicly
named in a messy divorce as leverage to get the doctor to
settle in ways his wife liked better than an even split, or
maybe even in a public trial. Since his wife didn't know
about the Family, though, the financial issues wouldn't
have been that much of a problem for him in the long run.
Since she wasn't aware (that's one thing that Family
surveillance works hard at finding out), he probably had his
shares and dividends held in the Bank of Golondrino where
they wouldn't show in any sort of normal search. If her
name wasn't on the account (likely, as their marriage
wasn't registered with the Family, either — I'd checked), it
would all revert to the Family.

Hell, for all we knew, he really had been a nice,
decent sort of fellow and he honestly thought that he and
his wife had agreed to go their separate ways. It's a bit late
to ask him now. That's my suspicious nature coming
through, most likely. Well, no, it wasn't. The suspicious
nature figured he'd been lying through his teeth and just …
having his way, as it were, with Becky. Considering, for
whatever it was worth, and that was exactly nothing right
now, that he might be one of the wronged parties here was
just giving him the benefit of the doubt, and like I say, it
doesn't matter one bit at this point. He's dead and probably
certain to remain so for the foreseeable future, which is
ultimately what really counts.

Alec's right about one thing. He usually is, although
I'll be damned if I'll admit that to him. I really need to quit
letting my emotions run me in this situation and put my
brain into first gear instead. This was, after all, the sort of
thing I do for a living. Truthfully more of an avocation

now, but still. "Well, if Becky didn't do it, and you and I both know she didn't, even if the Pima County attorney has other ideas, then who did? Who stands to gain?"

Alec didn't even hesitate on that one. "That's easy. His wife stands to benefit the most. Instead of half, since they were still technically married when he died, she now gets the whole enchilada. It's also possible, I suppose, that one of his patients might have been stalking him, although that strikes me as significantly less likely. Not just that I think he'd have been aware of such an issue as it came up, at least if he was worth a shit as a psychiatrist, but it also seems more likely to me that a patient would, on the one hand, be more likely to get him at home because he'd be easier to find there, and on the other hand, would probably be in it more for the emotional release of doing him in and a lot less interested in trying to frame his … his mistress, or girlfriend, or whatever term you want to use for Becky. In such a situation, I also suspect that a disgruntled patient would probably have killed both of them, not just him. That, to me, smacks of the wife more than any other reasonable suspect."

"And are the detectives and investigators looking at her?"

His face darkened. "Not that they'll tell me, at any rate. They seem to have decided that Becky did it, so they're more focused on trying to prove she's guilty than they are on seeing if there's anyone else who might have done him in and framed her or left her to take the fall. I think the wife needs to be investigated thoroughly. The honest truth, though, is that I have some real serious questions about whether that's going to happen."

"What about a random killing?"

Alec thought about that for a moment before responding. "No, I don't see it. Not only is her house in the sort of neighborhood where I think that would be less likely, but it seems to me that a random killer would probably also have murdered both of them, not just have killed him and left her behind. I mean, I don't know all that much about random killings, but it just doesn't make much sense to me. You know what you like to say about that."

Yeah. 'Once you look at it from the right angle, it *always* makes sense. If it's not making sense, you're looking at it wrong.' "Okay, so we're on the same wavelength here. There really is just no other choice, no immediately viable one, anyway, than the supposedly grieving widow. I'm going up to Scottsdale, see if I can find out something about her. I believe it's time for a good screw." Now Alec looked totally flustered. I smiled, sort of.

It helped to be back in the groove I was used to; I could sublimate my pain over Becky. At least at moments. *For* moments. Not as good as my usual emotional wall, but it would have to do. "No, not *that*. I keep a couple of 'spare identities' on hand for when I need to be someone else in an investigation, and one of those, the best of the lot, is Laura McCulloch, a salesperson in threaded fasteners. She's a handy person to be. If I'm around other women, believe me, nobody wants to know anything more about nuts, bolts and screws, and the line about 'need a good screw' either breaks them up or turns them off, depending on just how I deliver it and when. So they're not going to pry into me further. Men may, but if I just bat my eyes a little bit" — I demonstrated — "and perhaps confuse grade 5 and grade 8 bolts for a moment, or round heads and pan heads, then they don't even suspect that I'm not real. 'Poor little ol' me?' It works either way.

"But our Ms. McCulloch can be spending some serious weekday time working in greater Phoenix and of course, she's new to her job, new to town and she just happens to have the time to be doing something during the day or evening, or over her lunch hour, or whatever, that throws her into repeated contact with the newly widowed Mrs. Frankton." I made a face. "Besides, it keeps me away for much of the time when Tolliver's here. I'm sure he's the greatest lawyer we could possibly get for Becky since Perry Mason isn't available, and he's clearly dog people, which is a definite plus in my book, but there's something about his personal style that just rubs me the wrong way, and I can't help it. Can you manage with the dogs alone some of the time? Much of the time?"

Poor Alec didn't look happy. I have to admit that I wasn't either, but Tolliver had been right about one thing: I was the best person to actually clear Becky. The only one, perhaps. I didn't see any other choice about that, either. Just as he'd said, his job was to keep her from being convicted, if at all possible. But dammit, she needed to be *cleared*, not just freed. A not-guilty verdict wouldn't really prove anything substantive, however much it might get her out of this immediate mess, and it would still leave the finger of suspicion pointed straight at her for the rest of her life. All it would ultimately mean was that the prosecuting attorney hadn't proven his case adequately. Of course, if it did go to trial, the county attorney might hit the jackpot. Far better on that front as well to keep it from ever getting to a jury. I've got my job laid out for me. "Will you be gone the entire week?"

I reached out to lay my hand on his arm. Contact comfort. "No more than I need to. I don't know how I'll be able to run into her or at what time of day. Ideally she'll go to the gym at lunchtime or thereabouts. If that's the case, I might even be home some nights, although I figure I'll need to get one of those residence hotel rooms in Phoenix to make my presence there look legit, and I'll probably still stay up there during the week most of the time anyway, simply because the commute would be so horrid. But if the only time I can keep on making regular contact with her is when she goes out for coffee every morning at 6AM sharp, then I'll definitely have to be up there. It all depends on what I find. I'm inclined to stay there most weekday nights anyway, just to make my life a bit easier. I'll be here on the weekends, for sure, though." I grinned at him. "Like I'd miss the time I could be with you."

Now he *really* didn't look happy. I didn't think it was about my last comment. "Okay, I guess. Becky certainly needs the best help she can get, and right now, yeah, I think you're probably it, at least on that front. We'll do whatever we need to here." He looked at both dogs, who looked back hopefully. "Can we manage if Momma's got to be gone for a while? Huh? Can we?" They wagged their tails and Bruno cocked his head like he was trying really hard to understand what was being said to him. Alec turned to me. "When will you start?"

"Tuesday, I think. Daddy and Aunt Lori are flying in tomorrow, and we're all going in to see Becky Monday morning. I don't think they're staying over much beyond that. Well, Aunt Lori isn't, anyway. She needs to return to her own patients, so she'll be heading back to Denver right away. I don't think she's staying Monday night. Daddy suggested that he might stick around for a week or so." Aunt Lori is Becky's mom. Becky's father died several years ago. But my parents had been Uncle Colin and Aunt Beth to her just as her parents had been Uncle Jack and Aunt Lori to me, and all of them just barely removed from being parents to both of us together, so his coming here for Becky was just as inevitable as Aunt Lori's coming with Daddy for me would have been if the tables had been turned.

Alec's expression was neutral. "Well, he could have the pull-out in the living room and stay as long as he wants, by me at least. John and I can always use the office on Speedway. It's no bother to me either way. Well, not much of one, and it's not like you're going to be using it for the duration. When we get to the point where we're laying things out and generally spreading our papers around, we're probably better off there than here anyway."

"Sounds like a plan. In the meantime, I'm going to see if I can do something from here, like hack into her credit card records. If I'm really lucky, she bought gas or something that night, either here or in Casa Grande, and put it on a card."

Credit card files were generally pretty easy for me to get into by now, and this one proved no different. Changing something in them would have been a lot more difficult for me to do undetected, but I never did that. Her records proved somewhat inconclusive, if strongly suggestive.

Kendra Frankton had bought gas that night, but in Chandler, in the southern part of greater Phoenix, not in Tucson, Casa Grande or Eloy. Of course, any reasonable person might wonder just what she was doing buying gas at all at that hour; the receipt said the purchase was made shortly after 1AM. Chandler is the part of Phoenix that you reach first when driving in from Tucson. Not proof of much of anything, but certainly suspicious as all hell. Add in the fact that she'd topped off her tank around noon in Scottsdale that same day and it got even more interesting. Of course, if it meant a way to point the detectives in her direction, then I could let them take it from here, assuming I could ever get them to look at it in the first place. Hacked evidence isn't exactly admissible, but they can get it legally. Official warrants are a bit beyond my capabilities. Let's see what else I can find.

While I was at it, I pulled up the Family surveillance file on Jon Frankton again. Family surveillance wasn't something I could ever use for anyone else to see, but on occasion it came in handy. Since he was now no longer with us, I had no need to use it for anything other than my own knowledge and whatever edge it might give me in dealing with his widow.

Understand that Family surveillance is mostly intended just to keep general tabs on each of us and what we're doing. It's not complete, and it's not supposed to be, unless someone has specifically requested that it keep closer tabs on someone, such as a prospective successor. Then it becomes very complete, indeed. You'd be surprised at what it comes up with then.

But normal surveillance, well, if it caught you (assuming you were Family) robbing a bank, it would just note it. Nothing would happen because of the surveillance, at least. On the other hand, if you were arrested and convicted of such a theft, then you'd be bounced from the Family. You'd have one appeal, to the CEO. If the surveillance file said you'd robbed the bank, then, frankly, I'm not going to be especially interested in whatever you have to say. Family isn't starving, or being thrown out into the streets, so pleading necessity isn't exactly going to cut much ice with me, or so I think. I haven't had it come up, so far. Besides, if it were something you'd done really out of necessity, I'd expect you to be stealing food, not money. Not that I've been there, or will ever be in the future.

But I digress. Jon's file didn't have anything in it I hadn't seen already; I was just reviewing it. Not a lot of relevant information other than he and his wife meeting about three years ago and dating for pretty much a year before their marriage. Since he had apparently been leading the single life for almost two years when they first got together, he might well have been easy pickings, and if she had specifically targeted him, he was probably a sitting duck, especially if she had a few sexual tricks up her … well, up her sleeve. A small private civil ceremony, no relatives for either one of them. Nothing else seemed remarkable to me, at least not on this reading. I closed the file, although I would probably come back to it yet again at a later time.

I also needed to make a run to the store. I don't keep a stock of Laura's makeup and hair color. It's a handy identity, yes, but I don't use it so often that I keep those things on hand. Becky, makeup queen that she is, helped me set up hair color and basic, i.e. very minimal, makeup sets for several different colorations, brunette, redhead, brassy blonde and black haired, that I then assigned to different spare identities. As a result of her efforts, I now have a file on the computer that tells me which hair color, base color, blush and so on to buy for each, with substitutions just in case, all common major brands, so I just ran off a copy of what I needed for the brunette Laura. I know just enough about makeup to use those minimal things. Barely. I'm just *such* a dressy person, left to my own devices. I should quit that; sarcasm really isn't my strong suit.

Meeting Daddy and Aunt Lori at the airport Sunday felt more than a bit awkward. I mean, I love both of them dearly, and they had both been thrilled to hear about Alec and me (they'd met him for the first time just weeks before we got married) and thrilled for me as well when I became the Family CEO literally days afterwards. But they weren't here for anything like that; they were here because Becky was in serious trouble. It really put a damper on all of us.

The mood continued through dinner. Alec and I didn't feel much like cooking. At the house, we were largely living off leftovers these days, including portions of the incredibly huge stir-fry I'd made for us and Tolliver. Besides, with all of the stress of Becky's situation, neither one of us was really in a cooking mood. Luckily for Alec and me (mostly me) I keep the freezer well-stocked with chili of various descriptions. But since I'm the only serious chilehead among the four of us, we just went out to eat.

Daddy was uncharacteristically silent all through dinner. I could feel his eyes on me, but I was having some serious trouble trying to recapture the determined and capable feeling I'd had the previous morning, or even this morning. It would help me a lot when I could use the hair rinse tonight or tomorrow morning and don the Laura

McCulloch identity, letting me shuck, or at least sublimate, Amy Youngston Trevethen for the time being.

Actually, everybody's eyes kept coming back to me. Daddy was just the most obvious about it. Alec kept looking at me out of the corner of his eyes, checking on me every time his eyes stopped looking at Aunt Lori or, occasionally, Daddy. Aunt Lori kept glancing at me while she, hiding a great deal of pain, strain and concern herself, though not completely, kept up most of the conversation from that side of the table. Think 'stream-of-nervousness.' I mean, she hides it very well, just not perfectly. Not from me, anyway; I've known her as long as I've known Becky, so pretty much all my life. She's swatted my butt and kissed my owies, just like Mom did, so I know when she's covering up how she really feels. Besides, between my people-reading skills and my knowledge of her, I'm pretty good at reading exactly how she really feels underneath. She was scared to death for Becky, just like I was. Daddy's known her longer than I have, like pretty much all of *their* lives, so he probably wasn't fooled, either. Finally he asked one of the questions that were likely on everyone's mind. "How are you bearing up, Baby?"

He and I aren't confused about our ages, or anything. 'Daddy' and 'Baby' are relics of the trauma of losing Mom, not holdovers from my young childhood. We'd had a really rough time then, and both of us sort of reverted for a while. Later we decided to keep it up because it made us feel better, and going back to 'Dad' and 'Amy' didn't. But I digress yet again.

"Frankly, Daddy, I feel like shit. I can't get to see Becky, except on this goddam TV in the jail, I can't visit her but once a week and then only for a brief time, and … it's too hard for her. It's too hard *on* her. It's like something is dying inside her. There's no spark, no …" I had no better word. He and Aunt Lori took my hands while Alec put an arm around my shoulders and held me close. "It's not *fair*,

Goddammit!" That probably came out with more heat than it should have, but I was upset, to say the least.

Daddy's voice was flat. "Alannah!" I looked at him sharply; he was looking at me a bit oddly, too, although differently from Alec.

Alec had the strangest look on his face. "Now we're in for it. She's using the F-word." I turned towards him, puzzled. "Remember in Property class? When — what was her name? She sat two rows in front of us, was on the law review — called 'fair' the F-word?"

Then I turned back to Daddy. Calling me Alannah is guaranteed to bring me out of whatever internal mind-loop I've gotten into. "Is this my daughter I'm hearing? The tough, experienced PI? The Family CEO, able to leap huge investments at a single bound? Talking like a schoolgirl?"

Chapter 7

I shook my head sharply. "Okay, so it was a stupid thing to say. It's just … it keeps coming back to the same thing for me. This is *Becky*. I wouldn't begin to react like that if it were anyone else. Even …" I put my hand on Alec's other arm. "Sorry. Other than you, dear." Alec patted my hand in silent reassurance.

Aunt Lori's voice was gentle. "Don't be sorry, Amy. I understand about defenses, and you're allowed to be human. It's also not fair, either, nor is it your doing. From what you've said, you and Alec both did your best to convince Becky that she should stop seeing him. She made her own choice, and that's what left her open to having something like this happen. It's incredibly unfortunate and tragic that this happened to her, but nobody is blaming you."

It had to be costing her a lot to sound so … calm and collected. Becky is her only daughter, her only child, and just knowing Becky was in jail as she was, not to mention headed for a murder trial, had to be ripping Aunt Lori up inside. I knew what it was doing to my own insides; there was no way hers could be in any better shape. Probably not even as good. At least I had something I could try to do about it. Every so often, Aunt Lori's facade slipped just a tiny bit and I could see how it was really affecting her. I doubt that Alec could. But only for moments each time, even so. I guess there's something about practicing medicine that teaches you to hold a public appearance like that.

I made a face. "Nobody except me." Especially since I didn't feel that 'unfortunate and tragic' were really an accurate way to describe what was going on. Not if Becky'd been deliberately set up, as I was coming to believe.

Daddy squeezed my hand. "Don't beat yourself up over it, Baby. It isn't your fault. You couldn't have done any more than you did, and you couldn't have foreseen anything like this happening."

"Yeah. But when I hear that, it's my brain, not my heart, talking. Remember how I used to watch out for her as a kid?"

Daddy smiled. "Yes, and I remember when the school called to tell me you'd beaten up the boy who dumped her. I remember it all quite well. I also remember how proud of you I was then and how hard I worked to make sure you didn't know it at the time." (He had been? Huh. Sure fooled me.) "But she's a grown woman now, and she makes her own choices. You don't have to run interference for her any more."

I snorted. "Easy for you to say. My brain still thinks I need to, and telling it otherwise doesn't work all that well." It was very nice of everyone to try to help me feel better, but the one problem was that, just like I said, it really *didn't* work. I did tell Daddy that I was glad he hadn't brought *her* with him. He'd been in a relationship of sorts for several years with a woman whom I utterly detested. The feeling was mutual.

He just smiled. "Oh, she's been gone for quite a while, Baby. In fact, ever since I got your announcement from Golondrino."

I was puzzled. "Huh?"

"Oh, yeah. I got the announcement in the mail and opened it. I made some sounds of astonishment and pleasure, and she demanded to know what I was reading. I put it back in the envelope and said that it didn't concern her and I wouldn't let her see it. I'd never mentioned the Family to her, of course, and since I knew at that point that she and I weren't going to be together much longer, I certainly wasn't about to then. She got quite upset with me, and when I still wouldn't give in, she started packing.

When I got up the next day, she was gone. I haven't seen her since."

Well, that was some decent news in the midst of all this turmoil and bad news. Good riddance. Maybe now he could find someone more agreeable, or whatever. Somebody with talents outside of the bedroom, or so I presumed. I certainly couldn't see any other reason for him to have put up with her for as long as he had. But I also have to admit to being prejudiced as hell where she was concerned.

Everybody put on their game faces Monday morning, but Becky was still just as flat as ever. She didn't light up in the least, as far as I could see, with her mother, and she certainly didn't for Daddy, either. Delivering Aunt Lori to the airport afterwards, seeing her off, certainly didn't help, but she had a practice in Denver that she couldn't just put on hold for any length of time without more preparation time than she'd had. When she got out of the car, after the brief instant she took to collect herself and put her public face back on, she turned to Alec. "Did they take samples for toxicology screening when they arrested her?" Not having gotten the county attorney's discovery yet, Alec didn't know, but he said he'd find out. "Do that. I'm sure they did, but from her account, she may well have been, and probably was, drugged at the time, and she may still have some residual effects, even now. A number of the drugs she might have been given would definitely have shown up in her system for hours afterward. Not that her situation couldn't be the sole cause for the way she's acting now, but it definitely should have been checked out." That made sense. If she'd been drugged and by some inexcusable oversight they hadn't taken samples, then that could certainly help with the 'reasonable doubt' thing. Every little bit, I suppose. If we could show that she *had* been drugged, then …

Other than the little bit of makeup and the hair color that I buy as I need to, I keep a supply of the various things (there's a lot of overlap) that I need to transform myself into any of the several spare identities I keep in reserve. 'Laura McCulloch' has mousy brown hair, brown eyes and a bit of a sensitivity to sunlight, so not only did I dye my hair and wear tinted contacts, but I spent much of my time in sunglasses, even indoors. She's at least outwardly bustier than I am, so I dug out the padded uplift bras that I couldn't be bothered wearing for myself (I don't think Alec cares how much of me there is half so much as he simply does that it's me, period, the darling man. Besides, simply changing bras doesn't do anything to change the contents, obviously), and the couple of pairs of designer jeans and glittery t-shirts that I have for just such occasions. Like me, Laura can fade into the woodwork in the right circumstances, but what mattered a lot more to me was that she was very clearly not me.

I keep a wig in my natural dirty blonde hair color (and it's 'dirty blonde,' never 'dishwater blonde,' see?) for times when I had to switch back and forth from one of these assumed identities to being my own self on short notice, but I'd found it easier and better to take on her 'normal' coloration as my base when I was being her. I'd never before 'put her on' for weeks on end, though. This was going to be a new one for me.

Alec wasn't entirely thrilled at first with this brunette in his arms Monday night, but once his eyes were closed, or maybe it was just that the lights were out, he was sure it was me and everything else was fine. Poignant, but very fine, and I made doubly sure of it. I'd miss him, badly. There was no chance I wouldn't be spending at least some of my nights in Phoenix, starting with tomorrow night, and this would be the first time we'd been separated since we were married. Ugh. I knew I wouldn't be sleeping as well, either.

The most painful part of the entire transition, at some sort of emotional or psychic level, was when I slipped off the custom wedding ring — way too expensive a piece for Laura to be wearing — and replaced it with the plain gold band I'd started with over a year ago. I closed my fingers around the good one, and held it tight for a moment, feeling the impression it was making in my hand and the permanent one it had long since made in my heart and soul, before putting it carefully into the safe. I could still go back to it on weekends, which helped, a bit. Yes, I realize that it's just a piece of metal, objectively, but it means a huge amount to me, and seeing the matching one on Alec's finger makes it all complete, in some fashion. I think it's probably that internalization coming through.

The next morning early, I had Alec drop me off at the local car rental office. I didn't want to take the Beemer with me. Laura McCulloch was likely, no, make that certain, to be driving something a lot cheaper and more nondescript than my BMW X5, so renting a compact seemed like a good idea.

I got a short-term suite in Phoenix around lunchtime and managed to pick up Kendra Frankton before suppertime. I was parked about two blocks away, since I had found a good line of sight to her house, and had the bigger telescope sitting on a beanbag resting on the car window. It was hot enough to get uncomfortable in the car, but difficulties exist to be overcome, right? Anti-perspirant doesn't work all that well here, this time of year. So what? We desert dwellers are used to it. Anyway, state records had already told me that she drove a 2007 Toyota, and she now had her late husband's 2006 Lexus as well. When I found her, she was driving the Toyota. I caught a glimpse of the Lexus in the garage.

When the garage door closed behind her, I took advantage of the opportunity to have a granola bar from my stash. I try to keep a good handful of such things in my kit, as I never know when I'll have to spend my mealtimes sitting there watching somebody. It didn't bother me; I'd done it way too many times to be concerned. It was just how things were. Sometimes I'd live on such things for days on end, when an investigation required it.

If her credit card receipts were any indication, she did a certain amount — make that quite a bit — of clubbing, and I wanted to be ready if she left again. Among other things, I wanted to put a tracker on her car and I couldn't do that very easily when it was inside her garage.

She drove off again about an hour and a half later. She went right by me, and I had just enough time to slip the scope and beanbag off the window — one reason I use a beanbag instead of a window mount is because it comes off the window faster and easier, just for occasions like this — and lie on my back, arched backwards over the console, jabbed in the side by the shift and clutching the scope to my chest, as she drove by. Most people aren't all that aware of their surroundings, which makes much of my work a lot easier. I started the car — blessed air conditioning! — and followed after her at a respectable interval. I let too many cars in front of me at one point and would likely have missed her had she turned right, but instead she made a left turn and I could see her half a block ahead. When she pulled into the club parking lot, I took a swing around the block and then pulled in as well.

My trackers — I learned about them from Family surveillance — have some hellacious magnets. I walked by her car and 'dropped' my purse — it's a fake, with next to nothing of any import in it, just some crap to give it enough weight to seem real — and when I straightened up again, the tracker was well up inside her left rear wheel well. Now I could call it a night and go back to my suite. Well, motel, by my current standards. It's a helluva long way from the Director's Suite in Golondrino, the Family headquarters, and not just in distance. I booted up my laptop and logged onto the tracking program. Good signal, good location … I could drop into bed with a clear conscience, on that end, anyway. After I spent a half-hour on the phone to Alec, of course.

Alec and Daddy were doing just fine. Alec said he was learning a lot more about my younger years and my upbringing. I had to stop and think for a moment. Was I okay with that? I mean, it's not like I was concerned about any baby photos here, but … oh, what the hell. I really had no urge to keep my life private from Alec. Which, given my usual privacy fetish, was most interesting and such a change from my usual when I actually thought about it. Then Daddy got the phone. "Hey, Baby. How are you managing?"

"Oh, well enough. You know."

I could almost hear him smile. "Yeah, I guess I do. When's the next board meeting? Do you have to go?"

"It's about two and a half weeks or so. I should go, but I might cancel it. I haven't decided yet."

"Can you just suspend them for the duration?"

I snorted. "No way. I can cancel one with no problem. I can cancel two, but it's going to be talked about. If I cancel three in a row, that's the equivalent of submitting a resignation to the board without naming a successor. They could decide to re-elect me, but they could also put in anyone they wanted instead of me, and there's damn-all I could do about it. So I'd rather not cancel any if I can help it."

Daddy was slow in responding. He hadn't known; those were board rules. They weren't public knowledge in the Family, although they weren't secret or anything. They just weren't public because they only applied to the board. Actually, that one just applied to the CEO. There's a presumption, I guess, that since the CEO can dismiss any other board member at any time, he would simply get rid of any other board member who missed too many meetings.

Finally he said, "I see. Well, do what you must, Baby. I love you."

"Love you too, Daddy. Let Alec have the phone, again, please."

I said some things to Alec, quietly, that I'd just as soon Daddy didn't hear, but that I really, really wanted to say to Alec. Preferably in whispers straight into his ear, or even just demonstrate without saying anything, but this was the best I could do right now. Finally we hung up.

I'm hardly ever able to just drop off to sleep without reading first, and tonight was no exception. But Laura McCulloch wouldn't have been caught dead reading the sorts of heavy-duty investment books that I usually read nowadays, and I just don't do romances and other syrupy shit of the kind you might expect to find someone like her reading.

So on the very off chance that somebody might manage to check me out more closely than I would like, I compromised and settled on some science-fiction. Not Daddy's; he hadn't been producing much any more, and I'd read everything of his long ago, that which I hadn't edited in the first place. Just resting on his laurels, I guess. Some of his books had become cult favorites over the years; staying in print is good for the income, apparently.

I was happy about that for him, especially since all but one of the books still in print were ones I'd edited for him. Kind of like the one (also still in print) he'd assigned to me in lieu of a loan when I was setting up my business, right after I separated from my horrid first husband (why was I wasting my time thinking about *him*?).

His agent told me just last week that there were feelers being put out about another possible movie option, which would be quite neat as well as lucrative to have happen. Of course, I hardly need it now, but I can't exactly tell the agent that. Besides, he's got his own cut to get.

Anyway, so I cracked open one of my old favorite series. Strong woman protagonist (lots of other strong female characters, too), who started out as a common citizen and wound up, several books later (but the series is still going strong), indescribably rich and a sovereign head of state. I looked at myself in the mirror across the room. Did that sound familiar? I really hadn't considered myself in that light until right now. That put a really different spin on my appreciation for the series. Neat. I smiled to myself and went back to reading until I could turn off the light and drop off.

Chapter 8

Wednesday morning was a new day, or so I told myself. I woke somewhat groggily, probably from sleeping alone. Sternly I told myself that this was ridiculous. I'd slept alone for years before Alec and I were married and slept, alone, very well indeed for that entire time. The idea that I needed a *man* next to me in order to get a good night's sleep? I damn sure *wanted* Alec next to me. There's nothing wrong with wants and needs. But now I need to try to talk myself out of it for the duration.

No, I didn't need a *man*, *per se*, but obviously, I definitely did a lot better, now, when I slept with Alec. Besides, snuggling up next to him for the night really helped me feel very good, indeed. Wanted. Or even simply comforted, rather like when Becky and I used to sleep together. Whatever I needed at the moment. Oh, well, it is what it is, live with it. And he's not here, live with that, too. Diverting myself, I booted the laptop and checked the tracking program for the tracker I'd put on Kendra's car the night before. Here it was half past five, and she hadn't stirred. Well, her car hadn't, anyway.

I putzed around the kitchenette, making some very crappy coffee. I can manage without breakfast (not happily, but well enough), but I'm quite lost without coffee. Besides, the Family is so broadly invested in coffee now — my doing — that it's virtually impossible, for all intents and purposes, to buy even a cup of coffee without putting at least some tiny fraction of the cost into the Family coffers. I spent several minutes working at my sublimation of Amy Trevethen and letting Laura McCulloch take over, permeating as much of my personality as I could manage. Just in case.

By the time that the tracker showed any movement by her car, I was already in mine, waiting not far away, although out of eyesight. At home, I usually get in some serious exercising before breakfast. Out on a job, I get whatever I can, exercise and food both, and I manage without the rest. Since I'd be spending this week tracking her without necessarily trying to make any sort of contact, 'getting whatever I can' seemed like the most likely sort of meal I was going to have, beyond the thermos of lousy coffee I had with me. I'd have to do something about that for tomorrow.

Anyway, she left the house around half past eight and drove towards Phoenix proper. I managed to pick her up visually just before she turned into a small shopping plaza. I pulled in as far from her as I could reasonably manage and found a spot from which I could keep an eye on her. When it turned out that she was just visiting the cleaners, I simply made some notes on my little recorder and relaxed, just a bit. Her next stop was a coffee shop in another shoppette not too far away, and perhaps I could take a chance there.

I took my book on threaded fasteners, camouflage as though I were new at this job, just in case anyone asks, and went in. I ordered a large coffee, and when I had it fixed the way I wanted it (the Family got a bit more on this one; we own a substantial chunk of this chain now), I found a seat where I could sit and drink my coffee while keeping an unobtrusive eye on Kendra Frankton as reflected in the window while I appeared to be reading my book. Thank God for good coffee! I should probably dump the crap in my thermos and bring it in to fill here, but I couldn't take the time today.

It didn't take too long before Kendra was joined by a man, and their actions suggested that they were a bit more than good friends. Nothing improper, just that sort of touch and gesture, along with a kiss in greeting, not to mention body language, that suggested that they were lots more than casual acquaintances. Might be lovers, might just be rather good friends, but definitely somewhere in there. I murmured more notes, this time into my little pen recorder. Tonight I'd transcribe my notes and ship a copy back home for safekeeping.

When I saw them begin to get ready to leave, I stood up and dumped my cup into the trash. By the time they walked out, I was ready for them. I followed his car — a Lexus, he wasn't hurting — to his next stop at a medical office building, and in a great stroke of luck, was able to pull into the next parking space to him. I fumbled in my fake purse long enough for him to walk off before I got out and slipped another tracker up into his wheelwell.

Then I quickly caught back up with Kendra Frankton, who was by now at her gym. No little storefront exercise place, this; it was a full-line health club. More notes. Then while I waited for her, I did a quick check in the state DMV database; the fellow who'd met her was one Donald McGuire, M.D. His home address wasn't all that far from hers. A quick internet search on his name showed that he was an anesthesiologist. Interesting. Still more notes.

From the gym, Kendra Frankton hit a supermarket and then headed back home. She stayed there for a couple of hours before heading out again, this time to a mall. Laura McCulloch's t-shirts were a bit tighter than the ones I usually wore as myself (almost, but not quite, too tight for my shoulder holster), but I had a couple of those bigger ones with me, too. I pulled a gray one over the glittery one I was wearing and strolled into the mall well behind her.

Just window-shopping, one more nondescript face above a nondescript t-shirt among so many. I kept her in sight, barely, as she did much the same thing several stores ahead of me. She was paying no attention to her back trail, which certainly made my life a lot easier. Two t-shirts were rather hot out in the parking lot but were actually very comfortable in the cranked-up air-conditioning of the mall itself.

When she didn't come out of the fitness store she'd gone into for the longest time, I walked on by and made like I was looking at the machines in the window. She was back behind the counter with one of the store people, and the way they were caressing each other suggested that Dr. McGuire wasn't the only man on her line. Or that she was all that concerned about privacy. More notes as soon as I was away from the window. He wouldn't be as simple to trace, if I decided that I needed to.

One thing at a time, although I was certainly forming a definite opinion of her. Not a flattering one, either. I also didn't think much of her choice in men, for that matter, but perhaps I'm prejudiced. At least I approved of her late husband's last choice in women.

From the mall, she returned home, and the time she arrived suggested she'd be there until she began her evening routine. I took advantage of the break to go grab a late lunch, or perhaps an early supper, at a little Mexican place. If nothing else, it was a nice change from granola bars. It might be the only real food I got all day.

Shortly after suppertime, when she went back out to do some clubbing, it began to look as though tonight would be a replay of last night. I had a good idea of what was going on, because Dr. McGuire's tracker showed the same location on the screen. When I checked later, he had followed her home.

Alec had some news for me that evening. He'd found out who was prosecuting the case. "Michael Thorne, Esquire. I've never worked opposite him, but I've heard plenty of things about him. Nothing good."

Was this going to be important to my investigation? "Like what?"

I could hear a sour note in his voice. "Let's just say that he's got a mind like a steel trap. Once he's decided who the guilty party is, the trap is closed and he won't look at anyone or anything else. Exceedingly single-minded and absolutely unwilling to consider any chance that he may have made a mistake."

"Oh. One of these people who's afraid that if they're open-minded, their …"

Alec cut me off. "Don't even go there. I don't want to think it. If I'm going to be thinking anything about him in that regard, I want to stay with the steel trap analogy. At least if I let something slip about that in his presence, it probably won't piss him off too much and make my life a lot harder than it needs to be already. No, the only way that we're going to convince him of anything that requires him to change his mind is going to be to get somebody a lot higher than he is to rub his nose in it and spank him with a rolled-up newspaper. Preferably with an iron pipe inside."

I sighed. "I'm working at it, love."

"I know you are, honey. I just … well, John says it bodes well for a not-guilty verdict, and he's probably right about that. But seeing Becky, just like you, I have some real doubts about how much good that sort of result would do her. The only reason I don't think she's going downhill fast is that there's hardly any room left for her to go anywhere. It's almost enough to break my heart."

We commiserated for a while before hanging up. I fell asleep that night brooding instead of reading.

Thursday was largely a replay of Wednesday, except that Kendra had her coffee alone (I didn't go in) and she didn't make the trip to the mall. She took in a movie instead. I was beginning to get a picture that I could put together, one which would allow me to predict at least some of the places she was likely to go and when.

Friday morning I joined the health club she went to. I gave them Laura McCulloch's name and fake Las Cruces address, explaining that I was currently spending most of my weekdays here in Phoenix on my job and needed to be able to work out while I was here. Well, that story was partially true, too.

One of the minor aggravations was that I actually belong to the chain, in Tucson. It's where Becky and I go together. But that's as 'A.M. Youngston,' (I haven't bothered to change my name on the membership, and yes, I ought to do that one of these days) and I wasn't about to blow my cover on something as simple or as minor as a gym membership. Besides, I'd be billing the Family for this entire job, with Becky as my client, so this was going to be just another entry on the bill.

It took a bit of doing to get the club to agree not to mail anything to me at home, but after I explained about my husband and the certainty that he'd object, strenuously, to my doing this, they reluctantly agreed. Once the investigation was over, of course, it wouldn't matter, but I didn't want a bunch of mail coming back to them, or to the head office to be forwarded here, marked 'address unknown,' while I was still working here.

By the time Kendra came in, I was pumping away on one of the stationary bikes and working up a fair sweat. I'd taken advantage of the locker room facilities to switch to warm-up pants and another plain t-shirt, saving my good jeans and t-shirt. The pistol and shoulder holster were wrapped inside the t-shirt in my locker, although I still had on me two of the three Hideaway knives that I also wear every day. My favorite, the claw, was still in the back of the waistband of my good jeans. I didn't expect to need it here. I had two others on me, after all, and just how often do you get attacked in a health club anyway? Famous last words, a little voice whispered in the back of my mind.

Complacency always comes around to bite you on the ass when you least expect it. That's why they call it complacency. And surprise usually happens because you didn't see something in plain sight. That's why it's a surprise. I wanted to avoid both of those.

Kendra was heading for another one of the bikes. I had my iPod going, so we just exchanged nods as she climbed on and began pedaling a bit more slowly than I was. It may sound a bit odd, but I've got a 25-minute routine of bagpipe tunes, marches, jigs and other dance tunes that I use to keep my pace when I'm on a stationary bike and can't get the movies I prefer to watch on the bike at home. It definitely sets a fast pace, gets me moving and keeps me going. When it switches to the slow airs, I'm into my cooldown. Probably a part of the whole Celtic thing that I inherited from Daddy along with his mother's name.

Another nod, a smile and a friendly greeting as I walked by Kendra and headed to take a quick shower. Luckily my hair doesn't take much work, even as Laura. Little enough, anyway, that while I don't duck it under the water in a second shower for the day, I also don't worry about splashing it a bit.

She was coming in to the locker room when I was drying off. I gave her my 'new-around-here' routine as I got dressed and reapplied the minimal makeup that Laura wears, then had to fake a bathroom call before I put my regular t-shirt on. I just carried the t-shirt, wrapped around the shoulder holster and pistol, with me as I excused myself. No reason in the world to let her know I was heavily armed. The knife that's normally clipped below my bra I'd taken off when I got ready for the shower and slipped it into the pocket of my jeans. I could replace it when I put the holster back on.

By the time I came back, she was putting the finishing touches on herself. I merely told her (Laura tends to run just a tiny bit at the mouth) that I was heading back home to Las Cruces for the weekend. She was cool to me. Cold, really, but that was fine. I was just establishing myself at this point, and just in case anyone who mattered should see me driving south, I was establishing a bona fide reason for that, too.

It felt very pleasant to leave, get back into my car and let my voice shift back to my normal tones. Laura speaks with a slightly higher, more nasal and (frankly) slightly whinier voice than I do. Yeah, I know I don't have to do such things when the subject has never heard my natural voice, but it's mostly a matter of working at getting completely into character. I try to do it so that almost anyone who didn't already know me exceptionally well would never recognize me. Not, at least, when the hair color, clothes, voice, walk and general stance are all different. That's, for me, the real essence of a disguise. To wear it so well, so thoroughly, that you *become* that other person, and even people who know the real you don't connect the two. I work hard at it. Laura McCulloch was my best.

I'd gotten very used to, even somewhat in the habit of, checking for a tail last year. It's really a slightly enhanced version of Condition Yellow, being alert to everything going on around me. Once again it was the same old routine of getting off at random freeway exits, especially ones out in the middle of nowhere, wait briefly, occasionally check the sky for a watcher overhead, then zip back onto the highway and see if anyone else did likewise. There was nothing suspicious.

Actually, I would have been quite surprised if there had been at this stage. There are also other, more advanced techniques for getting a tail to reveal itself, but I doubted that I was facing any sort of organization here, or anyone trying to pull something really fancy on me. Not yet, anyway.

I could, I supposed, have set Family surveillance on her, but while it would, in the enhanced version, have given me wonderfully detailed reports on everything she did, there would be no way in hell I could ever get them into court, or into the prosecutor's hands, no way to explain them and frankly, having them would do Becky no good whatsoever.

Trying to use them, either in court or to persuade the prosecutor, would also open multiple cans of worms that I just didn't want or need to have to deal with, including that one to be avoided at all costs about 'what in the hell is this 'Family'?' My own investigations I could show, support and testify to in court if it came to that, and without involving the Family in any way. That made it all a no-brainer.

While I was driving south, I gave a lot of thought to Laura's backstory. My usual version of it has had her as a lower middle-class girl from a small town (Las Cruces, pleasant as it may be, isn't anybody's idea of a big city, unless they come from some place that doesn't have businesses on both sides of the street or extending for more than two blocks) whose conception of upscale shopping is J.C. Penney. As I thought about it, though, I suspected that such a woman would never be able to worm her way inside Kendra Frankton's life, or at least her confidence, which is exactly what I had to be able to do. I didn't have to be someone she aspired to, but whatever I presented had to be someone she could at least relate to and accept as within reach of her own level socially.

There were no written records of Laura's history, though, so I could change it as I needed to, and this was clearly such a time. Hm. Well, then, for starters, how about using Becky's childhood as a base? Only child of two doctors, grew up in Denver — I could certainly do that one. I'd virtually lived it, just as Becky had lived mine.

Then what? Why does she live in Las Cruces? Maybe I was simply kind of sketching this out in my mind, but it absolutely had to hang together logically. What if she'd gotten screwed over by her husband, and he'd left her — me, I mean — with next to nothing? So I had to go to work, and take whatever I could get? Okay, that hangs together, a bit.

But why Las Cruces? Another man? Well, yeah, that might do. Especially if my circumstances had thrown me in with a man of a much lower class ... and so 'Brian McCulloch' was born. I really hadn't wanted to marry him, but I was broke and had no choice. Hm. That doesn't say anything good for my independence, now does it? Pregnancy? Yeah, that might do it. *Would* do it. Then a miscarriage, which would certainly explain why there was no little McCulloch running around back home.

For later, of course, I suspected, or would come to suspect, that Brian was fooling around while I was stuck here in Phoenix on business ... I think that will work. I need to be someone who shops at second-hand stores and remainder stores, not because they're upscale, but because they're the best way to get upscale things for very few dollars when I don't have many. So I know about Tiffany's, and Oscar de la Renta, and Gucci and such (I do know about them, even if I don't give a shit about them. My weaknesses are Beretta, Colt, Steyr and things like that), but there's a definite financial reason why I can't shop in places like that.

Mom and Dad would probably help me if I asked, but I just can't bring myself to do that. Too stinkin' proud, or ashamed, or something close to one of those. Or both. Maybe *some* day I can reclaim my birthright. Especially if I can get rid of this no-good cheating husband that fate shackled me to. Yeah, I like that. I can play that part. Now if I can just let it out at exactly the right pace ... This is a bit like fishing. You need just the right bait, and it has to be presented just *so*. Once the fish bites, you have to play her so *very* carefully. That, actually, is one of the things I enjoy most about performing investigations like this. Which is interesting, or at least amusing, in its own right, since real fishing bores the shit out of me.

Chapter 9

When I pulled into my driveway, it was starting to look like a car lot. My own car was in the garage, but there was Alec's and one I didn't recognize that was probably Daddy's rental parked outside the garage. Now my rental. Oh, well. I marched into the kitchen and called, "Honey, I'm home!" Bruno was first in, and he stood up to put his paws onto my shoulders. He's not supposed to unless he's been invited, but I was so happy to see him that I buried my face against him and just hugged him as he licked my ear happily. Sasha and Alec came in just about together. Sasha's two normal gaits are 'stroll' and 'amble,' this must be 'stroll.' Letting Bruno down, I all but threw myself at Alec, but he was prepared for me and didn't even stagger. I gave him a kiss that could only hint at tonight — I'd missed him so! Then over his shoulder, I said, "Hi, Daddy."

Daddy arched his eyebrows. "Is that all I get? Your husband and one of the dogs get hugs, and it's just 'hi, Daddy' for your old man?" He was smiling.

Reluctantly I let Alec go (after another serious kiss) and stepped over to Daddy. "No, Daddy, that's not all you get." I gave him a good hug and a very nice kiss on the cheek. I know some people think that the whole 'Daddy' and 'Baby' thing is a bit screwy, or maybe unhealthy (Becky warned me they would, and she does, too, to some degree), but we're happy with it, so who gives a shit what anyone else thinks? He'd really been a good father to me and had worked very hard at it, especially through the turmoil after Mom's death and then my … experience. He still was one now, some two dozen or so years later, and I was very happy that he was still here, although the underlying reason could have been loads better, I admit. I needed more time with him.

By the time I was done, Alec was already fixing me a drink. Good, I needed one, a stiff one. Before that, though, I had to go down on my knees and say a proper hello to Sasha, too. Just because she wasn't the leaper Bruno was didn't mean she should be short-changed by any means. I buried my face in her fur and hugged her. Then, when I let her go, she proceeded to lie down and roll onto her back, pulling her back feet up, so I had to give her a good tummy rub. Naturally, seeing that, Bruno wanted one, too. I guess that's why people have two hands, to attend to two dogs at once. They seem to think so, anyway. I don't see any need to disabuse them of the idea.

Out of deference to Daddy's comparatively cold-temperature acclimation, we stayed inside in the air conditioning with our drinks. First I demanded an update from Alec. What had he and Tolliver accomplished while I was gone, especially beyond what he'd kept me apprised of over the phone, and how was Becky holding up?

They, the defense team, were supposed to be able to get into the crime scene next week early, so Tolliver was going to pick up the blood-spatter expert from California as he flew in later on Monday. Other experts had been consulted and retained as appropriate, but this was the first one who would actually work the scene. Becky herself was not doing well. In fact, Alec thought she was once again slipping downhill, such as she still had room to go in that direction, taking even less interest in her life and her situation than she had been doing the week prior. I could see the pain in his eyes, and I was quite worried about her myself. "Should they put her on suicide watch?" I asked Alec.

His face was grim. "I don't know. Somebody there at the jail may put her on it themselves, shortly, even without my suggesting it, which I really don't want to do. But I'm concerned as hell. Worried half to death, in fact. My worst fear about that is that if they put her on any sort of really intensive watch, it may wind up being so hard on her that I'm afraid it'll do more harm to her, psychologically, than doing nothing. I really don't have a clue as to where I should go with it."

I didn't know what to say to that. "You're still going in to see her every day, right?" He simply nodded. "Well, keep a close eye on her and do what you feel is best. I'm working the other end of this game."

"Oh, something else happened that you're going to want to see. I'd have sent it to you if you hadn't been coming home today and if I could have figured out how to do it."

"What?"

"It's on your security system from the office. I had someone walk in off the street this morning. John was leaving, and just as he was on his way out, this woman came in. Smallish, mouse-brown hair, kind of like yours is now, but a bit overweight. Not a lot, just a bit, well, thick-waisted and a tad soft in the outline, I guess I'd call her, if I were trying to be brutally accurate. She was asking for you. I told her I was your husband, I worked here too, and could I help her? She asked me, cautiously and sort of roundabout, without really spelling it out, whether I was Family, and I offered to show her my passport."

Nice touch. Alec isn't actually Family, himself, but the CEO's spouse gets a Golondrino passport for the duration of either the CEO's term or the marriage, whichever is shorter. Alec can think of some very adroit and handy ways to phrase things.

"Anyway, her name is Lissa McHugh. Lissa *Frankton* McHugh. She wants you to find her brother's murderer." My eyebrows went way up at that. "I told her that the police had a suspect in custody, and she waved that aside. 'That was just his girlfriend,' she said. 'His wife is the one that killed him.' She said that her brother had told her the same thing he'd told Becky, that they had an amicable separation and they'd agreed that they were free to go their separate ways while waiting for the divorce. But Lissa, who really, *really* despises his wife, hates her bitterly, in fact, said she warned him, not once but many times, that his wife probably didn't really mean it and was only using it to set a trap for him.

"Then at some point, Lissa figures that his wife must have decided that just holding proof of infidelity over his head during a divorce wasn't going to give her enough settlement leverage to satisfy her. That's the point at which she believes that his wife did the number on him, which kind of squares with our theory. Of course, the Pima County attorney isn't interested in what she's got to say, just like they aren't with me. She had a lot of interesting ways of describing Mrs. Frankton, which don't bear on the case but were certainly offering me quite a vocabulary lesson. She was pretty inventive in describing Mike Thorne, too."

I had to think about that one for several minutes. "So what did you tell her?"

"The truth, at that point and to a degree. That I was representing Dr. Swan along with the lawyer who was leaving as she came in — she then realized that she had recognized him — and that you were already on the case, looking for proof of the real guilty party. I didn't give her any more than that. There's more to what she said than that, of course. I questioned her pretty well, but that's the sum and substance of it. I used your office, not the front room."

So far, it didn't give me any more than I'd had before, really, although it definitely tended to confirm my suspicions. I'd have to get a copy of the security footage and watch it for myself. In my office … that was the best-covered part of the house. It would only take me a few minutes to get the recording, and I'd take a copy of it with me to review again during some of my 'leisure time' in

Phoenix. A break from watching Kendra would do me good.

"Okay, here's where I am. I've begun, just barely, to make contact with Kendra Frankton. She's seen me once in the coffee shop she goes to, where she meets the anesthesiologist she has on her string, although I kept my back to her then. I've also seen her with the fitness type in the mall shop where he works, although she didn't see me there. That's two men. She might have more, but I can't see where that really matters right now. I've joined the health club she works out at, and she's seen me there. I've greeted her and given her at least some tiny bit of the basics of Laura McCulloch. She thinks I'm on my way back to Las Cruces right now."

Daddy looked impressed. Alec merely nodded slowly. "Sounds pretty good to me. How long do you think it will take to get something out of her?"

I shrugged. "Next week or later. You know how these things go. If she decides to open up, I'm ready. I've decided to give Laura McCulloch a different backstory for this case, one more in keeping with Kendra's position in life. I figure that the usual one would make her shun me or ignore me, where this ought to make her at least a bit more willing to associate with me. Now Laura is going to have a background pretty much like Becky's, and I got screwed out of my birthright by one husband and knocked up and hooked up by my present lower-class one before I miscarried, and I'm working to build a nest egg that will let me divorce him. If and when I get the chance to lay it all out, that is. Until she starts to open up to me, though, all I can do is be there and keep on keeping on."

Alec had more. "Well, like I told you on the phone last night, the grand jury returned a true bill on Becky. Murder one and a couple of lesser charges. Arraignment is next week, and we expect a Trial Management Conference about eight weeks from now, give or take. Trial will start the following week."

He shook his head. "I don't know. John thinks we've got a strong defense case, but I have to admit, I'm scared as hell, although my lack of experience in cases like this is probably a major part of that and my feeling for her is most of the remainder. The prosecutor is bad news, Becky looks bad, emotionally about as flat as a very dead snake in the road, and that definitely won't look good at trial. I see some of what John's talking about, but … I'm not sure I should be handling this case. I'm too close to Becky on the one hand and I don't have the experience in this sort of high-profile public case on the other. I'm scared of doing her more harm than good, and she's awfully dear to both of us."

I got out of my chair to go touch and hold him in reassurance. "You're the best *possible* person for the job. She knows you, she trusts you, and there's nobody else she trusts as much or would do as much for. You've also got John to run the case with you. You've said yourself there's nobody better." I thought for a moment. "So I've got about eight weeks, maybe nine, ten at the absolute outside." Alec had a very sour look on his face. Daddy just sat silently, taking everything in. I looked over at him. "Have you got anything to add?" That could have sounded harsh, but I kept my voice soft because that was the farthest thing from my mind.

"Nope. I wish I did, Baby. She's like another daughter to me, as you know. But all I can offer is moral support, or whatever you want to call it. I mean, I know diddly about any of this sort of thing, as both of you know. Can we change the subject, or do we need to keep at this for a while? I mean, if you've got more you need to talk about, go right ahead. But if you're done …"

He truly did look uncomfortable, and there really wasn't much more that Alec and I could accomplish at the moment. I looked at Alec, and he just shook his head. "No, I think we're done for now. Why? Is there something you had in mind?"

"Well, it's kind of off the track, but I did have a thought, or at least a slight hope, that perhaps you'd like to go out west tomorrow and shoot some clay. I haven't been back to the club since I left Tucson."

I had to think about that for a moment. I hadn't been there much lately myself, even before all of this. Oh, what the hell. He was my father, and I wanted to spend some time with him, too. "Sure. Think you can shoot my gun?"

He snorted. "With your short arms and length of pull? I don't *think* so. I'll see if I can get one of the rentals from the club."

Alec spoke up. "You can borrow one of my Brownings, if you want. They're factory stocks, so they're longer than Amy's. In fact, I think they're exactly the same as the club has." Alec had a pair of Browning Citoris, one for trap and another one for skeet and sporting clays. The Citori is nothing fancy, it's a nice, basic over and under shotgun that works well enough and doesn't cost a lot. I'm going to surprise him with something a *lot* better, probably Italian and custom-made, once this is all done with, but business before pleasure.

Mine ... I've had my clay bird gun since I was sixteen. Daddy got me interested and involved in trap and then skeet when I was thirteen, and for my sixteenth birthday he offered to buy me a shotgun of my own, up to a certain amount. I had some very specific ideas about what I wanted by then, and the overage had to come out of what I had gotten on my shares. When Daddy heard what I had in mind, though, he approved it and we set up the order. I have a Beretta ASE-90, a model that they haven't made in a number of years now, although it's still one of the greatest Berettas ever made, in my admittedly rarely-humble opinion. It was brand-new on the market when I ordered it.

Instead of having two guns, one for trap and another for skeet and clays, I ordered it with two barrels fitted to the gun. One, the longest they offered, had interchangeable chokes, and I had that barrel weighted. That one was for trap, mostly. The other, just a little bit shorter, I ordered with fixed chokes and immediately sent it off to have it tubed with a sub-gauge tube set. What I wound up with was a gun I could use for any clay-bird sport, and I proceeded to do exactly that. Daddy had started me on trap first, and while I'd shot some skeet, most of my shooting at that point had been trap shooting, so I just ordered it with a trap stock in my dimensions, so it shoots high no matter what I'm shooting. Works for me, although it drives anyone else nuts if they try to shoot my gun on the skeet field, because they keep shooting over the targets. I loved the gun then — it was my first made-to-order gun — and I still do. I think it shows.

Suddenly fatigue and hunger set in. I guess I just took some time to fully let go of the stress of the week. "So what's for dinner? I'm starved."

Alec just said, "Depends on how soon you want to eat. I've got shrimp and sausage defrosted and ready for a paella, but if you need something faster, I can cook up some burgers and potatoes, sliced tomatoes or a salad on the side and do the paella tomorrow."

I love Alec's paella, but it meant waiting the best part of an hour. "I think I'll have the paella tomorrow. Burgers now, if you would be so kind, sir." He grinned and went to start dinner.

Daddy was still looking at me. "I really can't get used to you as a brunette."

I smiled. "You better. I'm not going back to my normal hair color until I'm done with this investigation. It's a twice-a-week job to color it and keep it up, but Laura McCulloch has to be on tap from now until I can get Kendra Frankton where I want her. Where I *need* her. Once

I've got her and I'm done, it'll only take me a couple of days to start to go back to my normal color. I'll wear a wig for the board meeting, if I decide to worry about it at all. It's not like my hair color is any of their business. Or concern."

I really wasn't up for much after dinner. I did have to put the guns and shooting bags into the car for the next morning. The club opens early in the summer so people can shoot before it gets too hot, and we were going to be there as soon as we could make it. But that only took about ten minutes. I told Alec he could stay up and keep Daddy company, but he decided that he'd rather come to bed with me (well, duh!) and I let the dogs out for a last spin as Daddy and Alec made up the pull-out.

I wish I could say that I paid off on the promise I'd made Alec with the kiss he got when I first arrived home. The truth is that by the time we were both in bed, I was already more than half asleep. I simply kissed him, cuddled into his side real close with my arm across his chest, his arm around me and I drifted off without even touching the book on my nightstand, much less doing anything more with him.

Chapter 10

Morning came early. I paid off Alec for last night's broken promise before we ever got out of bed, and Daddy didn't wake up until Bruno went to sniff him as I was taking them out for their morning spin. A light breakfast all around, coffee, of course, and we all headed for the club. Well, not the dogs. Neither of them was all that interested, and it was getting way too warm for them. The club doesn't have a lot of shade available, although they don't mind well-behaved dogs.

It was almost a first. Daddy hasn't beaten me at trap in years, but he creamed me today. I only broke 20 once, and my usual average is over 24. Well over. He was having a wonderful day — never hit less than 23 and he had two perfect 25's. Alec, when he shot, was in the low 20's, which is presentable for him, although he usually averages around 23. Of course, he had to use his skeet/clays gun, which may have had something to do with it.

Me, well, I guess my mind wasn't in it. God knows I certainly had a good reason. My mind was up in Phoenix, trying to work out how I was going to get closer to Kendra Frankton, and trap is first and foremost a game of concentration. My whole brain was just on an entirely different track, and it showed with a vengeance. So I probably won't mix business with pleasure, that pleasure, anyway, again. Not until this whole mess is done with. On the other hand, just spending time with Daddy, even under these circumstances, has a certain value to it, so it wasn't all bad by any means.

We left the club and just had to stop at a little Mexican place I knew out on the west side for a light lunch before heading back to the house. Over lunch, Alec asked Daddy about his writing. "Honest truth is that I haven't done any in a couple of years. I just haven't felt any stories coming to me, and I know better than to push it. I tried that once. Horrid book. It sold, but at the moment it's the only book I've written since Amy was eleven that's out of print."

Alec named one. Yep, that would be it. I remembered editing it. Not an easy edit at all. That was Daddy's second science-fiction book after Mom was killed. I told him when I first read it that he ought to deep-six it, but his agent seemed to think it would sell. It did, but just barely. Daddy looked at Alec. "Don't tell me you're a fan."

Alec simply smiled. "Well, no, not exactly. But Amy's got the complete set of your books and I have to admit that I've read all of them." He took a drink. "And didn't you also used to write …?" The little restaurant was sort of tight, so I wasn't at all unhappy that Alec had let his question end there.

Daddy just laughed. "You're kidding! That market is dried up and *gone*. I mean, you can find all of that sort of thing you want on the internet. If you want to read it, it's there. If you'd rather watch it, it's there, too. There's so much of it available for free that it's astounding to me that anyone can still charge for it and make any money, although clearly some do. No, when the market for that dried up, I just quit doing it completely. I never found it all that fascinating anyway. It just paid the bills, and when I found a story coming, I had to write it no matter what it was.

"I kept having this feeling that if I didn't write whatever came to me, either it would eventually disappear and nothing more would ever come, or else it would clog up the works until I finally got it down on paper. Or on a computer screen, more recently. At least with the science-fiction, the longer I waited before I tried to write whatever I felt coming, the heavier the emotional loading got. I mean, these are fictional characters. But if I tried to resist writing the story I felt coming, I wound up actually beginning to tear up over them. It's hell to cry over your own fictional characters."

It probably is. But at the moment, I had enough facts to worry about (and thinking of Becky, to get teary-eyed over), never mind fiction, and it was high time I got back to it. I checked the time. We really needed to get a move on, because Alec and I both had work to do. Before we went home, though, we took Daddy up not too far from Gates Pass to show him where we were buying land. I'd have to say he was impressed. Not by the quantity or cost of the land we were getting; he understood that for the CEO, money becomes a very minor thing. But he was clearly impressed by the sheer placement of it, and the expanse of view it had to the west. I still find it breathtaking myself and I hope I always do.

By now we had the inventory sheets from the crime scene. I spent several hours going over as many of them as I could stand, line by line. Alec and I knew Becky's house and its contents as well as anyone other than Becky herself, and we expected to know everything on the sheets. One thing stood out for me, though. The sheets listed an empty jewelry box from the jeweler I now used in Zurich. There was no necklace listed that could begin to match the one I'd given Becky from that jeweler last year — the necklace that had come in that very box. I pointed this discrepancy out to Alec, and he got all thoughtful. "I'll ask her about it tomorrow or during the week," he said as he made a note. "I don't know what it means. Could they have listed it as something else, or found it somewhere else?"

That was certainly a valid question. I scanned the entire file of sheets. Nothing like it was listed anywhere else in the house nor in her personal effects, and there was nothing else that could even begin to resemble the way that her necklace would have been described by any cop. The way that Becky felt about it, there was no question but that the necklace would have been in plain sight, because if it wasn't in the box, it was all but certain to be around her neck.

Given how the rest of the jewelry was described, I figured the description ought to be pretty accurate. Whoever had listed her jewelry had had a decent notion of what they were looking at. That was the only noticeable discrepancy that I found in the listings. If I got a photo of Kendra Frankton wearing that necklace, well, that would be a lot stronger evidence that she'd been there. Or if it turned up in her house.

I sent an email to Margarete, my secretary/receptionist in Golondrino, to check with the jeweler and find out how many such necklaces they'd sold. If I were really lucky, it would be a one-off. Let that one wait until Monday; I'd done what I could for now. Then I had a quick thought and I sent her another to contact the board members and reschedule the upcoming board meeting for a weekend, either the one before, which would be two weeks from now, or the following one, whichever worked better for the board members.

Then there were the crime scene photos to go over. Truly gruesome. I mean, there was blood *everywhere*. I figured you'd expect to find a void where Becky had been lying. I didn't, but other than a bit of shadowing, or whatever they call it, right up next to the bed, it was just acres of blood. The walls were spattered, some of the framed artwork was spattered — it looked like some madman had come in with gallon after gallon of reddish-brown paint and just hurled it around the room with total abandon. Well, maybe not multiple gallons, but definitely a whole lot. I'm not qualified to comment on blood spatter analysis, so I skipped to the medical reports and crime scene reports.

Frankton's body had been found supine, i.e. on his back, on the bed. He had multiple blunt-force traumas to his head and body. Well, that's being polite. His face was smashed into unrecognizability. His wallet was there, but they'd had to confirm his identity from fingerprints and dental records of individual teeth because his jaws had been shattered by the beating. Those teeth that hadn't been smashed in the process, that is.

His throat had been cut on the side next to where Becky had apparently been lying. Both sides, actually, but the majority of the arterial spray had been from that side, and either the cut hadn't gotten to the left carotid or that side had been cut later. I looked at the pictures again. No, the left carotid hadn't been cut; the cut was distinctly shallower on that side. Well, that would certainly explain the volume of blood on the side of the bed where Becky had been and the amount found on Becky's clothing.

I steeled myself. For just a moment, I reminded myself that it had to have been far worse for Becky, actually waking up in the middle of it. This was pretty bad even in photos, and I didn't have much experience in investigations of this nature. Hidden assets, secret trysts, juicy divorces and things like that were pretty much my usual fare. Finally moving up to the big time, I guess.

Cause of death was ultimately exsanguination, presumably from having his throat cut. That tends to do it, although getting beaten up that badly on the head and body isn't going to do anyone much good either, so he was probably already on the way out when whoever did it moved on from the beating. Cutting someone's throat also tends to let a lot of blood out to go all around the room, or so various TV shows would suggest. Judging from the photos of the actual scene here, the TV doesn't do more than barely suggest what really happens in such a case. Even Daddy was impressed by the photos. Maybe 'impressed' wasn't quite the right term.

It's amazing what you can find on the internet. I found what amount to actual courses on blood-spatter analysis. Not anywhere near enough to qualify me to testify in court, of course, but definitely enough that I could understand what I was looking at in the photos. Returning to them when I knew at least a tiny bit of what to look for and how to look for it, I assembled them in my mind. "Alec, have you looked at these carefully?"

"I thought I had. What did you find?"

"Put these together in your mind. There's a whole section of the bedroom that's missing here, and the photos from the surrounding area, like these" — I indicated three — "suggest that there should be plenty more medium-velocity spatter there." His lips turned in, the surest sign that his mind was working very hard.

Finally he eased up. "You're right. I hadn't looked at it like that before. Let's see — the area from just over the bed, around the ceiling fan and over to the far wall. Then toward the other wall *there*. We've got our own forensic experts coming in starting Monday afternoon. John said he'll bring the blood-spatter expert and a crime scene photographer, so we'll have our own shots of the room. *All* of the room. The others are flying in separately from all over the country as they need to be here."

Oh shit oh dear, this was going to get expensive. "Are any of them Family?" When Family members use other Family members professionally, the Family pays. That's how I was going to get my own bill paid, not that I wouldn't have done the whole investigation and never given a moment's thought to the bill, for Becky, even if I weren't the CEO. That payment creates a lot of incentive to keep everything within the Family whenever possible. That was also a primary reason — well, secondary, really, there was all of that experience and competence — for calling on John Tolliver.

"I asked John about that, and they're not. He says there aren't any independent forensic experts in the Family anywhere that he knows of, and he'd know about them if anyone did. But he's run into this before. He'll pay them out of his own pocket and then run their charges into his bill. That way it gets paid by the Family and not by us or Becky. He said that's how he's done it in the past, and nobody's ever challenged it."

Well, that should work. If anyone in Golondrino balked at the charges, of course, the problem would be bucked upstairs — to me. Better believe I'd approve this one. I mean, there's Family and then there's *Family*. At least for me, and probably for Alec as well by now, Becky was definitely very special *Family*. Not that I'd ever do anything against Family interests, but trust me, the Family could afford John's bill, *whatever* it wound up totaling.

Alec wrapped up whatever he was doing and headed for the kitchen. I figured I might as well, too. Even if I couldn't do much to help with the paella, at least the dogs needed to be fed. We spent some companionable time in silence getting their dinners ready, with a pleasant bit of kissy-face along the way. When that was done, at my request, Alec put me to work cutting up tomatoes and peppers for the paella. Anything to keep me busy and help me not think morbid thoughts about the crime scene on quite the same scale. Or about Becky's situation.

I had barely gotten started on that latter task when Daddy wandered in, probably tired of being alone, and sat at the kitchen table. We then filled the kitchen with talk about the shotguns, my favorite load, his favorite load and so on. Most diverting and, given the alternatives, most enjoyable as well. I didn't think I'd have any bad dreams tonight, but I have to admit that I was still caught up by the amount of blood in those pictures. Had it been Becky's or Alec's blood, or even Daddy's or Aunt Lori's, you better believe I'd have had some serious nightmares. But it wasn't, and I didn't have any particular attachment to the late Doctor Jon Frankton, thankfully, other than vicariously through Becky. Besides, the missing necklace was still eating at me.

Sunday morning came bright and early. I did omelets for everyone — sweet peppers, roasted chiles, some crumbled bacon, grape tomatoes and cheese, too much filling the way I usually do — and we put on the Sunday morning cable news program. Alec and I had each had our second mug of coffee by the time the show was over.

Then it was back to the old grind, going over the discovery Alec had gotten from the prosecutor so far. Neither of us found anything more of special interest, at least not yet. But the necklace still stood out, for me. It had been an extremely expensive necklace. Not that Becky wasn't worth it; she was that and more. She was not only a lifelong friend to me and almost as good, if nowhere near as long, a friend to Alec. Becky had also helped and supported both of us emotionally and personally during the run-up to my becoming CEO. I could probably say that without her, I might never have gotten to where I am and Alec and I might never have managed to get together. Nobody investigating the crime scene would have been all that likely to notice the necklace's being missing, or attach an appropriate amount of importance to it, but knowing how much she loved it, I damn sure did. Now I had something specific to focus on.

Chapter 11

Monday morning was no thrill. Yes, it was vitally important to visit Becky. As her attorney, Alec could pretty much come and go, but Daddy and I were the only other outside contacts she'd have all week, and he was going home this afternoon. She didn't look good at all. My overwhelming misery for her was pretty much a constant by now, but I could certainly see why Alec was worried about their putting her on suicide watch. I didn't think she would try to harm herself. I also didn't think she would try to fight whatever happened. Dammit, we *needed* her to fight. Time was short, but Daddy and I both tried to buck her up. Neither of us succeeded.

When I got back to the room I had rented in Phoenix, my first job was to check the tracking program and then see what emails I might have. The trackers provided an interesting pattern. Kendra Frankton apparently went clubbing every night, or at least her car went to the same club pretty much each evening. Donald McGuire had spent Saturday evening at the same club, and then his car spent the night at her house. Hm. Well, it was hardly a surprise, was it?

This morning, her car showed much the same sort of track as it had the weekday mornings last week. I love people who have a routine. It makes picking them up ever so much easier. Tomorrow morning I'd be at the gym when she arrived. Today I'd pick up the tracker from McGuire's car. He was certainly an interesting addition to the information, but I didn't have any real need to know his whereabouts on an ongoing basis. I also had to put another tracker under Kendra's car. The batteries were only good for about ten days, tops, and I definitely didn't want to push it.

I also had two emails from Margarete. The board meeting was no problem to reschedule, and the Family plane would be in Tucson to pick me up early Friday morning, about a week and a half from now. I was the second pickup, since it would first stop in Albuquerque for the two board members from New Mexico. The one from Hawaii was already in Europe on vacation, and the one from Germany preferred to go overland since he was so close, so the Family would send a limousine for both of them. We'd pick up the others on the way back.

Okay, that works. Some CEO's had specifically had themselves picked up either first or last, and it seemed to me as though it might have been some sort of ego thing. I don't work that way. My standing instructions were to pick me up in the most convenient way for the aircrew.

The necklace was less simple. The jeweler told her that they'd only made two such necklaces, and the second was still in their shop window. There were others in much the same pattern, but with lesser stones. Well, yeah, they'd kind of have to be. Those weren't important. I shot back an email to tell her to get back with the shop and give them whatever they needed to hold the one, although they could continue to display it if they wanted, and not produce another matching piece until further notice.

If I had to, I'd buy the second one, too. The first might never be recovered, and it was only money, after all. But not making any more just like it — that could be crucial. It wouldn't prove much to find Kendra wearing one of a thousand such necklaces, after all. One of one you could take to the bank.

I checked over my photo gear. I had brought the Leica M8 digital with the Visoflex and the 400mm Telyt, my usual gear. I get some very odd looks from other people in the business when I show up with that outfit, since it's rather antiquated next to modern digital cameras — but I get as good or better pictures, I get them faster and it's loads quieter. It works, and that's the most important part. I checked my settings and battery level, took a practice shot to make sure everything was working fine and I was ready to go.

I was in position to shoot some photos of Kendra on her way to the club door well before the time she usually arrived. She parked way on the other side of the parking lot, thank God, and walked towards the door. I got a couple of quick shots without even analyzing what I was getting. Plenty of time for that later. After she was safely inside, I strolled over to that side of the parking lot and, when there was nobody around, I quickly ducked down and swapped trackers in her wheelwell. Easy. Simple.

After I got back to my room, I pulled the memory card to get the pictures onto the computer. I gave the shots a quick once-over before I tried zeroing in on her neck. A simple pendant, no fancy necklace. Not that I expected to hit the jackpot so easily, but damn! Oh, well, tomorrow's another day, and Laura will be at the gym waiting. If nothing else, everything works just fine. That's important, even if I don't have the pictures I really wanted. Sooner or later, if there was any way on God's green earth, I'd get them. Oh, wait a minute, this is Arizona. Make that God's brown earth.

The only thing left, other than checking in with Alec, was my evening draw and dry fire exercises. I try to put in a half hour every evening before I get undressed. It was especially important tonight, because I wasn't going to be wearing my usual shoulder holster any more for the duration of this investigation.

That time in the locker room had made me just a bit more leery of letting the gun be seen, especially when I was wearing tighter t-shirts than usual, so I had brought my larger fanny pack. It's fairly nice leather, not great, and just big enough to hold the gun behind the body of the pack on a tear-away piece. It's made for it, actually. My left hand comes down and rips the front of the pack off its velcro so it hangs on the bottom stitching and the strap, which has two strands of very light cable running through it so it can't be easily cut off me. Pull the gun and as it comes up, the left hand meets it for a proper two-hand hold.

My problem is that there is a basic (and very sensible) principle that when you carry a defensive weapon, you carry it in the same place all the time. That way when you reach for it in the heat of the moment (trust me, if you *need* it, it's already stressful as all hell. I know from experience), you're always reaching to the same point. This was quite a drastic change from my usual shoulder holster, which made it all the more imperative that I practice. Longer tonight than usual, just to be safe. I dropped the magazine and carefully cleared the chamber, then I checked it again. Only then did I holster it and fasten the front of the pack back in place.

My own feeling is that anyone who carries a weapon on a daily basis is an accidental discharge waiting to happen. Good training and habits minimize the chance, yes, but figure it is *going* to happen sooner or later. There are two tricks.

The first is to maintain proper muzzle control, no matter what. As Col. Cooper used to say, never let the muzzle cover anything you aren't willing to destroy. If you dry-fire with the gun pointed at the dog, and you have an accidental discharge, I don't care how much you may dislike the dog, you are going to be very unhappy with yourself. You'll probably create one helluva mess, too, even if you miss. Or if you habitually aim at the neighbors' house through the picture window ....

Choose a safe target. Like that plaster bust of Beethoven on your mother's piano (yes, I did. And I replaced it. Out of my own money, not my Family dividends. Well, actually, yes, it was out of my dividends originally, but I kept a record, including accumulating interest, and eventually paid back, every penny, from earnings. Daddy didn't insist, but I *had* to. It was one of the things in the house that Mom had had, and with her gone, I couldn't possibly have just dropped the pieces of it in the trash and forgotten about it).

Daddy had his when he was young, too. A very nice tall colored glass vase — well, it was expensive, so I guess it was a *vahse* — full of flowers and water. Nailed that sucker dead center with a .22, or so he says. He paid that back, too. He didn't pay interest. Grandmother Alannah was rather upset, but understanding, as he tells it.

Anyway, the second trick is to learn from your experience. One accidental discharge is just waiting to happen. A second one strongly suggests, to me at least, that you didn't learn diddly from the first, and that does not incline me to trust you around weapons. Not, at least, within range of *me*.

Alec was fine. We didn't spend a lot more time on the phone than that; I was pretty tired and needed my sleep. I can hold it off if I'm doing something, but once I'm anywhere near my bed, it's almost like iron filings near a magnet. At least with Daddy gone, we could speak freely. We did.

Chapter 12

Once again I woke from a poor night's sleep. I'd spent most of the night moving around, trying to find Alec's arm to put back around me where it belongs. Sleeping alone is *cold* compared to sleeping with him.

Rather than drink the horrid coffee that was about as good as could be made in my suite, I made my way to the coffee shop where Kendra Frankton had met Dr. McGuire last week. Yep, there they were. No surprise, since I knew her car was in the parking lot before I ever got there. But I gave her a spritely wave and a very nice little smile before I took my coffee (blessed coffee!) over to a chair where I could see her reflection in the window.

I made like I was reading my book on threaded fasteners, although in actual fact I was just turning the pages at reasonable intervals and not even seeing what was on those pages beyond whether it was illustrations or text. I could already discuss various heads, lengths, thread types, pitches and hardnesses with someone in the field and at least *sound* as though I knew what I was talking about. That isn't far off of my actual level of knowledge, and that's all I need in this game, so the book was simply a bit of stage dressing at this point.

This time, for a change, I waited until she left before I got up to go. I made a production of checking my watch and then leaving, just in case she was watching me from her car. I don't wear a watch normally, but Laura wears one — a reasonable woman's watch, not one of these little dainty ultra-feminine things like Mom used to wear. Then I hit the gym, where she was already pumping away on her bike.

I gave her an 'Oh, hello again!' sort of greeting as I headed for the locker room. I came out with my iPod and earbuds in my hand and headed for a bike about three away from hers. Mustn't appear too pushy, after all. When I got back to the locker room, she was finishing up. That was fine with me. As I've said, as Laura, I could run just a bit at the mouth, but I needed to soften her — my — tones just a bit from last week. I apologized for spilling my issues on her last week, but explained that I was just starting a new job in a new city and was a bit nervous then. This week it wasn't all quite so new.

It seemed to work. I didn't get anything more than a noncommittal noise or two from her, but I didn't see the sort of irritated body language I'd seen last week. Definitely a step up, if a small one. The next couple of days were simply replays of the same. My only serious regret, such as it was, was that all she was driving these days, apparently, was the Toyota. I really wanted to get a tracker on her late husband's Lexus, just in case. But as long as it stayed in the garage, no dice. The batteries would probably die before I needed the damn thing anyway.

Alec did have one piece of news for me that evening. I'd been too tired last night to do more than simply check in, tell him I was exhausted, since this was after my exercises, and send him a kiss or two. Well, that and a couple of promises for when we were together again.

Tonight we actually had time and I had the energy to talk. What he had finally gotten out of Becky was that she and Jon had been out for dinner to a very fancy place the night he was murdered, one of the fancy resort hotel restaurants up in the foothills not too far from her house, and she had been wearing the necklace in question.

No reason why she shouldn't have been; it looked even better on her than I had thought it would when I paid the ridiculous price for it, and I'd known it would look absolutely beautiful on her then. Anyway, there was no sign of it anywhere in the arrest report or any of the other myriad forms that the incident had generated. *Gotcha*, I thought with a certain amount of triumph. Now if I could just catch Kendra wearing it …

By the time Friday rolled around, she was actually exchanging greetings with me. Cursory ones, at this point, but something. Not the time to begin telling her Laura's (invented) life story, by any means, but at least we were actually beginning to engage each other conversationally. Just beginning.

But of course, I had to head home to my husband in Las Cruces, or so I told her. I'd be back next week, unfortunately too late on Monday to be here for an early lunchtime, but I'd definitely see her here on Tuesday. She even said she was looking forward to it, although her body language and the tone of her voice suggested very strongly that she was simply being polite, barely, and really didn't give a shit.

I made a market stop on the way home. I was going to do fresh heirloom tomato pasta sauce tonight, one of my favorite recipes, and actually do some cooking myself. The kitchenette in the place I was staying wasn't exactly fixed with what I needed to make huge pots of chili, anyway, and what else is there for me to eat? So I'd go out when the pains got too bad and pretty much subsisted on coffee and granola bars or the like the rest of the time.

After I finally disentangled myself from Alec and the dogs, I found we already had four big heirloom tomatoes by the sink, drying. Three of them were my very favorite, the big, almost black ones with the most incredible tomato flavor. I guess great minds think alike. I washed mine, set them to dry alongside and separated out the ones I wanted for the sauce tonight. I set the smallest aside for a side salad. Life can still be pretty good, at least when Alec and I could be together.

I almost didn't get to make the pasta sauce. We started with a nice scotch each, and then poured another. Then we … well, we hadn't done *that* in the living room in months and months. Oh, God, but I'd missed him so. Finally, when we were done and had to move, I got up and pulled my t-shirt and jeans back on. Forget the underwear. I didn't need any more than that to cook in, but I've definitely gotten leery of sautéing things when I'm nude. Dangerous. Painful. I probably ought to get an apron.

Suffice it to say that I cannot begin to say how good it felt to sleep in his arms in our own bed again. I didn't wake up until more than an hour later than usual Saturday morning, with that difficulty in coming to full wakefulness that suggests a really good, really deep night's sleep.

I did some aerobic exercise before breakfast (no, not *that*, I was on the stationary bike) and worked up just a bit of an appetite. I didn't mention to Alec how disappointed I was that I hadn't gotten a container of chili out to thaw overnight. It was my own fault, after all, so instead I made do with toast, peanut butter and hot pepper jelly. Just sitting across from Alec at breakfast meant that, in my book, life was pretty much as good as it could be under the circumstances, no matter what was on my plate.

By now we had preliminary reports from at least some of our forensic experts. I spent some time poring over our crime scene photos. Unlike the ones we'd gotten from the Pima County attorney, ours were a complete set showing the entire room. Plus one of those 'virtual-reality' sorts of computer videos that shows you a continuous panoramic view of the entire room with just some movements of your mouse. Neat. The concept, I mean. The scene itself was still pretty gruesome, even in pictures taken well after the prosecutor's team had done their thing.

Then I hauled out the reports from Doctor Compton, the blood spatter expert. I spent several hours simply trying to understand his preliminary report and putting it together in my mind with our photos of the scene.

Now *that* was interesting. According to his report, the assailant had almost certainly been using his or her right hand when beating on the deceased. But I knew for a fact that Becky was a lefty. And care to guess which area of the crime scene made this most clear? Just that part of the ceiling that we hadn't gotten photos of from the county attorney. Gee, what a surprise.

I'd watched Kendra Frankton enough to know that she was right-handed. One more small piece. Very small, in this case; righties are what, five-sixths of the population? Something like that. Hell, Alec and I are both righties ourselves. It hardly did anything more than keep us suspicious of her. I was already suspicious as hell of her, and I didn't think that was likely to change. Well, lessen, anyway. It sure could increase.

His report also identified several other points in the blood patterns in the room. There was a handprint — right hand — on the bedspread. It appeared from its position and orientation that Becky had put her hand there and leaned over the bed to check on Jon. Blood on the phone, but we already knew that Becky had called 911 after she woke up. Some footprints, not many, that matched Becky's shoes. There were also some smudges on the floor that could possibly be footprints, but without any identifiable tread imprints.

His report also made reference to blood being found in the bathroom drains, almost as though someone went to wash up after the murder. Somehow, I couldn't see Becky, or any other reasonable person, for that matter, washing up just to then go lay down in a pool of the same blood. Maybe someone like, say, Kendra, had been wearing booties, scrubs and something on her head, and then washed up her face afterwards, before bagging everything to take with her? It made a certain amount of sense, anyway.

But going into the master bath, which is right off the bedroom, to wash up after the murder? And then walking back *out* through that same bedroom where the victim is lying? I mean, that's *cold*. It fits Kendra, of course. To a T.

The county attorney had the murder weapons; they'd been in the bedroom on the floor. A piece of black iron pipe, around two feet long, and one of Becky's kitchen knives, a big slicer. Not her favorite for kitchen use, I knew. She much preferred her santukos and only used the slicer for turkey or the like. Neither weapon showed anything but fingerprint smudges (ignoring a few old partials on the knife), as though whoever had been handling them had had gloves on.

So let me see if I understand the prosecutor's case theory. Becky and Jon got to Becky's place around 9:30 or 10 that night. After Becky opened the door, or let Jon do it with her key, either way, there were no prints on the key to say — hey, is that significant in itself? You think? — she gasses Jon, or maybe knocks him out, gets him to obligingly fall on her own bed (I happened to know what she thought of that bedspread, and she would never in a million years have done him there. But I couldn't possibly prove that to a court), beats him to a pulp with the pipe (which came from where?), and then she cuts his throat, just incidentally cutting it deeper on the very side where a lefty would be likely (or so I reasoned, as I tried to work such a stroke with my own hands) to make the *shallower* side of the cut.

She then removes the covering garments and gloves she had put on for the murder (*why?*), washes up (*why?*), discards those garments and gloves somewhere where the detectives and crime scene techs can't find them, gasses herself as well (disposing of the gas and apparatus where? and how?) and just manages to have herself fall into a pool of his blood right by the side of the bed. Or maybe just fakes being unconscious, and instead spends several hours waiting in the same room, or at least the same house, with her lover's body.

Oh, and let's not forget that her repeated beating on him was done with her weak hand, as the cast-off blood shows, and of course, she leaves the murder weapons in the bedroom before she gasses herself (yes, they'd done a tox screen, and she showed traces of anesthetic in her system).

Who wears gloves to murder someone in their own bedroom? And with their own knife? Come *on*! Get real!

Oh, and she must have dropped the necklace that she loved almost beyond description into the bag with whatever she had been wearing to keep the splatter off her clothes. The ones she was going to lie down in the blood pool while still wearing. Yeah, right.

How about this instead: She — or Jon, doesn't matter which — opens the door, or at least starts to, whereupon they both receive a blast of some anesthetic gas in the face. It's pretty obvious who has access to anesthetic. The killer pulls the key out of the door and wipes off any tell-tale fingerprints on it, if he or she handled it barehanded at all.

The killer, suitably dressed, of course, then drags Jon to the bedroom and pulls him up on the bed. Probably pulls Becky into the bedroom as well. Evidence? Well, the carpet showed signs of being freshly raked, but that could arguably have been Becky tidying up for the evening, or so a prosecutor would claim. Even though I knew she raked her carpet not at *all*, because again, I couldn't prove it in court. I once asked her why she had the carpet rake when she never used it, and she shrugged and said it came with the carpet.

Anyway, once Jon is on the bed, the killer begins to whale on him with the pipe. That's a very personal sort of assault, to say the least, and it was done right-handed, of course. Anyway, having worked out enough personal anger, and not incidentally causing enough damage to have all but killed him anyway, the killer then cuts his throat, slicing from left to right with a knife taken from the rack on the kitchen counter, finishing up by tossing the pipe and knife aside. Apparently to the right of where said killer was standing, for what little it may be worth.

Not as likely, or so it seems to me, the action of a southpaw like Becky as much as a righty like … among others, guess who. Finally the killer takes Becky's necklace, then drags her alongside the bed and drops her in the blood pool, probably on the so far entirely valid theory that she would wind up taking the fall for the crime and leave the real murderer free. Oh, and the murderer departs, after washing up, bagging the garments for disposal elsewhere and raking the carpet to clear up the drag marks.

Becky wakes up several hours later and, after gathering herself, leans over the bed to check Jon's body (handprint on the spread in the crime scene report, bloody smudges on the pulse point in his neck in the autopsy report), then picks up the phone to call 911.

Well, it hangs together and, modestly, I'd have to say I think it does so just a bit better than whatever the prosecutor seems to be thinking. I explained it all to Alec, including my reasoning. He listened carefully. "Yes, that's pretty much the way that John and I figure it had to have happened. We didn't think of the carpet raking, but you're right. You know, and to some degree I know, that she never rakes it herself. But you're also right that proving it in court would be next to impossible. So would the bit about the bedspread, which also hadn't occurred to me, but you're definitely right now that I think about it. She loved that spread. Other than that, we track. And John and I both think we've got a strong case for reasonable doubt that way."

I snorted. 'Reasonable doubt' might get Becky off, but nothing less than finding the real guilty party, or at least establishing conclusively, not merely probably, that she didn't do it would really do her all that much good in the long run. Yeah, she'd be free. But she was already eating herself up inside and doing a damn good job of it, too. Too goddam good. Simply finding that the jury couldn't convict her on the evidence offered was just not going to do anything to make her stop that. She needed to be *cleared*. Besides, just like Tolliver said, there's only one person who can do that right now, yours truly.

Sunday was another day. I woke to find us wrapped even closer together than usual, and since my hand was already in position, I figured I could wake him up the way he liked most. So did I. By breakfast, we were both ready for some calories. He wanted eggs, and I wanted my usual hot cereal with salsa and cheese. We both won. I fixed his eggs while he did my cereal. Steel-cut oats, this morning, with some cut-up fruit, salsa, a tiny bit of hot sauce (*very* hot), and a generous handful of shredded cheddar. His omelet was onion, some sweet peppers, one roasted chili, and a small tomato, all diced. We didn't have any small tomatoes. I diced the smallest of the remaining heirlooms, put some into the pan for him and added the remainder to the fruit in my bowl. Then I added some bacon crumbles to the small frypan for his omelet and took the shredded cheddar to top it with before it got baked.

As usual, I put too much stuff in, including eggs. Go to one of these fancy brunches and they do it all on a burner in front of you. They also flip it over in the pan, and the last time I tried *that*, Bruno caught it before it hit the floor and he and Sasha ate it in record time. I definitely couldn't have by then, as it was almost at knee-height when he got it. I actually did Alec's omelet while he did the dogs' breakfasts, then he did my cereal while his omelet (okay, technically I guess it was a frittata because it wasn't folded) baked. That way we were pretty much ready at the same time, and we were both very pleased with each other's efforts.

Made coffee while waiting for Alec to finish doing my cereal and we were waiting for his omelet to come out of the oven. Tune into the cable news show on the kitchen

TV instead of the living room because we ran a bit late. So what? It was Sunday, and as these things go, we had a grand time. Life was almost good, and if Becky had been safe and snug in her own house, or sitting with us, it would have been an absolutely incredible morning. I'm scared to death of losing her. I've internalized her to the point that I can't get my defenses up against her, and I don't dare let Alec know how much it worries me. He's got enough on his mind already.

Chapter 13

Alec was going to let John do most of the actual courtroom work in this case. John had the experience in huge, very public cases like this; Alec had the Arizona license. John would let Alec examine or cross-examine some of the witnesses.

Alec wasn't fooled any more than I was. These were witnesses whose testimony wasn't critical to any theory of the case and who wouldn't need any particular careful handling, like the deputies who'd responded to Becky's call. Assuming, that is, that there was any testimony we still needed to get out of them after the prosecutor was done with them.

No, neither one of us was fooled. The great John Tolliver would examine the critical witnesses. He had the experience, loads of it. It really was logical for him to take the testimony where the wrong phrasing, the wrong question, or worse, forgetting to ask a crucial question, the wrong touch with the witness — anything at all, really — could truly screw things up. That was why we'd brought him into the case, after all.

On a practical basis, as Alec reminded me, the simple fact that he was really going to be able to stand up during such a publicized trial and actually appear at the lectern was significant. It would be enough for him. He was definitely the student. The grasshopper. The padawan. Oh, jeez, cut that shit out. He was satisfied with what he was getting, and I damn well should be, too.

Besides, no matter how I felt about Tolliver personally, he really was a top-flight criminal defense lawyer. Almost as good as Becky needed. Well, not really. What she *needed* was Perry Mason. What she got was John Tolliver. Which was just about as good as we could do under the circumstances. Perry Mason didn't exist, Erle

Stanley Gardner was gone, Raymond Burr was gone (did you know he was short? I was surprised to find that out), and Tolliver, with Alec, was the best she could get. Along with yours truly. It would suffice. It would *have to* suffice.

Bright and early the next morning, it was back to the old grind. No, not the coffee shop, merely visit with Becky, try to ignite some spark of interest in her, die just a little bit more inside myself when I couldn't, then head back up to Phoenix and the surveillance. I absolutely hated being separated from Alec like this. I'd even put up with Tolliver to be back with my love, were that the choice. But Becky needed me to be here, so here I'd stay. Her needs are my needs. That, and 'this is Becky' seemed to be the watchwords of this entire case, at least for me.

I mean, I know I'm sounding a bit sappy about how I feel about Alec, and how much I miss him. Well, Becky always used to say that I should be putting down my feelings on paper, and dammit, that's how I feel, sappy or not. It also helps me not fret quite so much over the possibility of losing her, which, frankly, terrifies me at some level. Like I said, I've internalized both of them. In some way, it's a bit of a relief when I'm up here, away from both of them, and I can reassume the tough PI personality I cultivated for so many years. I just can't wrap myself in it to quite the extent I used to, now. Not with Alec as my husband and with Becky in such peril. It's a permanent chink in my armor. But I'll do what I can.

I'd never tried to maintain a role for this long before, either. Usually it was just put it on, spend a day, perhaps two, once in a great while three days in the role, and then I was done and could relax and go back to being myself.

Yes, it helped that I could go back to Alec and to being myself every weekend, but frankly, the role was starting to wear on me emotionally. I can't say that I disliked the 'daughter of two doctors' Laura McCulloch to quite the same extent as I do, or at least would have, the 'lower-middle class' Laura McCulloch, but in any event, I was getting damn tired of having to put this role on every Monday. It was really beginning to feel like punching a time clock. I also had no idea of what putting the rinse into my hair twice every week was doing to my scalp.

On the other hand, I knew damn well what losing Becky would do to the rest of me. If I were any judge of psychological states, even having the jury simply find her not guilty would still mean losing her, because she would be gone. Her body might still be there, at least for a while, but her spirit would have died during the trial, and a serious part of me would have died with it. It would be just as hard on me, I thought, as losing Alec would be. Some choice. She, Alec and I all deserved better out of life than that.

Not to in any way minimize what Alec was doing, because it, too, was absolutely vital for her, but more and more, it was looking as though I was the only person who could actually deliver on what she really had to have. If that was the case, then I simply had to suck it up and keep on doing what I was doing until I did deliver.

When I got back to Phoenix this time, the tracking program showed something different. Not good, just different. There was a stretch of road construction in Scottsdale, and according to the program, Kendra's car had apparently either parked or broken down there and stayed where it was from sometime Saturday until Sunday afternoon, when it disappeared entirely. Not good. Five will get you ten that the tracker came off — how, I've no idea, but probably on some major pothole or other bounce — fell into the street, and then eventually got run over and smashed. Luckily I had another here, the other one of the pair I'd been using on this job, as soon as I replaced the battery, and there were a couple of spares at home. Maybe I could reset it on her car tonight at the club.

Which meant, naturally, that this was one of the nights she either changed clubs or else just didn't go out. Don't know which, don't care. I did drive by her house, and there were no lights on inside. I hope you spend a sleepless night, you murderous, snake-hearted bitch. And not enjoying it.

Without Alec, I won't be far off that.

It also didn't look like she was going to be at the gym Tuesday, either. I got there at my normal time and still did my usual routine, and just as I was wrapping up, in she comes, almost breathless. I give her a polite greeting and we hit the locker room together, her coming and me going.

I try making some small talk about missing her, and she just laughs and says, "Oh, I had, um, an *interesting* night. *And* morning." Then she dropped her voice to a whisper. I guess she just had to tell somebody. "He's hung like a *horse!*" Oh, boy. How do I, as Laura, react to this? Finally — the moment I took to decide on a reasonable response was short enough to be interpreted as shock — I just ducked my head. I can't blush on command. Hell, like I've said, I can barely blush at all any more.

I simply said, "Oh, my." Let her interpret that however she chose. Then, so help me God, she laughed and apologized if she'd said anything I had a problem with! Well, no, not really, it's just TMI, so to speak. Too *damn* much information, honestly. Like I give a shit who's doing her and with what. Although it certainly explains why she wasn't in her usual haunts last night. Turn it off! I'm *Laura*! I'm *Laura*! I'm *Laura*!

I figured that I should merely be slightly embarrassed, so I faked it. Told her it was no problem, but I kept my eyes downcast to show that, well, not quite *no* problem, but … then I left her, saying I'd see her tomorrow, with luck, and headed out of the gym. Out in the parking lot, it only took me a moment to put the tracker up into her wheelwell. Yep, the other one was gone. Damn.

Those things are *not* cheap. But it's an expense of the job, and the Family can afford it, right? Who are *you* asking, Amy? You know damn well it can if anyone does.

Wednesday I found another place for my morning coffee and light breakfast. As I've said, the coffee I could make in the kitchenette was barely good enough to qualify for the name. I wanted — *needed* — something distinctly more drinkable. I wasn't too worried about running into her at the coffee shop, but I wanted to paint the image that I only made it there occasionally, while I hit the gym over my early lunch hour on a regular basis. Nice enough place, and they had wi-fi, so nobody thought it was strange that I had my computer out to work on. Of course, I'm on a cellular connection, not wi-fi, so I'm not going through their network, but they don't need to know that.

Yep, Kendra is at home, and right about now — yes! She's heading for the other coffee shop. Perfect. I'll hit the gym at my regular time. Maybe after her revelation yesterday, I can start to hint — suggestively, but only barely, I'm just a tad straight-laced — that I miss my husband while I'm here. That much, at least, won't be acting. Then, perhaps in a week or two, or more, whatever it takes, but after we've gotten a bit closer, maybe close enough for her to show me the local club scene or some such, I can hint that I suspect hubby is running around while I'm here. See where *that* leads.

But first things first. I've got to leave Thursday, not Friday, this week because I've got to catch the plane very early Friday for the board meeting. So I can set that one up today, because Laura would know ahead of time about the sales meetings Friday through Monday, wouldn't she? Of course she would. Duh. She's got to be there, after all.

At the gym, we arrived at the same time. I made some very polite noises about how good it was to see her and all that. Was that the tiniest spark of interest I detected? I mentioned having to leave early this week — aren't meetings the scourge of all mankind? — and all that sort of thing. By then we were on our way out to the gym.

She hopped onto a bike while I started with a weight machine, although I was careful to keep the weight well down from my usual. This wasn't a good time to demonstrate how strong I am. Oh, well, lots of reps and slow lifts will help make up for the lack of weight, at least to a point. After a while I joined her on the bike, and then she headed for the weight machine while I kept pedaling away.

I managed to see how much weight she used while looking barely interested, absorbed in what I was doing. Judging from the way she was straining at the end of her sets, she was up pretty much as high as she dared go. Based on that observation, she was lifting a comparatively impressive amount of weight. Not quite what I would be using to produce the same result, but a hefty portion of it nonetheless, as she'd set the weight up a bit from what I'd been using.

She might be a lying murderess, but I made a good mental note not to underestimate her strength. Of course, dragging Jon's body around and hauling it up on the bed wasn't something a weakling could have done. Becky's not all that light, either; muscle is heavy and she's a lot stronger than she looks, too.

Back in the locker room, I asked her for some suggestions of places to eat. It seemed like a decent way to open up a conversation. She asked me what I liked, and I told her Italian and Chinese. In practice, I rarely eat either one in a restaurant, outside of a serious weakness for pizza. But anything to help differentiate Laura from Amy, who's partial first and foremost to Mexican food and sushi.

Kendra offered me a couple of suggestions, although the ones I recognized were a bit higher-end than Laura, I mean 'I,' would be likely to be eating in these days. On the other hand, they were also the sorts of places she'd have grown up with in Denver, so I just thanked Kendra as I left and pledged to try some of them.

The next morning, I thanked her again for one recommendation of an Italian place. I actually had eaten there the previous afternoon — too early for the dinner menu, and way too early for Kendra to come in for dinner (very deliberately, just in case). It had actually been quite good, although not up to the standards of the little place in Lakewood, way on the southwest side of Denver, that I loved and which had spoiled me for restaurant Italian food. I'd taken Alec there about a year ago, when we were on a major investigation in Denver together. That, in fact, was where he'd first met Daddy and Aunt Lori, as they were dining there as well, quite coincidentally — it's Daddy's favorite, too, even though he lives clear across town.

Anyway, I said just enough to make sure she knew I'd actually been there, and then shut up. Until it was time to go home, and at that point, in the locker room, I made some noises about how nice it would be to be able to go have lunch with her, or even just coffee, when we were done some time, but I really, really had to get back home for that dratted meeting Friday, the ones over the weekend and even slopping over into Monday. I wouldn't be back in the gym until next Wednesday. Could we perhaps plan something tentative for then? Well, I hadn't expected her to jump at the chance. But she didn't turn me down flat, either. It would have to do.

Chapter 14

Driving back to Tucson always felt relaxing. I did most of my mental shucking of Laura on the drive, and by the time I reached Marana, I was almost back to my normal self.

This time, though, much as I wanted to, I couldn't just relax with Alec. I had to have a suitcase packed for the trip to Golondrino the next morning. I probably ought to leave some clothes there. It wasn't like anyone else ever used the suite. If the Queen of England showed up unannounced, they wouldn't put her in there unless I said it was okay. In Golondrino, I ranked her. Fancy that. Not that the second-tier suites were anything to complain about. But the Director's Suite was ours, mine and Alec's, for as long as I held the office, and leaving some clothes there would definitely make my life that much easier. I'll worry about that another time. Or maybe when I'm getting ready to come home.

It wasn't that big a deal; the board was used to seeing me in slacks and a blouse, or even jeans and a t-shirt (the first time when I barged in. Another story. Also on the plane each month). Alec wasn't packing. I looked at him, puzzled, and reminded him that we had to leave plenty early in the morning. "I'm not going this time," he said.

"Huh? Of course you are. I need you with me." He smiled, with no particular humor.

"And I'd love nothing better than to be with you, dearest woman. But Becky needs me *here*, and frankly, I think her need is much more crucial at the moment."

I couldn't argue with that. "Honey, I've been thinking. I'm going to cancel the next two board meetings. That should get us through the trial. Then we'll worry about where we go from there."

He shook his head. "Don't do that. Hold next month's as usual, although it might be better to hold it on a weekend, just like this one, if you can. But go ahead and cancel the one two months from now, because that one is right smack in the middle of the scheduled trial. That way you're only cancelling one, at least at this point."

I hated to admit it, but he was right. Like I told Daddy, I could cancel one meeting without any problem. If I cancelled two, then I left myself absolutely no leeway. "Oh, God, Alec, I've been looking forward to this weekend together for simply *ages*."

He smiled ruefully. "Yeah, I know. You're not alone, either, love. I just really have no choice here. You want me to be with you and I want to be with you, but Becky is just so damn fragile right now, and like you, I'm not seeing much animation inside her. We're her only lifeline to the outside world, and I just don't think I can go away and leave her totally bereft right now. Not even only for a couple of days. It's hard enough for me to keep from holding her, hugging her and trying to make her feel better. But that's an absolute no-no in there, and I'm afraid it would cost me my privilege of seeing her every day. That would be a disaster for her, far more than the simple lack of contact comfort is."

I caressed his cheek. "You're right, dear. We'll work extra hard tonight and Monday night to make it up, okay?"

I keep one of those clocked coffeemakers for times just such as this, when I don't have time in the morning to do much more than pour myself a cup on my way out the door. The next morning, I have to admit, we woke in plenty of time to have breakfast before leaving. We just had better ways to spend much of the time, and honestly, it wasn't like the plane would leave without me, or that I needed to be there two hours early, or anything like that. But I still didn't like to hold them up any more than necessary. They have a flight plan and they like to keep to it. Speaking as the CEO, I approve of that.

Most of the board members on the flight spent their time crossing the Atlantic sleeping. We'd done our socializing, such as it was, as they came on board, and they all noticed Alec's absence. I didn't explain; I'd wait for the meeting and tell everyone all at once. When they all pulled out blankets and pillows and put their seats down, I hauled out one of my ever-present investment tomes and worked at getting myself back into the CEO mindset.

At one point I looked up and snorted. Men! Not one had noticed, or at least remarked on, my new hair color. I punched the call and the cabin steward, knowing me by now, brought me a big mug of coffee before asking if I needed anything more.

Once on the ground, we all made our way through the cursory Swiss customs inspection — everybody knew each other by now, including the inspectors — and to the waiting limousines. My first trip here as CEO, there had been a different limo for each board member. Trust me, I put a stop to *that* immediately. I don't mind a certain amount of extravagance, but separate limousines for each person is just a complete waste. My policy, which went into place immediately after my first independent board meeting, was that if you had to go somewhere else along the way, you could request your own limo. You might just get one of the regular ones, with everybody else crowding in that much more, depending on the situation. Otherwise, three limos only and fill 'em up.

Three limos for all of us weren't exactly crowded, other than the time Becky came with us, especially since Bruno and Sasha had come as well. Of course, Becky can be so charming that nobody really minded. Ouch. That wasn't the best memory to bring up. Charm won't get her anywhere right now, if she can even muster any these days, and frankly, I think she's fresh out.

I know that if I wanted to get on my high horse, we could have gone through without any customs inspections whatsoever, since we are what passes for the government of an independent country. But while the Swiss never make any fuss about what we've got (we're not exactly smuggling contraband, after all), they like to know what we have, generally, and we want to maintain good relations with them. So we do our best to accommodate each other. They ask, we tell, nobody argues and everybody's happy.

Stepping into the Director's Suite, I suppressed the instant flash of loneliness. I'd never been here without Alec before. Damn. The routine was to let people settle in, try to recover from their jet lag and start the meeting the next morning, and this month was no different. I hung up my clothes, poured myself a glass of wine and then headed for a hot bath.

Reclining in the warm water, sipping wine, trying — still unsuccessfully — to relax, I had to admit that Alec had been right. I needed him here, yes, but Becky *needed* him there, and her needs were still my needs. Maybe even more so than before. That was just the way she and I were. It would have worked exactly the same had our situations been reversed.

Like I've said, there's Family and then there's *Family*. Alec seemed to be getting into much the same sort of mindset about her, too. I didn't feel up to going downstairs for supper, so I had it sent up. Eating alone wasn't much fun anywhere.

I couldn't decide if I'd be waking Alec when I called. I still couldn't always keep the time differential straight, but I knew he'd want me to phone him anyway. I was right; he had that sort of slightly fuzzy sound of the newly-awakened. Maybe he'd been napping. We swapped some pleasantries, regrets and such. Becky was pretty much unchanged. We closed with more endearments. Not all that satisfactory halfway around the world, but it was what we could manage. Sleep didn't come easily or give me all that much of a recharge. Oh, well, I hadn't expected anything different by now.

The next morning, early as it was, I found several of the board members already at breakfast when I came downstairs. We exchanged polite greetings, but I really had no interest in eating with anyone else right at that moment. I'd only come down as a way to help me get going. I sat over my coffee for quite a while.

I opened the meeting at 9am sharp, as I normally do. Before we got down to business, I told them that I had something important, personally important, to tell them. This, too, wouldn't be easy. I usually maintain a stronger front here, and I certainly could keep my defenses up with these men. The problem was the source of my situation.

They were all attentive. I explained about Becky, Dr. Swan, whom they had all met several months before, that time when she came with us to visit Golondrino and, not incidentally, do some shopping in Zurich, while Alec and I came for the board meeting. They had all found her most charming then, and they each remembered her.

They also remembered, for the most part fondly, Bruno and Sasha (one of the board members, I won't name names, is a cat person). We'd had no choice but to bring them then, since Becky normally keeps them when we come, and I absolutely will not kennel our fuzzy children.

I told the board members about the murder and the accusations. I was able to maintain, although it was quite difficult in spots. I worked hard at it. I told them, though only in general terms, about the investigation I was doing, trying to get the information to actually clear her and identify the actual murderer for the court.

Then I told them that as of the scheduled board meeting in two months, Becky would literally be on trial for her life, Alec was one of the lawyers representing her, and I would be unable to be present, so I had to cancel the board meeting for that month.

They began to exchange glances between themselves. Eventually they were nodding to each other. Finally John Barnsfather raised his hand to be recognized, and I offered him the floor. He looked at me and said, very carefully, that upon reconsidering his schedule, he found that he was going to be unable to make any of the board meetings for the next two and possibly three months. He turned to the other members and asked how many of them would be unavailable for a like time. Everyone raised a hand immediately save Jim Parkinstone, but when all of the others glared at him, he finally raised his hand, reluctantly, as well. I didn't understand.

Tobias Greibe asked John for the floor, and John yielded. Tobias turned to me and said (he has a light and very delightful German accent to his English), "We all remember the very charming Fräulein Doktor Schwan, excuse me, Swan, and we have also all been very pleased to serve over the past year with you as the Chief Executive Officer of dieser Familie." His English is excellent for business, but occasionally slips a little bit socially. It's part of his charm. "All of us as well understand the difficult position that cancelling two consecutive board meetings would put you into. Since there is no valid board meeting possible without at least fünf, excuse me, five board members present, you will not have to cancel any. There will be no board meetings for the next two to three months because none of us will be able to be here."

I know, or at least I've been told, that 'Fräulein' is out of fashion for adult women in Germany nowadays, unmarried or otherwise. But Becky prefers it and told him so, in her halting German and with a big smile, when she was here.

My eyes filled with tears. This was an expression of appreciation and support from them the likes of which …

well, I was speechless. It's not a feeling I have a lot of experience with. Finally I regained my composure. "I … we thank you. All of us, Becky, my husband and I. From the bottom of our hearts."

I considered something more, then figured what the hell. "I don't know if this would be seemly, but … I would truly like to give each and every one of you a hug in gratitude. I literally cannot thank you enough for what you are doing." At that, we all rose and they gathered around me for the hugs I'd promised. Even Parkinstone. I really don't know what I, or Becky, or Alec, have done to merit such caring and consideration from these men, but it is a memory, as cherished as it can possibly be under the circumstances, which will remain with me as long as I live.

When I could choke and cough my voice into some semblance of normality (none of them was fooled for an instant), I brought the meeting to order.

We spent the remainder of that day and pretty much all of Sunday, including our lunches (working lunches, in the room off the boardroom where I'd gotten my initial briefing on the job from the outgoing CEO over a year ago), looking over existing Family investments, discussing likely future investments, market trends and that sort of thing.

I knew, both from talking to one former board member and also from my first meeting with this board, that the board meetings, at least under the previous two CEO's, used to be times for people to challenge and try to tear down other board members' analyses and proposals, but I usually tried to see what sorts of common ground we could find instead. Consensus rather than confrontation.

I didn't have a lot to show for it yet, but there were certainly enough indicia to suggest that at the very least, it isn't a bad way to work. As several of them have remarked to me privately, it makes the meetings much more pleasant. I even have Greg Casaday and Ian McTolland discussing, earnestly and politely, their differences nowadays when I had been initially warned that in meetings, it was a good idea to keep them as far apart as was feasible.

Finally, as it was approaching suppertime Sunday, I had to wrap things up. "Gentlemen, it's been … a pleasure. I would ask for analyses and any warnings you may have to bring to my attention, by email, over the course of the next couple of months. I shall, in return, keep you all posted of what is going on back in Tucson, so we will all know if we will meet again in three months. Until then" — I choked, just slightly. They politely ignored it — "I will say good-bye. I am going to be leaving first thing in the morning, because it is vital that I return home as soon as possible to resume my investigation. Anyone wishing to make the trip with me will be most welcome. Otherwise, I will see you all the next time we meet. And again, I — we — thank you from the bottom of our hearts."

Saturday night I had been unable to sleep, despite being quite tired. After my call to Alec, I tossed and turned for over an hour, getting nowhere, until I finally decided to get back up and do something. Anything. I finally decided to reread one of the entries in the Director's Book. That's a book, very private, that is handed down from one CEO to the next. Each CEO signs into the book at the beginning of his tenure and — assuming he's able — out at the end. In the Book, Directors have usually detailed the ordeals they went through before being named to the post as well as their thoughts and ideas for the Family.

It would be truly a historian's treasure trove, were we able to share it, because it's a first-person history from the perspective of successive members of the 'merchant class' that dates back to the early 1500's. James Escarton, the founder of the Family, actually speaks of the incident which started him on his path to success, and that happened sometime in the early 1480's! But James directed us, the subsequent Directors, to keep the Book secret from all except, if we chose, our spouses. He was obviously a man far ahead of his time, but a very realistic one in terms of recognizing the difficulty of keeping secrets within a couple.

I could have gotten dressed and gone across the square to my office to read the original. Hell, as the CEO and the closest thing Golondrino has to a head of state, I could have walked across the square completely nude and nobody would have said more than 'Lovely evening, Director.' But thanks to my predecessor, I had a scanned version, quite encrypted, on my laptop, and that would do very nicely. I poured myself another glass of wine as the computer booted.

I flipped through pages until I found the one I was looking for.

12 April, Year of Our Lord 1748

I am devastated. I had tried to convince my wife not to journey to the Colonies, at least not without me. To allow me the time I needed in order to not only identify a prospective successor but to then design a proper ordeal and see that potential successor through it so that I could turn over the reins of the Family to a qualified successor in good conscience. She refused and took passage on the *Rose of Sharon*, a brig sailing for the West Indies.

I now have on my desk a ransom demand for both my wife and our daughter. I find I can hardly even give the smallest thought to the Family when my own family is in such dire straits. Devastated hardly begins to describe how I feel, but I lack better words.

I am in no small degree comforted by the knowledge that we have no interest in the pirate vessel which took my family. Ever since the disaster more than fifty years ago, when one pirate ship we had an interest in took a merchant vessel we also had an interest in, and in so doing cost us far more in the loss of the one investment than could possibly have been recouped by our share of the pirates' profits from the other, Emmanuel Roswald decided that the Family would no longer support pirate vessels. I am thus assured that whoever these pirates are, they have no connection to the Family.

I have commissioned a vessel to seek these pirates out and recover my family. She is, for all intents and purposes, a sloop-of-war, but one particularly heavily armed. Indeed, but for the promise of a significant sum over and above her cost, she would have been commissioned in the Royal Navy. Instead she has been commissioned in (as, I could say) the Navy of the Free Republic of Golondrino, although I expect none to recognize the eagle flag she will fly.

I write this to explain my actions, as I shall accompany her. My responsibilities to the Family are heavy indeed, but my responsibilities to my own family are, at least in my own mind and heart, even greater. I have no choice.

I do not know how long I shall be gone. It could be mere months. I might also never return.

The Family Board of Directors that has done yeoman service in finding and analyzing potential Family investments has the right, if the office be vacant, to elect a successor Director in my stead. I expect that they will do so before I return. To my successor, I can simply say that I am sorry that I could not make the orderly transfer of power to you that my responsibility to the Family indicates I should. Unfortunately, my responsibility to my wife and daughter requires otherwise.

Farewell.

David Youngston

Yes, that was the entry I was seeking, complete with the scattered water spots and inkblots that had to have been tears. Reading it has always been difficult for me, but doing so now in some fashion reassured me and vindicated my feelings. I might not be completely correct in being willing to subordinate the Family and my responsibilities to it to Becky, but at least I would not be unique. My heart went out to David Youngston. He was no ancestor of mine; Family history held no record of him, his wife or his daughter following that entry of his, save the following entry:

Pursuant to my election by the Family Board of Directors, I hereby accept the leadership of the Family. Given under my hand and seal this 30th day of October, in the Year of Our Lord 1748.

Harold Danielson

Clearly the Board gave Youngston six months before installing a successor. Whether this was considered his due, or they took that long to decide that he was not returning, or what, I don't know. The Board didn't meet every month, back then, I knew, but there was nothing in the Book to indicate either why Danielson was selected or why the selection happened at that particular time. Family financial history shows that Youngston was on track to be a particularly good Director, while Danielson was merely average. I finished off the wine, closed the laptop and went back to bed. At least somewhat comforted, I managed to sleep.

Chapter 15

Back in my suite Sunday evening, after the meeting had been adjourned, I poured myself a stiff scotch and carried it over to the easy chair that faced the window. I sat and sipped for a long time, watching the few lights come on below me and the mass of the mountain, the Piz Lad, looming over all of Golondrino as the shadows grew longer and finally took over completely, before I eventually went down to the restaurant for dinner. When I arrived, I found the entire board waiting for me. They insisted I sit with them, and only when they began to order did I realize that they had been waiting without dinner, just for me to join them. I was deeply touched, again, and I told them so. I also told myself that I wouldn't cry. Until I got back to my suite, I didn't.

This whole account has probably been one of the least interesting parts of this entire narrative, but I can't help it. On the one hand, as CEO, this is *the* function of what I do within the Family. Well, these meetings and the investments I make as a direct result of them. Anything else is just … window dressing. Making sure that I could skip the next several meetings without running afoul of the rules about my cancelling them, well, that was just so moving that I literally lack the words to properly express how I feel.

Anything that significant to me, I just have to relate. What's that old line? The good of the many outweighs the good of the few? Where the 'few' were Alec, Becky and me, I couldn't make that choice, not with a clear conscience, anyway. Well, no, that's not accurate. Frankly, if it came down to that for me, honestly, just as David Youngston ultimately decided for himself and his own family over the Family, screw the many. It's a matter of *Family*, after all. The three of us. But having the entire board be so moved, so concerned and so willing to help the three of us, well, Becky and me, anyway, I had no way to tell them just how moved I was. I tried, at dinner. I all but choked up.

When I got back to my suite, I simply bawled. Not just the board. That, plus Becky and her plight, and missing Alec … It was total privacy for me, so iron lady or not, I couldn't hold it in any longer and just let my emotions take over for as long as they needed to work their way out. When I was done, I called Alec, just briefly, had one last cup of coffee (caffeine doesn't keep me awake, thankfully) and requested an early wake-up call for the morning. I could have flown overnight, but since I don't sleep on planes, it's a lot easier on me to do it this way.

Alec and the dogs were waiting at the terminal when we arrived. It is so much more pleasant to fly to and from the executive terminal. You just can't go up to the gate with two big dogs in the regular passenger terminal any more. I'm not sure you ever could get the dogs in there like that. Hugs and kisses all around.

I looked at Alec for some encouraging news about Becky, but he had none. The best he could do was tell me that she hadn't seemed to have gotten any worse and she wasn't on suicide watch. Not yet, anyway. I wanted to get home, have supper — not necessarily in that order, but we did have the dogs with us — and fall into bed, in his arms.

Some pizza took care of supper for us. We let it sit while we got the dogs their dinners, a bit early, and then we sat down to the pizza while I told him about the board meeting. We saved some crusts for the dogs, who waited for them somewhat patiently. They didn't care about the turmoil, and we couldn't exactly explain it to them, after all.

The account of the decision of the board members to take it upon themselves to block the next couple of meetings so I wouldn't have to cancel them touched Alec as deeply, I think, as it had me. That they would have done this for Becky as well as for me … that impressed him, too. I guess she must really have won their hearts when she was there. Of course, she was good at that.

We'd just have to take her back to Golondrino again when all of this was over. If it ever was. Dammit, it *would* be. I had to keep framing it that way in my mind. I simply had no alternative, nothing else that I even dared consider, not if I were going to keep going, and as things stood, I had absolutely no other choice *but* to keep going. I owed it to Becky. I owed it to Alec. I owed it to us all. We *would* come through this, all three of us, and be together again. Any other possibility was just too terrible to consider.

Tuesday morning's visit with her wasn't easy, but I had to admit that Alec was right. She was no worse. Oh, sure, she'd talk, and she'd answer questions. But even getting those answers was like pulling teeth. She had to be coaxed to say anything, and she never initiated any speech at all, never asked a question of any kind. I tried to find something of the Becky we knew and loved in those dulled eyes. I failed.

Driving up to Phoenix that afternoon was less than entirely pleasant, because I use the northward drive to get back into character as Laura, exactly as I use the homeward drive to shuck her. Being able to be myself for a tad more than four days at a stretch had been such a relief, and now it was going back into the same grind I'd been in for what was beginning to feel like years. Oh, well, dammit, it's got to be. Live with it.

I also had to recolor my hair again. I debated before deciding to do it in the morning instead of the evening before. Using the rinse on my hair the next morning meant that I could do without until the following weekend. Was it going to help my scalp any? Dunno. It certainly wasn't going to hurt it, which I guess was what counted. By now, I have some serious mixed feelings about constantly coloring my hair for weeks on end.

By the time I pulled into the parking lot of the gym the next morning, I was completely back into character. Laura doesn't complain. Not that she doesn't have stuff to complain about; it's just that she's been so mistreated in her life, *by* her life, that she feels no real reason to complain any more, because it would just be a waste of effort.

Anyway, sort of like me, she's trying to rise above her history. Well, I used to be like that. Nowadays I don't have a lot more 'up' to go. Kendra was just pulling in as I stepped out of the car and adjusted my fanny pack. I have to be a tad careful; the gun inside, light as it is, makes the fanny pack quite a bit heavier than it looks like it ought to be. It's not a big deal, but paying attention to the little things is what really spells success in an operation like this. I gave her a smile and a pleasant wave as I headed inside.

For the first time, she opened the conversation and not about herself. "So how were your meetings?"

I put a sour look on my face. I'm pretty good at those, if I do say so myself. "Meetings are the bane of human existence," I replied. "Endless hours of sitting around and then hurrying up to wait. There's never anything in these meetings that couldn't be done at least as well by email or conference call while leaving us all out in the field. But they make the rules and they write the checks, so I guess they can do what they want. When they want us in, they get us in."

I was changing as we spoke. I was able to turn just enough away from her that she couldn't see when I palmed the hideaway knife, sheath and all, and unclipped it from my bra. I dropped it into my jeans pocket again and pulled my crappy exercise t-shirt on over my head. Designer jeans gave way to warm-up pants.

That may have exhausted her interest. We didn't speak again until we were about to leave, when she asked if I'd be around Friday. Was this a break? "Sure, as far as I know. Nobody's told me otherwise, at least not yet."

She simply said, "If you have the time Friday after we leave here, let's have coffee together."

Yes! Finally I had a good solid nibble on my bait. I tried my hardest to sound simply pleasantly interested. Sure, I'd suggested it last week, but looking too eager would be a disaster. "Sure. I can leave town a bit later than usual, no problem. What's wrong with tomorrow, or shouldn't I ask?"

I was strapping my fanny pack back around my waist and almost dropped it. It hit the end of the strap a lot harder than you'd expect, to look at it. Luckily it didn't hit the ground, so it made no noise, and Kendra was turned away from me and couldn't see it happen.

"Oh, I've got another commitment tomorrow right after this. But Friday I'm free."

"Okay. That's great. I'm looking forward to it." Be careful. You don't want to yank the bait out of the fish's mouth before the hook is well inside. As we parted in the parking lot, I sat in the car while Kendra drove off. Then I pumped my fist, below the window level where it couldn't be seen. You never know who else might see such things, or who they might pass it along to. "Yes!" I had her, at least one little bit closer to where I needed her to be.

Thursday we didn't arrive or leave quite together, so there was no opportunity to exchange more than cursory greetings. No problem whatever. The next day would be the first payday, even if a small one, for me in this game.

Friday came with rain. Rain with a vengeance. Desert monsoons can range from nothing at all — much of the time even in the so-called rainy season it doesn't rain a drop — to utter cloudbursts. I've seen the heavens open and absolutely pour sheets of water from before dawn until well after sundown, although thankfully not very often. The dogs don't like that, and for that matter, neither do I, since they need to be dried off before they get turned loose in the house. Bruno, with his short coat, is fairly easy, but if

Sasha's in coat, you just *cannot* dry her off completely. I sent a mental message of sympathy to Alec, just in case, although in practice it's often the case that weather hits Phoenix and bypasses Tucson, or vice-versa. Of course, substantial rain was also the one thing that could make Sasha do her stuff fast. Anything less and she ignored it. With all of her hair, I sometimes wonder if she even notices anything less. By now, her coat was grown back to a significant degree from her beginning-of-summer shearing.

Kendra was just walking into the club when I arrived. I walked a bit quicker — easy to do with all of the rain, although she had more of an excuse with her much fancier hairdo — and got into the locker room hard on her heels. A pleasant greeting, and then she explained that she was sorry, but she had to beg off coffee today. Something had come up.

Damn. Here I was looking forward to enticing her just a bit with some teeny tiny tidbits about my past and/or present. I'm the fisherman; she's the one who decides whether to take the bait or not. I just baited my hook, and she had nibbled. Now I have to wait for her to nibble again. How about another time? I suggested next Tuesday, and she said she'd make it happen. That'll work, I guess. Like I've got any choice here.

Shucking Laura on the way home this time wasn't as pleasant as last week. I didn't have a four-day weekend in Alec's arms to look forward to, even if it had turned out not to happen. I hadn't known that at the time. Sure, I'd have three wonderful nights with him, but it was back to worrying about Becky and poring over the evidence, looking for whatever else I might find to help derail the prosecutor's case. Or to bolster Alec and John's. The prosecutor's case didn't look like it was all that solid to begin with, but the more holes Alec and John could poke in it, and the stronger their case in the process, the better off we all would be.

Alec surprised me with chili for dinner. He knows my weakness — he damn well should by now — but he doesn't have much experience making it. I'm usually the one who does the dirty work over the pot, and I generally do it fairly often. I was running seriously minus on my chili balance lately, because I was eating out or getting take-out in Phoenix on the rare occasions when I bothered to eat at all beyond granola bars or the like, and frankly, I've never been all that impressed by most restaurant chili. This chili was fabulous, and I told him so. He confessed to following a recipe, and I had to laugh, because it's almost a point of honor to me that I never do that when I'm making a pot of chili. Some of this, some of that, sprinkle in some of this, add some of that, stir it up, let it simmer and I'm done. His was quite a complex recipe. Cook-off championship grade recipe, in fact. He'd carefully diced the meat and onion, browned it, added, seasoned and cooked just like the recipe said, and the result was as good as I could have produced. Better, possibly. Should I admit it to him? No, probably not, if it even matters. I'd make sure he knew how much I appreciated it.

He did. But that was later.

Saturday dawned clear as a bell, and we decided to chuck work for at least part of the day, because we just deserved a break. Packing the dogs into the car, we headed for Saguaro East, simply for a change. Saguaro National Park is in two parts. One, the smaller but arguably more spectacular, certainly my favorite, is west of the Tucson Mountains, hard up against Tucson Mountain Park and just north of the Desert Museum. Saguaro East is way on the other side of the city, up against and into the Rincon Mountains, which I expect are quite a bit older than the Tucsons. The Tucsons are very sharp and rugged, kind of like the Grand Tetons but on a much lesser scale, and the Rincons are more rounded and smooth. That, if I recall correctly, is supposedly an indication of greater age. But

what do I know? Geology is hardly my long suit. Both
mountain ranges were around long before I got here and
they'll be here long after I'm gone, I'm sure.

Anyway, we packed the collapsible water bowl and
plenty of water (it's a warm time of year, to say the least),
and we went to have a very nice hike. Before we did,
though, we went a bit further. There's a Farmers' Market
down in the Rincon Valley on Saturday mornings, they're
dog-friendly, and we took Bruno and Sasha for a stroll
through.

We all sampled some of the foods they were selling,
the dogs too — they loved the chili there better than I did, I
thought it was merely decent — and then checked out the
flea market behind. Nothing we couldn't live without. Also
nothing we wanted to find room for, for that matter. It had
been a hell of a time trying to combine our two households,
back when. Had a helluva garage sale, too. Then it was
back to the park and our hike.

One very non-feminine item in my fanny pack — I
didn't think I should go back to the shoulder holster just for
the weekends when I'd worked so hard to build the muscle
memory for drawing from the pack — is one of these small
multi-tools, and it's precisely for this purpose. Sasha just
had to sniff a cholla joint — the dreaded teddy bear cholla.

Cholla comes in a number of different forms. The
ones around here are generally either pencil-thin, with
scattered groups of spines, thick-cigar thick or thicker, also
with scattered spines, or teddy bear, which is thick-cigar
thick, but so heavily covered with spines packed so close
together that when the sun is just behind it, it looks like it's
covered in thick fuzz. Very pretty. Well, that 'fuzz' is made
up of very long, very sharp and *barbed* spines. Neither of
the dogs had gotten into any in about two years, so it was
probably time.

Of course, everything she did to try to paw or shake
the joint off just made matters worse, poor baby. Alec and I

both had to hold her while I got the tool out, unfolded the pliers and began pulling the spines. The first were the ones holding the joint onto her, and when I had it free I carefully flipped it well away from the trail. Then the remaining spines, one by one, until she got tired of our efforts and wouldn't let us continue. Bruno sat patiently and watched; he didn't seem all that sympathetic. We poured both of them some water in the bowl, and tried working on Sasha again after they'd drunk their fill. Eventually we got all of the damn spines out. Nasty things. That night Alec surprised me by taking me out to a very nice steakhouse. Life can be very good indeed, or at least it could be if we could ever stop worrying about poor Becky.

Chapter 16

Sunday was a whole new day. There was nothing of note on the cable news, although listening to politics for an hour almost let us put Becky out of our minds for the duration. I'm not sure which of us felt worse about her, not that it matters. Maybe he wasn't as terrified as I about the possibility of losing her. Maybe. Quite.

We got a call about mid-morning Sunday from Marilyn, one of Becky's officemates. Could she come see Becky with us this coming week? Oh, of course. I told her when and where, and she said she'd reschedule a couple of patients and be there for sure. Maybe it would cheer Becky up just a tad. Or maybe not, these days. Another call, this one on the machine when we arrived back home later, told us that Daddy and Aunt Lori would be down for the following Monday, just to see Becky. They'd get rooms themselves, no need to put ourselves out. I'd like to say how sweet, but the circumstances made it just a bit difficult to do that.

John had brought a very extensive stable of forensic experts to look at this case, but the necklace, if I could find it on Kendra, and the blood-spatter evidence still seemed to give us the best shots, at least in my untutored opinion. Like I've said, I'm not the lawyer here and I'm not going to try to be.

Finally I'd had as much in the way of crime scene photos and expert reports as I could possibly manage, so I tried to read something entirely disconnected from the case instead. Also not fruitful, because I simply couldn't concentrate on what was in front of me without having Becky's case and situation continually haunting me.

Finally I asked Alec if he'd like a walk. He did, and the dogs are almost always up for one, unless the sun is too hot. Today was cool, by local standards — Denver would have called it quite warm — so we all headed for the coffee shop once more. Iced coffee, this time. Both dogs love ice cubes flavored with iced coffee. Mostly we sat in silence, lost in our own thoughts. I hoped his were happier than mine. I doubted that they were.

Monday morning was overcast but dry. I re-colored my hair before we left for the jail. I could probably let it go through Friday without hitting it again if I didn't color it until Tuesday morning, but 'probably' is the issue. I tend to give my hair at least a quick wash every day, and that can thin out the temporary rinse pretty fast. This wasn't a situation where I could afford to trip myself up like that.

As I thought about it now, I probably should have used a more permanent color from the beginning and simply kept the temporary for touching up the roots, but I'm so used to only doing investigations like this one in a different identity for a couple of days at the most that I fell into the old pattern without even thinking about it, and now I've got temporary color and nothing else. Plenty of it, too. Oh, well, it is what it is. As long as the hair doesn't fall out and my scalp doesn't fry from the chemicals, I suppose I'll manage. I *am* managing, and I'm in my routine. I just don't particularly like it.

Alec sometimes says that a lawsuit quits being interesting the moment your name, or that of someone close to you, appears in the caption. Well, trust me, I could say almost exactly the same sort of thing about an investigation. It would have been a lot easier on me to do this for someone I barely knew or didn't know at all. So naturally I'm stuck doing it for one of the two most important people in my life. For both of them, actually. Shit! Of course, the case is the *People of the State of Arizona vs. Rebecca Ann Swan.* Double shit! If anything, it's worse when it's a criminal case. Triple shit!

Marilyn was very sympathetic Monday morning. I had to prepare her for Becky's condition, and even with that, she was shocked and quite disheartened by the level of Becky's non-responsiveness. It just seemed like nothing anyone could say sparked any activity behind those eyes. I got about that much response talking to the cactus. I simply felt utterly sick to the core of my being. And yes, I know that sounds sappy, but it also happens to be the simple truth. My best friend, the more-than-kid-sister that I grew up alongside, protecting and running interference for, comforting and being comforted by, was dying from the inside out by inches and there wasn't a goddam *thing* I could do to stop it.

Yeah, I know that nobody else will blame me — *does* blame me — for what's happened. Or for what happens from here on out. Daddy and Aunt Lori made that very clear the last time they were here. But shit! I can't just turn my own feelings off like that, no matter what anyone else might say. If I could, I'd be somebody else, and probably somebody I didn't even like.

I'd quit tracking Kendra's car last week when I pulled the tracker. It would have needed new batteries again anyway, and now that I'd pretty much established the necessary part of her routine and made contact with her, I didn't think I had to keep track of her movements on quite the same scale, although I still went to watch her at the club from time to time, camera in hand. This shift in emphasis left me with even more free time when I got back to the suite in Phoenix, so for lack of any better way to kill some time, I looked up 'suicide watch' on the internet.

Major mistake on my part. How horrid! At the very least, it suggested that Becky would be under constant observation. At the other end, she could wind up being kept naked in a bare cell with no sanitary facilities other than, I hoped, a floor drain. To tell the truth, thinking about Becky under such conditions made my blood run cold.

Then it had somewhat the opposite reaction, when I considered what I'd like to do to the person who had put her in her current situation, and that was almost certainly the woman I was going to nicely and politely have coffee with tomorrow, Kendra Frankton. The supposedly bereaved widow, who screwed horses, or something like that, and just mere weeks after the tragic, messy and very public murder of her husband.

Momentarily I enjoyed the thought of strangling her with my bare hands. Then I very carefully packed the thought, the image, and my outrage, away in the recesses of my mind. I didn't need to hide it from myself, but I definitely had to keep it firmly locked away while I was still on my investigation. After all, there was a chance — only an outside chance; I hadn't forgotten the comments made by Lissa McHugh — that Kendra hadn't done it, hadn't had it done and was totally innocent. And pigs might be flying by as I'm thinking. But even if she had done it, no, make that *especially* if she had done it, for me to give my true feelings away to her would be utter disaster or worse.

If she'd killed like that once (at *least* once, I reminded myself; as I said, I'd done some checking on her and this wasn't the only suspicious death/disappearance in her past), I didn't see where doing it another time would likely bother her, especially if she were the psychopath I was coming to suspect. Getting killed somehow isn't my idea of fun. I also figured it would ruin Alec's whole day, too. Not to mention leaving Becky in a real bad — well, worse — position than she was already in. Besides, if anything happens to Alec and me, Becky gets Bruno and Sasha. There isn't any backup. I worked on my resumption of Laura McCulloch and sublimated Amy Trevethen again.

Coffee Tuesday was sort of … anticlimactic. Well, that's not really accurate. Let's just say that it wasn't earthshaking, not that I expected it to be. Kendra was pleasant and polite, but neither particularly forthcoming nor inquisitive at first, beyond asking me where I was from.

That gave me the chance to talk, slightly disparagingly, about Las Cruces (it's really a fairly pleasant place, although it's not exactly a great metropolis), and then reminisce a bit about growing up in Denver. I asked her much the same, and she said she was a Phoenix native.

She was lying.

As I said, I'd done some research on her, back when I first began this investigation, and she had grown up in one of the less attractive parts of Los Angeles. First married at fifteen, she arrived in Phoenix at the age of eighteen, without any sign of a husband, apparently presenting simply as a recent high school graduate of some slight means, although she doesn't seem to have an actual high school diploma from anywhere. There was also no indication either of a divorce or of what became of her first husband, other than that 'slight means' that had pretty obviously been his contribution to her situation.

Jon Frankton had been her third husband. The second had disappeared while the couple was vacationing on a houseboat on Lake Powell. She claimed that she had been sleeping and that he liked to swim alone at night while they were anchored up in one of the lake's little tributaries, or whatever you call them.

A certain amount of suspicion focused on her, naturally, but his body wasn't found for several months, and between decomposition, fish, vultures and other scavengers, it wasn't even possible to assign a definite cause of death, much less point any fingers in her direction other than from simple, unsupported suspicion.

No, there was no concrete attached to his leg before he went to sleep with the fishes, or if there had been, the rope or whatever part of his anatomy it had been tied to had disintegrated before his body came to the surface. Nothing so obvious, in other words. Positive identification of the body had depended on dental records.

The poor bereaved widow was never really investigated for that one, either. Oh, and despite what her current driver's license said, her natural hair and eye color didn't appear to be the blonde/blue she currently showed the world. Her first driver's license said brown/brown. Nowadays she had no more body hair, so it wouldn't be a matter of her 'collar and cuffs' not matching. Or 'carpet and drapes,' if you prefer. The eyebrows were a bit of a giveaway, though.

She must live in her contact lenses, to be able to claim blue eyes with a straight face. I've gotten sort of used to wearing mine while I'm out of the motel room, but it's heaven to remove them after I'm in, and I'd certainly never try to claim they're my natural eye color. I also hide them behind sunglasses as much as possible.

As I thought about the danger of being married to Kendra, the term 'black widow' was beginning to come to mind, along with some memories of the various unflattering and, yes, very inventive characterizations that Lissa McHugh had used about her to Alec. Let's just say that I had found no reason to disagree with anything Lissa had said as yet. Those that I understood, anyway. I didn't expect that to change any time in the near future.

Luckily, one of my talents is the ability to present as utterly absorbed in what someone is saying to me. I can almost always also keep a mental recording of it on some unused track in my mind, too, so if I'm not really paying the conscious attention I should be, much less to the degree that it appears I am, I can usually play it back pretty fast and figure out what I should be responding to. Here, I paid more attention to her, although in fact I wasn't anywhere near as rapt as I seemed.

The more she thought I was looking up to her, though, the better off I was, as long as I didn't go too far and ruin the effect. Paying such attention usually makes people spill more than they otherwise would, too. Not this broad, though. She was a toughie, through and through. The appearance of the doctor's socialite wife only went so deep, and one good scratch ought to go right through that surface coating. I had to be careful not to give her that scratch. Not now, anyway.

When she paused, I was ready with a response. I indicated some sympathy for her recent bereavement, which she'd just laid out almost as though she had been the wronged party. Judging from her body language, it hadn't seemed like it was really all that important to her, but I had to say something, after all, and Laura McCulloch wouldn't recognize half the body language I do.

I gave her just enough background on the invented Brian McCulloch for her to realize that I'd married well beneath myself and knew it. She seemed thoughtful about that. Then I excused myself as I pulled out the overly-fancified phone that Laura uses ("a gift from Brian; I'd never choose something like this for myself") and checked the calendar.

I had an appointment in half an hour and had to leave. It had been a delightful time, etc. etc. We'll have to do it again real soon. Take care and I'll see you again tomorrow. All that sort of crap. Driving away, I felt somewhat … dirty. Not for what I'd be trying to do to her, but simply from having been with her. I just knew I'd be getting a whole lot dirtier before this was over. Oh, well, soap is cheap. I shower every day anyway.

Chapter 17

Having a chance to actually talk to her, at more length than simply passing in the locker room, especially given what I knew about her actual history, tended to strengthen the unflattering opinion I was already forming of her. She lied very smoothly, very smoothly indeed, and if I hadn't already known better, I'd have believed every word she said. Of course, I'd been suspicious of her before I ever met her, and having this much more proof in my own mind that she was a psychopath just added to the whole picture.

But it also raised a question. Why hadn't Frankton seen it? I mean, he was a professional mind-bender (Becky doesn't really appreciate the term, but I use it once in a while to twit her. She calls me a snoop in return), and if anyone should have been able to see through her, I figured it would be someone in the business.

On the other hand, Becky has said that even a professional can't always spot them, especially if they're good, and Kendra struck me as quite good. What do I know? But I had the advantage of having her history already, so I knew when she wasn't giving me the straight skinny.

He probably hadn't even thought to have someone look up her back trail. Pity. Lord knows he'd probably have been in better shape if he'd known about her. Of course, almost any shape at all, now, would be better than the shape he was actually in these days.

For just an instant, I wished, again, that Becky had been carrying on with Alec instead. At least she'd be safe. Not that the thought of sharing Alec with her didn't give me some serious pause. She'd never violate our trust like that, anyway. Nor would he. But at least I wouldn't have killed him in her bedroom. Or her.

Back to business. If the good doctor had seen through her, eventually, then I figured he'd probably have been a bit more careful. Knowing about her, then if he just had to have something going with Becky, it seemed to me like periodic lunches in public places, arriving separately, leaving separately, no physical contact, would have been a lot less … well, it wouldn't have given Kendra as much potential ammunition. Her lawyer probably wouldn't have been looking for 'the other woman,' under those circumstances.

Personally, from my own, thankfully rare, personal experiences with people like that, I would never give one any opportunity I could avoid for them to do whatever to me. And I'd *never* turn my back on one. Maybe he hadn't ever quite gotten to that point. Or maybe he'd never seen through her; she might have been too close to him by then.

Wednesday and Thursday passed without much of note. We exchanged our greetings at the gym each day, made some polite small talk and generally went about our routines without much interaction beyond that. Friday she offered to join me for coffee again, so naturally I took her up on it. Again, we didn't get into anything of importance, although I had to invent a job for Brian. It turns out that he's a construction worker (who knew?). Strong, fit, with good sexual endurance, told with downturned eyes and some slight hesitation. Up to that point, I had to admit, rather like Alec, other than the construction worker part. Not exactly someone who's interested in getting anywhere further in this world, also quite unlike Alec.

When she asked how we wound up together, I tried to beg off. Not too hard. Then when she persisted, I gave in and told her about the pregnancy, the marriage and then the miscarriage, doing my best to seem a bit — more than a bit, actually — embarrassed about the whole thing. I asked her more about Jon, and, with some careful effort on my part, she actually told me some things.

Mostly I found out that she resented his refusal to talk about his patients to her on a daily basis and, even more, she resented the amount of time he spent thinking about their problems when, by her lights, he should have been attending to what she imagined to be hers.

I was finally able to beg off on the excuse that I had to get home to Las Cruces in time to fix dinner for Brian. Poor little slightly abused me, you know? It worked, at least in that I was able to get away before I'd decided to throttle her selfish ass right then and there. Doing so would have been tacky. Bound to get me talked about. Out of character as all hell. It also definitely wouldn't have helped Becky, which in the final analysis was what really stopped me.

Driving home, for a few moments I thought I'd hit the jackpot. At one of the out-in-the-middle-of-nowhere freeway exits south of Phoenix, I had gotten off, as usual, to see if I was being tailed. Another car got off and sat behind me at the exit, so I turned left and started, slowly, to drive off towards God knows where. I mean, I'd gotten off at this exit almost every time I'd come through and never once had anyone else ever gotten off here. I figured maybe I actually had a tail!

But then the other car turned right and zoomed off. Oh, well. When he was out of sight, I pulled a U-turn and got back on the freeway going south. I didn't see another car like it all the way to Tucson. I guess all of these exits get used once in a while. For just a moment there, though, I had my excitement for the day.

But one thought kept coming back to me. If Jon hadn't seen her for what she truly was, then what had really been behind their pending divorce? I needed to do more digging when I could.

Alec wasn't home when I arrived, so I just hung out with the dogs and worked at making them feel very special. For starters, they both got a real good brushing, not that

Alec had been stinting them on that. They're always happy when I don't divide my attention other than between the two of them, much as they love Alec too, and we — they and I, not Alec and I — hadn't had as much time alone together, as it were, since Alec and I had gotten married.

Not as much as they would have liked even before, for that matter, since Alec and I had spent most of our free time together even then. I had just had some, well, let's just say some significant psychological quirks that I needed to get beyond. Becky would have had a more dignified name for them, I'm sure, but what the hell, they're gone now and that's what really matters. I keep trying to make up for lost time when he's with me, or maybe I'm just so joyous about actually being as close with him as we are now. Like *that* distinction matters, especially to the dogs.

He finally got home just about the time Bruno and Sasha were finishing up their dinners and I was just about to pour myself a drink instead of waiting to see if Alec wanted to help me drink a bottle of wine.

Surprise! He wanted to take me out to dinner. My choice, so we kissed the dogs and drove several miles east on Speedway for all-you-can-eat sushi. Not perhaps the very best varieties, but plenty of nice rolls, good quality and enough to leave us with that 'Thank-God-we-didn't-order-one-more' feeling. We passed on sake with dinner, preferring to come home and open a bottle of wine to share with the fruit flies in the back yard.

That was the first glass. The second glass we had in the bedroom.

Saturday we again decided to have a bit of fun. Just like the previous weekend, we'd pretty well worked ourselves to death over the evidence and the investigation already, and we both needed to recharge a bit. The Desert Museum beckoned; we hadn't been in months. The dogs were well satisfied to be left home in the air conditioning, which was good for all concerned, since they couldn't go into the grounds anyway.

We strolled, we sat. We watched the animals. The javelina were out, for a change, and lizards were active near several of the remudas where we sat, as well as in the enclosure outside the front gate, and for a real reward, there was a gopher snake out hunting before it disappeared into a rodent hole. Neat. I don't associate much with snakes, but I think they're fascinating creatures. I certainly know enough about them to know which ones are dangerous and which ones aren't; gopher snakes definitely aren't, unless you're a lizard or a rodent.

Finally we wound up with coffee in the coffee shop up by the entrance and gift shop. We couldn't avoid the case completely, though. Alec had heard rumors that the crime scene would be released within a week or so, that the investigators for the Sheriff's Department had gotten everything they could from it. "Can you find whoever's best at crime scene cleanup?"

"I doubt that there are any Family firms doing that."

"Unfortunately. Oh, well, so sad, too bad. It's only money. Get the best there is as soon as we can do it and have them do whatever they need to. Thorough is better than cheap. Haul shit away rather than try to clean it, at least the cloth and such, if there's a choice. Any word on the little rug?"

"Yes, I forgot. They'll let me have it — they say they didn't damage it — next week if we'll stipulate that all the blood on it is Frankton's. I couldn't see any harm in doing that, since they haven't found anyone else's DNA anywhere in the room. Just his and Becky's, I mean, and so far, none of the blood is hers. John agrees. It's kind of stiff now; I've seen it. But it's probably worth trying to clean. I'm sure Becky would be upset if we didn't at least try."

"Got that right. Find whoever's best at cleaning those, either here or in Phoenix, and we'll take it in as soon as we have it. Anything else going on?"

"Not really. John won't even be here again for the next couple of weeks; he says he thinks we're pretty well set up by now, there shouldn't be any surprises or anything happening here that I can't handle and he's got cases he needs to attend to elsewhere."

My feeling of relief really wasn't rational. I hadn't seen him since the first time he came, and I hadn't had any other contact with him, either. I just had this utterly irrational response to having him either in my house or in my office, because dammit, he rubbed me the wrong way.

Not a racial thing, just one of those instant responses you sometimes have to people. It was definitely irrational. I already admitted that. But he was also what Becky needed, so I kept it zipped. Yes, she needed to be cleared, not simply gotten off on a 'not guilty' verdict.

However, I also had to consider the possibility that she couldn't be cleared before the trial was over. If she got off, then there would be that much more time to clear her without having her sitting in jail. Probably sitting in her own filth by then, I thought, remembering the descriptions of suicide watch. Tolliver was definitely the best person to get her that verdict. Oh, well. I could manage.

Sunday at the airport wasn't as … well, pleasant wasn't a word I'd use to describe any of this, so let's just say 'unstrained' … as the last time we'd picked up Daddy and Aunt Lori. We took them by their hotel, waited while they got their rooms, and then went to the house. This time we'd cook dinner in.

Sitting out in the back yard, I watched Aunt Lori closely. She seemed more … fragile? on edge? something, anyway, than she had the last time she'd come. Well, naturally. The whole thing had to be an on-going unending horror for her on much the same sort of scale it was for us, if not even worse. She also couldn't give in to her feelings the way that Alec and I could. There was nobody really close to her to help and support her as Alec and I had each other, in terms of the feelings she kept bottled up all day. She also didn't have anything she could do to help with the case, in the sort of way that Alec and I were both actively doing something for Becky.

I didn't think the visits were all that vital for us, although I strongly suspected that Alec's daily visits to see her and sit down with her were probably the only real lifeline Becky had. It was more that we had things that we could do for her, Alec with the court case and me with the investigation. All Aunt Lori could do was fret and stew. Not a good recipe at all. Then she couldn't possibly let her patients see it, so it just got held in until after the day's work was done. How horrid things had to be for her! This wasn't the most productive line of thought, but at least it helped me keep my mind off how bad I felt. Jeez, but that's some trade-off.

Conversation this time made their last visit seem positively animated. Of course, with nothing to show at this point for everything we'd been doing, we really didn't have a huge amount to talk about, either. None of us felt like putting words out just because there weren't any flowing between us at any given moment. Eventually Daddy asked me about the board meeting. Finally! Something I could talk about without … well, no, not if I told him what had happened.

But what the hell, it was better than sitting and doing my own stewing. So I told him about what those lovely men had done for me and for Becky. Aunt Lori had tears running down her face by the time I was done. Daddy pulled his chair over by hers, even closer than he had been, and just held her close. She turned her face onto his shoulder as best she could and just began sobbing. Alec and

I both went over to her to try to comfort her, but Daddy had pretty much monopolized her for that.

Monday morning's visit with Becky was still horribly difficult. When you could get her to respond to questions, it was in a monotone, with no animation to her voice whatsoever. Her face was equally inanimate. She wouldn't look us in the eye, never offered anything beyond a direct answer to a question, never two words when one would do, and she volunteered nothing. We all tried pleading with her, trying to explain how vital it was that she try to fight. She *had* to fight, she had to help us.

It made no impression on her at all that we could see.

The only thing that keeps me from talking about how it was breaking my heart was seeing, and knowing, what it was doing to her mom. Aunt Lori looked almost shrunken, she was so hurt and miserable. It seemed to radiate from her, or perhaps my own pain was simply resonating with hers. Daddy was in nearly as much pain, as best as I could tell, but without having to bottle it up all day, every day, and put on a public face the way she did, he might be a little better able to cope with it or at least keep it from building up in the same way. When our half-hour was up, he put his arm around Aunt Lori's shoulders and helped her out. I tried to help from the other side, but there just wasn't enough room in the hallway for three abreast.

We took them directly to the airport from the jail. When we dropped them off, they appeared to be doing a little better than they had immediately after the visit. But as we pulled away from the curb, I watched in the mirror — Alec was driving — and I saw Aunt Lori start to crumple. Daddy caught her and wrapped his arms around her, holding her up. My hand went to my mouth, and Alec simply said, "I don't think we were supposed to see that." My tears dripped onto my t-shirt unnoticed.

When we got back to the house, my mind was made up. I couldn't go to Phoenix right away. I'd stay home with Alec. I needed the comfort, the contact with him, badly, and I could still leave early the next morning and make the gym at my usual time. We let the dogs out for a spin, since they'd been locked up for several hours, and then sat on the couch together. I'd have been on Alec's lap, but I'm — unfortunately, at least right now when I could really use it — more than a bit too muscular and not well-enough padded for that. I get uncomfortable for him to hold that way, and I cut off his circulation.

Instead I just curled my feet under me on the seat cushion and leaned into him while he held me. We stayed like that for several hours. I wasn't exactly crying. Well, I wasn't sobbing. My tears simply flowed freely. That night I again cuddled as close to him as I could, laid my head on his shoulder and once again cried myself to sleep. I don't know what's worse — feeling like this, or being unable to be the tough PI I've spent so many years becoming and how vulnerable that makes me feel.

If there's a difference.

Chapter 18

Tuesday morning came way too early. Breakfast was both abbreviated and fast, for us. Well, for me, anyway. I needed to be on the road as early as I could manage, since I was likely to wind up in the ever-present traffic jam that some wags like to refer to as the Phoenix rush hour. Why do we call it a rush hour when the last thing you can do in it is rush anywhere? I worked extra-hard to get into my role as Laura and had pretty well succeeded by the time I reached Chandler.

As it was, I didn't get to the gym until a couple of minutes after Kendra. Not late enough to be any sort of problem, but I certainly didn't leave myself any room to spare. I wasn't so far behind her that there would have been any question of our going to coffee afterwards. For some reason, though, she said she couldn't make it and postponed until Wednesday. Oh, well, if nothing else, I can use the exercise.

One of my larger problems, when I could relax and let myself come back to the fore, was that the slow pace of the investigation was really starting to wear on me. I wanted to take some giant steps and achieve some great results. You know, Perry Mason sort of stuff. Or Sherlock Holmes. Something of that sort. Of course, whenever I looked in the mirror, all I saw was me, Amy Youngston Trevethen. Unless I saw Laura McCulloch. Either way, I guess I'd have to do. But I needed to find something to do in my downtime besides brood. And, of course, question myself, which I was getting all too good at.

Dammit, I *was* up to this, even if I hadn't ever done a case like this before. If nothing else, because there wasn't another person in the entire world who both cares as much about Becky as I do and who can do this. God knows that neither Alec nor John Tolliver were even thinking about doing what I'm trying to do, much less doing it. Not that I blame either of them for it, they're doing what they can do here, and yes, Alec probably does care as much about Becky, now, as I do. He just can't do what I'm doing.

Nobody else is doing it, and unless and until the prosecutor decides to get off his ass and actually investigate someone who might really have committed the murder, nobody else can or will. There's just me, and Becky needs me. She needs me *here*, doing what I'm doing. Which is the best reason of all for continuing to do it and do it to the absolute best of my ability. Pep talk concluded.

Wednesday coffee with Kendra proved to be interesting. We did seem to be drawing a bit closer together, if that was the best way to put it. One of the first things she asked me was about how I dress. "Well, the truth is that since I'm going into hardware stores and places like that, all I really need to do is look presentable. I could probably get bigger orders and make more if I had real boobs instead of these tiny things, but I can't afford implants. The best thing I can do under the circumstances is these super-pushup padded bras. They do work. When I was in training, my trainer suggested it to me and my sales picked up by about twenty percent. But the guys in the hardware stores really aren't all that concerned with how I dress as long as it's reasonably nice."

Kendra smiled. I had a momentary flash thought of sharks and piranhas before silently repeating the mantra of "I'm Laura. I'm Laura. I'm Laura." Then she reached across the table and took my chin. She gently moved my head this way and that. "Well, have you considered using more makeup? Not a lot, but maybe just something to, say, accentuate your eyes? I mean, some mascara and a touch of eyeliner, perhaps with some eye shadow, could make a world of difference, and it's a lot cheaper than silicone."

I had to laugh, just a bit and with a little barely-evident discomfort. Laura wouldn't really like to get much into the specifics of implants, I figured. But in response, I simply said that I'd never really learned how to use makeup like that (the absolute truth), which was why I didn't have any.

No problem, Kendra had the answer for me. She told me to go to a specific department store in Scottsdale, to a particular cosmetics counter and ask for one specific makeup consultant. I guess that's the one she went to. Tell her what I needed, not for dress-up, but just to try to highlight my eyes a bit, nothing too spectacular or bold, and let her take it from there. Well, why not? I could probably use the experience myself. Laura, who would be looking up to the probably slightly amused, and thankfully tolerant, Kendra, would be sure to do it. I allowed as how I had some free time this afternoon and I'd definitely go.

Until that time, I had some Family board members' reports and analyses to go over, so I worked hard to shift back into CEO mode for a while. Sitting in my suite, I got so absorbed in what I was reading and doing that I ran over my planned time to leave for the store. Oh, well, I guess sales calls can run over, too, can't they? Of course they can, don't be ridiculous. I worked hard to get back into character, successfully, as I got into the car.

I got to the counter in an evident hurry, only to have to wait while the consultant finished working over a different guinea pig. Once she began to work her magic on me, though, I stopped noticing time. Actually, I found it quite soothing, even though I suspect that most women wouldn't. Several interruptions for customers, occasional points when she had to go find something that wasn't handy, but just being able to sit there without thinking about the Family investments on the one hand or working to maintain my pose as Laura on the other while I was being worked on was very pleasant for me.

When she was done, the mirror showed me a face that was — well, it was clearly my own, but quite a bit more striking, especially in the eyes, and yet not so clearly the product of lotions and potions as to look fake. It also gave me a much better understanding of why Becky was so emphatic about using makeup and doing it well.

I certainly didn't need it for my own everyday use, since it would have made fading into the woodwork that much harder. But Laura would have been astounded, so I made the appropriate noises. Then it came time for the sales pitch. Were I being myself, and in happier times, I'd just have bought the entire package and worked hard at being able to put everything on properly, just for Alec. Becky would have helped me do it, I know. The total package, though, would have been way beyond Laura's modest reach, and I absolutely couldn't break my cover like that, especially since Kendra seemed to know this woman, even if only slightly.

I finally settled on just the eyeliner and mascara, with some free goodies thrown in, just as the 'real' Laura would likely have done. But I might come back to one of these cosmetic counters for a package for myself some time when Alec and I were going to … let's not even go there. Don't *dare* go there. I'm Laura. I'm Laura. I'm Laura. Think about Brian, think about tight money (not the easiest transition after directing the shifting around of about a hundred billion in investments earlier this afternoon), think of my image in Kendra's eyes, and most of all, even if slightly out of character, think of Becky.

That worked. My mood went south in a hurry, to the point that some small part of my reaction showed on my face. The consultant took what she saw as unhappiness at the amount I was spending, which also worked. And yes, if Laura could replicate the application I'd been shown, she probably would have made up the cost in her increased sales in fairly short order. Or so I presume, having never actually sold a threaded fastener in my life.

Kendra noticed the difference instantly on Thursday morning. She beamed and asked me if I didn't think that was a serious improvement, and of course, I had to admit that I did. It didn't really survive exercise, but I was able to reapply it fairly well after I got dressed again. Kendra offered a tad of advice, although I noted a faint undertone of amusement, as in 'helping out the poor little girl.' Oh, well, let her have her fun. I'm playing a much bigger game here, and this is just more chum in the water, so to speak. The less she thinks of me, the less she'll be on guard against me. Yeah, right.

Thursday afternoon I spent glued to the computer, digging deeper into Kendra's background, Jon's history and so on. I reread Jon's Family surveillance file, and when I decided I didn't like what was there, in terms of some of what I thought it might be glossing over, I requested the raw data for the time they'd been married. That would take a bit of time to come in, although they should have it all digitized already. I rewatched Alec's questioning of Lissa McHugh, and picked up some possible subtle clues there, in addition to a couple of invectives I hadn't known before. Then I tackled Jon's email account.

He really wasn't very imaginative with his passwords. He also kept copies of what he sent out. He really should have cleaned out his files more often. Not that it didn't make my life a lot easier, because it certainly did. By the time I'd finished with his account, I had several dozen emails between him and Kendra to chew over.

Most of them were fairly innocuous, but a couple of them clearly suggested that he had been the moving party in the divorce. I tried to remember the file her attorney had given me. Yes, he had been the petitioner and she the respondent, not that that really says anything certain. But some of the things he didn't quite say suggested that he'd found her doing things he didn't approve of and that he figured she wasn't going to change.

I kind of wished he'd spelled out just what those were, instead of statements like 'you know what I'm talking about,' but I had enough to give me some general ideas. They were certainly in line with the clues I'd gotten from Lissa's statements, too.

I really wanted a chance to dig around in his computer — well, Kendra's, now. I could just barge in, I suppose, but if she were home this evening, that would at the very least be a major dumb move, and I filled my quota of dumb moves years ago. That meant replacing the tracker on her car, and hopefully she left her computer on all day. That would have to wait for next week, since I wouldn't be doing anything with it over the weekend.

Coffee Friday was nothing special. We chatted a bit, I praised her choice of makeup and consultants, that sort of thing. Like I said, nothing special, just deepening the acquaintance a bit. As I shifted back to Amy on the drive back to Tucson, I did begin to wonder how Alec would respond to my new look.

I'm not sure he noticed it, at least at first. He couldn't have reacted any more strongly to me than he did anyway, and I didn't exactly pull back and play coy so he could get a good look. I buried my face in his shoulder as soon as I got out of the car, when he met me in the driveway. God, but his arms felt so *good*.

It was probably close to half an hour later when he tilted his head, and said, "You've done something with your face." I laughed and told him about my week. What I hadn't already told him over the phone, that is. We had a very pleasant evening, considering Becky's plight and how it kept hovering over us and everything we did, as usual. God, she was so much between us when we were together that she might as well be living in the house with us. Of course, if she were here, we wouldn't have quite the same pall that kept coming over everything we did these days, would we?

The weekend was a bit disappointing, at least in terms of my being with Alec. The trial management conference was scheduled in two weeks, and trial starts a week after that. Things were really beginning to come down to the wire, and building the case organization that John and Alec needed for the trial took precedence over everything else.

Over coffee after Saturday breakfast, I asked Alec what were the odds of the case actually going to trial as scheduled. "I'd say that a run-of-the-mill felony case might well be postponed. We're not up against a speedy trial deadline here, yet. But for a nice, juicy case that's generated at least region-wide, maybe even nationwide news coverage, I'd suspect that the chance of that happening is essentially zilch. Figure this one will go as scheduled. Even for a lesser case that could well be postponed, we'd still have to have it all set up, just in case."

"Oh, of course, I know that. I was just wondering. My biggest problem is that I've got nothing concrete on Kendra yet. Damn it! I've gotten to know her well enough to know that she's dangerous. *Way* dangerous, and how Frankton, as a professional shrink, could have missed it the way he obviously did totally escapes me. In fact, I'd swear on a stack of bibles that she's the murderer. She had the motive, the means and the opportunity, and so far, I've not seen one single thing or heard one word from her to suggest that she has any conscience whatsoever.

"At the very least, Becky had no motive. You and I both know that, even if, once again, we couldn't prove it. And she's got a serious conscience, too. But where the prosecutor won't see it and won't look at Kendra, then I've got to find something to let you rub his nose in it in open court, and I don't have anything like that yet. I don't even have any good likelihood of getting it, much less in *time*. Shit, shit, *shit*!"

Alec patted my hand. "We'll do the best we can. If we can't get her cleared, we can at least get her off. That'll give us some additional time to find something to show the prosecutor who's really guilty."

I snorted. "You and I both know that's not going to be enough. Remember the OJ trial? *He* was found not guilty. The news coverage pretty well stopped looking at the case, but people's opinions of his guilt never changed. If Becky's not convicted, what makes you think that anyone's going to be looking at the facts if we can't clear her until later? You know as well as I do that just getting her off is not going to be enough. Look at her now. Look at how she's taking all of this. Do you really think that a not guilty verdict will be enough?"

Alec shook his head. "No, you're probably right about that. Nothing less than an actual exoneration is likely to do the trick. Just getting her off and leaving her looking to the world like she merely escaped a guilty verdict because Tolliver's an excellent lawyer is probably going to leave her almost as devastated as she is now. But a guilty verdict … sure, we'll appeal all the way to the Supreme Court if we have to, but she won't be getting any better along the way, that's going to be years in the process, and she won't be free while we do it. Oh, I almost forgot to tell you. She's getting a psych evaluation the end of this coming week."

I wasn't sure what to make of it. "That doesn't sound good."

"It's probably not. It'll be with the prison psychiatrist, not an outside contract shrink. Becky did say, finally, after I pressed her several times, that she knows him and he doesn't like her. It's hard to tell, as emotionally flat as she is these days, but I think the feeling's mutual. She didn't offer me any insights on him, so I checked him out with Marilyn, and she filled me in. Let's just say that it isn't good. He's no star, professionally, to put it politely, and he wasn't doing all that well on his own, which is probably why he took the job. He also tends to use drugs more than he needs to, or so she says. Prescribe for people, I mean, not use them himself."

"So he's going to try to drug her into cooperation. That would certainly explain at least a part of why they don't get along. I've talked to her about it in the past, and Becky really, *really* doesn't like drugs. She'll refer patients for them when they absolutely need them and she sees no alternative, but she wouldn't ever get along with someone who used them at any opportunity or as anything save a last resort. *Very* last. Nor would she want to. It's such a basic difference of treatment philosophy, and she feels that most of the shrinks who push drugs at any opportunity are simply sloppy, professionally. Or worse. I mean, I'm sort of reading between the lines, there, but I expect it's pretty close to what she'd say, at least if she were sure she weren't going to be quoted."

Chapter 19

"I think he'll have an uphill battle if he tries that with her. She told me that she won't take drugs, period. It's the most animated I've seen her since this all started, and that's still not much. But she said that she absolutely will not take any psychoactive drugs."

"What did she say? Exactly."

"She said she'd rather be dead than drugged. She said she absolutely would not take any psychoactive drug under any circumstances."

"'Rather be dead than drugged'? She's still in there. We've still got a chance to get her back." It wasn't easy to listen to, but I'd heard her use those exact words far too often. If she was still using them, I had that much more reason to believe that underneath all of the depression, all of the blackness, the Becky we knew and loved was still there. If she was in there, we could find a way — some way, any way! — to reach her and lead her back. We needed to. *I* needed to. I think Alec felt that *he* needed to, also, in much the same way. Failure was not an option.

One way or another, I felt a certain, if tiny, amount of encouragement that she could find enough within herself to be so adamant. But at the same time, I couldn't help but think that something to at least take the edge off her depression might help her now. And what would the prison shrink do if she refused to allow herself to be drugged? Especially when he didn't like her to begin with? I shuddered to think.

I spent most of the weekend making copies, assembling notebooks, indexing a couple of secondary depositions and whatever other minor chores I could do to help set up the case for trial. Overall, rather boring, to say the least, but it helped John and Alec, and it also helped me feel that I was actually doing something to advance the case.

It also reminded me of why I decided not to practice law after law school, not that I really needed reminding. I did spend close to an hour each day, a break from the routine, just brushing and loving the dogs. I hadn't had enough time with them lately, so we all spent the time just being together and loving each other. Then back to the grind.

One major problem is that this was real life, not TV. Legal cases take a certain amount of time, and while it can be stretched out, there is damn-all that anyone can do to speed them up. Investigations such as I was doing during the week, well, there was also no way that I could hurry up the process of worming my way into Kendra's confidence without blowing everything. I'd spent enough evenings watching her at clubs that by now I was completely satisfied that she never wore any serious jewelry to them, either her regular club or the occasional alternative I'd found by the simple expedient of following her for a couple of evenings.

It was certainly not outside the realm of possibility that she did on weekends, but I'd established pretty well in the early days of this investigation when I had the tracker on her car that she almost invariably went to the same club every night, even on weekends, so it didn't seem to me like she would suddenly change her level of dress to that degree, just for the weekend.

Her alternative club, where she went about once every two weeks or so, was usually a weekday thing. That necklace was the one thing I figured I absolutely had to tie to her, if it were at all possible. I suppose I could burgle her house and discover it there, but that was too chancy.

Committing a felony, the likelihood of alarms that I couldn't bypass in time, the accusation that I had planted it — no. I needed to find it around her neck. That was the best, maybe the only chance I'd have to produce enough evidence to really clear Becky's name and not simply get her off. Barring a confession in open court, of course. Would I be that lucky? Don't be ridiculous. Like I said, this is real life, not television.

Before going to the gym Tuesday morning, I went back to the coffee shop that Kendra frequented. I managed to park just a couple of spaces from her car and, just in case she was watching me, got out carrying my book and fanny pack precariously in my arms. Then I let them cascade out onto the ground rather spectacularly as I passed her car. As I knelt down by the rear wheel of her car to pick them up, I slipped the new tracker up into the wheelwell before going in to continue my study before exercise.

Coffee Tuesday after the gym was just a bit different. For the first time, I hinted, very faintly, that I thought that Brian might be fooling around on me while I was spending my weekdays in Phoenix. Kendra is way too smart to let it go over her head, but I didn't get any reaction that I could see. That was fine; I really wasn't looking to get any, not yet.

Laura would probably have been way too embarrassed to go into more detail, at least at this point, and I had to maintain my role in all ways and at all costs. But this was one of the more important hooks I figured I could lay out there.

On the one hand, if Kendra eventually took me up on the … invitation? … and gave me some instruction about how to rid myself of such a troublesome man, that might be very good. It certainly couldn't hurt. But mostly, I wanted to manage to get just that much closer to her, one wronged woman to another. I worked very hard to portray the sweet dutiful wife, despite my societal comedown, feeling possibly a bit betrayed. But trying to hide it really well and bear up under it. Just not, quite, succeeding completely.

That evening the tracking program showed her at her club, so I gave her computer a try. No good; apparently she'd shut it down before leaving the house. Damn. A little later, when I called Alec, I told him that he should know that he might be cheating on me. As I rather expected, he was pretty much speechless. When I thought the silence had gone on long enough, "Oh, and by the way, your name is Brian. Brian McCulloch. In case you ever need to know."

"So this is just another part of your act." He sounded relieved. "Trust me, I'm not having conjugal visits with Becky."

I had to laugh. "Oh, yeah. Don't worry, I know you're not, love. She probably wouldn't be up for it these days anyway. Wish she were. No, I'm just trying to draw Kendra out a bit, very gradually. I'd love to know how she played her husband, but mostly I'm still trying to get a little bit closer to her. Carefully, since I think I'm probably safer snuggling up to a rattler, but I'm continuing to try to get some hard evidence on her. I need *something*."

"Well, keep trying. I'm still trying to show the prosecutor that there's something there. Of course, he's still just as adamant that he's got the guilty party. I think I could blow a hole through his case with a shotgun and he wouldn't change his mind. Come trial, of course, that's exactly what John and I plan to do."

Alec couldn't see me shaking my head. "What a jerk."

"Yeah. You be careful, Amy. I love you."

"I love you, too, dear. God, but I wish I were there. I am so damn tired of being up here, playing a role like this. I want to relax and be myself. There, with you."

"I know, love. I wish you were here, too. But we're both doing what we have to."

"How was Becky today?"

"Much as I wish I had something positive to report, all I can say is that I'm positive that she's still the same. I know we've both said this a bunch of times already, but I still feel that the only reason I don't think she's going downhill is that I don't think there's any more *down* for her to go. Not, at least, while she's still sane and rational.

"I'm sure there's something worse, but as long as she doesn't go there, I can maintain some little bit of hope for her. If the time comes that I can't get through to her at all, then I'll *really* start to worry. I still wish I could get away with more than just touching her hand with a fingertip before the deputies come down on us. She needs the contact."

Well, if there were anything that would make me feel as good as I could about being up here like this, that was it. As much as I wanted to feel Alec's arms around me, as much as I wanted to hold him while we slept and be held in return, we were both doing this for Becky, and that made it all worthwhile and doable. Not to mention absolutely imperative on other levels.

Wednesday evening I lucked out with her computer. She drove off for her club, and for whatever reason, she'd left her machine on. I rummaged around through piles of files. Then I found a couple of files that had been encrypted. Those I worked on for a while, and eventually found a password that worked on one of them. Kendra wasn't much more imaginative with her passwords than her late husband had been, thank God. To my surprise, I found a collection, short, but there, of names, addresses and credit card numbers. None of them either Jon's or Kendra's, naturally.

Well, *that* was interesting, and while it may not have been the entire reason for the divorce, it certainly fell into line with the sort of things I'd picked up from the emails and from some of the hints from his sister. I could certainly see why he wouldn't want to have anything further to do with someone who'd be doing that, especially on his computer. Was there more? There might have been, but I'd seen enough for my purposes. I backed out of her machine, being careful to leave no traces, and shut down my program.

By the time we went to coffee Thursday, I was getting a bit of a reaction from Kendra to Brian's suspected infidelity. Mostly, at this stage, a bit of tsk-tsk level sympathy, but even a teensy bit of a response was enough to satisfy me right now. She even commiserated a bit with me on Friday, the poor little girl going home to her possibly-cheating bastard of a husband.

Way deep down, below the Laura level, I felt more than just a bit dirty, dirtier than usual, as I headed south out of Phoenix afterward, but by the time I'd checked two or three times for a tail and had pretty well shucked the Laura mindset, as I drove through Marana, I was in as good shape, mentally, as I was going to be. My physical shape was really benefitting from the regular visits to the gym, but as I've probably already said, the only real mental relief I got, other than times when I had to be the CEO during some of my mid-week downtime, was when I got to spend time home, with Alec, Bruno and Sasha.

Weekday evenings weren't too bad, but there was always that little bit of Laura that I kept active to help me reassume the role the next morning. Oh, but it felt so good to be greeted with the enthusiasm Alec and the dogs always showed me when I arrived. There were times when I regretted only having two hands to offer everyone, and this was one.

One bright note, sort of. Becky's psych evaluation had been postponed until Monday afternoon. If nothing else, this would give me the chance to see her again and try to buck her up a bit first, not that I expected it to do a lot of good.

Dinner was no more than usually subdued; Becky's situation still pretty well cast a pall over everything, except when something temporarily overwhelmed it, like my arriving home. Alec was grilling a steak, potatoes in foil on the back of the grill, and I was fixing side salads on the table outside as he cooked. Finally I just had to say it. "Tell me everything's going to work out. Help me *believe* it."

He shook his head. "You … I wish I could. What I *can* tell you is that we're doing everything we possibly can. John and I are giving Becky every bit of chance we can to win the case at trial. It's gotten to the point that I begin to wonder if the prosecutor has something against her personally, because I simply cannot imagine him taking this weak a case to trial. I'm all but certain that she'll be found not guilty. The place I can't get to is being certain that she'll really be cleared, instead of just getting off. I can also tell you, and I'm deadly serious about it, that we're all doing everything we can do. I mean, I know what John and I are doing, and as much as I can, I know what you're doing too. I can't think of anything more that any of us could be doing. If it's possible to clear her, we will. Beyond that …"

"I was afraid you'd tell me something like that." I felt my eyes brim and overflow. "I hope you don't mind some tears in your salad."

Alec came over to me, put his arms around my shoulders and gently wiped away the tears. "Every tear of yours is precious to me, Amy. I just wish I had more to offer. To both of you."

I sniffed. "I wish she were here in this hug with us. Anything but where she is now."

Alec nodded. "Yeah. Me, too."

The evening was quiet. When we finally went to bed, we had the rest of our usual welcome home, but it, too, was very subdued. I didn't cry myself to sleep … quite.

Chapter 20

My weekend was more trial preparation. This time I spent almost all of it listening to different variations on Alec's opening statement and his summation. He wasn't planning to do them; those were going to be John Tolliver's big moments. But only an incompetent idiot would completely depend on John's being there when so many things might happen to him between now and then, and Alec was neither. If any of those things did happen, of course, Alec was still Becky's attorney of record and it would be his responsibility to jump in and run the entire case. Time, tide and all that.

Even if the judge were willing to grant a continuance should something happen to John, it would mean that much more time behind bars for Becky, and that was utterly intolerable to both of us. Make that all three of us. But the speeches weren't easy to listen to.

What an utter understatement. The process was sheer hell to sit through. I couldn't refuse; it was way too important for all of us. Potentially crucial, in fact, so I had to do my bit, even if that was just listening and offering cogent commentary. If it hadn't been for Becky, it would just have been a replay of our trial advocacy courses in law school. He had always valued my comments and reaction, and even then I could coach him on his delivery style, too. I couldn't have passed without his helping me write my statements in the first place.

If Alec had to deliver either the opening or closing, he had to have the absolute best ones he could possibly have with top-notch delivery. We went over them enough times that I lost count, especially the opening. Closing arguments — summations — were too subject to changes according to what had actually been presented at trial, so the best he could do with that for now was to base it on what he knew he and John would definitely bring up at trial and what he expected the prosecutor to show. But it might be, almost certainly would be, revised and rewritten right up almost to the point that he put his notebook on the lectern to deliver it.

The opening, though … that he had to have down absolutely pat, and to suit his own style, he had to be able to deliver it entirely without notes, other than perhaps the most sketchy ones. Just single words or phrases, printed really large, that he could see at a glance. Or even better, none at all. He had to be able to present it to the jury and not only make them believe it, but make the jury members believe that *he* believed it.

It was Sunday afternoon when he finally found what we both felt was the right combination of tear-jerker and pull-no-punches story, our account of what had happened along with the promises of evidence and testimony that we either knew we had and would present, or that we knew the prosecutor didn't have but should have had to make his case.

Not that I hadn't cried over the earlier versions; I knew the case far too well already. So did Alec. He had to know it in that sort of detail; I didn't. I could cry over it. He didn't dare. All of the emotion he wanted — *needed* — to put into it had to be done with his words and his voice, not with his voice breaking. He did, and did it damn well, too. But I'd gone over way too much of the evidence myself already not to have those sorts of feelings and reactions myself. And dammit, this was *Becky*.

I wanted to do something entirely different for dinner, so I pulled out a cookbook that I rarely use and found a nice sauce to put over fish. I sometimes wish I could lose myself in cooking; there's something so pleasant about it, especially when I'm in such turmoil in the rest of my life. But I found, again, that some turmoil is so great that nothing overcomes it completely. It was at least a partial respite, though. I so rarely fix fish that it was a pleasant diversion from chili and such-like. Although it was definitely a spicy sauce; some things are just constant, and for me, chili — real chili, not the supermarket powder — is not a seasoning half so much as it is a food group.

Monday morning's visit with Becky was just another chapter in the same dismal book. More than anything else in the world, I wanted to put my defenses out front and shut out all of these horrid emotions.

For her, though, that wasn't an option. I'd have to tough this one out. I felt utterly sick about my best friend, and the possibility of losing her was one of the worst things I could think of. I'd have given almost anything to be able to skip these visits with her — but I simply couldn't. I've never been one to shirk my responsibilities, and no matter what happened, she would always be my best friend and erstwhile kid sister. Who was I kidding? She really was, genetics and parentage be damned, and I'd have gone on making these visits even if I'd known for a fact that she and Jon had had a major blowup and she really had killed him. Knowing as I did that such a thing was completely beyond her, knowing how she had felt about him and being utterly convinced that she was being railroaded by the Pima County Attorney, I had even less choice.

None of that made me feel any better. I'd have taken her place in a heartbeat if I could have. If nothing else, I could, I thought, have coped a bit better with that sort of situation. Although — this struck me as I was thinking that — was she wondering if she had actually done it during the time when now she has no memory? I sure hoped not. That could only send her further down the spiral to nowhere. Or maybe it just explained why she couldn't break out of it on her own. Either way, it wouldn't do her any good, that was for certain.

All that mental nattering carried me through to my exit from the freeway. Then I simply had to wend my way through the Phoenix surface streets to my rented suite. This time I locked the door behind me, dropped my cases and flopped face-down on the bed. I let my emotions take over for several minutes before I sat up, shook myself mentally and decided to get back down to business. Get up, dress up and show up.

Of course, I had to wipe my eyes, and if I'd been wearing any of my new makeup, I'd have had to take off the remains and reapply it. I'm not a crier; it's not in my nature. But sometimes, once in a great while when my defenses are down, things just get to be a bit overwhelming. And dammit, this is *Becky*. Somehow, everything kept coming back to those three words. This is *Becky*. Everything in my life right now, or so it seemed, kept returning to that concept. Except, perhaps, for 'her needs are my needs.' But that just emphasizes the situation, doesn't it?

My emotional whirlpool was interrupted by the opening notes of Bond's Viva — my cellphone. My own, not Laura's fancy one, which uses a different ringtone. I looked at the screen; it was Alec. Why was he calling me during the day on this phone? He knew to call Laura's anytime before about 8 or so in the evening, just in case I was with Kendra. "Yes?"

"Amy, love, Becky's had her evaluation."

I felt a chill run down my spine. "And?"

"He's put her on suicide watch. Highest level." Now my blood ran cold all the way through me. "I managed to con and bull my way into the observation side of the interrogation room it was being done in. A new guard, I think; apparently I wasn't supposed to be there. Anyway, the psychiatrist greeted her by name, and she simply responded, 'Frank.' Apparently there's a bit of a history between them. I mean, I know I told you that before, but I saw it for myself today. Not a lot of history, I'd say, from what I saw, but they certainly aren't each other's favorite people, and it definitely showed on both sides.

"Anyway, the evaluation itself … well, let's just say it was duller than dogshit and let it go at that. Afterwards, though, the psychiatrist said that, in his opinion, she was seriously depressed and he'd like to put her on anti-depressants. Becky simply said, 'No. I won't take them.' He said that he could order her given them anyway, and that was the one time I saw some animation on her face. She gave him a really angry look — it only lasted a second or two — and said, 'No, you can't. Not without a finding that I'm incompetent, and you won't do that.' I mean, that's more words in one statement than I've heard out of her since her arrest. Anyway, he finally nodded his head, and then he said that she left him no choice but to put her on suicide watch.

I caught him in the hallway after, and while he wasn't very happy about my having seen it all, to say the least, he told me much the same thing, that he had no choice. In his opinion, he said, she was sufficiently depressed that she represented a serious danger to herself, and his duty in such a case was to prevent any sort of suicide attempt or other self-inflicted harm if that was at all possible. Since she wouldn't take the drugs, and she was right that he couldn't order that if she were competent, which she is, in his opinion, even if only minimally, he had no choice but to put her on the highest level of suicide watch. Then he just turned and walked away."

I felt absolutely sick. To think of Becky confined naked in a bare cell — there might have been worse possibilities, but at this stage, I certainly couldn't think of any, and even on later reflection, I still don't have any idea what they might have been. My tears were flowing again, dropping to the floor unnoticed. My stomach was churning. We passed a couple of minutes in other conversation — neither of us was in much of a talkative mood — until we finally hung up. I pulled a pillow to my face and just bawled.

I must have cried myself to sleep. I seemed to be doing that a lot, for me, in this case. I doubted that it would be a pattern, at least not unless or until something worse happened to Becky, like a conviction. Or … but I refused to go there in my mind. I checked the clock; it was after midnight. I got undressed and crawled into bed. I lay there in the dark for over an hour before I could get back to sleep.

When I finally did, sort of, I was restless and tossed and turned for what was left of the night, in and out of sleep. What dreams I had were a horrible jumble. I'd be pleading with Becky to let me help and she'd turn her back to me. Or she'd beg me for help and when she'd reach out for my hands, I couldn't raise my arms from my side. That sort of thing, with variations that didn't change the overall themes. When 5 o'clock rolled around, I was still tired. Not having Alec around was bad enough; this was far worse.

Tuesday morning I had to have a serious talk with myself. My anger — rage, really — over what had been done to Becky, if it broke through my cover, would at the very least blow every bit of effort I'd put in to trying to get close to Kendra Frankton. Which certainly wouldn't help Becky one bit.

When I actually got out of bed, I regarded the pillowcase. I hadn't bothered to use my own, and it was heavily colored with my hair dye. After I was showered and dressed, I hauled it to the office. The clerk didn't say anything, just gave me a clean one and tossed mine into the laundry. I kept repeating my mantra of 'I'm Laura. I'm Laura. I'm Laura' all the way back to my room. By the time I came out again, I was completely back into character.

It was time to escalate things with Kendra again, just a tad. I used a very light touch of 'poor little me' as I repeated the sort of things I'd said before about thinking Brian was maybe getting serviced somewhere else while I was here during the week, to the point that he hadn't even been all that involved with me this past weekend. Not to the point of sniffles or anything, just some general sadness, or at least wistfulness about it.

I was trying, very carefully, to get just a teensy bit closer to her, and maybe it was working. She actually expressed some degree of sympathy for my plight (in her words, not by her body language) and asked if I'd ever considered ridding myself of him. I told her that I couldn't afford a divorce, that that was one of the things I was trying to do by working at this job. She seemed to digest that, and we moved on to other subjects.

Before we separated, though, she had invited me to come to the club with her the next evening. Trying to cheer me up a bit, I suspect. I made the minimal protest that I didn't have a thing to wear, and she told me that my usual working clothes were just fine. So it's a date. Some drinks, some music, some dancing … whups! I absolutely cannot dance. That's not a choice on my part; I can't as Amy, and so I can't as Laura, either. Trying to fake it when I'm dangerous to any partner who's not wearing steel-toed workboots, is simply impossible.

I love to listen to music, but I have all of the musical abilities of a bullfrog, and I think Becky got my share of gracefulness as well as her own. She moves like a tall cat and dances very well, where I tend to move more like a bull, a slightly clumsy one at that, unless I'm extra-special careful, and dancing just is not within my capabilities. Oh, I'm plenty coordinated, and if it's something like shooting, or fighting, where I can move for a purpose and not think about what I'm doing, I can do it quite well. I just can't move to music to save my life or my partner's feet. I didn't describe my failings in quite that sort of detail, but she simply said that was fine, we could just enjoy the music and have a few drinks. Maybe she'd do some dancing if someone asked her, maybe not, no big thing.

Chapter 21

It turned out to be a very pleasant evening, as these things go. It was definitely helping me snuggle up just that much closer to Kendra, when I could ignore the image of getting up close and personal with a scorpion. I worked real hard at that, and I made sure never to touch a drink that I wasn't handed to me by a waiter or that I'd taken my eyes and hands off afterwards; I simply couldn't afford to take any chance with having something slipped in by anyone. I wound up abandoning several drinks barely touched, but that was merely money. I finally got to the point that I'd excuse myself to hit the bathroom, then set my drink on an empty table as I went by, just to keep the almost-full glasses from piling up on ours.

By the time I got back to my room and called Alec, he was asleep. I woke him, poor dear. He didn't have any more good news, other than to remind me of the trial management conference the next week. That was definitely going to cut into our weekend, but I suppose it can't be helped. Becky's case takes, *has to take*, priority over everything else. Hell, Becky's case was the *reason* for all of this. Friday over coffee, Kendra actually managed to surprise me. Did I have, or could I get, a fairly elegant outfit? She was throwing a very nice party at her house a week from this coming Sunday, and I was invited!

If she was ever going to show up with Becky's necklace, that was definitely my best shot. I replied that if I couldn't dig something suitable out of my closet, I could certainly buy something over the weekend. Were pants appropriate? I don't own any dresses or skirts (true). Oh, sure, pants are just fine. Just something really nice. Well, as nice as you can manage. And no, I didn't miss that little put-down. Little did she know. But I very carefully didn't let that show, either.

Driving home from Phoenix, letting myself become Amy again, I felt my spirits soaring, at least by comparison with how I'd been feeling ever since this whole mess began. I finally had a real chance, even if only a slim one, to get exactly what I needed. Since next Monday was probably also the beginning of my last trip to Phoenix, I was bringing home everything I wouldn't need for my last week. When I pulled into the driveway, the four of us had a most warm homecoming. We finally settled the issue of who would get attention first by having Alec and me hang onto each other with one arm each while each dog got the other arm. We switched off periodically so both of them got attention from each of us. Not completely satisfactory for any of us, but it worked. As much as we don't ever want our furry family members to feel shortchanged, humans had to come first, even if not by much.

Mid-morning Saturday, Alec decided to take a break so we could go out. I wanted to head up to La Encantada, a very upscale little shopping plaza in the Catalina foothills, where I could find something suitable for Kendra's party. Not that I needed anything that would knock her socks off, so to speak, since I still needed to keep up appearances as Laura, but certainly nice enough that I wouldn't have to put up with any of the sort of 'well, if that's all you could manage' crap. I'd had quite enough of the snide little putdowns, at least ones I didn't absolutely have to endure, thank you very much.

We'd parked toward the south end of the parking lot, down in front of AJ's, the gourmet supermarket, and started walking up toward the clothing shops that are north of there. Suddenly I got one of the worst shocks of my life when Kendra Frankton herself stepped out of another shop in the direction I was heading! Luckily, she turned away from me and went on in that direction. "Ohmigod! That's Kendra!" I hissed to Alec. "Go follow her and see what she does."

He was flustered for a minute, but then reached for his Bluetooth as I spun on my heel. As I stepped off the curb, heading back to the car, my phone rang. It was him. "Yes?"

"What was *that* all about?"

I sighed. "Are you following her? The blonde? The tall leggy one in the lightish blue top, that just came out of Ann Taylor and walked away from us?"

He was silent for a moment. "Yes, I'm on her. That's Kendra?"

"You bet, my dear. That is Kendra Frankton herself, in the flesh. Damned if I know what the hell she's doing here, she should still be up in Scottsdale. But I absolutely cannot risk being seen here, with you, in this hair color, even without my padded bra and fancy t-shirt, when I'm supposed to be in Las Cruces with my cheating hubby Brian. Even though Brian, as far as she knows, looks like you. Or maybe *especially* since Brian looks like you, and you have never figured out how to look slightly disinterested in me."

I heard a chuckle. "She's meeting somebody. A man that just came out of … let's see. It must be the Apple store. He's … oh, around my height, give or take, brown hair, clean-shaven, thin, with prominent ears."

I was a tad puzzled. "Prominent ears?"

"They're going up the back escalator. I'm following. Yeah, prominent ears. They stick out a bit."

Now I'd figured who he was. "That's probably Dr. Donald McGuire, the anesthesiologist she sees over coffee a bunch of mornings. Sometimes over breakfast, too, as near as I can tell."

"That fits. He's trying to hold her hand. She keeps shaking him off. It looks like they're thinking about lunch. They've stopped walking. I'm going on into Frost while they have their discussion. He's looking at the restaurants … hold on a moment." I heard a door whoosh! "She's shaking her head. They're heading back your way." I heard the door open again. "Shit!" His breathing got a bit heavy. "They went down the escalator, but there's a crowd on it behind them. I'm heading for the other one and maybe I can pick them up." As he trotted towards the other escalator, he kept talking. "You know, she looks a bit familiar. I've seen her somewhere before — oh, my *God!*"

"What is it? What happened?"

"I just realized where I've seen her before. The last time we were at Becky's for dinner! She's the woman who came to the door while we were fixing dinner!" A moment's pause. "Coming down … Got 'em! I'll let them get just a bit further ahead of me. Amy, they're heading in your direction."

I looked around at the nearby cars in the parking lot. Just on the other side of the aisle I was in, two cars away, I saw what looked like the Lexus I'd seen Dr. McGuire driving in Phoenix. Shit! "Alec, if they're heading back to their car, I think it's right across from me." I sank down in my seat so I could barely see over the dash. So Kendra knew where Becky lived? Well, by now, I was more than convinced that she was the killer, so I guess it wasn't all that much of a surprise. I could worry about it some other time, if I even needed to. After a couple of minutes, I saw them approach. "They're coming."

I sank down the rest of the way. I had my window partly open, so I could hear as they pulled out of the space. Not atypically for a summer weekend, there was someone already waiting for their space as they pulled out. I sat back up. "Meet me at the end of the aisle toward AJ's. I'm going to try to follow them." I closed my phone and dropped it into one of the recesses in the console as I started the car. Picking Alec up, I tried to catch up with them. Well, a couple of cars behind them.

They went up to the upper level and out on Campbell heading south. I managed to keep within three cars of them, but then they zipped through the light at Sunrise just as it turned yellow and the (expletive deleted) careful driver ahead of me stopped just like she was supposed to. Shit! By the time the light had turned again, at least a dozen and a half cars had turned into Campbell, and Don and Kendra would be more than halfway to River. From there, there was no way of telling which way they'd gone. Shit! I pulled around the corner and drove back into La Encantada. Alec simply looked at me, questioningly.

"Hey, I still need an outfit. I figure this is probably the place she's least likely to come back to now, right?"

"Well, I suppose."

As we walked up towards J. Crew, I let myself relax just a bit. "God, I'm sure glad she didn't see me. If I'd been wearing my wig, I'd have been willing to try bluffing my way through it, at least if I'd actually gotten face-to-face with her before I spotted her. As it is, though, with this hair color, I'm way too much like the Laura she knows to be able to pull that off readily. I'm just lucky you were able to follow her."

"Why's that? I didn't get any sort of information from it."

I squeezed his hand. "Alec, dear, most such investigation is fruitless. In this game, you do a lot of tailing, a lot of observing and a lot of sifting, all for just a few tidbits that may be useful."

He snorted. "That doesn't sound all that exciting."

I grinned at him. "Hey, think about all of the motions in your average court case and how little actual movement they cause. That's why you're the lawyer and I'm not. It's also why I do this and you don't." I opened the door. "Oh, and if I'd run into her as I walked into the store, it would have been lots worse. Then you'd have been my cheating husband, Brian, and, without my prompting, have had to look somewhat disinterested in me, which, like I say, is not exactly your strong suit." He just chuckled some more.

The sales clerk helped me, and it didn't take long before I had a nice enough outfit, black slacks, black jacket and some silky blouse sort of thing that would do the job. Nice enough without looking like it would break Laura's bank, dressy enough without overdoing it, quite classic, actually, and the sort of thing that Laura could have bought just now or had hanging in her closet for five years or more. Utterly timeless, in other words.

We then headed up the front escalator (I wanted to get something from Frost, the gelato place) and when I got to the top of the escalator, I looked around. As my eyes fell on the window display in St. John's, I was astounded. There was the most beautiful long Oriental-ish jacket-type thing there.

Now understand that I'm about as far away as you can get from being a clotheshorse. I normally buy jeans and t-shirts on the internet in quantity, and hardly ever wear anything beyond that. But this really caught my eye. All but knocked it out, in fact. I just had to go in, and when I left the store to find Alec sitting on the bench outside, I had another entire outfit. The jacket, another pair of slacks, and another top, any one of which cost more than the entire outfit I'd gotten downstairs. Quite a bit more.

Kendra would never see it, though. This was for Alec. When this was all over, we were going out someplace real special. There's hardly any place in Tucson that you have to dress up for, but there are a couple where this sort of outfit wouldn't be out of place. I could also think of one or two places we'd been to in Zurich where it would fit right in, too.

I still needed some jewelry to go with Laura's outfit. I finally found something workable, a modest pendant and earring set, in a jewelry store in Tucson Mall. It's not easy to find clips these days. Becky and I had both gotten our ears pierced as teenagers, but I hadn't kept mine up and the holes had closed within months. This place was happy to put clips on whatever I bought, and that completed the 'ensemble.' I was set.

Even though Alec was largely absent — not physically, just intellectually — for the rest of the weekend, we still made the most of what time we could share. I fixed meals, I took the dogs for walks, just the three of us (they were thrilled, of course), and I really enjoyed myself as much as I was able. I even took them to the coffee shop alone, stuck my head in the door to ask someone to fix me a large coffee, and the pups were in seventh heaven. Sleeping with Alec, our arms around each other, was, by now, the most incredible treat.

By this time, I'd gotten so sick and tired of what was going on in Phoenix, not to mention of being Laura and being around Kendra, that just being home, as myself, knowing that Alec was there, and being with the dogs, brushing them, walking them, enjoying being with them, loving them and being loved by them, was an absolute delight. I did everything I could to avoid thinking about Monday morning, when I'd return to the same old grind.

Chapter 22

Return to the grind I did. My usual Monday morning routine was on tap once more — shower, color my hair, dress once more in the padded bra, snugger t-shirt and designer jeans, see Becky again and stifle my tears and worry, then hop, well, crawl into the rental and head north once more. At least I was on the downhill slope now. On a hunch, I'd pulled a couple of big cable ties from my electronics bench and rolled them up into my hip pocket. They didn't take up a lot of room, and I just figured what the hell.

If I couldn't manage to get what I needed pretty damn soon, I'd have to come up with some completely new idea, and I'd just put so much time into this particular quest that I hated even the idea of having to abandon it unfulfilled. Hauling Kendra bodily into court didn't seem all that likely at the moment, but one never knows. One way or another, Becky needed me to do something damn quick. With the end in sight, and nothing concrete to show for all of my efforts as yet, I was really beginning to get antsy.

I consoled myself with the idea that if I got what I needed this coming Sunday night, then I could head back to Tucson on Monday and we'd be home free. I'd have enough proof to positively clear Becky (as positive as it ever gets in this game, I reminded myself), and I could shuck this persona as well as the clothes and toss both back into the depths of my dresser where, hopefully, I could leave them for one hell of a long time. Damn, I was sick and tired of Laura! Even the daughter-of-two-doctors Laura had worn way too thin for my taste by now. If I'd been living the lower-middle-class Laura for this amount of time, I'm sure I'd be almost certifiable by now.

Coffee Tuesday with Kendra was simply another pleasant meeting, at least as pleasant as it could get while, as always, I was trying to ignore (or overlook) the predatory nature of the person I was with. Laura is pretty good at that sort of thing. As Amy, of course, I would have trusted Kendra just about as far as I could toss her — make that toss her car. I could probably manage to get a couple of feet out of her, if I had to.

Once again, as I related it, Brian had seemed a bit distant while I was home, still enough to continue to suggest that perhaps he was getting serviced someplace else while I was stuck here in Phoenix. As an aside, this wasn't a problem I actually had; I knew exactly who Alec was spending time with while I was here. I certainly wasn't jealous of John Tolliver, and I heartily approved of whatever time Alec could spend, was *allowed* to spend, with Becky. She needed it.

But as Laura, I kept my thoughts on the imaginary Brian. In character, I couldn't afford to let my mind wander. When I'm with Kendra, simply taking the *chance* of letting the role slip was *way* too dangerous. Even a moment's inattention — "I'm sorry," I said in response to something she said that I'd missed. "I guess I was … my mind was somewhere else." For once I couldn't replay whatever had been said while my mind was off doing its own thing. This is *not* good. Pay *attention*, girl! You *know* better!

A half-smile from Kendra. Reminded me of a cat looking at prey that just hadn't noticed it yet. "Whereabouts? If it's any of my business, I mean."

Amy would have had a different response. I'm Laura. I'm Laura. I'm Laura. "Oh, back in Denver, I suppose. I'm not really sure, just sometime in my life back when …" I let it trail off. Let her fill in the rest. On the one hand, I was impressed by how far and how quickly I was worming my way into her confidence. On the other hand, that persistent image of snuggling up to a rattlesnake wouldn't go completely away.

Oh, well, one way or another, it shouldn't be much longer. Jury selection in Becky's case started this coming Monday morning, right after the court heard whatever motions both sides might have, so it couldn't be all that much longer. Sit on that! I don't know anything about that! I'm Laura. I'm Laura. I'm Laura.

But yes, I told her, I'd made arrangements to stay over the weekend, and I had brought an outfit to wear. It was nice enough, I thought; it had been given to me by my parents a year ago last Christmas and I hadn't really had any good chance to wear it yet. No, Brian didn't know I'd brought it. He really doesn't pay any attention to my packing any more, and he probably doesn't even know what the outfit looks like anyway. He's never paid a lot of attention to my clothes, and nowadays he doesn't seem to pay all that much attention to the contents, either.

Kendra simply smiled a bit and observed that it would be convenient if something happened to Brian. I worked hard not to seem too interested, but I did look at her at that one. Just a bit wide-eyed, the poor little girl who's trying, but who is just a trace too innocent, or perhaps isn't quite up to the world. "What do you mean?"

She waved it away. "Oh, nothing, nothing. Just that if something happened to him, it would certainly solve your problems."

I put on a half-smile. "Yes, I suppose it would. But it's kind of hard to predict accidents."

"Yes, it is, isn't it?" She had a slightly odd look on her face, but nothing I felt safe in asking about. I tried just looking at her curiously for several seconds, but she didn't offer anything more, so I left it there. Maybe something would come of it later. Of course, it certainly gave me some personal confirmation of my belief that she was the one who'd done in her late husband. Not that I'd had any real doubt remaining any more, but still …

Afternoons were beginning to drive me quietly nuts. I really had no more need to investigate anything about Kendra. By now, whatever chance I had of getting what I needed came down to the party Sunday. She and I weren't going to a club again until the next evening.

On a whim I found an indoor shooting range quite a ways from where I'd been seeing Kendra, so I rented the necessary protective gear, bought some ammunition and gave the little Kahr from my fanny pack a workout. By the time I'd run through a hundred and fifty rounds, my hand was sore and my accuracy was where it belonged.

Pistol skills are very volatile, requiring constant practice, and it's a tough little gun to shoot well anyway. If I don't hold it just so, it hurts the hell out of the base of my right thumb. Given the time to take a proper grip, of course, it's no real problem. I've always figured that if I had to pull it out and shoot it in earnest, a sore thumb was the least of my worries, especially compared with making sure that I hit what I was shooting at and fast. Working on the muscle memory to take the right grip without thinking about it couldn't ever hurt.

I usually put a hundred rounds or so through it every week or two, and I'd been neglecting that lately. Then, of course, I had to buy the basic items I needed to clean it afterwards, too, since I hadn't brought any of that with me either. Not a great additional expense, really; just another detail. I could have let it go, but that would have been sloppy at best, and there was no reason to have a dirty gun under my pillow where I always kept this one at night, here.

Finally I left the range and decided to treat myself to a decent supper, Mexican, of course, something I rarely did when alone like this. Eat out, that is, not have Mexican food. That's my usual fare when I eat out alone, here, there or anywhere.

I checked in with Alec after I'd gotten back to my room, but he couldn't spend a lot of time on the phone. No problem; I hadn't expected him to, with this major a trial bearing down on him the way it was. I'd gone through other, far less crucial trials with him before, and when the time came that the actual trial loomed over him, he barely knew I was around. That was before we were married, of course, but I knew I had to allow him his space right now. If I'd been home, he'd have noticed me at dinner, perhaps, and once we got into bed. Not otherwise.

Besides, Tolliver would be around pretty much full-time from here on out anyway, too. But we had enough time — always! — for some murmured endearments and a couple of long-distance kisses. Nothing like having his arm around me while I slept, of course, or mine around him. I consoled myself with my book for a while before drifting off into some marginally-satisfactory sleep.

The next morning I headed out for some coffee and a light breakfast before making my way to the gym. Thinking about Alec in final preparation for the trial brought back thoughts of law school, which led to memories of graduation and how Alec found me several years later, when we were both single again.

God, talk about wool-gathering. I hadn't thought of those times since … well, since before Alec and I got married. I hadn't thought of them much then. Mostly I spent my time, especially during the run-up to my becoming CEO, giving (at most) some small acknowledgment (well, not always so small) to my consciousness of Alec and then stuffing the thought into the deep, dark recesses of my mind. Major mistake on my part, but so it goes.

I was about to check the time on my cellphone when I remembered the three-quarter size watch that Laura wore. I'm still not used to wearing one, even after these several months, because as Amy, I usually only wear one when I'm on a plane. It was just about time to leave for the gym. I carefully packed up the memories — almost any memory of Alec is sweet, now — and tucked them away in one of my mental cubbyholes. Not to forget or ignore, just to keep them safe and out of the way while I was working. I'm Laura. I'm Laura. I'm Laura.

Coffee and even clubbing Wednesday were as close to enjoyable as I could get under the circumstances. If I'd had Alec with me, and Becky had been safe and sound, with us or elsewhere, I would have had a grand time. Good music, good drinks and coffee, and Kendra was even quite pleasant, at least for her. But nothing special on Thursday, when it was just coffee after the gym.

The only thing that stood out was on Friday at the club, when Kendra — she'd had a bit more to drink than usual — said something about perhaps I could give Brian a longer leash, let him think that he had my blessing to go do whatever he wanted while I got the goods on him when he did. I managed to appear as though I was utterly surprised by the concept, but at the same time, on another level where it wouldn't show, I realized that I'd just had my suspicions of her completely confirmed. Not about her husband's murder, necessarily, but certainly about how he'd been played by her, and how Becky had been set up. Oh, my. Did I ever have the right target in my crosshairs.

Chapter 23

That evening, instead of reading, I spent quite some time lying in bed in the dark, just staring at the ceiling and thinking about how this whole thing was going to play out. Not the situation with Kendra, but with Becky, presuming that I could actually clear her. At the one end, we could, at least in theory, deliver her to her house, shut the door and go home. Yeah, right. Your very best friend, yours and Alec's both by now, has just been isolated in jail for three months, depressed like you can't even *understand*, and you're going to put her back, alone, in the house where her lover was murdered while she lay there unconscious, in her bedroom that's now scrubbed clean of virtually all signs of habitation, of almost all signs of human existence, and *leave her there*? I don't *think* so.

Okay, so we take her home with us. Well, hully gee, what a surprise. She can sleep on the pull-out in the living room. That gives us the chance to keep an eye on her, see how she's managing, and besides, the dogs will love having her around.

Uh-huh. So she's been all alone, bereft of all real human companionship she could trust and believe in beyond pretty much daily visits with Alec. No touching allowed for three months, and you know how tactile you and she both are, at least with each other. Now you expect her to manage alone on the pull-out? Well, she might. It's possible. The real problem is that while all three of us are fairly asocial — yes, Becky's a party animal, but she never really gets *involved* with other people, she just enjoys the whole party experience — we tend to cleave to each other. Close. *Very* close. Like all the times she and I would sleep together in one bed, for comfort, when we were younger. And even later, like after my divorce when we first got together in Tucson.

Let's be honest here. It's not likely that she'd be okay all alone in the living room, even with the dogs for companionship, is it? Who would she naturally turn to for comfort and companionship? Us! So then what? Am I going to invite her to sleep with me and Alec? The first reaction was an instant 'NO!' But then the little voice weighed in. "How about all of that stuff about 'her needs are my needs'? Remember, as you've said so often, 'this is *Becky*.'" Dammit, her needs *are*. And it *is* her.

So yeah, if she can't handle being all alone on the pull-out — and like I say, she could have either or both of the dogs, if they'd be enough, but to continue just in case — make that *since* they almost certainly wouldn't be — then she'd kind of have to sleep with us, wouldn't she? No other choice, is there? Not that I'd give her an invitation. I'd leave that one up to her. I've got my preferences, even if I have to give in to her needs.

Just sleep? Aaaargh! Oh, *God*, I don't want to go there. That makes my stomach hurt just to even hint at it. Besides, Becky wouldn't violate my trust like that.

But is it a violation of my trust? Or is it a manifestation of *her* trust? Huh? My stomach didn't stop hurting, but *something* raised the question. How does *that* work? Let's play with that one for a bit. Who do I trust? Really trust? Well, there's Alec and Becky, of course. There's Daddy, and Aunt Lori, and Carol, Daddy's first girlfriend after Mom died. And of course, Bruno and Sasha. Who else? Forget about it, there isn't anyone else. Like I said, I'm somewhat asocial.

Who does Alec trust? Me, of course, and Becky. Bruno and Sasha. Probably Daddy and Aunt Lori, because of me, although that's less certain. Also not important at the moment. He's never met Carol, although he might take her on faith because of me.

Who does Becky trust? Me, Alec, Aunt Lori, probably Daddy and maybe Carol. Oh, and Bruno and

Sasha, especially after they protected her that time last year. Who else?

When she was telling me about her training, I remember her saying that going through therapy herself — apparently you have to do that in order to be qualified as a psychologist, something about having to experience being on the other side (but you don't have to be sued to become a lawyer) — opening up to her therapist was the hardest thing she'd ever done. She still kept some things away from him (like the Family) that didn't jeopardize her therapy, and she said she'd probably never be able to do it again with anyone, under any circumstances. Not that she actively *distrusted* him, but simply that she's like me and doesn't fully open up to anyone. Except me and Alec, that is. On that basis, I think we can pretty much stick with the same list.

So if she needs anything more than just comfort and companionship, do I still look at it as a violation? I mean, on one level, it is, yes. Clearly. But the fact that she would trust enough, Alec and me both, to be that open about her needs with us — oops, there's that whole 'her needs are my needs' thing coming into play again, too.

I don't want to do this.

My stomach still hurts.

I *really* don't want to do this. It makes my stomach hurt, it makes my heart ache, no matter which way I look at it, and it's just an incredible amount of anguish. But I started this, and it's got to be resolved. Remember the CEO's motto: No Dithering.

Shit! Let's try this from a different angle. I'd give her the shirt off my back. I'd give her more than that, but the bra won't fit. We know about the shoes, her feet are bigger than mine, too. So if it was absolutely what she needed, would I give her Alec?

My stomach churned at that thought, and my heart ached. Even more.

But if it meant the difference between Becky living or not, then could I possibly refuse? Knots began to form in my gut. I could feel the start of tears, and angrily I wiped my eyes. I *do not* cry, I thought furiously. It didn't work; the tears continued to flow. But all I'm doing here is thinking this whole thing out. Or trying. There's no decision being made about this, nothing's happening right now. My gut relaxed, but just fractionally. My heart continued to ache.

Would I have to *give* him? I couldn't give him up. I just *couldn't*. I don't think there's any way at all that I could turn my back on him and walk away, even for Becky. Yes, her needs are my needs. But if I lost him, then *I* have an overwhelming need, and *he's* what I would need. Even if her needs are my needs, that doesn't mean that one trumps the other. Talk about anguish! There's got to be a solution, I thought. There's *got* to be. I won't *accept* the idea that there isn't.

Well, would I give up part of him?

Huh? Which part? No, seriously.

Would I … *could* I … share him with her?

Once, for a while, or forever?

I played with that in my mind for quite a while as my guts did the most amazing dance all around my aching heart.

The whole concept hurts to consider. As I look at it, though, forever actually doesn't seem to hurt quite as much. Quite. Why is that? Once … that's … well, it would hurt, and it would feel kind of like he and I were being used, too. But if she really needed him that badly (and if he were willing, I reminded myself. He's got a say in this, too. Duh!), and trusted us that much to let us see that need, try to meet that need, for *her*, I could manage. I think. I hope. It's not like the two of them would be sneaking around behind my back and carrying on for a lengthy period.

Am I just rationalizing here? Probably. Probably, hell! Damn right I am! But I'm just thinking it out. And dammit, I *will* find a solution that works. Because nobody else is going to, and frankly, the alternative of losing Becky for good, just like losing Alec for good, is the most terrifying thing I can conceive of.

I want to bring my armor up. I'm tough, and I use my defenses all the time to help me stay that way, *be* that way. But I can't build that sort of an emotional wall between me and either Alec or Becky. Doing that would make me hard, not tough. I love both of them deeply, and if I can erect that sort of defense against them, it would also be a defense against my feelings *for* them. Once I do that, I'm no longer the person I think I am. That I *need* to be, for myself.

How about for a while? Definitely harder to take. There's still, well, either once or for a while both feel like violations. Even if I don't look at it like it's a breach of my trust in her, because I'm allowing it, it's still a violation of the relationships involved. Even if I'm willing to — ugh! — accept it. Sort of. Both of them are. Going on for longer makes it worse. Yes, she's worth it. She means that much to me, so I'd accept it. But it would definitely hurt, no matter how much I accept it.

But forever? That doesn't feel so much like a violation as it does a commitment. A different sort of commitment, I added quickly. A different sort of relationship. One that includes all three of us, together. I … I could live with that. I think.

So why doesn't my gut unknot at the thought? The anguish should go away, shouldn't it? If I've got the right answer? Or do I? Dammit, I don't want to do this! Any of it!

But I have no other choice, do I? Do any of us?

Let's try to look at it more analytically. What are the pros? Well, it would meet her needs, if they go that far.

She might not need it, I reminded myself. I can hope, right? It would keep the three of us together, and if that's the way we went, she certainly wouldn't be out trolling for someone else. That probably played a significant part in her getting into this situation in the first place. She wanted a close relationship of her own, badly, and I knew it. There were two people she couldn't hide her desire for such a relationship from, me and herself.

I don't think Alec had a clue, any more than he did that she'd been interested in him. She'd concealed it very well, and let's face it, he's a man, which automatically means he's not as perceptive. But if she were in a successful relationship with us, then she wouldn't be casting about for another one and potentially winding up in trouble. Again. Besides, she really is my more-than-sister; I worry about her. Over and above this whole situation.

All of this, of course, is assuming that she's willing and that needy. Also that Alec is willing, although some of the things he's said in reaction to her condition and what she's going through at least suggest that this wouldn't be entirely out of his realm of possibility. That is, if we can make a go of it, of course. I mean, it's got to be a successful relationship, right? If it's not successful, then I've just screwed everything up. Well, if it blows up, anyway. If it works for a while and we then kind of drift away from it … maybe that wouldn't screw *everything* up, at least.

What are the cons? Let's see. Sharing Alec — the knot in my gut tightened, for just a moment. My heart hurt worse, also just for a moment. Three of us together — hell, simply the two of us wasn't always smooth sailing, although Alec and I both had the experience of the horrid relationships in our past to help us work that much harder at it. But three? Half again the problems? Give me a *break*. Probably more like three times. Cubed. There's also the issue about until the new house is built, three of us together in that tiny place? Shit, I'd noticed the crowding when Alec moved in. What would another adult in there be like? Although after Becky's … experience, she's probably got as much incentive to work hard as we do.

Her needs. My needs. This is Becky, remember.

Yeah, it does keep coming back to those, doesn't it? I don't want to do this. I don't want to even *think* about this. But somebody has got to, and I don't see anyone else stepping up. Forget that, there isn't anyone else *to* step up. I figure Alec won't, and nobody else is even going to give it a second thought. That means it's up to me. All of it.

So who gets the pullout during sex? I mean, this is more mechanics than theory. I've already reached my conclusion, even if I'm a tad slow in admitting it. But it would sure help to have something at least a little bit more detailed than just a blank canvas entitled, 'Alec, Becky and me.'

Living with us is no big deal. Not when push comes to shove, and in that house, that's exactly what it would be. We can tuck an armoire for her clothes in any number of places. We can have a vanity for her makeup. One person cooking at a time, mostly; the kitchen isn't all that comfortable with two working, but we can rotate. That's certainly doable. Enough chairs in the dining room, and there are already three in the kitchen, too, because it's been the three of us eating together there so often anyway. The garage and driveway together will hold three cars, even if it sometimes takes a bit of shuffling to get out whoever's in back. Those are the easy parts. Sex isn't.

Hell, if it weren't for the sex issue, it'd be easy. I'd just tell her to move in, sleep in our bed with us and be done with it. No worries. But as I said, who gets the pullout? Dammit! Why won't my gut ease up?

Oh, come *on*! If Becky can't sleep alone on the pullout, and she needs someone so badly as to sleep with us in our bed, then why would she accept being exiled to the living room just because we're …?

While we're at it, could I stay there, knowing that she and Alec are …?

Which means all three of us, together in the bedroom, for everything. Goldfish bowl time. More knots in my gut. Tight and churning to boot. But her needs … *her* needs.

If it starts, can we work it out? If everybody wants to, I presume we can. There's no way that I can see to give it a trial run. In for a penny, in for a pound, or something like that. If we start it, we have to do so with the intention of making it work, regardless. The *absolute determination* to make it work. All three of us.

I can do this.

Do I want to? Let's not go there. It's a question of need, not want. I absolutely don't want the alternative, and that's something I can say for sure. So yeah, I think I can do it, since I have to. Not having any reasonable alternatives will do that to you.

Is there any other solution I can find? Who gives a shit? If Becky doesn't need this much, then it'll take care of itself, because we'll find however much of whatever she does need and provide it. I won't push her where she doesn't need to go. If she does need this much, well, this has just defined the outer limits of where I'm able to go, I think.

More to the point, I believe it'll work, if we do have to go that far. That's good enough for me, I guess. It's going to have to be, because it's all I can give. All I *have* to give. And I'm not sure there really is anything else, other than completely giving up Alec. I've already ruled that one out.

I turned onto my side and pulled the sheet up to my chin. I guess I've figured out what I'm doing. Once again, remember the CEO's motto: No Dithering. Now all I need to do is lay it all out for Alec, most carefully, and then wait to see what Becky wants. Needs. The knots were still there, but they didn't cinch up tight. Maybe this was the right decision. I hope it is. That's all I recall thinking before sleep took over.

Saturday was a difficult day. I had this persistent feeling that I should have awakened with Alec instead of alone in my suite, but with motions and jury selection beginning Monday morning, I could spend the entire weekend with him and outside of bed, all I'd see would be the top of his head as he prepared for trial. Even if I were there, this most definitely would not be the time to talk to him about Becky, him and me. So while sleeping alone was disappointing, and I missed the dogs as well, there was just not enough reason for me to drive back to Tucson for one day.

Instead I explored Phoenix just a bit more. Once again I wound up in the huge used bookstore — there are a couple of outlets from the same store in Tucson, but each individual store is different — and spent some relatively enjoyable time going through their investment books — nothing special — checking out Daddy's books in their science-fiction shelves — not a huge number, but a few — and wound up in cookbooks. I actually took two of them away with me, figuring that I'd try something new and different for Alec when all this was over. Kind of silly, since I've already got more cookbooks than I have space for in the kitchen, and there are several I hardly ever use, but the two places where I can, and still do, lose myself are at the range (shooting) and at the range (cooking), so to speak. And these did look interesting.

There was also one small but encyclopedic work on chili peppers that I just had to have. I never even knew some of them existed. Now that I did, I'd have to work at trying to find them and learn to use them. Maybe I'd have to learn to grow them. One way or another …

When Sunday rolled around, I was up early. Not by choice, but simply because of when my eyes popped open. For probably the first time since Becky's arrest (what a God-awful way to mark time!), I was ravenous. I decided to go have a good-sized breakfast and then, an hour or two later, I'd hit the gym. Not the one Kendra and I had been going to, but another one of the same chain way out on the west side of town where I could go as 'A.M. Youngston' instead of Laura McCulloch. Someplace where I could really give myself a good workout without having to worry about Kendra hearing about me or what I was doing. Or walking in while I was working myself to the max. I mean, I felt *good* today (as these things go) and I wanted to make the most of it.

I was well into the Sunday Phoenix paper when my omelet arrived. I like my own better; they're overflowing with meat and vegetables, smothered in chili, salsa or guacamole as the mood strikes, and that sort of thing. They're also not half so pretty, because I do put way too much stuff into them. But every so often, I remember what the clean-up is like and enjoy eating out instead.

The Arizona Republic is a very nice paper on weekdays. The Sunday Republic, though, is no better than the Tucson paper, in my opinion, other than editorially; it's not quite as far to the left as the Star. No matter, I mostly just wanted something to take my mind off and it did that admirably. Finally folding it all up to leave for some later diner, I headed out to the west side of Phoenix where that other gym was.

Working out at the gym let me blow off a lot of pent-up emotion. I also worked myself to a frazzle, a lot more than I did whenever Kendra was around. I'm always careful near her never to show her just how strong I really am or how much endurance I can actually muster. Now, with all the privacy in the world, in the anonymity of my plain t-shirt and work-out pants, I could actually tax myself to the fullest. My legs were wobbly when I got off the bike. My arms and legs were like rubber when I finally quit the weight machine, and my stomach was so sore when I finished my crunches that I couldn't even sit up at first.

It was absolutely glorious! Why I hadn't done this more times over the past couple of months escaped me, but at least I'd done it now. I have to admit that I'd let up just a little bit myself since Alec and I were married. Not enough to lose the physical edge, but I didn't need to keep the body quite as hard. Just a bit more like Becky, letting the contours soften just a tad. But it just felt so good to really stretch myself again instead of holding back the way I had to on most weekdays.

Finally it was time to head back across town and begin to get ready for the party. I hardly dared hope I'd find Kendra wearing the necklace.

Chapter 24

Putting my makeup on was still a bit of a challenge. I had to remove it and start over twice before I was satisfied with the effect. Finally I had everything in place and could start to get the outfit on. I checked it over carefully for previously undiscovered tags and pins, found one of each and removed them. Then into the pants, add the top and finally the jacket on over it.

The pendant and earrings I'd gotten just for this purpose … damn, but those clips were uncomfortable! Live with it. They didn't bother me half as much as getting my ears pierced again would have. Nothing I couldn't manage to bear for a couple of hours, and while they were nice enough pieces, they were certainly nothing special and could, *would*, disappear into the depths of the jewelry box on my dresser, the one that holds piles of various things and precious little jewelry, as of tomorrow.

I turned this way and that, checking every aspect of my appearance in the mirror. It didn't have to be one hundred percent perfect, but it certainly had to be as close to perfect as Laura would have made it, and since I'd made sure that she seemed to look up to Kendra, I figured she'd take special pains with her appearance for an 'elegant party' at Kendra's. Wanting to make a good impression. Finally I was satisfied.

When I checked the clock, though, I was still too early. I figured I should arrive about ten to fifteen minutes after the start of the party. It wasn't a sit-down dinner party or anything like that, so the time I arrived wasn't critical. That much time ought to still seem interested enough without being too eager, or so I presumed. This sort of thing isn't my strong suit, to say the least.

That left me with a half-hour to kill, so I took off my jacket, folded it carefully and laid it on the bed before sitting down in a chair in the front room of the suite to go back to my book. Triumph as the heroine not only escaped from her confinement but took the bulk of the entire population of the prison planet with her! I sure hoped that was an omen for tonight. By the time I was ready to leave, I had just enough pages left in the book to get me to sleep tonight, assuming that I wasn't so tired that I simply dropped off. Or so keyed up that I couldn't get to sleep at all. Either one seemed like a reasonable possibility at the moment.

I stepped out of the door of the suite repeating my mantra to myself. By the fourth 'I'm Laura,' I was behind the wheel and once again completely in character.

When I arrived, the party was just getting started. That was fine; I simply hadn't wanted to be the first person to arrive, nor to get there after almost everybody else was there. It was a familiar sort of party for me, and it would have been for Laura, too. The daughter-of-two-doctors Laura, that is. Uncle Jack and Aunt Lori used to have such get-togethers at least once a month, sometimes more often, especially around the holidays.

When Becky and I were small, we'd have sleepovers at my house with a babysitter during them, because Daddy and Mom were at the party. Usually when the babysitter tucked us in, as soon as she was out of the room, we'd wind up tangled up together in one bed.

When we were old enough, we'd still be there, but just the two of us, alone. Still slept tangled up together.

Older yet, and we got to dress up and go to the early stages of the parties before going off to bed in Becky's room. By the time we were seniors in high school, we were full attendees at the parties. I found them interesting enough, but never all that enticing; Becky was always far more the party animal of the two of us. She worked the room and loved the experience. I tended to stay in one place. But we did quite nicely, I thought.

Enough reminiscing. Repeat the mantra silently to myself as I hit the bar to get a glass of sparkling water with just enough scotch — not really cheap scotch, but a long way from single malt, it didn't escape me that none of the liquor was all that good — to give it a tad of color. I wanted the camouflage, not the alcohol. I mingled and found that most of the couples were people Kendra had most likely met through Jon, or perhaps through Donald McGuire, who was there as well. Medical types, in other words. No problem, I could always mingle with people like that. After all, I'd been doing it much of my life.

As usual, I spent most of my time listening and very little of it actually talking, if you don't count agreeing, asking a few germane questions and the like as talking. I don't; they're part of real listening. Not that I expected to pick up anything of value to me, but people who listen tend to fade into the woodwork in people's memories, where those who talk stand out. I work hard at not standing out, not being memorable.

I'd probably been there for fifteen or twenty minutes, I wasn't keeping close track, when I first saw Kendra. She was wearing basic black, much as I was, except hers was a dress, and her back was to me. I could just glimpse the back of the necklace she was wearing, and it clearly wasn't Becky's. I wasn't happy about that, to say the least. The swirl of people then moved me away from her and I lost sight of her in the crowd before she could turn around and see me. Well, I could leave, I suppose, but I had the entire evening and nothing else scheduled. Might as well stick around, at least for a bit longer. Have enough of the canapés to make a light supper of it, too. A bit of a change from things like chiles rellenos, if nothing else.

Next, I wound up in an extended conversation with another woman who had grown up in Denver at much the same time as Becky and I had, in pretty much the same milieu as Becky had, although just enough behind us and in a different part of town that we hadn't known each other.

That was just plain lucky; it would definitely have been difficult and could have turned into an absolute disaster for me if she had, and recognized me. We played the 'do you know' game for a while, and I could honestly answer that I did know a few and I knew of a few others (I actually knew her father, not well, from Uncle Jack and Aunt Lori's parties). Naturally, those that I knew best were ones that she knew simply by name or reputation and vice versa. I planned it that way; three or four of the people she named besides her father were people I actually knew fairly well, again from Uncle Jack and Aunt Lori's parties (two of them were Family) and they hadn't all gone to that big hospital in the sky yet.

But since Laura McCulloch, or Laura Johnson, as she was growing up, didn't really exist, I couldn't take the chance that she'd check me out with them. Oh, I probably could have, since this particular play was almost certainly going to ring down its final curtain tonight, win, lose or draw, but old habits die hard, I suppose. I hate cutting off my line of retreat.

When I saw Kendra again, it was about three-quarters of an hour after I got there. Call it a half-hour or so after the first time I saw her. This time she was facing me, and she was wearing a very nice squash blossom necklace. Silver with lots of turquoise and coral, very fancy indeed. But — I replayed in my mind the last time I saw her — not what she had been wearing before. Seeing me, she made her way over to me and asked how I was enjoying myself. "Oh, it's a very nice party. It reminds me of the ones my parents used to give when I was growing up." She smiled. "That's a very nice necklace you're wearing," I added. "Lovely, in fact. Navajo?"

"I think so," she said. "I picked it up in a place above Sedona, up in the canyon." I knew the place; Alec and I had stopped there ourselves when he and I were just beginning to investigate the Family board members, well over a year ago now. I had a couple of pieces from there myself, including a lovely pair of earrings, given to me by Alec, that almost made me want to get my ears pierced again. Almost. Not that I offered Kendra any of this, of course. I'm Laura. I'm Laura. I'm Laura. Then she added, "Just stick around. You'll see some others." I must have looked puzzled, because she added, "I'm wearing a number of different things tonight. I don't get much of a chance to wear my best jewelry, so I'm changing from time to time."

My mind suddenly clicked. "That's such a nice piece. May I get a photo of it?" She agreed, so I pulled out my cellphone and got a good shot of her with the necklace. Not that I gave a damn about this one, but if she showed up with Becky's necklace, I wanted to be simply taking one more picture of several, not suddenly going bananas for the very first time over a stolen piece connected to her husband's murder. That might make her suspicious. Make that 'would be certain to.' I didn't dare let myself forget the sort of person I was dealing with here. Shooting her in her own living room during the party would probably be the height of bad manners, and I'm quite sure Emily Post would back me up on that. Of course, having her kill me during it would rank right up there with it and probably bother me a hell of a lot more. I thanked her, we separated and mingled in other directions for a while.

I admit, this jewelry-switching bit struck me as a tad odd. How many guests at a party notice each other's jewelry beyond the beginning of the party? If even then? Tiring of meaningless conversation, I took a seat on the sofa for a while and eavesdropped a bit. Sharp hearing is a real plus in this job, right up there with the ability to fade.

Two women behind me were talking about it as well. Some of the remarks I'd have to characterize as downright catty, but from what they were saying, a number of these parties Kendra threw wound up having a certain element of show-and-tell to them. Clothes, furniture (!), jewelry, that sort of thing. Each party had a central point, something she just had to make public.

There were also usually some new guests each time who were the prime targets of the display, like that short brunette in the black pants outfit tonight. Hey, I thought, that's me! But I simply sat there as though I hadn't heard anything. I got the distinct impression that those two wouldn't even be there except that they enjoyed the social occasion. Their husbands were off across the room, apparently. It didn't sound as though they had a lot of use for Kendra. Well, join the club.

The evening went on in this sort of vein for several hours. I took in a quart or so of fizzy water and, with all of that, perhaps one good shot of scotch, total. By now I knew where both of the readily accessible bathrooms were, from experience, and I'd gotten about four pictures of Kendra in different jewelry, all of it quite nice. She'd worn more than that, but those were the pieces I figured I should really respond to, and if I were the targeted guest, so to speak, I might as well play the part to the hilt.

Chapter 25

I didn't see her when she came out next. I was standing, talking to one of the women who'd been behind me earlier, when Kendra came out. My first warning was when she said, "Oh, that's a truly lovely necklace indeed. I wonder where Kendra got it?" I turned around. Jackpot! Kendra was wearing Becky's necklace.

I have to admit that it looked almost as good on Kendra as it did on Becky. Emotions aside, that is. Also interesting, as their coloration is so different. Becky is almost dark, approaching Mediterranean in coloring, while Kendra's fair enough to make people accept the 'blonde' hair and 'blue' eyes without a second thought. Truth to tell, I wanted to knock Kendra down, remove the necklace forcibly and stomp her face into the sort of mush she'd made of her late husband's face. But doing so would be tacky. Bound to get me talked about. I'm Laura. I'm Laura. I'm Laura. Laura would never do anything like that, she's much too nice. Almost saccharine, in fact.

I made my way towards Kendra and pulled out my phone once more. Kendra just got a half-smile on her face and held still, but I hadn't failed to notice that her eyes had been cold all evening. Not just to me; that seemed to be their natural condition, at least in this sort of crowd, but they had never been quite that cold to me before. I was careful not to let any of my feeling of triumph show.

I stood around her for a few moments and told her how magnificent the necklace was. She seemed to like that. I asked her where she found it, as I had a couple of the other jewelry items she'd been wearing, and she responded that this one had been a gift from her late husband. His last gift to her, in fact. Yeah, right. Thieving, murderous bitch. I'm Laura. I'm Laura. I'm Laura. I smiled at her and praised his taste, both in jewelry and in wives, obviously, and she preened just a tad. Then I excused myself to hit the bathroom once more.

I didn't need it, this time. Oh, sure, I could find something to get rid of, but my real motivation was to get that picture someplace safe. I set it up to go to Alec's email, and once it was sent, I breathed a quiet sigh of relief. No matter what happened now, my best proof that Kendra, not Becky, was the guilty party was out of my hands and in the place it would do the most good. Then, just to be safe, I sent another copy to my own email. I pulled my pants back up, flushed and readjusted my fanny pack. The small but noticeable weight of the pistol was quite reassuring at that moment.

Back out among the crowd, I noticed that it was beginning to thin just a bit. This is my big chance, I thought. I looked around, but there was no sign of Kendra. Well, give it a few minutes. She's probably changing her jewelry again. I went back to the bar for another colored fizzy water.

She came back in about five minutes later, wearing yet another necklace. She must have quite a collection. Working my way over to her, I apologized for having to leave, but said that it was getting late and I'd been up early, so I really needed to head on out and perhaps I'd see her at the gym tomorrow. She didn't seem to react, but simply told me good-bye. Her eyes didn't warm a bit, and her body language suggested an utter lack of interest as well. Possibly some anger on top of it, but I had no idea why that might be.

Back in the suite, the first thing I did was call Alec. I almost felt guilty waking him up, but when he heard about the picture, he got so excited that he had to go boot up the computer to check for it. We spent several minutes in a mix of casual conversation and murmured endearments while we waited. Then there was no sign of it in his email. No sign of it in mine, either.

What frickin' corner of the goddam ether had it gone to? It was his address; that was already in the phone, and we both sent emails back and forth from phone to computer and vice-versa on a fairly regular basis, even just quickie 'I love you' or 'I'm thinking about you' sorts of notes. Hell, I'd sent him three or four of those just this past week and gotten one back.

I pulled out my phone once more and sent the picture to him again, as well as to every other email address the two of us had that I could think of. Several times. I probably sent out more than a dozen copies, all told, and finally one showed up where he could find it. I breathed a deep sigh of relief. No matter what else happened, I'd done what I could to clear Becky. I sent him a kiss and told him to go back to bed, I'd be home tomorrow.

Then I busied myself packing up everything left of what I'd been spreading out over the past two and a half months or so that I hadn't taken home already. When I'd gotten most of it contained, I had worked off most of my emotional high and was pretty much ready to turn in.

I'd done pretty well on the book. I could have managed another page or so, if the book hadn't ended just when it did, but it was a close enough thing that I just turned out the light and let the darkness take over. Sleep, blessed sleep and all that, although I kept one hand touching the pistol under my pillow.

I actually overslept the next morning, for me. Usually I'm up around five or so, but this morning the clock said it was almost six when my eyes came open. Oh, well, this time it hardly matters, does it? Tonight I'd be in Alec's arms again where I belonged. I felt so good, in fact, that I wished Becky could be there with us. Probably just a reaction to her situation. I showered, dressed and started carrying my things out to the car.

There was a breakfast spot between the place I'd been staying and the freeway, and I found, to my delight, that they even offered small omelets. I settled on a two-egg thing with plenty of salsa and cheese, some meat, and drowned it in coffee. Very presentable coffee, considering. Then I finished working my way through the morning newspaper while I waited for the coffee to work its way through me.

I was in no hurry to get out of Phoenix. The rush hour traffic would largely be going the other way. Besides, Alec would be in court by the time I got home, and he might not even be trying to use the picture right now, this morning. I mean, it was motions and maybe even the beginning of voir dire, not the trial itself. Well, whatever they decided to do with the picture, that was up to him and John. I'd done my part. It was a bit after 9:30 when I finally hit the road headed south.

Colonel Cooper, may he rest in peace, would have been ashamed of me. I'd spent all of this time, very appropriately, in what he would have characterized as 'Condition Yellow.' That's an alert and watchful state, not worried, but aware of what's going on around me, just enough that nobody can sneak up on me or threaten me without my knowing what's happening in plenty of time to react appropriately. Today I felt such a sense of triumph over what I'd finally done and relief that it was all over that I went to Condition White, which is essentially oblivious. Most people spend most of their lives in Condition White, but it's not healthy for someone who is packing a weapon.

Or someone who is being followed. As I found out I was. The hard way. Stupid me. Dumb, idiotic, complacent, stupid me.

There are a couple of major truck-stop type gas stations south of Casa Grande, down around Eloy. I was finally in need of a pit stop once more, so I pulled off the freeway and into a parking spot away from the building. If I'd been thinking straight, as I said, I'd have been checking for a tail long before I got there. I should have been; it's

211

gotten to be pretty much of a habit. But I just felt so *good* today about what I'd finally accomplished, as well as so good about finally being *done* with Phoenix, with Laura and most importantly with Kendra, that I'd just driven on by the out-in-the-middle-of-nowhere exits I usually got off at to try to get a tail to show itself. Besides, I'd been checking every time I'd made this trip and never found anything worth mentioning. Why should this time be any different?

Someday I'd like to ask a dumb question like that without having it turn around to bite me on the ass. Today just wasn't going to be my day, though. I was doing just fine until I came out of the station with the predictable cup of coffee in hand, headed back to my car. I heard a familiar voice holler, "You've had it, bitch!" I whirled around to see Kendra running towards me, blood in her eye, holding a two-foot length of iron pipe over her head, ready to bring it down, hard, on mine!

Chapter 26

Shit! I backpedaled furiously as the pipe whanged! off the car. A two-foot long piece of iron pipe? Where had I heard that before? Don't bother answering, I'm busy at the moment. I tried tossing the cup of coffee at Kendra, but she simply dodged it and the lid didn't come off. Pity; it was nice and hot. Oh, well. So sad, too bad.

Some part of my mind said that the car rental company was not going to be happy with me. The more immediate part of my mind firmly told it to shut up, we were busy at the moment. I made a grab for the pipe, but Kendra pulled it away from me before I could do more than get my fingertips on it. Those threads on the end of the pipe hurt as they went by, but it was simply a scrape that I could ignore.

I faced her warily. I suppose I could pull the pistol and shoot her, but dammit, if you have to shoot someone, it's not like TV and I am most definitely *not* the Lone Ranger. You *do not* shoot their gun or whatever else they're holding out of their hand. You shoot for the center of mass, i.e. the torso. You put *multiple* shots there and pray that they work, because sometimes they don't. Shooting Kendra like that stood a good chance of taking her out of the game permanently, and as good as it would feel for the moment, and it definitely would, it wasn't going to help Becky at all.

There was also a significant chance that it wouldn't be enough to make her stop trying to kill me, at least before she managed to hit me. That would not be good, either. In any event, shooting her would also put me in line for a lot more explanations, which I really didn't need to get into at the moment. Trust me, any Pinal County attorney could, if he chose, make my shooting her seem like a total overreaction on my part, and that would also not be good, either for me or for Becky.

Better for me to try to handle her on her own terms, because the absolute last thing Alec needed was to have Becky on trial for murder in Pima County and me on trial for murder, or even just manslaughter or assault with a deadly weapon, in Pinal County. And of course, being in jail would almost certainly cost me my position as Family CEO, if only from missing too many board meetings.

As Kendra drew back for another try, I leaped up onto the hood of the car. Thank God for rubber soles. When she came towards the front of the car, hoping to get a hit on my ankles or knees with her pipe, I jumped to the roof of the car and kept going. I hit the ground behind the trunk running, and got a couple of dozen feet between us before I turned to face her again. Nice safety margin, for as long it would last.

Probably it wasn't going to be long enough, because she definitely wasn't giving up. Oh, no. She had blood in her eye, specifically mine, and she was quite vocal about it. She discussed my ancestry, my sexual habits, my breeding, whatever I'd been trying to do with her and almost anything else you can imagine. Plus quite a bit that you'd almost certainly never think of. I didn't bother replying; I was too busy trying to stay out of her reach and saving my breath for more important things, like continuing to stay out of her reach and trying to figure out what to do about her.

Some people just have to talk while they fight, but I've never understood why. That two-foot piece of pipe wasn't exactly helping me figure out how to deal with her, either. Whenever she thought she was within range, she'd take a two-handed hold like it was a baseball bat and try a swing at me. Four or five of those swings landed on various parts of the car. The rear window was history, as was the driver's side rear window. The bodywork was suffering, too. Clearly, she was furious and, judging from the way she was hurling invectives, totally out of control. The car was the least of my worries. Staying alive was the major priority in my mind at the moment. Damn near the *only* one.

Bottom line, the car was expendable. I wasn't, and if just one of those swings landed, I'd look like her late husband before she was done with me. This much I was sure of, even if her doing that to me in public might mean the end of her career. Of course, she could well be so out of control because she'd figured out that I was going to end her career anyway and she wasn't willing to go quietly. Personally, I was a lot more concerned about the possible end of *my* career. I spent a lot of time bouncing around the parking lot, mostly backwards, until suddenly I tripped.

I went ass over teakettle, and Kendra took advantage of my mishap to get up close and personal. I rolled frantically to stay clear as her pipe clanged! off the pavement around me several times. Finally I was able to get to my feet, although I had to move extra fast to keep away from that deadly piece of iron when she came up on me as I rose running. I almost fell over again as I went, but I managed to get my feet moving faster than my body was falling and eventually regained my balance as I again opened some distance between us.

There were some people over by the building watching us, but they didn't seem too eager to get in the middle of our little dust-up. Given Kendra's weapon and her eagerness to use it, that was probably good sense on their part. Of course, this seemed to be the one time in history when there were no Highway Patrol or Border Patrol people congregating here. Damn. Just my luck.

I'd have given a lot to have had Bruno with me right now. He has a way with people like Kendra. I think it's the loud snarl and the big white teeth. He's been trained to use them to best effect, too. I was at a distinct disadvantage here, having neither worth mentioning. Oh, well, no point in wishing for what I don't have, is there? Besides, he might find the pipe a bit hard to handle, too.

By now I was back to my car. She got closer to me, and wham! went another dent in the trunk. I was going to have some real fun explaining this to the rental company. Assuming, of course, that I came out on top of this little … incident. If not, I probably wouldn't be worrying about what to say to them. Probably wouldn't be worrying about anything else, either, and that was an outcome I'd definitely like to avoid. It'd ruin my whole day. Not to mention Alec's and Becky's.

Finally I quit trying to play her silly game. But as I decided to go for the pistol with my right hand, Kendra managed to catch my right arm a glancing blow. Nothing horribly worrisome; no bones seemed to break or anything like that. I was moving away from her as it hit, so it mostly just slid along the arm. But the entire arm seemed to go numb about the time that the pipe glanced off the bone in my elbow, and I definitely couldn't use it to try to hold a gun with at the moment. Pulling the gun and dropping it struck me as worse than not pulling it at all, so I just let it be. Besides, Kendra just might know how to shoot, and the last thing, *really* the last thing, that I needed to do was give her my only serious long-range weapon. I still might have to use it myself.

I wanted to stay out in the parking lot rather than be trapped between the cars, but retreating from Kendra didn't always leave me any choice. I made a massive leap up onto the hood of the car, except that this was the Cadillac Escalade in the next stall. Jeez, but they're tall. Clang! The owners were likely to have fun explaining that, too. Why should I hog all the fun, anyway? I made my way up to the roof of the big SUV and stood there bent over for a second, hands on my knees, trying to catch my breath. Down below, Kendra did much the same, although she never took her eyes off me. In the background, someone shouted.

Neither of us paid them any attention. "Goddam lying bitch," she said. "Screw salesman my ass! Consolidated Bolt never heard of you, you lying piece of shit!"

Well, duh, of course they hadn't. That job was just as real as Laura McCulloch, i.e. it's made up out of whole cloth. The entire persona was fake, so why wouldn't the job be fake as well? Not that anyone had ever called them looking for me before. I'd picked them because I managed to get my hands on a bunch of their forms and literature. Lots easier than making up my own and getting it printed. It wasn't like I was actually going to *sell* any of that stuff, after all. They were just window dressing.

Someone was still yelling in the background, but nobody was yet brave enough to try to separate us, so I didn't pay any attention. Neither did Kendra as she went on. "I tried to call them to check on you, but they had no idea who you were. They don't even *sell* in Phoenix. You knew that, naturally. You've been lying the whole time."

Got that right, bitch. That's why it's an assumed identity. It's not real, get it? Anyway, Consolidated sells to the eastern US. There's another fastener company that sells out west. But trying to explain all of that seemed like a real waste of my time and energy. Besides, she didn't want an explanation, she wanted my ass. Dead. Speaking for myself, as I've said, I kind of objected to that on general principles. Some specific ones, too.

So where did I slip up? I'd put so much work into maintaining this cover for so long, I was having trouble trying to figure out where I went wrong. Was it something I said? Something I'd done? Not done?

Chapter 27

"You and your goddamn cell phones!" she hollered as she suddenly took another swing. Cell phones? That was it! It had to be! When I'd taken the pictures of her yesterday evening, I'd used my regular cell, not the overly gaudy one that Laura had always used in her presence. One she'd never seen, and Laura wasn't in any position to have more than one, especially a second one as expensive as my regular one. Or have any need for a second one, either. But Laura's prettified phone didn't have a camera at all, so far as I knew, and if it did, the camera probably wasn't much. That phone was just a prepaid piece of shit that I could toss in a drawer until I needed the identity, any of my spare identities, actually, without racking up a regular monthly bill, so I'd just automatically grabbed my regular cell, which had a decent camera in it, to take the shots.

Luckily I'd sent the photo to Alec already. Since we'd made sure he already had it before I went to bed last night, we could get Becky cleared no matter what happened to me here.

Although for some strange reason I had an objection to getting killed in a gas station parking lot. I hopped to clear the pipe as she jumped up and swung for my ankles. Before she could reverse her swing and try again, I was down on the far side of the Cadillac and heading away once more, trying to keep that reasonable gap between us. I spent a lot of my time backpedaling, working hard to maintain that distance. Oh, and ignoring the audience we were starting to gather. One of them, maybe the owner of the Escalade, tried coming towards us, but Kendra took a vicious swing in his direction and he retreated. Sensible of him.

She had to have been suspicious of me before that; the cell phone just wasn't all that great a failing, by itself.

Of course, I had to remember the sort of psychopath I was dealing with. I also couldn't afford to forget that she is significantly stronger than she looks. Yes, I'm stronger than she is, but not by a huge amount, and she's the one with the pipe here. I was armed, yes — I flexed my fingers, my arm and hand were recovering from that numbing blow — but like I'd said, shooting her stood a decent chance of killing her, which wasn't in Becky's best interests, although it was beginning to look as though it might be in *mine*. In any event, doing it would mean yet more explanations.

Using one of my Hideaway knives, well, they were designed for opening people up where God hadn't provided a natural orifice, and besides, they'd require that I do something I'd been avoiding this whole time, specifically getting up close and personal with her. As long as she had that pipe, I wasn't about to do that without some real careful planning, and besides, my need was to take her out of the fight, not remove her from the human race.

Although that certainly might improve the gene pool, I have to admit. Opening her up surgically — the knives were good for that — was little better than shooting her. Messier, yeah. But if I had made up my mind to go ahead and kill her, there was absolutely no reason for me not to just shoot her from a reasonable distance and be done with it. All things considered, though, I'd be better off letting the state do that, if I had the choice. Fewer explanations to make that way.

Was it my imagination, or had she slowed down just a bit? I knew from our times at the gym that I had more endurance than she did, but just like with strength, it wasn't all that marked a difference. She probably was, since my breath was beginning to rasp as well and I hadn't been wasting mine telling her everything about her past and what I wanted to do to cut her future short like she was me. By now we'd made a number of circuits of the various cars parked there as well as a couple of gas pump islands.

Several of the cars had picked up dents from her pipe, and my rental was by far the worst of the lot.

A couple of the people watching — I risked a quick glance — looked like they wanted to do something but couldn't figure out how to do it safely. This was ridiculous. I couldn't just keep running around the parking lot. If nothing else, someone was sure to call 911 sooner or later, if they hadn't already, and that would bring the local sheriff, if he wasn't already on the way. That would have meant more explanations and even more chances for her to find me distracted. It would only take one good blow and I'd be history in short order.

I judged her swing and began to carefully close the distance I'd been keeping between us. She watched me warily, and when she thought she could get me with a lunge and swing, she took her chance. I ducked back just long enough to let the pipe go by, then I stepped in close. Real close. I tried a sharp blow to her solar plexus, but she turned in her follow-through and took it in the side. Shit!

I took a good hold of the pipe with my left hand, but she spun with it and almost yanked it out of my grasp. I slapped her in the face as I brought my right hand over to grab the pipe as well, but I wasn't able to put as much weight behind it as I'd like, so it didn't bother her a lot. She tried to knee me while we both wrestled over the pipe, but I was expecting that and pulled her in even closer to me as I turned my hip to her so she couldn't get a good blow in. Then I pulled back a bit, which put more weight on the pipe, and as we both bent over, she head-butted me in the face.

I saw stars. She'd gotten me a good one in the right eye. It'd definitely color up nicely and probably swell up to boot, if I lived long enough, but I never let my grip slip on the pipe. I returned the favor when she brought her head back up, and blood spurted from her nose. If nothing else, her tone changed as her nose clogged up, and it made her that much harder to understand. Not hard enough, unfortunately. I did have to commend her vocabulary; I hadn't ever thought of even half of the insults and slurs she came up with. She could have given her sister-in-law lessons. The things she was saying did call her supposed breeding into question, but then I'd never been under any illusions about that anyway.

The next time she tried to knee me, I was ready for her and again I shoved into her. I got too close for the blow to hit, and in pushing her backwards, I managed to knock her back into a car, hard. I'm not sure which one, since I wasn't paying a lot of attention to minor details like that by then, but her head slammed into the trunk and it seemed to daze her just a bit. I was able to get the pipe out of her hands and I just threw it behind me as hard as I could.

Before she could recover, I grabbed her head and beat it on the trunk a couple more times as hard as I could. Her eyes seemed to roll up in her head and she became dead weight in my hands. I wasn't about to take any chances, though, because she might have been faking. I pulled her off the trunk and dropped her face-first onto the pavement. Actually, I didn't simply drop her, I helped her get down really quickly. I wasn't gentle about it, either. It didn't do her nose any favors, like I gave a shit about little details like that at the moment. Being gentle with her was not in my game plan any more, if it ever had been.

I knelt on her waist and dug in my hip pocket for the cable ties. Thank God for whatever impulse had led me to bring them along. One of them secured her wrists behind her, and another around her ankles left her pretty much at my mercy. I didn't have a lot by then. This whole episode — never mind that it had been my own stupidity that let her get the drop on me and get so close from the beginning — had just been that much more shit that I hadn't needed. I dragged her to the rear of my car, opened the trunk and began trying to pull her into it. Somebody behind me was protesting, but nobody tried to stop me. Somebody else came and gave me a hand getting her up to the level of my car's trunk. He was probably glad to see the end of us.

Despite her floppy knees, we were able to get her close enough to her feet to be able to tip the top part of her body into the trunk; once we'd gotten to that point, getting her feet in was easy. I did have one afterthought, though. I reached in and broke off the inside trunk latch. Assuming she regained consciousness, and she probably would, the last thing I needed was to have her pop the trunk lid from the inside and wave at other cars as we went down the freeway.

I thanked my anonymous helper as I hopped in and made tracks out of there. I checked the clock on the dash. It had been less than twenty minutes since I'd pulled in, and that included the time I'd spent using the rest room and getting a cup of coffee. I don't think the fight itself had taken more than about ten minutes, all told. Time sure flies when you're having fun.

I was about two miles or so down the freeway, going at a very careful and reasonable speed with the wind whistling through the open passageway where the side and rear windows had been, when I saw a sheriff's car running lights and siren north on the other side of the freeway. He might have been heading for the gas station, but I had enough of a head start that with any luck, he'd probably never find me. If he did, well, I'd worry about that if it happened. Just about then I heard a thump, and then another. Apparently Kendra had awakened and was trying to kick whatever she could. No worries there; she wasn't going to undo or break those cable ties. I headed on into Tucson.

Chapter 28

I pulled up to the curb outside the courthouse and gently drove the car up onto the sidewalk. As I went around the back end of the car and opened the trunk, some uniform came out from inside, looking a bit upset with me. "Hey, lady, you can't park here."

I thought of a couple of snappy returns and then decided against them. This was going to be more than enough fun without aggravating him unnecessarily. Opening the trunk, I began trying to haul Kendra out. She was pissed. Uncooperative, too. Of course, she'd been kicking anything she could for the last twenty miles or so, at least. Thank God I'd had the foresight to break off the emergency latch.

"I'll get you for this," she said. Quite loudly, too. "I'll gut you like a fish. I'll carve you up like a piece of meat." The uniformed officer by now was almost to the car and, judging from the expression on his face, utterly shocked. By now I had a pretty good idea of how to punch her buttons, so I tossed a couple of insults showing her impotence back at her. Then she said what I'd been hoping for all along: "I'll *kill* you! I'll kill you just like I did that no-good cheating husband of mine!" Oh, I think I know how to push her buttons by now, all right. Imagine me buffing my fingernails on my currently somewhat well-padded chest. Not really doing it, of course. I had other things to worry about at the immediate moment.

The officer stood stock-still. I guess it caught him totally by surprise. I looked at him. "You heard that?" He nodded, still a bit shocked. I had my little pen recorder going as well, but having a real live person who had heard it, especially someone with a badge, was very nice. Then somebody in a suit came up behind me. I turned and he flashed me a detective's badge.

No Other Choice

"I heard it, too. You would be …? Oh, it's you, Ms. … Youngston, isn't it? Still finding trouble, I see." Surprise of surprises, it was the same Detective Jackson who had come to the house both times that it had been shot up a little over a year ago. Still with a bit of a smile, too. Well, nobody had drawn a gun on me yet. Nobody had demanded that I turn Kendra loose, and I had not one but two witnesses with badges who had heard her confess to killing her husband. That ought to be admissible as an excited utterance, with any luck, at least from what I remembered of evidence class. I figured I was doing pretty well, all things considered. There was also probably no need to explain to him right now that I'd gotten married since he'd seen me last. Irrelevant shit like that could be ignored.

"I'm glad to see you too, Detective Jackson. Could one of you gentlemen help me get her into Judge Ramirez's courtroom? You just heard her confess to killing her husband, and Dr. Rebecca Swan is on trial there right now for that very murder. Well, it's just motions and voir dire at the moment, but it is getting underway. I'd kind of like to do something about that." The detective and the uniformed officer exchanged glances, then Detective Jackson nodded. The one in uniform reached for the radio on his shoulder and said something into it.

A couple of minutes later we had several more uniformed deputies, I think they were, out to help us. I clipped the cable tie around her ankles and happily turned Kendra over to their tender care with the detective following along. Most of the blood from her nose was on the trunk carpet, not her blouse, so she didn't look perhaps quite as much the worse for wear as she could have. I grabbed the laptop bag from the car as I went.

At the metal detectors, we almost had a major malfunction. They wanted all of the metal on me, which meant, for starters, my pistol and all of my knives. I didn't have a huge issue with it, not when clearing Becky was in

224

the offing, but it seemed that with a pistol, I was supposed to use a different door where they could log it in and properly secure it.

I finally settled the issue by field-stripping the pistol. I dropped the magazine, ejected the chamber round and then pulled the slide back to align the witness marks, popped the slide stop and slid off the top unit. They got the magazine, slide, slide stop, recoil spring and barrel, which meant the ammunition and virtually all of the metal parts, and I kept the frame, which is almost entirely plastic with a few minor metal parts in it. I had the part with a serial number, so they didn't actually have a gun, legally, and I didn't have enough metal on me to speak of, so I was considered harmless, or so they figured when they finally got beyond being utterly puzzled.

Having Detective Jackson urging them to let me through probably helped, too. The Hideaway knives I simply stacked in the little basket and let them hold those with the slide and such until I came back. I left them the computer bag, too. It was just easier and quicker than having them inspect it and then let me carry it. Not only did I have my hands full already, but I had other things on my mind than anything as unimportant at the moment as my laptop, since I was quite satisfied that nobody was going to break the encryption I had on it without a ton of work. I also figured if it weren't safe with several deputies watching it, where would it be?

They weren't exactly happy about it all, but they couldn't find any really compelling reason to stop me now. Detective Jackson simply seemed very amused by the whole routine. He had it easy. Just the flash of a badge and they let him pass without worrying about the buzzing of the metal detector.

Neither he nor the uniforms would crash the courtroom. Well, they had to work here, I didn't. Detective Jackson and I consulted briefly. He said he wouldn't do it himself, but he'd certainly follow me in if I went and he'd stay if I needed him to corroborate what Kendra had said. Whatever works.

Kendra had apparently begun to figure out how much trouble she was getting herself into, since she was now reduced, mostly, to muttering. Nothing really comprehensible, but after listening to her up in Eloy, that was simply a relief. I grabbed her waistband and just took her from the uniforms. I could say they were surprised, but that seemed like a serious understatement. Dumbfounded would likely be more accurate. Bending her over with my other hand on her collar, I leaned down and said to her quietly, "You're just a wuss. You're nothing but a weakling and a pussy. You couldn't kill a fly."

Then, putting all of my strength behind it, I used Kendra's head to push open the double doors, quite sharply, and shoved her bodily into the courtroom, which fell silent at our entrance. She sprawled inside on the aisle floor, and the only words spoken after we stepped in were hers: "You bitch! I'll kill you the same way I did that no-good sonuvabitch cheating husband of mine!" Quite loud. She was seriously pissed, just as I'd hoped. The resulting silence in the courtroom lasted for several minutes.

Alec caught my eye and both winked and winced. I guess he saw the shiner. Luckily the eye hadn't swollen shut, although it was definitely puffy. I'd been feeling it, cautiously, on the drive from Eloy. What the hell, I was here in time. Cavalry to the rescue and all that. Nobody else moved. Finally the judge broke the silence, and he was clearly furious. "Just what is going on here? Who are you, and what the *hell* do you think you're doing in my courtroom?"

I met his eyes without blinking. "This, your honor, is the wife, well, *widow*, and murderer of Dr. Jon Frankton, which, I believe, is what this trial is all about." The worst he could do was hold me in contempt, right? I hoped that was all, but for clearing Becky, anything he might do to me would be fine just about now. "I believe the court heard her say so just a moment ago. There's also a photograph I took last night, which the defense has, of her wearing the unique one-of-a-kind custom necklace that Dr. Swan was wearing on the evening that Dr. Frankton was murdered and which was not found at the crime scene. The empty box for that necklace, which Dr. Swan was given a bit over a year ago, was found and inventoried in Dr. Swan's house by the crime scene investigators."

The judge harrumphed. I guess you'd call it that, anyway; that's how it sounded to me. "And you would be?"

"I'm Amy Trevethen, an investigator with A.M. Youngston and Associates, your honor." Goodness, was he about to come over the bench at me? I certainly hoped not. It would definitely be tacky, and likely unpleasant, at least for me. He was seriously offended by what was going on, that much was clear.

Then he settled back down. "Are you any relation to defense counsel Trevethen, here?"

"I'm his wife, your honor."

By now the entire gallery was quietly abuzz. I ignored them. "His wife." Was that a question? Seemed like just a comment, but I'd answer it anyway just in case.

"Yes, sir." I nodded as well, but the court reporter couldn't pick that up.

"And if I asked, would you also be Dr. Swan's sister? Don't answer that, I really don't care." I'd had my mouth open to respond, but at that I shut it again. There was no need to go into that. That was good for me, because I don't know to this day which way I'd have jumped on that one. Becky in command of her faculties would have backed me up either way. Now? God only knew. He went on. The judge, I mean, not God, although there's precious little distinction in a courtroom. "And you know when Dr. Swan got the necklace because …?"

"Because my husband and I gave it to her, your honor."

Another harrumph. Then the judge turned to the prosecutor. "Mr. Thorne."

"Your honor?"

"Did your office investigate this woman" — he gestured at Kendra — "for the murder?"

Now the prosecutor looked very unhappy. Well, I would have been, too, in his shoes. "Uh, well, no, your honor, we, we didn't. We believed we had the guilty party in Dr. Swan, here."

The judge's attention was riveted on the prosecutor. "Mr. Thorne, do you mean to tell me that you didn't do an exhaustive investigation of all reasonably possible guilty parties, specifically including the victim's wife?" His tone and body language strongly indicated that he was still very upset with somebody. I really hoped it wasn't me. Or at least not *just* me.

The prosecutor got to his feet. "Your honor, the defendant was found at the murder scene, covered in the victim's blood, and all she could offer as an alibi was the claim that she'd been unconscious and had no idea what had happened from the time the two of them arrived at her house until she woke up, she claimed, several hours after midnight with the victim dead on her bed."

The judge's complexion was growing steadily more florid. "You're not answering my question, Mr. Thorne. I specifically asked whether you were telling me that you and your office failed to exhaustively investigate any and all of the possible guilty parties, specifically to include this … woman." He again gestured towards Kendra where she lay.

Kendra had finally quit struggling, and she'd shut up again. It seemed as though she might really have begun to figure out how deep a hole she was in and decided to quit digging. Damn good idea on her part, if more than a bit too late. Well, too late for her.

I took a moment to look around while the prosecutor took the heat. Lissa McHugh was sitting just outside the bar, immediately behind the defense table. No other familiar faces beyond the three at the defense table, and most of the gallery looked like press of some kind or other. Probably were, with any remaining openings filled by whoever from the public could get in. Most trials have few if any people in the gallery, but when the press wants in, they fill it up pretty well. This was a juicy and very public murder case, and one way or another, the gallery was standing room only.

The prosecutor choked a bit. "Um, no, your honor, we didn't. I — I guess I'd say we were in error."

Alec and John had both gotten to their feet. John spoke first. "Your honor, we'd again move for the immediate dismissal of all charges against Dr. Swan."

The judge turned to them. "Sit down, both of you, shut up and wait your turn." Both of them did as they were told. I just stood there with Kendra on her side, lying on the floor at my feet. Nobody else moved. The judge showed a bit of a smile. It wasn't a pleasant smile; it reminded me more of a predator about to pounce. "Well, Mr. Thorne, what *do* you say now?"

Thorne hung his head for several seconds, but the judge waited him out. "Your honor, this really doesn't change anything. Dr. Swan still has no reasonable explanation for the time period during which the murder occurred ..." — Alec and John both stood again, Alec with his notebook open in his hands and John with his mouth open to speak. The judge didn't say anything to them, he just waved them back into their seats.

"Mr. Thorne, you are *seriously* trying my patience. I have here" — he held up some major paperwork — a defense motion to dismiss, and one of their exhibits to that

motion is the result of the toxicology screen your office —
your office! — conducted on the defendant. It shows traces
of anesthetic in her system, several hours after the murder.
Are you disagreeing with your own evidence?"

That sent the prosecutor scurrying through his own
papers. I wanted to smile at Becky or at Alec, but I didn't
think it would be a good idea to call attention to myself at
this point. I stood there keeping my face as expressionless
as I could manage.

"Your honor, there are several ways that Dr. Swan
could have gotten that anesthetic into her system. She could
have gassed herself" — the judge stopped him in the
middle of his sentence.

"Mr. Thorne, did your office find any such
anesthetic or means of administering it in Dr. Swan's
residence?"

The prosecutor straightened up and faced the judge.
"No, your honor, we didn't."

The judge's face suggested that he felt quite a bit of
disgust with what he was hearing. He wasn't alone. "And is
it your contention that Dr. Swan gassed herself and then
managed to dispose of the gas as well as the means of
administering it before the deputies arrived in response to
her call?"

"Your honor, she had sufficient time after
awakening" — the judge waved him into silence.

"Mr. Thorne, your office also indicates in its own
reports, which defense experts agree with, that the assault
was almost certainly committed by a right-handed assailant,
as shown by blood spatter evidence at the scene. Yet your
own reports indicate that Dr. Swan is not right-handed,
isn't that correct?"

I think the prosecutor was beginning to sweat. I
would have been, in his position. Of course, I never would
have been in his position. "Uh, your honor …"

"Mr. Thorne, this defense motion to dismiss claims that you have failed to establish even a *prima facie* case for guilt, to the point that your case is so riddled with reasonable doubt that the only real question is why you arrested and charged Dr. Swan in the first place. And they have done so, *on every issue*, with *your own* reports and evidence. What evidence of their own that they offer merely bolsters what your evidence already states. Having looked over everything I can find in the file, I am strongly inclined to agree with them.

"Now, having *clearly* wasted my time on a case you cannot possibly win, you put me in the position of having the wife of defense counsel haul in the widow of the victim who screams out *in open court* that she killed her husband. The widow, I would add, that you never investigated for the murder. What have you got to say about that?"

Finally the prosecutor found his voice. "Uh, your honor, we'd, uh, we'd move to dismiss the charges against Dr. Swan and charge Mrs. Frankton, here, with the murder of her husband." He didn't sound happy *at all*. Couldn't blame him. Not for that, I mean. Of course, in his position, I wouldn't have been so dumb as to rule out the wife without a good investigation first, but he'd made his bed, let him lie in it.

"No, Mr. Thorne, I'm not going to let you get off that easily. Feel free to charge Mrs. Frankton. She's your problem, deal with her. Somewhere else. My first question to you is whether you mean to dismiss the charges against Dr. Swan with prejudice. You do, don't you?"

The prosecutor nodded; he still seemed a long way from happy. Like I've said, not my problem. The judge continued. "I'm going to let the record reflect that you have so moved. But I'm not really satisfied by letting you withdraw the charges you filed against Dr. Swan, not when you've taken this case as far as you have on as little supporting evidence as you've shown. Now that your motion is on the record, I'm instead going to grant the defense's motion to dismiss.

"I've gone through the evidence that the defense has offered with their motion. *Your* evidence, mind you. If there is one thing that stands out to me, it is that not only is there no possible way you could ever expect to win this case, but if the jury were by some miracle to come back with a guilty verdict, I'd have to overturn it, because there is *not one scintilla of evidence* that I can find to support your case." He dropped the motion on the bench, and the sound echoed through the courtroom.

"You allege no motive that I can see for which you offer any evidence beyond naked supposition. There is nothing other than simple ownership of the knife to tie the murder weapons to the defendant. I presume you were intending to try to convince the jury that Dr. Swan wore gloves while killing the victim in her own bedroom, with her own kitchen knife, and then left the weapons in plain sight. Is that right? Good luck.

"You have evidence which specifically supports the defendant's account and not only do you ignore it, you offer no reasonable explanation to counter it. You have evidence which specifically suggests that someone other than the defendant committed this crime and yet you failed to investigate anyone who even simply fitted the evidence to the extent of being right-handed. As you yourself are, I note." Thorne had the grace to color at that one.

"I have better things to do with my time. *This court* has better things to do with the time." The people in the gallery, all of the media, anyway, were all scribbling like mad. Yep, that was the rolled-up newspaper with the iron pipe inside. Thorne's problem, not ours.

The judge turned his attention to Alec and John, who got to their feet once more, if not quite as quickly as before. He said nothing at first, until Alec took Becky's elbow and gently got her to stand. "Dr. Swan, I am, as I indicated, dismissing all charges against you. With prejudice. That means that you cannot be charged again, no matter what they may find in the future. Do not cause me to regret that decision. Under these ... extreme circumstances, I rather wish I could offer you some sort of apology, but that is beyond my power. As soon as the bailiffs are done with you, though, you will be free to go."

Everybody at and behind the defense table was excited, shaking hands and clapping each other on the back — except Becky. She just continued to stand there, motionless. I saw, and I hurt for her. So bad.

I had just taken a step towards her when the judge called my name. "Mrs. Trevethen!"

I turned back to face the bench. "Your honor?" Now what?

"Mrs. Trevethen, and you too, Mr. Trevethen and Mr. Tolliver, understand this. And remember it well. This is a one-time deal for you. Perry Mason does not practice in this court, and will not *ever* practice in my courtroom. Is that understood? If any of you pulls a stunt like this *ever* again in my court, you're going to be in the county jail contemplating 'contempt of court' for a long, *long* time. *Ever!* Understand me?"

Three voices almost as one: "Oh, yes, your honor. We understand." Then he adjourned the court.

The bailiff, with his attention on Kendra, was caught by surprise, so he was a bit late with "All rise!" as the judge swept off the bench. The gallery was ready to descend into pandemonium. I really hadn't been prepared for the number of press present, I guess. I should have been, given the publicity that this case had garnered already, but one way or another, I wasn't. Publicity had been the last thing on my mind, so let's not even go there. Just so they didn't sniff out the Family, that's all I ask.

Their focus wasn't really on me, or anything to do with me other than with my last-minute entrance and the attendant drama, anyway. I guess it was sort of Perry Mason-ish after all, huh? Erle Stanley Gardner, wherever you are, eat your heart out.

Then the bailiff came for Becky, saying that they had to process her out. It would take another two hours or so, but he told us where we could meet her and just when. She simply went with him, never looking at us and still showing absolutely no emotion at all. God, what would it take to give her some life back?

A couple of uniforms came to take charge of Kendra. Tolliver, all business now that his part was done, just stuck out his hand. "I'll be on my way, then. It's been a pleasure." That was to Alec. He turned to me. "I told you that you were the person she needed. Congratulations." I took his hand. At this particular moment, he couldn't rub me the wrong way any more. I was too thrilled to have actually cleared Becky.

Then Tolliver added one last comment. He dropped his voice, pulled my hand towards himself and leaned in close to me. "And *Ms. Youngston* — best of luck in everything. You seem to have quite a bit of luck, but if my wishing can add any, believe me, you are welcome to it and more for all you can get. I'm delighted with the job you do, both as an investigator and in your other … ah … work." I just kept shaking his hand numbly while he said that. Just like at the airport, it was just about the last thing I would have expected to hear.

Then he disengaged and picked up his litigation case. I think he left. I guess he did; I haven't seen him since. I turned to Alec and hurled myself into his arms. Pretty hard, when you figure I started from no more than about eighteen inches away, and I'm solid. He actually staggered a little. Several reporters were thrusting microphones at us, which we ignored. I noticed, barely, a number of flashes going off. We'd probably wind up on the front page of the Daily Star tomorrow. Oh, well, who gives a shit?

When we finally broke our clinch, Tolliver was long gone. Alec and I really wanted to shy away from the cacophony of questions being fired at us, but after what felt like several minutes, Alec just held up his hand. When everybody clustering around finally fell silent, he said, "We won't answer any of your questions at this time. We would just like to say that we are very, *very* pleased to see justice finally done here and to see an innocent person be turned loose from the jaws of the legal system, freed from the accusation of a horrible crime of which she was another victim, not a perpetrator. That's all. Thank you all very much." It didn't stop the questions, but we ignored them as we left. Eventually even the hardiest gave up.

While he'd been talking, I'd been throwing papers from the defense table into his case any which way. We then made our way through the reporters and walked out of the courtroom. "Coffee," I said. "I need to talk to you about some very important things, and you just know that neither one of us can make a move without coffee." Alec just smiled. Little did he know what was coming.

Outside after retrieving, reassembling, reholstering and resheathing my weapons and reclaiming my laptop, I wasn't surprised to see the car being hooked up by a wrecker. I thought about protesting, but I finally figured I'd just get it out of hock and turn it back in to the rental company in the morning. Or, given all of the damage Kendra had done to it, maybe I'd just pay the rental company for it and forget about it. At the moment, I really didn't give a shit. It was just money, it's going on my bill in any event, and either way would be easier than doing something now. I made a mental note of which tow company was hauling it off. Just in case.

Chapter 29

We found a coffee shop fairly quickly, not too far away, where we could sit well off by ourselves. Yes, both Alec and I are quite private by nature, even though for somewhat different reasons originally, but this discussion was going to be one I *really* didn't want to have overheard. I'd rather not even have it, truth be told. I just had no other choice in the matter, or so I was still utterly certain. Not if I were going to be true to myself, to my image of myself, to Becky and to everything I'd been telling myself to keep me going for the last three months.

I'd been gaming it out in my head ever since the other night, and now it was time to begin to put my plan into action. I dropped into my chair fairly heavily. "God, but I'm glad *that's* over."

Alec looked at me with some concern. "Care to tell me about the black eye?"

I smiled a bit wanly. "No biggie, really. It probably looks a bit worse than it really is. Kendra … took exception to some of the things I've been doing. She tried calling Consolidated Bolt about me, and when they denied knowing who I was or having any sales people in Phoenix, she figured out I was a fraud. She waylaid me at one of those truck stops in Eloy and came after me in the parking lot with a piece of iron pipe, to tell you the truth. It got a bit exciting for a while, but I managed." I didn't feel any need to replay the entire fight for him at the moment, so I changed the subject. One of my better talents.

I wasn't sure I wanted to do this. Hell, I *knew* I didn't want to. It almost made my guts knot up just to think about it. No, scratch 'almost.' The only problem was that they knotted up even worse when I considered the alternatives. I'd already gone over this with myself, and I felt — still feel — that as much as I didn't want to do it, I had absolutely no other choice whatsoever.

There were two things I definitely could not do, as I saw it. The first was to leave things to go as they would while I did nothing, because they would go *way* south, left to their own devices. The second thing I couldn't do was spring it all on Alec without some sort of warning, or at least some softening up. Those were the only alternatives I saw. If I was missing any, so what? I had to work with what I could figure out. What I *had* figured out. "What sort of shape do you think Becky's going to be in when we pick her up?"

Alec sipped his coffee and said nothing for almost a minute. "Frankly, not good. I've barely seen any bit of life in her eyes since the last time we all had dinner together. What little I did see was only the time when she told me she'd refuse to be medicated. Well, that and the time the prison shrink was suggesting she take the meds. Other than those, nothing. Not a single bit of animation whatsoever, including in court today, even after the charges were dismissed."

I hadn't seen any then, either. I smiled faintly. Not in any way how I felt, but I needed to set something up here. Just like the other night, I couldn't have begun to say where it had come from, but even with as much thought as I'd been giving it then and since, I still hadn't reached any other conclusion about where it was probably going, and God knows I'd been looking. I was afraid that I was right. I wanted to be wrong. I desperately wanted to find another way. The closer I got to actually having what I'd thought out come to pass, the more I hurt. My poor aching guts were in knots. I did *not* want to do this, but I still felt that I had no other choice.

I was also afraid I'd shock dear Alec out of his socks if I just laid it on him cold, and given my own … misgivings, now there's a nice, understated word for it, I figured that I had to do it just so. I would. 'There is no try. Do. Or do not.' "I didn't think you were looking at her eyes. At least when we were heading out to go swimming, I thought you were looking at something else of hers."

That got me a sharp look. "You're trying to steer this conversation somewhere." Well, yeah, I was. I'd sorta hoped it would take a bit longer for him to figure it out, but I guess that wasn't all that subtle, was it? Subtlety, at least when I'm in my own persona, isn't really my strongest suit. I mean, I knew that he liked looking at her (and I certainly don't blame him for that), but we didn't need to discuss it, so that comment was probably a bit of a giveaway.

So I went with my strong suit and changed the subject again. "What do you know about suicide watch?" I asked him.

He still had his eyes pinned on me. He knows me too well. Mostly I like it, but once in a while I'd like to be able to maneuver him, just a bit, without his being aware of it. Not today, apparently. I also wish I didn't feel that I had to do this. To either of us. "Not a hell of a lot. I mean, I know what it implies, but I don't know the mechanics of it, if that's what you're talking about."

"Yes, that's exactly what I mean. I've had a bit too much time on my hands the last bunch of weeks, and one of the things I did was look it up on the internet." He snorted. Well, yeah, there was a lot of information on the net, and some of it was even accurate. "And then I called Marilyn and checked what I found with her. What I had read was accurate, and it's … well, it's horrible. And yes, love, I am using that word most advisedly. There are several levels of it, and from what you told me, thanks to that jackass prison psychiatrist, Becky was on the highest watch level. Do you know what it is? That's being kept naked in a bare cell, without even a toilet. Go on the floor, because it's the only choice. Even at some of the lesser levels, suicide watch is so … well, the word that keeps coming up in the accounts is 'dehumanizing,' that it seems to me that it would almost be kinder to let people kill themselves rather than subject them to that."

He mused for a moment. I always know how hard he's thinking when his lips turn in. "Okay, so it's horrible. I can't argue; I don't know enough about it, although the idea of our Becky being confined naked in a bare cell like that kind of turns my stomach. Makes me want to take her in my arms and make it all go away. But you still aren't telling me where you're trying to go with all of this."

Of course I'm not, dear. I've got to take some time to do it right and set you up for everything. Although that 'our Becky' suggested he might not be quite as hard to bring around as I'd feared. But damn all lawyers' single-mindedness, I thought, with a smile to myself. I took a deep breath. In the tighter-than-usual t-shirt and padded major-uplift bra I was still wearing, Laura's bra, it was significantly more noticeable than usual. His eyes flicked just where you'd expect. Men can be so pliable. What was it somebody once said? The primary biological function of women's boobs was to make men stupid? I knew Alec. I didn't think I could depend on quite that effect. But keeping his mind where I wanted it, or at least away from where I *didn't* want it, yet, likely couldn't hurt. I wish I could have been diverted so easily. I was still in a horrid turmoil over the whole thing, and I was probably going to stay that way for a while. Damn!

"She's been in absolutely terrible shape." He nodded. "Being on suicide watch for two weeks, if it's done anything, has made it even worse." Still nodding. "You've seen her house now, after we've had it cleaned up. Unless she uses her guestroom, she can't exactly go back there to sleep tonight. She's been in jail for … what, eleven weeks or so? Call it three months, close enough. Frankly, I think that after going through the experience of having her lover murdered there in her own bedroom while she was unconscious, waking up to the body on her bed, covered in his blood, especially given how brutally and messily he was killed, and then being arrested, held and at least going through the start of a trial for the murder, I don't think she's going to want to be alone tonight anyway." He stopped nodding; the sharp look was back. Okay, let's see if I can break this down any further. "Look. She's been alone, all alone, except for you and, from time to time, me, but just on TV, ever since she was arrested."

Now he looked just a bit puzzled. Good. I hope. At least he's thinking. "Not hardly. I mean, there've been jailers, probably matrons or whatever they call them, the county attorney has tried to question her, she was evaluated by the prison psychiatrist — she's had plenty of human contact since then."

"Huh uh. They don't count. For her, they *can't*. They were all the enemy, all simply part of the horrible experience she was going through. That doesn't exactly make them even human, from her standpoint. The only people she always had that she knew and trusted were us. You know she's like me; she doesn't completely trust or open up to anyone outside of the three of us. Sure, Marilyn came once, and Daddy and Aunt Lori came a couple of times, when they could. But on a day-to-day basis, you were it, and I was the only other constant. Do you see it?"

Now he was nodding again. Use some of that gentle fishing sort of ability you use in your investigations, girl. You can do it. You know where you want to go, but you have to lead him, you can't drag him. Well, not exactly. You know where you *need* to go. You don't even know that you really want to, you just know that you have to. No, even that's not correct. You really, *really* don't want to go there, given a choice. You're just utterly certain that there *is* no other choice. This is a unique situation and a totally unique set of circumstances, so maybe, just maybe, a unique solution is going to be needed. Is going to *work*. And something, *anything*, that works, right now, is vital.

The only thing that matters, in fact, because saving Becky and helping her find her way out of her horrible depression, the hell she's found in her own mind, is the most important thing you have to do in the entire world. The *only* thing, right now, that you have to do, because if you can't do it, nothing else matters. So now you have to lead him along to the same place. Ever so gently. Lay the bait in front of him and s-l-o-w-l-y pull it in. You can do it. "She's been in really, really bad shape. You've seen her, you've been with her. I don't think she's going to snap out of it simply because they turn her loose."

"No, probably not." Still nodding. Maybe I should have been a salesman. Yeah, right. Selling threaded fasteners all over the west. God save me.

"She's not going to want to be alone at her house."

"I'd say almost certainly not, when you put it like that. And definitely not with the way her bedroom is right now."

"So …" I drew some rings on the tabletop with my fingertip. "What would you say to her staying with us?"

He relaxed. Clearly he didn't see where I was headed with this. How could he? I barely could myself, even after my analysis the other night, and it was, I thought, still just a possibility, not a certainty. Might not work even so. God, how I hoped it didn't work out that way. But I was dead certain to my core that it would work out exactly that way, at least in the end. I was just as certain that it *had* to go that way or else it would wind up being a total disaster. Those were the only alternatives I could find. "Oh, of course. She can have the pull-out. No problem at all."

I kept drawing rings and didn't meet his gaze. "What if she needed to stay with us for a long time?"

He was drinking, but he stopped at that and held still for a moment. I could almost see wheels turning. I hoped I didn't completely strip his gears when I finally got it all out there for him. "Um, well, it'll be tight as long as we're in that house, but ... sure. Whatever she needs. She's been awfully close to us for as long as we've been together here in Tucson, she's probably the best friend either of us has at this point and she's been your best friend all your life. I can move my study across the alley into the office and we can set that room up as a bedroom for her. However long she needs."

Now I looked up at him, until I could see his eyes, but just barely. Softly: "The rest of her life, even?"

That rocked him back. He clearly hadn't considered it that far, which made it utterly certain he hadn't considered the rest of the way I could see this potentially going. Probably going. Likely going. Or oh-shit-oh-dear-it's-going. I wasn't completely sure I really wanted it, deep down, but I just knew, somehow, where it would likely — make that almost certainly — lead and how it needed to end up if it did.

Did I just say I wasn't completely sure I wanted it? Hell, no, I didn't want it! I didn't want to have anything to do with it! Who in their right mind would? But Becky wasn't *in* her right mind now, and not having anything to do with it included letting things go where they certainly would if I turned it down. In Becky's current condition, that would absolutely be worse. I *hate* feeling trapped like this. Her needs are my needs. My new mantra. What the hell, at least it's better than 'I'm Laura,' three times over.

Becky, in her professional persona, would have said that this was a decision that needed to be made from strength, not weakness. At this point, I was all but certain she had no strength left to tap into. As her protector, I had to have the strength for both of us. It was a self-appointed position, yeah, but that had happened many, many years ago, and like I'd told Daddy, I'd never completely given up the job, at least in my own mind. I don't know *how* to give it up.

Did I have that strength? If I did, was I doing this from my own strength? I do and I *would*. Weakness would be letting things go to hell on their own. They still might, no matter what I did, but if they were going to go there, I'd be trying to steer us away from the abyss for all I was worth, all the way as we went. When Alec's lips relaxed and turned back out, he was nodding again. "Yeah, I guess so. The rest of her life, if that's what she needs."

I reached for his other hand. I loved this man so, but I still feared I was going to shock him out of his socks when I got all of this out. He squeezed my hand in return. After a minute or so like that, I asked, even more softly, "What if she needs more than that?"

He stopped and let go of my hand. The sharp look was back once again. "Just what do you mean by that?"

I took another deep breath. I was just a bit hunched over this time; I wasn't trying to take advantage of whatever frontage I have. I just … oh, *God*, I was miserable. *So* miserable. I had to go on, though, since the alternatives were worse, and I couldn't just leave it. I had to have everything settled between us when we went to get her. *Strength, girl*, I repeated to myself. Several times. It helped. Not a lot. "You know she and I used to sleep together as kids, right? Even after that, for comfort, like when we moved in here together? What if she needs to sleep with us now, like that? What if we need to cuddle with her and soothe her?"

Now his look was truly piercing. "You mean, like just cuddle and *sleep*? In the same bed?"

I met his eyes without blinking. "Yes. Just cuddle and sleep." One baby step at a time. Absolutely cannot rush this one.

"Um. Hm. It's going to throw a real monkey wrench in between the two of us, you realize." He was

smiling, not broadly. But I hoped it was a good sign. And boy-o-boy, was he right about the monkey wrench.
Speaking of wrenches, this was still a major wrench for me. It was going to get worse before it got better. If it ever did. Maybe this was all she'd need. I can hope, can't I? Yeah, right.

"Isn't she worth it?"

"Well, yes, she is. But…"

Should I leave it there? At least for a while? I tried the last of my coffee, but it was cool by now. Good. An excuse to temporize just a bit. I stood up. "I need a refill. Want one? No? Back in a jif."

My mind was moving a lot faster than my feet, although the feet weren't moving in circles the way my mind was. It might not come to this. Maybe I was barking up the wrong tree. And all of the power I now had as the CEO wasn't going to do a damn thing to help here. I strongly felt, though — *somehow* — that I not only knew where this was going to go, but where this *had* to go, at least if it went anywhere at all. Maybe, more accurately, where I had to *make* it go, or keep it going if it went in that direction at all, until it stopped of its own accord. Becky's accord.

The only alternatives I saw were disastrous, so if I had anything to do with it at all, this was it. Her needs are my needs. I couldn't simply spring this on the dearest person in my life. Even for the sake of the other dearest person in my life. Not without a great deal of care — and of anguish, for me. Anguish, hell. What's the word for the sort of extreme misery I felt? I'm not sure there's such a word in the English language. I kept clinging to the idea that I could be, had to be, strong for everybody. Well, for Becky, anyway. Alec could probably manage to find his own strength, if it came to that. I had faith in him. Thank God. There's only so much I can carry by myself, and this is pretty close to my limit. Awfully close.

When I got back to the table, I set the cup down and stroked his hand for a couple of moments. Like I said, he knows me too well. "You're not done with this, are you?" Well, he didn't look upset. Not yet, anyway. He also didn't pull his hand away. If I had to characterize his expression right now, 'slightly bemused' was probably the most accurate. Wait until he's heard it all. At that moment, for the first time, the possibility of losing Alec over this whole thing flashed into my consciousness. With a major explosion of fear. Make that utter terror. Was there going to be a successful way through all of this? For any of us? Or was I simply dooming all of us to the most incredible pain?

I was doing this in the first place because I couldn't choose between him and Becky, but if that became the choice thrust upon me, then there would be nothing but pain as far as I could see, either way. Misery, my ass. Major terror. The most wretched pain and horror I could imagine. More. But, for whatever little comfort it offered me, and it was damn little, at least if it cost me Alec, he would just be walking away. If the cost were Becky, she'd have taken her own life, and that would absolutely be worse.

Wouldn't it? Of course it would! He might come back. *Could* come back. Becky … no. You don't come back from Rainbow Bridge.

"No, I'm not really done, I guess." Back to drawing rings, interspersed with drinking coffee. My bladder wouldn't take a lot more of this abuse before it started sounding the alert, but this had to be done and it had to be done just so. "What if she … what if she needed you?" I held up my hand as his mouth opened. "I mean, it's not just sex. Think of it, at least for her, as … oh, as an affirmation of her freedom. An affirmation of *life*, for her. Something she desperately *needs*, and at least as important, something she trusts us enough to ask us for. Like I said, we're the only people she really, truly trusts."

His mouth shut again. This time I didn't try to fill the sound void; I just waited for him. I really, *really* didn't want to go here. This, perhaps, was what was really knotting my guts up. It was definitely a major part of it. Alec and I had such a wonderful sex life, now, and here I was possibly risking it all, in fact, even possibly our entire life together, on what amounted to a hunch. My stomach burned. I waited. I prayed for an antacid. My prayer went unanswered. I waited.

Oh, my, what an interesting study his facial expressions made. How I could be so outwardly calm in proposing such a thing was, at some level, sort of amazing to me as well, especially considering the level of turmoil I felt inside. Finally he just looked at me. "Is that what you want? I mean, you're an active partner here. I realize that a … a man's arousal has no conscience, but *I* sure as hell do, and if this were going to happen, I'd have to be awfully concerned about how you'd react, too. First and foremost, in fact. Yes, I love her dearly. But that's … God, but you're asking a whole hell of a lot. You *are* asking that, aren't you?"

He paused for a moment. "Besides, if we agree to this between us, neither you nor I have any idea how we'll feel about *us* once we head down this path."

Well, that was certainly a reasonable response. Fairly honest, too. "I know I am, and I'm trying very hard to be as honest as I can be with you, too. I'm not entirely certain how I'd react inside. Well, not entirely, but I expect I'd hurt, badly. At the same time, I know that her pain hurts me horribly, too. If anything happened to her, a serious part of me would die along with her, just as if something happened to you. *Just as if.* You deserve me whole, not in pieces. Oh, you dear man. I'm … I don't know exactly how to say this. I …"

He reached for my hand, held it very gently. "Just lay it all out. Quit beating around the bush, stop trying to set me up or take these incremental little steps to wherever you're going. Put it all out for me. I'll sit here and listen to whatever you say, and I'll give it whatever fair and honest consideration I possibly can. No matter what it is. I'm beginning to get a … maybe a glimmer of a ghost of an idea of where you're heading, possibly, but I want to hear it from you. I might be wrong. I rather hope I am, but just tell me. All of it."

He was looking directly into my eyes, trying to project to me all of the calm and confidence that I wish I could feel on my own right about now. Could he sense the degree of turmoil I was in? I hoped not; it would make him hurt, and I didn't want that. Never that.

"Okay." Two or three deep breaths. The hell with what my chest was doing; this was to keep me calm and collected, and that wasn't easy. Wasn't really working at all, to tell the truth. Finally everything came out in a rush.

"If there's one thing I've realized over the past couple of months, it's that she's … just as important to me as you are. *Just as important.* I'd be just as hurt, just as lost if something happened to her as I would be if something happened to you. I … I'm not sure I could stand it if I lost her because I didn't do something I could have done. *Should* have done. It's that whole kid sister/protector, closer-than-sister thing all over again. Well, partly.

"I mean, yeah, she might snap back from this on her own. Pigs might fly, too. But what I can see as a very likely outcome, probably the *most* likely outcome, of this whole experience is her being so lonely, so needy, so *desperate*, that she needs the — oh, call it whatever you like, but she could very well need not just to sleep with someone for the companionship she's been without for so long, but actually need sex, just for the same sort of reason. Now that she's lost Frankton, she has nobody else to turn to, nowhere else to go. As I see it, if she does come to us, to you, for it, it won't be because *we* can't trust *her*, but because she feels she *can* trust *us*. Both of us." Tears were running down my cheeks. Alec reached across the table and gently wiped them away.

"And you want to know if I'm willing to provide it."

"Well, sort of."

"So you're still not laying it all out. C'mon, give." His voice was gentle, and he was smiling. Sort of. I guess that's a good sign. I hope.

Several more deep breaths. The tears were still flowing. Would this ever be easy? "Okay. No, I don't want to share you with just anyone. I wouldn't even be willing to share you with a good friend, if I had such a friend. But this isn't just a good friend, this is *Becky!* I'm *terrified* by the possibility of losing her, just as terrified as I am of the possibility of losing you."

I paused for a deep breath. It didn't help. "I know this sounds more like I'm still being a schoolgirl than the CEO, but dammit, it's *true!* Nothing in the world terrifies me like the possibility of losing her. You. *Either* of you, because you're both ... I've internalized both of you. Whatever armor I can present to the world to keep myself tough, you're both inside it. All the way inside. That's why I'm willing to do this. Any of this. It's the only reason, but jeez, what a reason! So if she ... needs like that ..." I ignored the tears. "I mean, her needs are my needs. I keep coming back to that."

"Yeah, I've heard you say it often enough. Even in your sleep, once or twice. Well, just for the record, I'd rather not be shared, either. I'm not into that sort of thing, and you are very definitely all the woman I want or need. Ever, as long as we both shall live. I think those were the words, weren't they?" Oh, God, what a wonderful man. What have I ever done to deserve him? Why on earth would I risk losing him by doing this to him?

"To be honest, I've never considered such a thing in my life. Well, my adult life. I was a teenager once, I admit. But you're right that she is very dear to both of us, and very special, and all of that. If she needs that, and if you really need me to give it to her … shit. I don't want to, you know. Hurting you like that, and you've already admitted that it would, is not something I'm even sure I can do, at least like that. But just for the record, if I decide to do it, can I at least put up a bit of resistance, or do I have to jump her the moment she makes a move in my direction?"

I smiled through the tears. "Of course you can resist. It'd probably look suspicious if you just gave in willy-nilly."

"Apt choice of words." His tone was quite dry.

What do you know? I can still blush. Then I paused. There was still one piece more, and he deserved to hear all of it. He'd asked for it. The knot in my guts twisted a bit tighter. Would this blow the whole thing? Was I risking my own future here? As well as his? And hers? "Oh, hell. You asked for everything." I paused. He simply watched me. Then, very softly, "Would you be willing to marry her?"

I thought his eyebrows were going to climb into his hairline. "This is more of that terror, isn't it? Well, I'm not giving you up. Not even for Becky, precious as she is to both of us. No way, no how, not ever. That's final."

Oh, what a dear, dear loving man! To think that I had held him at arm's length for years because I was scared. Well, terrified. Idiot! Me, I mean, not Alec. I reached for his hand. He didn't, quite, pull it away. "Not to lose me, dearest one. *Never* to lose me." His arm and hand relaxed. "That is *exactly* the choice I couldn't make — the one choice I could *never* make. To save one of you, *either* of you, at the cost of the other. That's what I'm trying to avoid, and that's exactly the sort of terror I'm talking about. What I'm asking is whether … would you be willing to …

to bring her *into* our marriage? The three of us, together? To save all of us?"

Now his brow furrowed and his lips turned in. Major thought on that. But his hand didn't pull away or even twitch that way, which was comforting. Well, he'd said to spill all of it. Now I had. Time to wait, because I had absolutely nothing more to say here.

Finally he spoke. The first thing he said was, "Is that *everything*? You've now given me everything you've been trying to lay out so ... carefully?" I looked him square in the eyes and nodded, slowly. It really was. My gut relaxed, if only fractionally. My eyes were brimming, but there didn't seem to be any more actual tears coming at the moment.

"Well, that's ... that's a different sort of thought. Radically different." He paused some more. "You think it's going to be necessary?" I shrugged. "But you think it might be." I nodded. "How would this work? Two of us in the bedroom, one on the pullout? What do you have in mind for this ... this ... *arrangement*?"

I squeezed his hand some more. Did I feel an answering squeeze, just slightly? Or not? "Never, Alec. If we were to do this, it would be, it would *have* to be, because she had been so traumatized by all of this that she couldn't be alone. Couldn't be *left* alone. We would be doing this because she could not *handle* being pushed away and left alone, which is exactly what sending her away for that would be. Which would, or at least could, mean all of us in one room. In one bed. Together."

He looked, well, dubious. "And sex, all in one room, all in one bed, together? How would *that* work?"

He had me there, but I was in too deep to back out now. Not holding anything back was at least letting my anxieties and worries subside just a bit. A bit. The knots in my gut loosened, just a tad more. The tears were flowing again, but I continued to ignore them. I shrugged.

"Honestly, I don't know. I guess … I guess we'd let it sort itself out. I think we'd have to, because we'd have no other choice. But if we're all in this together, and we all want to be, then I think we can … can manage to work it out somehow between us."

I sighed. "Oh, Alec, I don't want to lose you. I don't want to lose what you and I have together. It's *so* special, and you mean so *much* to me. But I don't want to lose *her*, either. She means too much to me, too, and I've worked much too hard getting her cleared to let her go now, can't you see that? And you have, too."

Another pause. "Shit! There's that schoolgirl talk again. I really need to stop it. But the real question is that if she's that needy, that desperate, do you see any other way? I don't want this. I *really* don't want this. But as much as I don't want it, I'm still more worried about her, *for* her, and what losing her would do to me. To both of us, really, because if it happens to me, it's going to impact *us*, and badly. It's a really difficult choice for me. Damn near impossible, in fact. But I think I'm making the right one here. Hard as it is, and God, is it ever. I just don't see any other way. She hasn't got anyone else, and she's almost certainly going to be needier than she ever has been before. She just doesn't have any alternative. Frankly, at this point, neither do I."

Alec sat there in silence for several minutes, just staring off into the distance. Finally he looked at me again. "The honest truth is — my first impression, anyway — that I think it would make me feel used." I had my mouth open, but he held up his hand to stop me. "I also think it would be using you, too. Using both of us and using our relationship as well. Is that the way we want to work it?"

He had me there. Dammit, it *was* using us. He was right about that. How do I balance that one? Slowly I nodded. "You're right, it *would* be using us. My biggest issue is that I still keep coming back to the point that I can't afford to risk losing her by turning her away. Not just having her leave, but killing herself, because at this point I think she would, and that's utterly unbearable to me. Do you have any suggestions? For myself, I'm willing to let myself be used, for that. Only that, and only *her*, but — oh, hell, for me, it keeps coming back to 'this is *Becky*.' But I can't commit you to that."

It was a good minute before he responded. "It's going to depend on just what she needs. If she's living in the house with us, even if she's sleeping on the pull-out, it's going to be crowded. Longer-term, like I said, we can certainly move the study into the office and give her that room. No problem there. If she wants to sleep with us, just sleep and cuddle, it's going to be worse, or at least more complicated. As I said, it's going to throw a real monkey wrench in between us. Nothing we can't live with, though, I expect, at least for a while, given that particular alternative. I suppose my biggest question, if we go as far as you're talking about, would be, 'who's running this relationship?' All of the relationships here?"

A wry smile from me. "You would have to ask something like that, wouldn't you? I … I guess … is that me doing it? Or letting her do it? Either way … shit. I cannot *handle* the idea of losing her, and that's what I keep coming back to. Everything else is kind of secondary at the moment. I mean, I'm willing to do just about anything, short of giving you up, rather than risk that. And I'll even give up half of you to keep from losing her, if that's what it takes."

He began stroking my hand with his thumb. "Well, for starters, why don't we just see how it plays out tonight? None of this is so earth-shattering that we need to commit right now. There may not be any other way, but if we're going to do whatever she needs right now, then let's let her have some input before we commit to anything long-term, shall we? There may not be any other way, at least in the short term.

"But here's a question I haven't heard any answer to. Are relationships like that stable? I suspect they're not, unless you've got a horrid power discrepancy, like in those polygamous communities you hear about up on the Strip, and I don't see much of that here. I could be wrong about that, but I don't want to see you hurt, either, Amy. You're far too precious to me, too. I think I could probably manage it — if we were going to make it permanent. Or try. My greatest fear would be of getting into a relationship like that and having it poison all of the relationships. You with her, you with me, me with both of you and so on. How would we avoid that?"

Shit! I hadn't even considered that! I smiled at him through my remaining tears. "Damn realist." He grinned back. "Do I understand you? If we were able to make a permanent go of it, you'd be willing, but without some assurance of that, you're … reluctant?"

He shrugged. "Fair summation, in a nutshell, although reluctant might be a bit of an understatement. Some assurance is all; I know there are no promises and I'm not looking for that. I mean, I wouldn't be at all surprised if she comes to sleep with us tonight. Or even for some time. Our sex life may be kind of … lacking, for a while. Can you manage that? I suppose I can, for that sort of reason, and not resent it.

"But just like you don't want to put barriers in front of her, let's not push her where she may not need to go, either, okay? Oh, and one other question. If we're not in that sort of relationship, but she's living with us and sleeping with us, even just some of the time, what do we do when she walks in, um, on us? She might not ever do it, but I'd have to figure it'll probably happen sometime, if only by mistake. Maybe we can't predict her reaction, but you'd better give some thought to yours." He got a sour look on his face. "I think I can predict mine, unfortunately."

The tears were gone now. I sniffed and then blew my nose on one of the napkins. "I think the three of us could make a go of it together, and you're right, maybe it won't come to this. I really, *really* hope that we don't need to do this at all. Maybe we can help her pull herself together and we won't even have to go into this. But ... the idea of losing Becky, of all people, still scares and hurts me worse than anything else I can think of short of losing you. Truly, I'm not even certain that losing you would be worse. It might simply be just as bad, and both of them utterly horrible and unthinkable. Losing her because we turned her away, or shut her out — *that* would be utterly unbearable.

"Far worse than her walking in on us, although you're probably right about your reaction. Mine, well, if that happens to you, my reaction isn't going to be all that important, is it?" I gave him a sideways grin at that.

His voice was so soft it was almost a whisper. "No, it's probably not. I understand what you're saying. *Everything* you're saying. But let's just pull her in for an extended physical and psychic group hug and see what she needs, first, instead of trying to construct something that we don't know if any of us even wants or can keep. I also think it's time for us to be getting ready to go pick her up."

Chapter 30

We were both waiting for Becky when they let her out. When she finally appeared, she had what she would have called the 'flat affect of the terminally depressed.' She was so much worse than she had seemed while she was in jail, and she certainly hadn't looked very good then. I hadn't really looked at her in the courtroom, other than to note her complete and utter lack of reaction, even to being cleared of all charges. I'd been too busy paying attention elsewhere, most especially to the judge.

She now looked so emotionless, so utterly drained, so oblivious to what was happening around her that it made her professional poker face seem positively animated. She dragged her feet and walked as though she was almost lifeless. She probably was, at least emotionally. When she reached us, we gathered her in for a long group hug.

"I'm destroyed," she finally said. "My life, my home, my practice, my career … I've probably lost my office as well. I'm totally alone. I've got nothing left at all." Just the desperate sound, the tone of her voice was like one more knife in my gut; the utter desperation and desolation of her words were even worse. This was my very best friend, closer than any sister could ever have been to me. The best friend I still felt, in my own heart, that I was supposed to look out for and protect. As close to me as Alec, in fact. Yes, I'd been right about that. I just wanted to weep for her. But I couldn't, not now. If anyone deserved a good cry, it was her, and she had to do that for herself. I wouldn't take that away from her by crying, too. I couldn't. I loved her too much.

"No, you haven't lost everything," I told her. "It's all current. Alec and I have taken care of everything. Money is not an issue. It will *never* be an issue." Trust me, I'd see to that. Being the Family CEO would be good for something. "Your house has been cleaned up, we've had people in taking care of the yard and the pool, your mortgage and office rent are current, and Marilyn tells us there are even two or three of your patients who said they believed in you no matter what and would wait for you. And know that you're not alone and *never* will be. We're here for you. For *you*."

Somehow, I didn't really think that two or three patients were going to make her feel all that much better, given the patient load she'd had before all of this, but at least it was something more than the nothing she likely had been expecting. There might be more who'd come out of the woodwork now that she'd been cleared. Time would tell. Whatever we could do for her, we would. *Whatever*.

I was right; it didn't help much, if at all. She just stood there between us, tears flowing freely and her whole body shaking. I let Alec hold her, mostly, since her greater height would have caused some real problems in getting her face onto my shoulder compared to leaning on his chest and shoulder.

Finally I worked at breaking through to her. "Hey, even if you need to keep crying, and I wouldn't blame you a bit if you did because I'm sure you need to, you can do it somewhere else. We don't need to stand around here. C'mon, let's go. Let's get away from here. I'm sure Bruno and Sasha would like to see you, too." I pulled her gently towards the car.

We had Alec's car, since my rental had been towed away, but he'd have been driving in any event. I sat in the back seat with Becky, just holding her while she continued to cry. I hoped she was letting out all of the pent-up emotions she had kept bottled up inside her for so many weeks.

I was also certainly relieved that Alec and I had discussed everything to a significant degree in the time we had had before she was released from custody. We were actually in our driveway before the flow stopped. My t-shirt was soaked by now, not that it mattered, but eventually she did stop her tears. Or maybe she just ran out of water to make them from. Then it turned out that she had thought we were going straight to her house, so Alec backed out and we headed up into the foothills.

When we pulled into her driveway, she sat in the car with the door open for the longest time, simply looking at her house. Finally, with absolutely no enthusiasm whatsoever, she got out of the car and slowly walked to the front door. Alec had already unlocked it. Once inside, as we'd expected, she couldn't stand the idea of spending the night there. No surprise; what she'd gone through her last night there had been truly horrific, and being all alone in the house now would probably be impossible for her, stirring up horrible memories that could only have — *had* to have — festered inside her for all those weeks while her incarceration had left her without any interest or ability in resolving the turmoil they had produced.

Her master bedroom wasn't usable in any event. The three of us went into her bedroom to pick up whatever she needed, and even though I'd seen it since it had been cleaned, it now seemed somehow unbearable, with her standing there looking around at the wreckage.

Well, it wasn't wreckage now, it was just bare. I mean, like *bare*. The carpet and padding were completely gone, down to the concrete underneath. Gone too were the mattress, boxspring, bedspread, bedding and curtains. The bedframe stood in the middle of the room, the headboard was leaning up against the wall and could use refinishing. The nightstand and dresser needed it worse. The lamp on the nightstand looked a bit odd without a shade. Every bit of cloth that had been in the room was now gone. The walls and ceiling were a bit patchwork where they'd been scrubbed clean of blood, and repainting was going to be necessary, too. The flatwork on the walls was still there, but some of the frames showed evidence of serious cleaning and needed refinishing as well. The crime scene cleanup people had really done a number on the room.

The only thing that had completely escaped their clutches was the small silk Persian rug that Alec had managed to rescue from the investigators, and we'd had that professionally cleaned. They tell me that silk rugs are almost indestructible. I'd seen the rug both before and after the cleaning, and I had to admit that it was all but impossible to tell it was even the same rug. It now looked almost brand new again. Since it had been a gift to Becky from Uncle Jack, one of the last things he'd given her before his death, I also knew she'd eventually have been devastated again by losing it, had that happened.

At the moment, I still had it wrapped in plastic and stashed safely at our house. Becky was just standing there, shuddering, eyes mostly closed, while Alec dug around in her garage for her suitcases and garment bag. When she wasn't able to give us much coherent direction, we packed them ourselves. Every bit of underwear and such from the dresser, and then lightweight outfits from the hanging clothes until the suitcases and garment bag would barely close. We could always come back for more another time. It worked.

When he returned from putting them in the car and could take over being with her, I grabbed whatever I could from her bathroom and vanity in the way of makeup and such, since Alec had no idea whatsoever of what to take there. As I've said, I don't use the stuff myself to speak of, but Becky certainly does, and she'd need it to put herself back together, if we could only spark the interest. I knew enough, now, to know which things were the most vital to take, just barely, but the little makeup case was full when I was done.

I'd have to say she looked almost sad as Alec locked the front door behind her. That was understandable as well, although a significant improvement on how she'd been in her bedroom. Becky had been living in that house ever since she and I had both moved out of the office/house on Speedway, more than six, close to seven, years ago, now. She had so many good memories of her house. So did we, although she also had the one really horrible one that I expect more than outweighed everything else.

When she was better able to handle it, we'd see to having the rest of her belongings packed up, removed and put into storage or just moved, replace whatever needed replacing and put the house on the market. No problem. Anything that could be fixed with money was not going to present any difficulties at all. Like I said, being the Family CEO was going to be good for something, no matter what else happened to the three of us. I'd make damn sure of that. Becky was welcome to stay with us, cramped as it would be in that little house, for as long as she needed. The rest of her life, if she chose. That was settled. Was I as comfortable with it as I'd tried to present to Alec? With that much, sure.

The three of us had a lot of talking to do, and dinner was merely a beginning. Sasha stayed by Becky's side, almost glued to her, all evening, and it looked like every time Becky would start to tear up, Sasha would lay her head or a paw on Becky's leg for attention. She could be quite insistent when she chose to be. Sasha the therapy bear. It seemed to help Becky.

We'd all been at it for close to an hour after dinner — I'd had to go into a bit more detail about how I got the black eye — when Becky suddenly realized that I was a brunette. I said, in Laura's voice, my tagline of "Need a good screw?" and then told her about Laura McCulloch and the rest of what I'd done with Kendra Frankton, as well as how Kendra had set Jon up. That occasioned some more tears, although simply tears and not the whole-body paroxysms she had shown earlier.

I guess he might have been a really great fellow after all. Mentally I hoisted a toast in his honor.

It was probably after midnight and a couple of bottles of wine later when she had recovered at least some of her perspective on life, not a huge amount, and we finally got around to calling it quits for the night. I had her take the dogs out back for their last spin while Alec and I set up the pull-out in the living room for her. It might not be the most homey sort of place to sleep, but as Daddy could attest, it was a reasonably comfortable bed and would certainly serve the purpose if she decided to use it. Or if she slept at all.

Alec and I exchanged a meaningful look as we worked. Well, we'd done what we could. What would happen would happen. Alec and I had had it out to the best of our ability, and now the next step was in Becky's hands. As late as it was, though, inner turmoil aside, I still couldn't just drop off to sleep. It's a bad habit of mine, I suppose. I was reading in bed — another investment book, of course, it seems like I read almost nothing else nowadays, at least when I'm being myself, while Alec, next to me, was just about drifting off — when there was a tentative tap-tap at the bedroom door.

Chapter 31

Okay, that was expected. I hadn't wanted to suggest it to her, since we had to let her go where she needed to at whatever speed she needed to go at. I didn't want to drag her where she wasn't ready to go. Or didn't need to go. Where I still didn't really want to go myself if I didn't have to.

Alec opened the bedroom door. Becky had on a nightgown that was almost thick enough to be demure. Not that any of us were strangers here; we'd all spent much time in and around her pool nude over the year following our marriage, she and I for years before that, and the two of us had freely traipsed around the house nude when living together, both in college and in the Speedway house. There were certainly no issues remaining around nudity for the three of us.

She might find that nightgown a bit hot with all five of us in the bedroom, even with the ceiling fan going and the air conditioning cranked up, but she was welcome to sleep in skin like the rest of us if she chose. Now that we were going to leave the bedroom door open — there was no point to closing it again with all of us inside — I figured Sasha would likely go sleep on the tile in the bathroom or the kitchen. She normally only slept in the bedroom by choice during the cool months, and she'd come into the bedroom, trailing Becky, naturally. Her coat was pretty much grown back out now from her summer shearing, and she really preferred to sleep on tile instead of carpet these days. It got kind of interesting getting to the toilet when she was sleeping in the bathroom, but at least she has enough white in her coat to show up with the nightlight I kept on in the bathroom precisely for that purpose.

I put my book up and turned out the light. Three of us together in a king-sized bed didn't leave a lot of room for any one person, but Alec and I were used to sleeping close together. Very close. I turned onto my left side and pillowed my head on his shoulder while his right arm held me close. Becky snuggled close on his other side, mirroring me. I did note some slight surprise when Sasha laid down against the far side of the bed, shaking all of us as she hit the bed and floor together. After a while I drifted off.

I really had no idea how much later it was when I came awake, and I couldn't find out just what time it was because the clock was behind me. I had slept surprisingly well; when my eyes opened, the room was fully lit. The sun was up, Alec and Becky were both still asleep, and both dogs were sitting there, staring at me over Becky. No wonder I woke up.

I considered my position. My arm was across Alec, my hand on Becky's upper arm. Her position still pretty much mirrored mine. Alec's right arm was around me; I could see his other hand on Becky. Oh, well, if it's time for breakfast, it's time for breakfast. Or brunch. Whatever. This was a day when we could all afford to sleep late.

I wondered whether our nights were going to continue like this. Does it matter? Other than interfering with Alec's and my sex life, probably not. What the hell, if I can get a good night's sleep and it helps Becky, then it could be lots worse. At least he and I would be together, even if rather more … chaste than we'd like.

I withdrew my arm gently; Becky's eyelids flickered open. Alec's did, too, as soon as I eased myself out from his encircling arm. I simply smiled at both of them as I got out of bed.

A little bit later, I was mixing the dogs' breakfasts when Becky came into the kitchen in her robe. "Coffee's ready," I told her. She didn't say anything as she fixed herself a mug and sat at the table.

Finally she broke her silence. "You weren't surprised by last night." A statement, not a question.

"Hold on a minute. Dogs *sit!*" Bruno and Sasha both sat. Of course they were hungry; this was more than an hour later than their normal breakfast time. I set the bowls in their usual places. "Dogs okay!" To Becky, "Let me get my own coffee." After I'd sat down across the table from her, I regarded her as intently as she was me. "No, I wasn't. Not really."

"Neither was Alec."

"Nope."

"Had the two of you … discussed it before?" She was holding her mug in front of her face, making it more difficult to read her expression.

"What? Your coming to sleep with us? Yeah, I kind of led him into it yesterday, before we picked you up."

"What if I'd wanted more than that?"

Let's not address the question directly, shall we? I set my mug down and looked her square in the eyes. "Do you?"

She set her own mug down. "I … I don't know. I know I needed the comfort, the feeling of someone next to me. I haven't slept that well in … well, in months."

I smiled. "We're glad."

She was quiet for two or three minutes, thinking about that. Alec wandered in, already dressed — I thought I'd heard the shower — and fixed his own coffee. He took the last chair, turning it around so he could cross his arms on the back and just looked at both of us as he sat down. Sasha, done with her breakfast, came over and sat down next to Becky, leaning into her leg. Becky petted the dog absently. Finally she broke her silence. "It's terribly moving. Both of you obviously care for me a great deal, and it's something I really, really need right now. But … I can't stay here forever. I need to find my own way back. I" — I cut her off with a hand on her arm.

"Becky, dearest, you can have whatever you need. Sleep with us as much as you need. Stay here as long as you want. We'll get started working on your house and get it back into shape." I could see her shudder. "Even if it's just to sell the place. You can stay here with us for as long as you need. We're here for you. I mean it. Whatever you need, however long you want." Alec and I exchanged brief glances. Well, we'd just have to see where it led, wouldn't we?

And she did. Sleep with us, I mean. By the time Daddy and Aunt Lori arrived the following week (they'd been planning on being here for the trial anyway), we'd shifted Alec's study into the office and turned the room he'd been using into a bedroom for Becky, although she still came to sleep with us every night, soon after we all turned in. We'd used the pull-out for her bed, since the armoire and vanity we put in made the room rather crowded, but we still opened it up every night until after they left. Having Daddy and Aunt Lori here did seem to help Becky steady herself a bit, but that's about as far as I could claim. The real evident recovery was Aunt Lori's, as she seemed almost back to normal. They only stayed a week, but we had a pretty good time, all things considered.

Chapter 32

Becky started seeing patients again a few days after their visit. I think she initially had five patients to begin rebuilding her therapeutic relationships with, and she managed to schedule them into only two days a week. It was somewhere around two, perhaps three weeks after that when I came back inside with the dogs one morning, getting ready to fix their breakfasts, when I found Becky at the table with her coffee, tear tracks running down her face. I raced through the dogs' morning prep and sat down next to her, not even bothering to get my own coffee. I put my arm around her shoulders. "What is it, love?" She didn't answer, except to shake her head.

The day, one without patients, for her, went by without her being willing to talk to either of us, or even say much of anything at all. Then she and I went out to dinner — Thai food — alone that evening. I thought she might be in need of some talk between just the two of us, without Alec around or possibly about to walk in on us. It took some work on my part to get her going, but when she did, it wasn't pleasant to hear. "I really don't know where to begin. I've … I've got some serious problems."

I did my best to look as absorbed in her as I felt. "How could you not? C'mon, dear, tell me about them." Then I just waited.

She was silent for the longest time. Finally she spoke. "Shit!" Just then, naturally, the waiter came with our dinners and she stopped again. I kept on waiting. "You know, psychology is an absolutely wonderful profession." The acid all but dripped from her voice. "It not only lets you understand just how and why you're screwed up, it makes sure that you know when and how you're getting worse, not better." A tear ran down her cheek, but only the one. She ignored it.

"I'd hoped to be working on getting out of your lives by now. Feeling a bit better, maybe finding some other therapist to go talk to, even trying to find another relationship and another place to live. But I *can't*. I ... you and I, we've never been all that social." I nodded. "When we were younger, we never really formed close attachments to anyone else, and other than with Alec, we still haven't."

Where was she going with this? I wondered. Her pain was horribly evident, but I had to know more about what she needed before I could suggest a solution, even the one that Alec and I had agreed on. She continued.

"Understand that a therapeutic relationship is a form of intimacy, especially for the patient. I can't do it. I don't mean with my own patients, that's no problem. But I can't do it for *myself*. I can't open up to a therapist, I can't, I don't *dare*, even try to bring someone new into my life. When I simply think about it, I shut down emotionally. Completely."

She stopped for a mouthful of dinner. I was just about to take my first bite when her eyes bulged a bit, her face turned sort of red, and after a fast drink of water, she managed to cough out that she'd gotten my dinner. I took the bite I was still holding on my fork, and she was right. Hers was just mildly spicy, where mine was significantly hotter. We swapped plates. "It's good, though. You'll love it."

Staring into her eyes, I said calmly, "Okay, so you've got a problem. That's perfectly understandable after everything you've been through. Is there a solution? Or a way through it? Help me out here. Talk to me."

She flared her nostrils. "Amy, I want to have relationships. I want to be *able* to have them. I want to be able to have a sex life. I want ... I want to be *normal!*"

"Don't we all? Keep talking, love. Tell me all about it."

She began playing with her flatware. "Marilyn and I have been out to lunch a couple of times. She's broached both subjects, getting me into therapy, and my finding another relationship. My only reaction is to run! I've not told her, I've just begged off. She's a wonderful friend, for an outsider, and I know she wants whatever's best for me, but … I've become relationship-phobic. Far more than I ever was before. I don't trust, I don't *want* to trust, and the idea of opening up to someone just makes me want to bury myself. Or run away. It doesn't matter whether it's another therapist, or someone to share my life. I don't want to do it, and I *can't!*"

She looked around the room and lowered her voice a bit more. "I can barely talk to Sasha, and I know *she's* not going to repeat what I tell her. I trust her! And I need her! I find myself reaching down for her, even now, when I know she's not here. And when we get home, we'll find her lying just inside the door, waiting for me. So happy to see me, so concerned about me, so worried if I hurt. That's what I want in a man, and I can't find it because I can't get that close to anyone." She was crying quietly by now. I reached out to hold her hands as she continued.

"I can't handle any more losses, and when you develop wonderful relationships, you … you always set yourself up for the possibility of loss. The loss of Jon was way too traumatic for me and now I can't even allow myself any possibility of having it happen again, in any kind of way."

"Alec and I talked about this, you know."

"Amy, this is one of my problems. I'm close to *him!* I — I *want* him! And he's *yours.* I can't do that. I can't do it to *him,* and I can't do it to *you.* I'm afraid that if I keep living with the two of you, I may, but I can't live *without* you, either. And I can't live with anyone else." She sniffed loudly. "I'm so terribly messed up." More tears were making tracks down her cheeks.

I squeezed her hands in reassurance. "I'm not threatened, love."

"But Amy, I could" — I squeezed her hands harder and gave them a shake.

"I know exactly what you mean, and I said I'm not threatened, Becky. Listen, dear." I looked around. The tables near us were vacant, thankfully. Leaning closer to her, I said, "I spent a very difficult night during my investigation, thinking about what you might need and how we, Alec and I both, could provide it. How we could help you cope. Then he and I discussed it together before we picked you up." I took a deep breath. This wasn't going to be an easy question, but for her sake, I had to make it look like it was at least a lot easier than it really was. "What do you need? Do you need him for a night, or do you need to have an ongoing relationship with him?"

She looked astounded. She probably was. "Amy, I can't do that! I can't do it to you, I can't do it to him! I mean" — I shushed her gently. If nothing else, her voice was getting a bit loud. The restaurant wasn't *that* big.

"Becky, dear, I'm not offering to give him up. Let's be straight about that. But outside of that, whatever the three of us want — *all three* of us — and can agree on is fair game. I've had it out with myself, and he and I have already talked about it. Let's eat up and go home. We can talk this out, all three of us. I promise."

What's beyond astounded? Flabbergasted? It fits. "Amy, I — " I laid my hand on her arm.

"Not here, Becky. Save it for when we're home. We can do this. Together. Trust me."

Becky had been right about one thing. Sasha was lying just inside the door. As usual, she attached herself to Becky as soon as we were in the house. As Becky bent down to tell her hello, I went into the living room to give Alec a kiss. Then I simply said quietly, "We've got a bit of a problem. We — all three of us — need to talk." I stepped back so he could stand, but his eyes never left me. Slowly I nodded. Finally he shrugged. Just then Becky and Sasha came in from the kitchen as I went over to give Bruno some attention.

Alec gave her a quick kiss as well. "Is this a time for wine?" Becky and I both nodded; we hadn't had any alcohol before dinner, for a change. "Be back in a minute."

How to do this? I waited for Becky to figure out which seat she wanted, which turned out to be the sofa, and I took one across from her. When Alec came back, I nodded at the other easy chair. That would put the three of us in approximately an equilateral triangle, which seemed an appropriate positioning to start with.

It was one hell of a discussion. It was so hard on Becky once she got going that I can't even put down her actual words. It's all I can do to relate what she talked about.

Initially, Alec and I mostly listened as Becky talked in much more depth than she had before about that horrible night, her arrest and her time in jail. How she had felt, what she'd been told in her initial interrogation before she asked for her lawyer, what she believed people to be whispering behind her back, that sort of thing. Some element of paranoia in it, she admitted, but not without a certain amount of reason and truth behind that. How much worse it became for her when they put her onto suicide watch.

Alec didn't look pleased when she got onto the subject of John Tolliver, because it seemed that his entry into the case coupled with his failure to go meet with her in jail gave the personnel some additional excuse to talk about her likely guilt. Or presume it, because his cases tended to be quite high-profile ones, and his clients were generally regarded as guilty, even if lucky in their choice of lawyers.

I'd never even considered that possibility, but the flip side of that coin was that had the trial actually gone on as planned, we had definitely needed somebody of his caliber to defend Becky, and frankly, there were damn few lawyers with that sort of ability and track record. None of the others were Family. To tell the truth, I had been thrilled to be able to get him and on the Family's dime to boot, and I'd do it again in a heartbeat even knowing what I know now, although I might well insist on his going to see her. As CEO, of course, I carried enough weight to do that.

In any event, by the time Becky was done with that portion of her account, her pain was so great, so agonizingly evident, that we'd both abandoned our chairs to sit close on either side of her to offer what comfort we could. That's where we stayed.

From there, she moved on to her current issues. As she noted in the restaurant, all of us tended to be fairly asocial, other than with each other. We've got some casual friends, sure, even some fairly good ones, but no other deeply close friends. We've pretty much been fine with it, as these things go, but Becky was really caught in a bind now. Her experience with Jon's murder had made her so fearful — her term — as well as even more unwilling to open up to anyone that she couldn't even bear the idea of forming a new close relationship with someone else. *Anyone* else.

She had plenty of time to find a potential partner, but in order to do that, in her professional opinion, she needed some extensive therapy, and there were multiple problems there. First, she knew, at least casually, almost all of the people in her line of work here in Tucson, which meant she couldn't go to any of them. None of them were Family, which would have meant some serious expense if she were to try one of the few she didn't know.

The money wouldn't have been any problem; I'd see to that, and I told her as much. But the second, far greater problem was that she was convinced that she literally could not open up to someone even in such a setting. As she'd told me years ago, doing that had been the hardest part of her training, and she hadn't opened up completely then, although what she'd kept hidden, mostly the Family, hadn't compromised either her therapy or her training. Now, though, she could feel herself becoming increasingly withdrawn, and the more withdrawn she became, the more she needed therapy.

At the same time, the less she would be able to open up to a therapist as she would have to do in order to actually be able to work with one and develop the necessary trust. God, what an incredible mess!

That led to her wishes for a normal life. And a sex life. Her *need* for them. She laid out what she saw as all of the insurmountable obstacles in her life right now, her inability to trust, to open up, to accept the possibility of intimacy or even just the exploration of the possibility with someone new. How — irrational though she admitted it was — she so feared another experience like she'd had with Jon.

And so on. It was heart-wrenching, to say the least. Oh, hell, it was loads worse than that. I just don't have words to describe how I felt, and judging from his expressions, Alec wasn't any better off. Her misery just hit us to the very depths of our beings.

As she wound down, I gave Alec my best imploring look, trying without words to remind him of our discussion. He simply nodded slowly.

I guess I had to broach it. "Becky, there's a solution here. I ... I can't call it an easy one, but there's a way through all this."

She shook her head. "I know you said that, back at dinner. But you can't" — I laid a gentle finger across her lips to stop her.

Alec took advantage of the silence. "Becky, your needs are our needs." They are? *Ours*? I'd never heard him say *that* before. Will wonders never cease? "You're important to us, as important as we are to each other. Do you need to be with us?"

Her tears stepped up a bit. "I am with you, but I *can't*! I can't have you, I can't abuse Amy like that, I can't use the two of you, I can't, *I can't*, *I CAN'T*!!" She was all but yelling at the end. Sasha came over, shouldering the coffee table aside and endangering our wineglasses. When she got in, she laid her head in Becky's lap, hard. Becky just bent over her, stroking her while the tears kept falling.

I looked at my glass. Empty. So were the others. "Alec, is there another bottle handy? I think we're going to need it." I simply waited, holding Becky and trying to reassure her by holding her close and stroking her hair and her back, until Alec got back and refilled us. I wanted him there to help, especially after his last comment. "Becky, what would be wrong with having all three of us, together, as a group?"

"Oh, Amy, no! Groups like that aren't stable! They're … they're perverted. They're" — Now it was Alec's turn to stop her.

"Becky, how are they perverted?" Leave it to the man to key in on that, I thought with a smile to myself. Not really fair, perhaps, but still …

Now she seemed a bit flustered. "Well, they … they just *are*. I mean, three people together, how could it not be?"

"Becky, if it's three people who are together because they love each other, they're in love with each other, and they can, and do, meet each other's needs, what's perverted about it? Especially if they're the only ones who *can* meet those needs?" I was impressed. He'd obviously been giving the whole concept some serious thought.

Still flustered. "Well, three people together, I mean — it's not normal!"

I had to chuckle. "Becky, you're straight, right?" She had an almost horrified look on her face, but nodded. "Well so am I. Very much so, trust me. I love you dearly, but I have no interest in you in that area. All the times you and I slept together, we never had any issues about that, did we? We're not talking about the three of us having orgies together. That's not what this is about. We're talking about three people forming a family together, because we love each other and fulfill each other's needs. Isn't that what good working relationships are all about?"

"But I'd be using both of you. I'd be abusing your relationship, your trust."

Alec weighed in again. "Becky, you wouldn't be abusing *anything*. We're inviting you. If that's using us, then we're volunteering. We're *offering*, so even if it's using us, it's not *abusing* us. This would be, *is*, our gift of love to you. Like I said, your needs are our needs. You have a need, a desperate need. You've just spent a whole bunch of hours telling us all about it. We can meet that need and help *you* meet it. What's wrong with that? Especially since nobody else can?"

She shook her head. "Relationships like that aren't stable. I can't come in and wind up breaking up your marriage, or having to leave and be out on the streets. I just *can't*."

My turn. "Becky, I've been doing some looking. It's not easy to find any sort of serious research on triad relationships, polygamy and such. But from what little I can find, it doesn't appear that those sorts of relationships are necessarily any less stable than conventional marriages. There are four triads within the Family, did you know that? Two of them have been together for more than ten years, one for almost twenty and the fourth, one that's all Family, is approaching its thirtieth anniversary. So there may be some instability, but it's hardly a given and probably isn't all that different from the stability of couples. I also believe that if we go into this determined to make it work, we can. Don't you? Really? I mean, we've got a helluva lot of incentive, you know?"

"But … do you really want to share Alec?"

I snorted. "Hell, no, I don't want to. But it's the solution I see. I've seen it since … well, since a couple of days before I barged into the courtroom. I told you I spent an evening shortly before then just trying to figure this out. Remember? The bottom line is that there are two things in the whole world that absolutely terrify me. They leave me utterly unable to face going on, either as CEO or even just …. Those are losing Alec and losing you. Nothing else scares me like either of those do, and frankly, I can't even say which would be worse. *Nothing* terrifies me like those. So for you, dear, in this kind of a situation, I would. Not for anyone else. *Anyone*. My willingness to share Alec isn't really the issue. Our doing, our being *willing* to do, whatever it takes to help bring you back to a normal life is. And Alec is just as determined as I am. Right?"

He was nodding. "Becky, if you and I went back to the bedroom, made love, and then you went back to your own bedroom, or moved out, *that* would be using me. Using *us*. We could. Amy would let us. It would hurt her, but that is the gift she'd give you. And she'd smile through her tears as you left to resume your life, because she loves you that much." Becky turned to look at me, shocked, and I nodded, slowly, looking straight into her eyes. He was right about how much it would hurt, just as he was right about the rest.

Alec went on, though. "But *I* won't. I cannot, *will not* hurt her like that, no matter how willing she is. And, to be honest, and I apologize to you for this, no matter how much you might need it. I'll admit that if I were going to stray, you'd be my only choice. But I'm not. As long as the relationship is me husband, Amy wife, and Becky friend, that's how it has to stay. How it's *going* to stay, and as I said, I'm very sorry, but that's where I stand. What we're offering here is a commitment. You and us. All three of us, together. A commitment is an entirely different matter to me."

Oh, God, what a special man! And to think I'd been too scared of a relationship to allow one with him for years. But I had to chime in here. "Yeah. The Three Fates. The Three Furies. The Three Musketeers."

Becky wasn't quite whispering. "MacBeth's three witches."

Alec smiled. "Snap, Crackle and Pop." I reached across Becky to slap him. Lightly. But she smiled, sort of. Sasha looked up at her and, apparently deciding that her charge was better now, backed out carefully to lay down a couple of feet away, although her eyes never left Becky. Bruno still hadn't moved, other than to roll over onto his stomach and watch us from time to time. He'd been lying over by the TV all evening. Of course, when it was just the three of us talking, even loudly, he could sleep through almost anything.

Becky looked at the dregs in her wineglass. I was just about to ask Alec to get some more wine when she said, "I think I need some coffee instead." She peered at the cable box under the TV. "My God, it's almost five o'clock! We've been talking all night!"

I stretched. "No wonder I feel so tired. I, for one, need a nap. But these two" — I gestured towards the dogs — "need their breakfast, and a spin outside first. Who's up for what?"

Becky stood up. "I'll take them out." I think she probably wanted a few minutes alone to digest what we'd been talking about. Alec offered to make coffee, so that left me to do their breakfasts. When we'd all had our coffee and the dogs had eaten, I repeated my intention to take a nap. Becky came with me, and Alec followed us.

Later that morning was, well, interesting. Becky seemed a bit more accepting of, or at least willing to look at, the solution we had proposed, pun intended, I guess, although she wasn't willing to commit to anything before she had some food in her. I probably shouldn't call it morning, since it was getting close to noon when we finally sat down to something resembling breakfast.

She fixed her coffee and sat down as I put her plate in front of her. Sasha came, sat down next to her and leaned into her leg as usual; Becky petted her, also as usual. Such an inseparable pair now. I was putting the other plates onto the table when she spoke. "Amy, you said you came to this decision before the start of the trial." I nodded. "So this wasn't a surprise to you, either."

"Let me get my own coffee." After I'd sat down across the table from her, I regarded her as intently as she was me. "No, not really."

"And Alec was ready to … to go for it as well."

"Yep."

"Had you discussed it with him before, too?" Just like that first morning, she was again holding her mug with both hands in front of her face, making it more difficult for me to read her. Sasha was looking at her elbow, probably wondering if it was safe to insist on more attention. Or wondering if her input were needed.

"Oh, yeah. Just as I told you, we'd gone through it before we picked you up from the courthouse, and then more recently, whenever you were working and we were in bed together."

"Everything."

"Yep."

She set her mug down. "How did you know?"

"Which part?"

"All of it. I mean, it's such a … it's so different! You knew I couldn't sleep alone, didn't you?" I nodded some more. "And then what I was saying last night?"

"Well, that wasn't something I'd necessarily expected. I didn't think you'd build to it in quite the way you did. Not being the mind-bender" — Becky got an odd look on her face.

"Snoop." A wan smile.

I grinned back. "Yep. Not being schooled like you were, I figured it'd hit you right away. I've been sort of hoping you'd pull through, since it never went beyond all of us sleeping together. Obviously, though, you've been getting worse, or at least not better." She nodded. "But that doesn't change our positions. If we're the only people you can have a relationship with, then that's what we'll do for you. Alec spoke for both of us last night."

Just then Alec showed up to fix his own coffee and sit with us. I continued. "He said your needs are our needs, and he's right. We love you, dear, and we want to see you happy. We want to see you healthy. We can't do a lot. We can't offer you formal therapy, because neither of us knows how, and as you've said to me so many times, we're too close for that. But we can certainly use that closeness. We can offer you a loving family to join, the one family you've said you could be a part of, now, as you are. To help heal you. We're making you that offer. It's what we have to offer, and it's everything we *can* offer."

Becky picked up her spoon and twirled it in her fingers for a few moments. Then she stirred her coffee, unnecessarily. Without looking up, she asked, "Amy, how did you know about all this?"

I shrugged. "A hunch. And a feeling."

She was quiet for two or three minutes, thinking about that. Alec and I exchanged puzzled looks over our breakfasts as Becky continued to pet Sasha. Finally she responded to what I'd said. "A hunch." I nodded. "And a feeling." I kept nodding. She buried her face in her hands and her shoulders started shaking. Alec and I both reached for her, but she waved us away. "It's fine. I'm laughing! For the first time since this all began, I'm *laughing*!"

She paused for some of her coffee and then leaned over to hug the dog. "I should probably throw away my license. One big furry dog, a hunch and a feeling, and here I've spent years in college, graduate school, internship … for what? You two and Sasha did more for me last night and this morning than any of my colleagues could possibly have done in days, probably even weeks." She wasn't really smiling, but compared to the last four months, and especially last night, it was far and away the happiest and most engaged we'd seen her. That felt very, very good, as these things go. It could have been a lot worse.

I put my hand on her arm. "Becky, dear, look. I just put two and two together. I wasn't sure what was going to happen. I had some strong suspicions, that's all. It might not have happened, and if you hadn't needed it, then that would have worked, too. To be completely honest, the longer we went without it coming up, the more I hoped you wouldn't need it.

"I had a lot of qualms about this, too. Still do. But if we make forming this family of ours into a successful relationship and keeping it that way our top priority, I think we can do it and make it work. I'd worried for weeks, the whole time I was trying to work Kendra, pretty much, that I'd lose you. Alec has, too, I'm fairly sure." He was nodding.

"I eventually realized that if I lost you, I'd lose a serious part of myself. Some part of me would die inside, along with you. *Just as if I were to lose Alec*. A different part, but no smaller or less important a part. What that said to me was that if you needed somebody, and had nobody else, then I — *we* — had to be that somebody. A unique solution to a problem that we'll probably never see happen again, at least to people in our sort of situation. Especially given our general asocial nature. When you finally got to that point, we were ready."

Alec broke in. "And it means all three of us, together."

Becky looked at him. "She gave you all of it." He nodded. "You're okay with it."

He shrugged. "I don't know. I'm not completely sure how I feel about it, but I believe I can manage it, as a commitment, not a … a fling. I certainly don't want anything to happen to you, any more than Amy does. You're just as important to me as she is, even more so now than you were that first night a month ago. When Amy put it to me, she led me into it slowly, bit by bit. It might have been easier to do that with you instead of just laying it on you cold like we did, but you needed something fast, or at least that's how it looked to me this morning, and I'm sure it did to Amy, too. I'm … well, I'm as okay with it as I'm going to be, at least until I can see it's going to work. And yeah, losing you would tear me up inside, pretty much the same way it would to lose Amy."

"But you won't just have sex with me."

Alec gave her a loving smile, but shook his head. "Becky, I made a vow to Amy. She may choose to let me, but *I* promised. I'm not going to do that. I won't break that promise, and I won't hurt her like that. As far as I'm concerned, either it's a commitment for all of us or it's not going to happen. Assuming I can do anything with all of us in one bed, of course."

Becky smiled at me. Not broadly, but definitely a smile. "Amy, you married a Boy Scout."

"You can marry him, too," I responded. "The offer's still open."

Then she sat up straighter as his last sentence hit her. "All of us in one bed?"

I took over. "Becky, if you can't sleep alone, and you can't open up or trust except with us, would you want to be stuck in your bedroom while Alec and I …?" She shook her head.

"Believe me, dear, I am damn sure not going to be sent there just because you and he are together. If we're in this together, we're all in it *together*. We're doing this so you'll never *have* to be alone, and it seems to me that shutting you out just because Alec and I are together would be the worst kind of alone for you. It definitely would be for me. Besides, one of the biggest potential problems in relationships like this, when it arises, from what I've read, seems to be jealousy. It's a little hard to be jealous if we're all together."

Becky was silent for several minutes as she got more coffee. "How do you and I … uh, interact?"

I chuckled. "However we like. Becky, you can read, sleep, watch TV or do whatever you want. Other than eating crackers in the bed. That's what I plan to do. Read, sleep or watch TV, I mean. I'm not looking for a two-on-one scenario," — I glanced at Alec, who was just shaking his head and smiling slightly — "and there'll also be plenty of times when the two of you are together and I'm busy. And vice-versa. You can even leave the room if you choose, because nobody's talking about holding you prisoner. But it would be *your* choice. Come out to the living room and watch TV. Read. Whatever. Hell, kibitz if you need to. But if we're all together as much as we can be and want to be, even during sex, then it seems to me that jealousy is going to be sort of out of the question."

"That seems a bit perverted."

Alec stood up. "If the two of you will excuse me, I'm going to go brush the dogs. In the living room. Well, Bruno, at least. I find that I'm not entirely comfortable in this discussion at the moment. But Becky, let me leave you with this thought. What we're offering is out of love. It's not an attempt to take advantage of you, or to disadvantage any of us. You'd be free to do what you liked. As would

Amy if the situation is going that way. It may be a bit more — public — between us than any of us is used to, but it's not perverted. I'm not looking for that two-on-one scenario either. We just want to make sure, as sure as we know how, that you don't feel shut out. That you don't *ever* feel shut out."

I took his arm. "Alec, we're not trying to shut you out now, either."

He smiled gently. "Didn't think you were. But the only one who's going to have to perform every time and under all circumstances seems to be me. I've said what I have to say, and since my part is pretty well settled, you two can figure out how you're going to work things between yourselves without any further input from me. Don't worry. I won't be far away if you need me, and I'll be there no matter what the two of you decide." He gave Becky's cheek a light caress. "No matter what *you* decide. Besides, precious little is going to happen before I learn how to manage with both of you with me anyway." We both laughed at that, although perhaps we shouldn't have; it did take some time to learn that. For all of us.

After he left, Becky threw up her hands. "I guess I can't fight that. Who can be upset by being loved like that?"

I grinned at her. "Why on earth would you want to fight it? The way I look at it, all's well that ends well. We've made our decision, we love you, and you're here. You're home, with your family."

She finished her coffee. "I was right. I can't argue with being loved like that. Well, I said I'd try, and I meant it. I … let's do it."

Finally we did figure out how to work the relationship. Everybody worked at it, very hard, and we managed. We had our share of failures, but, surprisingly for me, at least, it was mostly Alec who insisted on our getting beyond them. He kept us together when they happened, he helped us ignore them and accept them as simply temporary problems that we would get past, and every time, he would simply gather the two of us in and hold us close while we all talked our issues and problems to death. We learned to talk *everything* out, in depth, and eventually the problems stayed dead and buried.

At that point, we really began to function as a wonderful team. More than managed, eventually. Actually, as I had kind of expected, figuring out how the three of us would function in that tiny one-bath house turned out to be harder, and there were occasional times when it would have been all but impossible had we not had the office to use as well.

We made sure that Becky was never alone, as long as she felt she needed it. At least one of us was with her at all times, me, Alec or (on the very rare occasions that we were both absolutely unable to be there) Sasha, who had obviously decided to hang with her at any possible moment. Well, she was always with Becky, and continued sleeping on Becky's side of the bed, no matter the weather.

Sasha also became a regular fixture in Becky's office, and those few patients who couldn't manage with her in the office simply never came back. Just as before, one of us always dropped the two of them off and picked them up, every day she went in to work. And no matter what's happening, we all sleep tangled up together like a litter of happy puppies. That's the way we like it. Enough said.

We might not be able to formally legalize the relationship, other than in Golondrino for the Family, and that's simply registration, not legal recognition outside of there (the Family doesn't concern itself about such things), but we needed a ring for Becky. The board meeting was the following weekend. We got a fourth limo, just for the five of us, and we went into Zurich proper to stop at the jeweler's so she could be measured before heading for the hotel.

By the time we left on Tuesday the ring, matching Alec's and mine, was ready. More for the memory than the necessity, on our way back we went to Las Vegas first and returned to the same chapel where Alec and I were married. We brought the dogs to be witnesses this time, though. They sort of crowded the little chapel, and the fellow who ran it wasn't at all sure about having two good-sized dogs along for the ceremony, but they're very well-behaved dogs, money talks, and it spoke loud enough here to reassure him that having them there was the right thing to do (as in the punchline of that old joke, "Ah, faith, why didn't ye *tell* me the poor creature was Catholic?").

I even had them put their pawprints, as witnesses, on the fancy certificate that I'd had done up for us in lieu of the marriage license we couldn't get for three. It would be framed and hung in the bedroom as soon as we got back home. I did find my heart skipping a beat when the guy running the service got to, "Do you, Rebecca Ann, take Alannah Meav and Alexander Forsythe …"

He stumbled over the vows the first time through; we had omitted 'for richer and for poorer' since it really didn't make any sense in our situation. 'Poorer' was not in our future any more, that was for sure. He also had a minor difficulty with 'as long as you three shall live.'

When he had gotten through them, though, Becky said, as calmly and definitely as I've ever heard her say anything in our lives, "I do. With all my heart, so help me God, I do." Then when it was, "Do you, Alannah Meav, take Rebecca Ann and Alexander Forsythe … ," I said exactly what Becky had. As did Alec when it was his turn. And do you know, it felt *right*. *Absolutely* right.

But I did make a mental note for the new house. Buy a bigger bed. And build the house bigger, but since we hadn't even begun to design it yet, that would be the easy part. So far, at least, the three of us seem to fit together as though we were meant to be this way. Who knows? Perhaps we were.

Epilogue

Six months later, we were all still content. It actually felt as though all three of us had been together since long before Alec and I were married, and in some ways I suppose we have been. The general lack of friction between us, now that we'd settled in, was simply amazing on those occasions when we even bothered to think about it. Well, maybe 'lack of friction' isn't completely accurate. We have our fights and the occasional blow-up like anyone else. But we all have one overriding concern that we keep coming back to, that of losing what we have, and what Becky has so desperately needed, so we get over them quickly and work very hard to resolve them, not simply sweep them under the rug.

Are we living a fairy tale? Maybe by anyone else's standards we are, but if we are, who gives a shit? And what's it to anyone else anyway? It's our life, and we're very happy with it. But it's by no means a 'living happily ever after' sort of thing. I was right about one thing. There are a *lot* more difficulties in a triad than there are with only two people. On the other hand, we like what we have, and we are, as I say, bound and determined to make it work, *whatever* it takes, and that may be the key. Sleeping all tangled up together makes it hard to hide or hold on to hard feelings, too.

Becky did quite a bit of research on triad relationships while she was building her practice back up — she and Sasha are up to 22 patient hours a week, now, and still climbing — and we all spent quite a bit of time discussing what she'd found. She did have to admit, with just a trace of sheepishness, that what I'd found out about triads' stability seemed to be as accurate as we could find from what little literature there is. Most importantly, though, what we have works, at least for us.

I also asked the other Family triads how they managed — through the Family, not directly as the CEO — and got some tips from them for us to consider as well. Mostly we just find our own way, but the absolute imperative for all of us is that we *will* find a way. We *do*. There is no 'try,' and there is no 'do not.' (Yes, we all loved Star Wars when we were growing up.)

We don't entertain a lot, not that we ever did. Marilyn and her husband have been here a couple of times. It's not really a surprise, but the dining room here is quite tight with five. I think Mark is still wondering if Alec is incredibly lucky or, alternatively, cursed by having two wives. But he won't ask directly, and we're certainly not telling.

The three of us were sitting in the back yard over coffee the other morning and I asked Becky if she ever felt that she'd be better off in a more conventional relationship with somebody else. She thought about that for several minutes before answering. "No, I don't think so. As good, perhaps, if I could ever have gotten there, but definitely not better. Before everything fell apart, I probably would have thought differently. Well, no, I'd never even considered something like this, so that was really the only choice I had. Jon was a very special person to me, and I truly thought — think — that he and I could have had a good relationship together. Perhaps not as close as you and Alec," — she smiled warmly at him — "at least at first, but it might have gotten there in time. Since he was Family, I think the four of us could have become really close. Not this close, of course."

She smiled again before launching into how the experience had all but overcome her. "I literally was lost by the time the case was dismissed. I'd been so traumatized, emotionally abused and drained that I had no reserves left at all. None whatsoever." She took a deep breath. "Dear God, listen to me. It makes me sound like such a weakling.

But I felt so utterly trapped by what had happened, and the totality of it all was more than enough to overwhelm me.

"When you invited me into your home, you were literally throwing a life preserver to a drowning woman. I had, I felt, nobody but the two of you in the entire world, and had you closed me out, I would have been left with no one at all.

"I've been … oh, envious, I suppose I'd say, of the relationship the two of you had had ever since you were married. Even before, I guess. Not jealous, simply envious, because I wanted to have such a special relationship, too. Just continuing to live here with the two of you the way I was doing would not, in the long run, have been all that much better. It might have kept me going, but just barely, especially after that first month when I could feel my problems getting worse. Now I have a family *here*, a family that I love and frankly, I *want* to be in this family, forever."

She paused before going on. "I worried about my own reactions when you brought it up. Was I responding to you simply because you were helping me, rescuing me? Was I agreeing to this out of an utterly unhealthy degree of neediness, not to mention my … fear of getting into another relationship with someone else, instead of from a real love and desire to make a family out of the three of us? I went to sleep that … that morning thinking about it, and continued to think about it all the next week. I debated with myself. I agonized. I … I prayed. I'm still not sure to whom, but I tried. Oh, God, how I tried.

"The other side of that coin, of course, was that I'd known and loved both of you long before you became my only outside lifelines during that awful time. It also made a really major impression on me when you were willing to let me share Alec when I so badly needed someone. Even if he wasn't willing. Damn Boy Scout."

She was smiling at that comment, and Alec simply smiled back. "The point when I really, truly knew that what

I was doing was utterly right was in the chapel, when I was asked whether I took the two of you to be my spouses and so on. At that moment, I knew, for sure, that it was right. That's why I didn't simply say, 'I do.'" I understood. That was when my own reservations had completely disappeared and my poor, abused gut had finally finished coming untied. "Amy, you do understand that you came up with a — I guess I'd call it a global solution — that went way beyond what was really needed?"

I shrugged. "Don't know about 'way beyond.' At the time, I was desperate and needed a solution that would work right then and there lots more than I needed the perfect solution some time later. This was the one that occurred to me. Why? Do you want out?" I smiled as I said it.

"No, I don't. I'm serious. I'm here by my free choice. I love our being a family together, and I want it to go on this way. Forever. I never would have expected it, never could have thought about such a thing before, but … I wouldn't want to be anywhere else, now. Even now that I think I could, at the least, manage with some effort to develop a workable therapeutic relationship with someone."

I took a long drink of my coffee. "You remember what Heinlein said. 'Love shared is love multiplied.' I guess I thought I'd see how it worked in practice."

Becky looked a bit skeptical. "Amy, that's a nice-sounding platitude — in fiction. In real life, that sort of thing is a lot more likely to cause some real trouble."

I shrugged. "Hey, I needed something and I needed it right then. Besides, look around. For us, so far, it seems to be working. Doesn't it?" I grinned at her; she returned it. I turned to Alec. "How about you? How do you vote? Are you comfortable living the male fantasy?"

He snorted. "Fantasy, my ass. This is by *no* means such a dream. Two women, one man and no worries about the next hour, next day, next week — *that's* a fantasy. No. This is an ongoing project, a family that needs constant care, attention and dedication, not to mention a lot of endurance on my part. For me, I'm here with my family. That it's unconventional isn't important or even relevant to me.

"That I could find a family like this to suit me so much surprises me just a bit. Well, more than just a bit, I have to admit, but I adore the two of you, I have loved both of you, one way or another, for years. I meant what I said that night, Becky, that were I going to stray, you would have been my only choice, and now that we're all together, well, Amy was right. *This* is right, at least for us. Without how we are, without what we went through, it almost certainly wouldn't be. The sex … Amy, you were all the woman I ever needed in that regard. Or, at the time, all the woman that I ever wanted. I never fantasized about anyone else, even this dear lady."

He reached across Sasha to touch Becky's hand, and she smiled at him. "That Becky is here with us, too, now, is that much more delightful, yes, because we fit together so well. I frankly don't give a damn about the sex, from that sort of voyeuristic side. I'd love both of you just as much if there were no sex involved whatsoever."

Becky and I exchanged glances. Yeah, right. Then we smiled at each other and nodded knowingly. Alec went on as though nothing had happened, although I wouldn't bet that he'd missed it. "That there is simply makes everything so much … better. The bottom line is that I'm utterly delighted with the two of you and I want the two of you to be just as happy with each other and with me. Need I say more?" Both Becky and I were shaking our heads and smiling. Alec truly has a way of saying exactly the right things.

Becky turned to me. "Amy, you're so strong, I don't think that spending that time in jail would have affected you the way, or at least to the degree, that it did me. I just couldn't handle it." She was getting back into the emotions of the whole experience, I could tell. "They *broke* me, Amy. Jail was bad enough, but when they put me on suicide watch and left me there, it *broke* me." A tear ran down her face, followed by several more. Her shoulders started to shake. Alec got to her first, but we were both holding her in moments, laying our heads gently against hers. When she indicated that she was better, I went back to my chair.

"Becky, we can all be broken. Let me tell you something about so-strong me." I took a last swallow of my coffee; it was almost too cool to drink. "Think back to my ordeal for becoming CEO." A prospective Family CEO has to be subjected to an ordeal, designed by the outgoing CEO, to test the successor's ability to overcome the most severe challenges. It is not — *must not be* — public knowledge (although I'd told her, after swearing her to secrecy. Alec had gone through it with me, so he already knew), and it *must* be kept secret from the candidate until afterwards. This is all a charge from James Escarton, the Family's founder. Overall, it works, for the Family, and has for centuries. But it can be — is! — very hard on the candidate, who doesn't have any idea what's going on or what he will become, at that point, assuming he makes it through successfully.

"Here's what I haven't told you. Either of you." I nodded to include Alec. "When they had us tied up in the kitchen here, blindfolded and gagged, they broke *me*." Becky looked aghast. Alec's face darkened. "My greatest fears right then were two. First, that if they killed us, as I felt absolutely certain then that they were going to, then turned the air conditioning way up as they left, nobody would find us until you came to get more food for Bruno and Sasha." I leaned down to hug Bruno, who licked my ear happily. Sasha was sitting between Alec and Becky — smart girl! — and getting petted by both of them.

"I wasn't half so scared of dying, myself, as I was of having you come in and find our bodies like that. That absolutely terrified me. Then, when I thought they were burning Alec, that was more than I could take. I told them they could have anything they wanted. I'd turn over my notes, quit the investigation, go away, never cash another Family check — *anything* to make them stop hurting someone I loved so. Especially when I'd finally *really* found him and had just gotten through my own problems around him.

"But" — a wry half-smile through some tears of my own — "it's real hard to make yourself understood through a gag, you know? So nobody knew except me, to my shame then, and now the two of you. By the time I could have said anything intelligible, when I got my gag off again, I had the upper hand. Well, an equal chance, anyway. Rachison was on the floor, hugging himself and only semi-conscious, and I was at least in a position to actually fight Beindorf when he came in."

I took a deep breath. That had been a really difficult time. Suddenly Alec was there, holding me, wrapping his arms around me, and Becky right behind him, maneuvering to my other side to do the same. My word, but it's good to be so loved. They both put their heads up to mine and we just stayed that way for several minutes. It felt so damn *good*.

Alec finally spoke. "God, I wish I'd known. They'd never have made it out alive if I'd known. Amy, I …"

I held up my hand. "Alec, dearest, it's *done*. Remember what Ray Fields said to me later? That it was important for me to know whether I could be broken, and if so, what it would be like within me as I approached that point? I honestly believe he was right. Now. Because what I've really come to understand from it all is *me*. I can be

broken, yes. But not, I think, by or for myself. You two —
and yes, you two little beggars, too" — I fondled both dogs,
who had maneuvered for some of the group hug themselves
— "are both my strength and my vulnerability. Having all
of you with me makes me more than I am by myself. Much
more. It also creates an avenue of vulnerability for me. But
knowing that, I can prepare and guard myself from that
angle that much better when it's needed. That's all to my
benefit. So hard as it was at the time, and yes, it really was,
and even shameful to me then, I don't regret it now. I've
done lots of thinking about it since, and I've really come to
terms with it. For myself."

It was true, I had. Maybe it had even been
necessary, although I'd pass on that particular thought. It
certainly had been really difficult. Now, at least, though, I
could go ahead and detail my ordeal in the Director's Book,
which I'd been putting off so far. Now that Becky was a
part of this immediate family, my spouse, she could
actually see the Book (and has) as well, instead of simply
hearing some things about it as my confidential advisor.

I seriously doubt that the Founder had ever
envisioned a successor with not one but two spouses when
he directed us to keep the Book so confidential, but times
change, don't they? It's not like it's anyone else's business,
after all. And the Director's Suite is more than big enough
for all three of us, even without exiling one of us to either
of the ancillary bedrooms; we'd proven that already,
repeatedly. All five of us, actually, as with Becky part of
the family, there's nobody here to keep the dogs while
we're in Golondrino, so they come too. They're a real hit
with the hotel staff.

When Christmas rolled around, we had some really
major gifts and reasons for celebration. As our first
Christmas together as a functioning family, of course, it
was particularly special just on that account, and we made
some personal gifts to a couple of charities we wanted to

help, anonymously, as we've continued to do ever since. We had finally gotten the initial sketch of a plan we could approve of from the Family architect we'd brought in to design our new home, so we could start on it as soon as we got title to the last parcel, as we did a month later.

Becky got to open the largest package. I'd tagged it from me to all of us, but Alec gallantly let her do the honors. When she got it open, she just looked at the framed artwork for several minutes before turning it so Alec could see it. "So what does it say, Amy? Is it Japanese for 'sushi spoken here'?"

Alec looked at it intensely for another minute or two. "It's not Japanese, it's Chinese. Marjorie used to have something like it hanging in her room when I was a kid. Let's see — hers was Tranquility, she told me. But it only had one of these — oh, my *God!* That's what Heinlein called the ideogram for Trouble!" Becky looked utterly confused, so Alec explained. "Here. It's in three parts." He gestured to indicate them. "This one is a roof, and it indicates a house. This one is a woman, and one woman under a roof is Tranquility. This one — I don't think the ideogram really exists, but this is what it would be if it did — is two women under one roof. That's what Heinlein said in one of his books was the Chinese symbol for trouble."

I snorted. "Yeah, he did. But for us, think of this as being Double Tranquility. Because that's what we're going to make it. And make *of* it." It's going to hang in the entryway of the new house, once we're in it. And we're working very hard on that 'double tranquility' angle. 'Trouble' it definitely isn't, at least for us.

We also received what was, for Alec and me, the most welcome gift of all, the first resumption of Becky's sense of mischief, when (two days earlier) she brought home, of all things, what she told us was a Festivus pole. It looked like a piece of aluminum conduit stuck into a flowerpot to us.

We had to look it up, as neither Alec nor I knew what Festivus was (neither of us had been *Seinfeld* fans). Alec then said that we could certainly put it up in the living room with the Christmas tree (which left precious little area in the room in the first place, although the pole doesn't take up much), but if we did, then we would have to go whole hog. The airing of grievances was brief, like nonexistent, since we already had that out every night, such as it was.

For the feats of strength, we decided we would have to arm-wrestle, with the loser having to make the coffee (such a penalty!). Alec beat both of us fairly handily, but Becky's been working out and getting back into the condition she was in before everything fell apart, and while I did manage to beat her, it was almost a close thing. She lost in good humor, and naturally, Sasha trailed behind her as she went to the kitchen for her penalty. Alec, Bruno and I followed.

Then, about an hour before the turkey was done, Daddy and Aunt Lori called. The only odd moment was when Aunt Lori asked, "Becky? Are you going to live with Amy and Alec forever?"

Alec and I exchanged glances. What was Becky going to say to that? "Mom, we're all together. That's how we're going to stay. For the rest of our lives."

"But I mean ... they're married."

"Mom, we're *all* married." Long pause.

"What do you mean? All ... all three of you? You're all ... married? Together?"

"You bet, Mom. We're all together. For ever and ever."

In the ensuing silence, I could hear Daddy in the background say, "Well, *that's* different."

Aunt Lori's voice got just a bit quieter. "Rebecca? Is this truly what you want?" Names are funny things. Aunt Lori only calls Becky that when she's especially serious or concerned. Daddy makes sure to call me Amy then; when he calls me Alannah, he's either trying to get my goat or shock me. It works, too.

"Oh, God, yes, Mom. It's just what I want, and it's what I need. It's what we all need."

Aunt Lori was quiet for several seconds, considering what Becky had said, I guess, before she went on. "Well, it's certainly not anything I would ever have expected, but … bless you, dear. Bless all of you." We all chorused our thanks to her and to Daddy as well, when he chimed in to add his own blessing.

Well, now they knew officially. After they got better accustomed to the idea, they seemed to be fine with it. Overall, it was, we all agreed, the best Christmas we had ever had in our adult lives. We hope it's just the beginning for all of us.

About The Author:

Insurance sales, collections, and even the practice of law get old after a while. A.J. Kohler did all of those, but is mostly a retired attorney who practiced law in Denver before heading south for a warmer climate. Winter sports were never an interest, and shoveling a driveway, not to mention careening around town on ice- and snow-covered roads got real old, real fast, so the desert beckoned and a love affair blossomed (with the desert; the partner was already a commitment).

If there is one thing that A.J. would say about Tucson and the desert to those who aren't familiar with it, it's this: Out here, gardening is a blood sport. Cactus is often not friendly to work with, but the results are worth it (after you've healed up).

A.J. lives on the outskirts of Tucson with a partner of the opposite sex and two long-coat Akitas, also of opposite sexes.

About The Author:

Insurance sales, collections and even the practice of law get old after a while. A.J. Kohler did all of those, but is mostly a retired attorney who practiced law in Denver before heading south for a warmer climate. Winter sports were never an interest, and shoveling a driveway, not to mention careening around town on ice- and snow-covered roads got real old, real fast, so the desert beckoned and a love affair blossomed (with the desert; the partner was already a commitment).

If there is one thing that A.J. would say about Tucson and the desert to those who aren't familiar with it, it's this: Out here, gardening is a blood sport. Cactus is often not friendly to work with, but the results are worth it (after you've healed up).

A.J. lives on the outskirts of Tucson with a partner of the opposite sex and two long-coat Akitas, also of opposite sexes.

Social Media Links:

Facebook: https://www.facebook.com/aj.kohler.39

No Third Choice:
https://www.facebook.com/NoThirdChoice

Website: http://www.ajkohler.net/

Other Solstice Titles
by
A.J. Kohler

No Third Choice

Amy Youngston is Family. It hasn't done much for her until one day, when Raymond Escarton Fields, the head of the Family, hires her to find out who's trying to kill him.

The Family has many doctors, lawyers and other professionals, but in all of those thousands of cousins, there's only one private investigator, and that's Amy.

She takes the case, but when some party or parties unknown start by bugging her office that very night, it's clear that she can't handle this alone. The only person she can turn to is the one close friend she has (of two) who isn't Family, and, because it is secret, he doesn't even know about it. Until now, because Amy has to tell him. She's not supposed to tell outsiders, but he has to understand what's going on, doesn't he? She could tell him if she married him, and they're certainly close enough, but . . . let's not go there. Amy's got some serious problems with intimate relationships, especially with Alec. Problems she'd rather not think about (but they still keep coming back).

When Amy finds that there's as much of a target on her back as Fields had told her was on his, she begins to wonder. Did he hire her because she was the only choice he had – or because he had it in for her? Without some handle on the bad guys, there was no way she could find the answer to this question except to carry on with her investigation.

The most frustrating part for Amy is that there doesn't seem to be any reason for someone to want to kill the head of the Family. Of course, the same can't be said for whoever it is that's sending her repeated messages that she's in their crosshairs as well. Especially when they ambush her and Alec, tie them up and proceed to torture them in her own kitchen. As they say, expecting to be killed in the immediate future tends to get one's attention. They've definitely got hers.

Ripped in Two

Reesa's not looking for a relationship, she's after for a killer. Sometimes, though, it's easier to think outside the box when you don't start inside it, and it's not like he doesn't have some involvement with these murders already. Jeff's not bad to look at either, and he's willing to settle for just going to lunch from time to time. That works for her.

Then again, as many times as he's been involved with the murders, maybe he's the killer himself.

Or maybe not.

Of course, life would be so much easier if the star local TV crime scene reporter didn't insist on putting her front and center all the time and sneering at the fruitless efforts of both the Tucson Police and Pima County Sheriff's Departments.

One way or another, Reesa won't rest until the killer is brought in. Better if he's a stranger, but if it's this private eye who's working to be her friend, so be it. *Whoever* it is will be going down.

Bet on it.